DEAD RECKONING

A CORNISH CRIME THRILLER
BOOK 3

BERRICK FORD

HARVEY
BERRICK
PUBLISHING

Copyright © 2025 by Berrick Ford

All rights reserved.

No part of this book may be reproduced in any form or by any electronic or mechanical means, including information storage and retrieval systems, without written permission from the author, except for the use of brief quotations in a book review.

From *The Poetry of Robert Frost* by Robert Frost published by Vintage Books. Copyright © 1969 Holt Rinehart and Winston, Inc. Extract reproduced by permission of The Random House Group Ltd.

CONTENTS

DEAD RECKONING	v
Cornish Crime Thriller Series	ix
Prologue	1
Chapter 1	13
Chapter 2	21
Chapter 3	29
Chapter 4	45
Chapter 5	60
Chapter 6	76
Chapter 7	93
Chapter 8	103
Chapter 9	117
Chapter 10	123
Chapter 11	129
Chapter 12	145
Chapter 13	153
Chapter 14	162
Chapter 15	171
Chapter 16	181
Chapter 17	194
Chapter 18	208
Chapter 19	218
Chapter 20	231
Chapter 21	245
Chapter 22	256
Chapter 23	264
Chapter 24	281
Chapter 25	288
Chapter 26	300
Chapter 27	308

Chapter 28	326
Epilogue	338
What to read next...	341
The Cornish Crime Thriller Series	343
Acknowledgments	345
Forensic File	347

DEAD RECKONING

DEAD RECKONING – A Cornish Crime Thriller #3

When Besnik Domi, the feared enforcer for organised crime gang, the Hellbanianz, is extradited back to Britain, PC Tamsyn Poldhu has to face the man who tore her family apart. Detective Inspector Rob Rego's job is to make sure that the case against the killer is watertight.

But the Domi brothers have a long reach, and when threats are made against both Tamsyn's and Rego's families, they have a choice to make.

And it might not be justice.

DEDICATION

To Wendy
A kick-ass WDC, a pioneer for women in the police in the
1980s.

CORNISH CRIME THRILLER SERIES

#0.5 *Dead Start*
#1 *Dead Water*
#2 *Dead Man's Dive*
#3 *Dead Reckoning*
#4 *Dead Shore*

PROLOGUE

Tamsyn had not been to court before.

When the door to the witness room finally opened and the usher called her name, Tamsyn thought she was going to be sick.

She stood on shaky legs, tucked her police bowler hat under her arm and entered the courtroom, wishing she felt ready to face a killer.

It was eerily silent as she followed the usher who directed her to the witness box, and she felt her cheeks burning as everyone's eyes focused on her. She placed her hat on the chair behind her, then standing erect, she looked straight ahead, hoping to portray confidence. But when she placed both hands on the table top, her palms were damp. She only barely resisted the urge to tug at her constricting uniform or wipe the sweat from her forehead, and she tried very hard not to twitch.

She stood looking at the row of lawyers seated directly in front of her: five men and three women, like a flock of crows in their black robes and formal wigs.

A murder of crows.

The judge sat alone; rimless glasses perched on a fleshy nose. His was the only gaze that seemed neutral.

Tamsyn discreetly cast her eyes at the twelve members of the jury who were all watching her curiously. She didn't glance up at the public gallery where anyone who was interested in the case could gaze down at the theatre below, and she definitely didn't want to see Detective Inspector Rego watching her. It was enough to know he was there.

The man they'd all come to see sat behind a reinforced glass screen, flanked by two uniformed prison officers. Besnik Domi: enforcer for the organised crime gang, the Hellbanianz; drug tsar; money launderer; murderer. Tamsyn could feel the cold stare of his shark-like eyes. She felt utterly alone, but repeated the mantra that her sergeant had taught her: *remember who is on trial here, remember who is going home tonight.*

Even though he was seated below, the defence barrister appeared to sneer down his long nose at her. Tamsyn had never encountered Sir Malcolm Sloane KC before, but when she'd heard that he was going to be defending the man who'd tried to kill her, she'd Googled everything she could find about him. That had been a mistake because what she'd read had filled her with dread and loathing: the man was ruthless, defending murderers, terrorists, arms dealers, and criminal gang members. He rarely lost a case.

His junior counsel sat behind him, looking alert and expectant, ready to collect the pearls of wisdom that Sir Malcolm prepared to cast before swine.

Tamsyn's head snapped towards the usher when he asked if she wanted to swear or affirm.

"I'll swear," Tamsyn said, her voice low but steady.

She placed her hand on the Bible, and then the usher asked her to repeat the oath after him.

"I swear by Almighty God that the evidence I shall give shall be the truth, the whole truth, and nothing but the truth."

She was relieved that her voice didn't waver and remained steady.

As the prosecuting barrister took her through her evidence-in-chief, Sir Malcolm scribbled endless notes, occasionally nodding at something his junior counsel whispered to him.

At the end of the questioning, Tamsyn felt calmer and more confident.

Those feelings didn't last for long.

Sir Malcolm's black robes swirled around him as he rose from his seat, a Darth Vader of the courtroom, and he stared at her for several seconds, his pale blue eyes unblinking. Then he glanced down at his notes, turning the pages slowly, before taking the top off an expensive-looking fountain pen and putting an asterisk next to several questions.

Tamsyn had been warned that this was all theatrics, mind games to unnerve the witness. Unfortunately, it was working.

"Constable Poldhu, good morning."

"Good morning, sir."

"Please could you tell the jury how long you had been a police officer at the time of the alleged offence, Saturday the 1st of April earlier this year."

As if Tamsyn needed to be reminded of the day she'd nearly died.

"Three months."

"But your first day as an active police officer after those few weeks of training, I believe that was Monday 27th March: is that correct?"

"Yes, sir."

"So, at the time of the alleged offence, you had completed only one week as an active police officer: is that correct?"

"Yes."

"And how old are you, PC Poldhu?"

"I'm 21."

"I believe it was your birthday last June, so you were just twenty at the time in question?"

"Yes."

"I must be getting old when police officers are so young," he said, giving a self-deprecating smile to the jury who appeared to appreciate the joke.

Tamsyn knew what he was doing; knew that he was working to undermine her credibility because she was young and maybe even because she was blonde. But knowing his game didn't stop him hitting his target.

"You're too pretty to be a police officer."

Besnik Domi had said those words to her, and now he was sitting in the dock, staring down with dark, amused eyes.

She knew that Domi was as guilty as hell and as evil as the Devil himself. But within the legal system was a presumption of innocence until guilt had been proven.

Sir Malcolm's comment had sowed the appropriate seed. Tamsyn could see what the jury had been led to think: that she was too young and inexperienced to know what she was talking about. There wasn't a thing she could do to stop them, except refuse to crumble.

But with the precision of a surgeon, Sir Malcolm began dismantling her evidence piece by piece. He didn't bully or belittle her, knowing juries didn't like that; instead, he calmly and clinically challenged every word she'd said until she felt uncertain of her own name.

"In fact, you didn't see the defendant kill Saemira Ruçi, did you, officer?"

"No."

"Did you see him with her at all?"

"The CCTV..."

"I'm asking you: what *you* saw, what *you* heard..." Sir Malcolm took a pleased breath then continued. "In fact, you didn't see the defendant with Saemira Ruçi at all, is that correct?"

"Only on CCTV," Tamsyn replied stoically.

Sir Malcolm responded coolly.

"A poor-quality image where it is not possible to positively identify the defendant."

It was true: the CCTV image of victim and murderer was blurry, and the man in the dock had been identified by his sweatshirt, a tenuous link at best.

Tamsyn's resolve began to crack; sweat dampening her shirt under her arms and in the small of her back. She knew that Domi was guilty, knew it with every breath in her body, but proving it was not as straightforward as she'd believed.

Sir Malcolm let his last comment linger portentously, appearing neither annoyed nor impatient. He was building a defence, one implacable sentence at a time, working towards a crescendo that threatened to overwhelm her.

"So, according to your version of events, there were just four people on the boat that night: the defendant, your uncle, your grandfather and you. Quite the family affair."

"George Mason was not my uncle."

"You had called him 'Uncle George' your whole life."

Tamsyn was silent.

"Did you see the defendant aim a gun at your grandfather?"

"No, but..."

"Perhaps you saw the defendant kill George Mason?"

"No, I didn't see it, because I'd already jumped overboard when Domi tried to shoot me!"

"So, you didn't see who shot George Mason, did you?"

"No, but there was nobody else on the boat!"

"How can you be sure? You said yourself that you were highly distressed after your uncle, George Mason, shot your grandfather; in fact, you believed him to be dead. We can all understand that your memory of that night would be hazy. In fact, there was someone else on that boat. Didn't you hear them moving about? There was a fifth person, wasn't there, officer?"

The barrister raised his eyebrows.

"Well, there was Morwenna," Tamsyn replied hesitantly.

Sir Malcolm was taken aback, clearly not having expected that answer.

"My dog."

"I beg your pardon?"

"She's a Jack Russell," said Tamsyn, causing a ripple of amusement around the court.

The barrister was clearly not amused.

"Yes, well we were talking about humans," he said tightly, "not canines."

"Then you'd be missing out a key part of what happened," Tamsyn said, looking him in the eye. "When the defendant attacked me, she bit him, and that's when I jumped overboard."

Sir Malcolm was surprised that she'd managed to pull him off track, but he was too experienced to let it bother him for long. Instead, he turned it to his advantage.

"I'm glad you find this a laughing matter, officer, because I do not, and nor do the members of this jury."

"I wasn't..."

Sir Malcolm cut her off and Tamsyn began to shrivel under his steady assault as he caught her up in knots of her own making, leaving her sweating and tongue-tied; worse still, he'd made the jury question her evidence.

He drew himself up, his pale eyes scything through her.

"I put it to you, PC Poldhu, that your version of events is not the full story. You were a novice, still in your first week with the police, your first week! And in your distressed state, believing your grandfather to have been murdered by the man you called your uncle, it's completely understandable that you don't have a full grip of what occurred. It's also understandable that you don't want your uncle's memory, a close family friend in fact, to be sullied: we'd all understand that."

He drew himself up for the kill.

"But the facts of the case are this: George Mason was a criminal who had been smuggling drugs for years, something that he made plain to you. He was the one who had a connection with the victim; he was the one who was seen with her, who worked with her, who called her on her mobile phone; and he is the man who killed her."

The verbal torrent left her breathless whilst Sir Malcolm breathed so hard that Tamsyn half-expected fire to shoot from his nostrils.

"Is it not the case, PC Poldhu, that my client was merely

a useful scapegoat, a legitimate businessman who was in the wrong place at the wrong time and became entangled in your uncle's web of deceit, and that Mr Domi is wholly innocent of the charges brought against him."

"No, I..."

"Can you really expect this jury to believe your half-baked version of events? That a *dog* saved you? At best, you have been shown to be naïve; at worst, incompetent. You don't know what happened that night: isn't that the truth?"

Tamsyn clamped her mouth shut. She knew that whatever she said would be twisted against her. Detective Inspector Rego had tried to warn her, tried to tell her: *"No one ever wins an argument with a barrister."*

But she'd been so certain of herself, so certain of the truth, so sure that the jury would recognise the truth when they heard it. And she'd been wrong.

The man who'd hit her, who'd pointed a gun at her, who'd threatened to kill her, who'd tried to shoot her, he was watching her now, a faint smirk lifting one corner of his mouth. Then he glanced away, seemingly bored by the proceedings.

"PC Poldhu," Sir Malcolm repeated, "would you please answer?"

"I..."

Tamsyn couldn't speak. She simply couldn't find the words.

Sir Malcolm glanced at the judge who gave Tamsyn a long, cool, look.

"Just answer the question please, officer."

"I have sworn on the Bible and have said nothing but the truth. I have come here to assist the court," she stammered.

But before she could say another word, she was thrown to the ground.

Her ears were ringing and she felt like she was choking.

Who pushed me?

Then she realised that the room was full of thick, black smoke, and flames were licking up the side of the room.

Sir Malcolm was on the floor just feet from her, eyes squeezed shut, his mouth opening and closing. His wig was comically askew and he clutched his right hand to his chest. Several of his fingers lay next to him.

What? That's not right.

The rest of the lawyers had vanished, papers strewn about where they'd been sitting. As staff and jury fled for the fire exits, Tamsyn felt as if she was watching a silent, black-and-white film. She couldn't stop the ringing in her ears.

Suddenly, DI Rego was there, shaking her arm roughly, his mouth moving, but the words were muffled and didn't make sense. He was shouting at her, shouting something urgent. He tugged on her arm again, then put his mouth close to her ear.

"BOMB!" he yelled. "There's been a bomb!"

She touched her head and her hand came away red, but she didn't know if it was her own blood or Sir Malcolm's.

Dimly, she heard Rego again, the words muted as if she were underwater.

"...walk?"

She frowned in confusion.

"Tam ... you walk?"

She nodded groggily as he pulled her to her feet.

Smoke filled the windowless room making her cough and her eyes water.

"...you help...?"

Rego gripped her arms, shaking her urgently until she looked at him.

"We ... help them!" he yelled, pointing at Sir Malcolm and then at Judge Whittaker, whose chest was sheeted with blood. "...them out!"

The heat in the courtroom was growing and sweat stung her eyes, but each second brought greater clarity.

She blinked and nodded at Rego, then tottered across to Sir Malcolm who was no longer moving. She didn't know if he was breathing or not and there was no time to check for a pulse. She had to get him out. She had to get them both out.

Kneeling behind him, she slid one hand under his neck and the other between his shoulder blades, lifting carefully and sliding herself closer until Sir Malcolm was slumped in a sitting position half on her lap.

The police manual instructed that the next step was to put her hands under the casualty's armpits, then grip his forearm and wrist, but Tamsyn's hands tangled in Sir Malcolm's robes as the flames licked closer. She had to move *now*. Her muscles protested as she straightened her spine, adrenaline fuelling her strength as she shuffled backwards, but Sir Malcolm was heavy and it was getting harder to breathe as smoke spiralled around them.

From the corner of her eye, she saw Rego staggering from the courtroom with Judge Whittaker slung over his shoulders in a fireman's lift.

Tamsyn inched backwards, but with her hands still caught in his robes, she didn't have a good grip on Sir Malcolm. The heat was becoming unbearable until finally a weak sprinkler system was activated, sending clouds of steam hissing into the vaulted ceiling.

With her boots slipping and sliding on the wet marble floor, she'd managed to drag Sir Malcolm as far as the corridor outside the courtroom when a camera flash briefly pierced the haze. A man with a camera swept past, photographing the scenes of chaos.

"Help me!" she wheezed, but her voice was too weak to carry far, and she was inhaling too much smoke.

When Tamsyn saw a second figure running towards them, hope cut through the agony of trying to drag the 16 stone barrister.

She screamed for help, but only a hoarse, hacking cough erupted from her throat.

It was enough.

The figure swung towards her.

In utter disbelief, Tamsyn saw the muzzle flash of a machine pistol pointed in her direction, and shards of coloured plastic flew through the air as the green exit sign shattered. She fell backwards with Sir Malcolm on top of her, recoiling as other rounds hit the side of the court building, shattering windows which had survived the initial blast.

Bullets arced across the atrium, peppering the stucco ceiling, pocking the walls, and sending chips flying from the marble floor, but Tamsyn was pinned down by Sir Malcolm's dead weight. She struggled as her lungs were compressed, trying to wriggle free.

The gunman spun in a circle, his extended arm still holding the weapon. He looked straight down the barrel at Tamsyn.

He walked towards her slowly, his finger slipping from the side of the trigger guard to the trigger itself.

Tamsyn's mind floated outside her body, and she was calm. She'd always known this time would come. From the moment she'd seen the drowned body of her father when she was just ten years old, she'd known that death came to all people, good or bad. And on this day, death wore the face of her nemesis: Besnik Domi.

He prowled towards Tamsyn, his steps unhurried even as smoke swirled through the weak sprays of water. He smiled, and used the machine pistol's elongated barrel to move her hair from her face, gently, almost lovingly. He said something in his own language then blew her a kiss.

And pulled the trigger.

CHAPTER 1

Detective Inspector Rob Rego stepped onto the podium in his borrowed jacket, mouth set in a grim line. Flashes from an array of cameras blinded him and his eyes watered for the second time that day.

Assistant Chief Constable Gray clapped an overly-familiar hand on his shoulder and subtly steered him off to the side then took up a flanking position as Assistant Commissioner Shinawatra from the City of London Police stepped forwards.

She was a small, severe woman in her early fifties who exuded authority, and as she opened her mouth to speak, the room fell silent, only the continuing clicks of camera shutters penetrating the ominous weight in the room.

Christ, thought Rego, *we're like a recruitment poster for diversity in modern policing: Asian woman and biracial man.* Then he glanced at his boss, Assistant Chief Constable Gray: *and the ginger tosser.*

"Good afternoon, ladies and gentlemen," Shinawatra began. "Thank you for coming to this press briefing. My name is Assistant Commissioner Chalita Shinawatra and I am the Gold Commander for this incident. I'm here with colleagues Assistant Chief Constable Ian Gray and Detective Inspector Robert Rego from Devon & Cornwall Police."

Rego wondered why nobody from the Metropolitan Police was on the podium with them; they had resources that the City Police couldn't even dream of, and he was fairly sure they'd be taking the lead further on in the investigation, whatever Shinawatra said.

There was a soft clatter as fifty cameras pointed towards Rego and Shinawatra, along with a few half-hearted snaps of Gray.

"On your chairs you will find details of our 24/7 telephone hotline for information, and the website where mobile phone footage can be uploaded." She paused, her voice filled with gravitas. "I can confirm that at 10:09am this morning, Monday 21st October, police were called to an incident at the Central Criminal Court, London EC4, where an explosive device was detonated in Court 1. A male detained person escaped from custody where he was standing trial for murder, drug trafficking, and seven counts of money-laundering. My colleagues from the southwest were giving evidence at the time."

Gray frowned, and Rego was irritated and impressed in equal proportions by the subtle way Shinawatra deflected any possible hint of blame from City of London Police. She continued smoothly, giving more details, including the orchestration of the attack, diversion, and subsequent flight.

"This incident enabled the defendant to escape from custody. An automatic weapon was discharged in the court following the explosion. The defendant and now the man suspected to be behind this attack on the Old Bailey is Besnik Domi, an Albanian national. Domi is a very dangerous man, and if seen, he should not be approached under any circumstances. Instead, we ask anyone who thinks they have seen him to dial 999 immediately and we will respond with the appropriate resources. Domi could be anywhere in the UK: through his criminality, he has contacts across the country. We believe Domi may still be armed, so again I repeat, if seen, do not approach this man, dial 999. This is a recent photograph of him," and she pointed to a large screen behind her.

Domi's mugshot was displayed along with a blurry CCTV image of him speeding down a pavement on the back of a motorbike driven by an unknown male.

Shinawatra paused, taking a moment to let her eyes travel across the assembled journalists.

"It is with deep regret that I have to inform you that as a result of this incident, Sir Malcolm Sloane, a senior member of the King's Counsel, was taken to the Royal London Hospital where he later died."

Rego tried to hide his surprise because he hadn't known that Sir Malcolm had passed away. His injuries hadn't seemed that significant.

"There is also a police officer in hospital who was injured during the attack. She is currently under armed guard. The injuries to this officer are not life threatening but the officer is currently undergoing treatment. I'm not prepared to disclose the extent of her injuries."

Shinawatra held up her hand as the journalists demanded to know more about the injured officer. She ignored their questions and continued with the briefing.

"The Central Criminal Court is currently closed. Army bomb disposal experts have conducted a thorough search of the whole building and determined there are no secondary devices. An extensive forensic examination is being conducted. This is likely to be ongoing for some time, and we ask that the public bear with us. We appreciate there is some significant disruption in the local area while those enquiries continue. No doubt you will have seen video footage of the road outside the court in the local area being blocked: we are working with partners from the City of London Corporation, the London Fire Brigade, London Ambulance Service and the Metropolitan Police to remedy the local issues caused by the criminal gang whom we believe to be responsible. We are grateful to the Mayor of London for his ongoing support and resources made available to us."

Rego kept his expression deadpan as Shinawatra finally mentioned the Met at the end of a long list.

He hated politics getting in the way of police work. It happened too often, and he glanced at Gray.

Shinawatra carried on reading from her notes whilst still making regular eye-contact with the assembled reporters.

She's done her media training, Rego thought cynically.

"Court 1 of the Old Bailey has sustained significant damage and will be closed for the foreseeable future. However, the overall structure of the building has not been compromised. Some of the court staff have been affected by this abhorrent attack, and counselling will be made available to all members of staff or members of the public in the building who have been affected."

Then she returned to the most critical part of her communication.

"I would urge anyone with mobile phone or any other footage to upload it onto the website address you can see on the screen, and the same information is on your briefing sheets. If anyone has information but is unable to access the website, please contact us and an officer will come to you."

"Is this being treated as a terrorist incident?" asked a reporter from the front of the pack.

"Was Sir Malcolm assassinated?" shouted another.

"How much damage was done to the Old Bailey?"

"Who was the female police officer?"

"Do you think Domi has left the country?"

Rego was wondering the same thing. Part of him hoped this particular criminal had fled abroad, but the other part wanted the bastard to rot in a British prison for what he'd done. And he was pretty damn sure that there most definitely was an ongoing threat to the public whilst Domi remained at large.

Shinawatra ignored the barrage of questions.

"It is not my intention to extend this press briefing. As you can appreciate, I have a lot to do and I need to get back to Scotland Yard to liaise with my colleagues from the Metropolitan Police. There is a fast-paced investigation with a considerable amount of information that needs analysing. You will see an increased police presence in the area for public reassurance, so thank you for your time this afternoon. We will have further press briefings in the forthcoming days."

She turned to leave but the assembled journalists were unhappy with her closing statement and yelled out more questions. Some of them turned to Rego instead, but he said nothing, glancing once at the crowd bristling with microphones and unanswered questions, then followed Gray and Shinawatra from the podium.

As soon as they were out of the journalists' earshot, Gray drew Rego to one side.

"I'm heading out to a top-level meeting with Assistant

Commissioner Shinawatra and the Met's AC for Frontline Policing," he informed Rego. "There's no need for you to stay in London, so you'll be travelling back to Exeter with the rest of your team now."

It was a statement, not a question, but Rego shook his head.

"No, sir, not until the morning. We're staying at the hotel for another night."

Gray had already started to walk away but paused and looked over his shoulder.

"Has that been authorised? We do have a budget to work to, and we have to be accountable."

Rego stared at a space to the left of Gray's epaulettes.

"One of my team is in hospital, sir. I'd like to see her first."

"Ah, yes. That girl..."

"Police Constable Poldhu."

"Yes, I know her name, Rego. You seem to be joined at the hip with her," and he gave Rego a speculative look.

"She was integral to the Domi case, sir, and a key witness," Rego said tightly.

Gray glanced at his watch. "Very well. I want your report in my inbox by tomorrow morning. Carry on," and he strode away.

Rego watched him leave, running a weary hand over his head, fingering the small sticking plaster that covered a cut above his eye.

I'm fine. Thanks for asking.

He had a headache that was off the Richter scale, and two paracetamol and an ibuprofen had barely put a dent in it, but he'd walked away from the scene. He'd been very lucky.

And he had a lot of work to do. For a start, he wanted to

get back to the Old Bailey and check on the retrieval of exhibits and documents from the damaged courtroom, and hope that nothing significant had been lost for when Domi was recaptured, re-tried, and convicted of his crimes.

Rego took off the borrowed suit jacket but had no idea who to leave it with, so simply hung it on the back of a chair and pulled on his overcoat, trudging along the damp, chilly streets, deep in thought. This part of the city was always quiet once the working day had ended, all of life moving to Soho and the West End while the offices belonging to banks, law firms and money-makers sank into darkness one window at a time. But several streets before he'd even reached the Old Bailey, the blaze of huge LED floodlights erected to help the road crew, fire fighters and forensic teams shrunk the shadows and made him shield his eyes.

Domi's gang had planned everything like a military operation, including hijacking a Blue Circle lorry carrying eight cubic metres of ready-mix concrete which they'd used to flood the street, slowing any chance of pursuit. The spill had also stopped paramedics getting to the wounded and the London Fire Brigade getting to the fire before more serious damage was done to the century-old building.

With forensics on the scene, every centimetre of pavement and road were being photographed, and every piece of rubbish examined, recorded, and taken away in the unlikely event that it held trace evidence.

A massive bulldozer was scooping the semi-set concrete into huge skips that were being hoisted onto articulated lorries and guided through the narrow streets past the baroque silhouette of St Paul's Cathedral.

The Old Bailey was a crime scene and being there wasn't Rego's job, but he wanted to check in with the scene search officer. Although, as documents were scanned into the court system and stored electronically, most trials these days didn't have a lot of paper.

Rego was given an ill-fitting forensic suit to wear as he made his way inside. He showed his ID again, wrinkling his nose at the stench of smoke and dirty water.

He found the crime scene search officer sifting through debris and documents pertaining to the case, at least half of them completely sodden from the building's sprinkler system. It had done more damage than the incendiary device, and maybe Domi had planned that, too.

He met her weary gaze, clearly irritated to be disturbed, so decided to get out of her hair. He had no business being here. He gave her a brief smile, thanked her and the team for their work, received grunts in reply, and left the scene to the officers who were paid to process it.

He needed to get to the hospital.

CHAPTER 2

Tamsyn lay in her hospital bed stinking of smoke and bone tired, but pain and the ringing in her ears kept her wide awake. Every part of her body ached and she felt as if she'd lost a run-in with a double-decker bus. Her head thumped so relentlessly that she was nauseated, and every breath she dragged into her lungs burned.

But more than that, she was scared. Every time the door opened, she nearly jumped out of her skin, and her erratic heartrate showed in spikes on the monitor above her bed.

Why am I alive? Why am I still alive? The words beat an insistent tattoo in her brain.

When Domi had pointed the gun at her, it felt as if she'd fallen off a cliff, as if her body was in free fall and her mind frozen. She hadn't even been able to close her eyes, staring into the gaping barrel of the gun, watching, utterly unable to move.

She'd seen Domi pull the trigger; she'd seen the moment he killed her. She'd expected to die, and in that split second, she'd mourned the life she'd never have.

But she hadn't died, and she didn't know why.

The TV was tuned to the BBC News with the sound off and the subtitles on, so she'd seen the entire press conference. They'd spelled her boss's name as 'Reagan' on the subtitles and she wondered if they'd correct it in later broadcasts. She saw the explanation of how Domi had escaped then the announcement that Sir Malcolm had died.

I didn't save him. I couldn't even save one person.

She hadn't liked the man but he shouldn't have died today.

Her throat felt as if it had been sandpapered and her breathing was as noisy as that of a lifelong smoker. Another fit of coughing had her reaching for the oxygen mask.

She was too busy hacking up a lung to hear the quiet knock on the door, but then Rego was standing next to her, helping to fix the oxygen mask around her face. She gulped in lungfuls of cool air, her breathing gradually easing.

"Do you want some water?"

She nodded weakly, and Rego used the bed's remote control to raise her into a sitting position, then he carefully removed the oxygen mask and held a plastic beaker to her mouth as she took a sip.

This brought on another coughing fit, and she was too wretched to care when he passed her a bowl made of recycled cardboard to spit into.

Finally, the coughing subsided, and she lay back in bed, utterly spent.

Rego sat in the chair next to her.

"Well, I won't ask how you are," he said, drawing a reluctant smile from her. "Mimi and Sid have been asking after you."

Tamsyn nodded, her eyes closing.

"I've spoken to your grandparents..."

Tamsyn groaned quietly and opened her eyes again.

"...obviously, they're worried, but I told them that you'd be out of hospital in a day or two." He paused. "Look, I know you said you didn't want them to come here, but I can get a car to bring them tonight. They'd be here in seven or eight hours."

"No!"

"Okay," Rego said resignedly. "But if you change your mind..."

"I won't," she croaked.

Rego nodded, although it was clear that he didn't agree with her decision.

"Domi?" she coughed, her eyes hopeful.

Rego shook his head tiredly.

"A Crown Court Bench Warrant has been issued for his arrest. There's a manhunt under way with an all-ports bulletin, and he's on the Interpol Red Notice."

"Sir Malcolm? I thought..."

"I'm sorry, Tamsyn, he didn't make it. His heart stopped on the way to the hospital – maybe it was the shock. There was nothing you could have done; there was nothing anyone could have done."

It had all been pointless. Everything she'd done had been for nothing.

Rego was still talking.

"There's something else I need to tell you – there was a journalist at the court and he took a number of photos of you with Sir Malcolm."

Yes, that was it. I remember seeing a camera flash. I remember Sir Malcolm's dead weight pinning me down. And then Domi...

"And there were more taken outside while we were waiting for paramedics." He watched her pale face closely. "The photos are already circulating online and we're expecting them to be in the newspapers by morning. So far, they don't have your name, and we're hoping to keep it that way. Our press office at Exeter have been informed and are dealing with it."

Tamsyn flung an arm over her eyes.

Rego wasn't surprised by her reaction.

"Yeah, I know. Look, Tamsyn, I've spoken to Inspector Walters at Penzance and also DCI Finch at Exeter and they agree with me that this on top of Domi's interest puts you in a vulnerable position. I've made some calls and they're assigning you a protection team from MO19 while you're in hospital."

MO19 was the firearms unit of the Metropolitan Police which meant that Tamsyn would have an armed guard to watch over her.

Tamsyn squeezed her eyes shut and shook her head weakly.

"It's not your decision," Rego said gently but firmly. "I've also been ordered to tell you that you're on sick leave for the time being ... and you won't be allowed to come back to frontline duties if there's even a hint that Domi is still in the UK."

Tamsyn's eyes opened wide.

"No!"

Domi had taken so much from her: her security, the way she lived, and now her work, too. Fury coursed through her even as she felt utterly impotent. She was a police officer, sworn to uphold the law, and she wanted to do her job, she needed to do her job. Yet again, she'd been sidelined because of him. Tears of frustration burned behind her eyes but she refused to give in to them.

"No!" she wheezed, almost retching as she coughed violently.

Rego waited until she'd finished, then held the beaker of water to her mouth again. She tried to hold it herself, but her hands were shaking too badly.

"Tamsyn," Rego said patiently, "when we were debriefed, you reported that Domi tried to kill you, so while he's still at large, the level of threat is very high. Your grandparents were asked if they'd like to go to a hotel for a few nights, but they declined. I did get them to agree to having extra security measures at the cottage instead: there's CCTV being put in, a panic alarm linked directly to Penzance nick, dead bolts on doors and windows, and there'll be passing patrols until the threat has been downgraded – which means when we receive intelligence that Domi has left the UK."

Tamsyn's eyes were wide and fearful at the realisation that this had put her grandparents at risk.

Rego understood how she felt: when you started in the job, no one anticipated the toxic fallout on relationships and families. He was worried about her.

"I'm arranging for you to have an armed escort back to Cornwall, so there'll be an Armed Response Vehicle and a driver."

"Sir, I don't think..."

"Devon & Cornwall Police have a duty of care for you, and until intelligence indicates otherwise, the threat risk is high. This is real, Tamsyn. The Met's Firearms Silver Commander and his tactical advisor have both endorsed their risk assessment that you need armed protection."

A loud knock made her start, and Rego stood up to peer through the small window before he opened the door.

Tamsyn caught a glimpse of a man in a police tactical uniform. Rego spoke quietly to him for several minutes before allowing him into the room.

"Tamsyn, this is PC Joe Quinn from MO19. He and his team will be ensuring your safety while you're at the Royal London. Quinn, this is PC Tamsyn Poldhu."

Joe Quinn's ready smile was framed by quick, grey eyes and a thatch of light brown hair, but it was the weapon slung over his shoulder that drew Tamsyn's attention.

Technically, every police officer in the UK was trained with firearms as the Captor incapacitant spray was considered a firearm, but Tamsyn had never fired a gun and it hadn't been part of her training. Her mind flashed back to Domi and her heart missed a beat. Above her bed, the monitor beeped in sympathy.

"Good to meet you," said Quinn, his gaze roaming the room as he spoke.

Tamsyn nodded weakly.

"Right then," Rego said, stifling a yawn. "I'll get off now. I need to give your grandparents another call to let them know that I've seen you and that you'll be in touch with them tomorrow. But if you need anything, just call me, okay?"

"Thank you, sir."

Rego nodded, then turned to the young MO19 officer.

"Look after her, Quinn."

"Yes, guv."

Rego took one last look at Tamsyn, then left the room.

Quinn spent the next minute checking each corner, under the bed and the *en suite* bathroom, then much longer looking out from the small window in all directions. Tamsyn's breath stuttered when she realised that he was working out if there was any way a sniper could get an angle into her room.

Surely, Domi doesn't care that much about killing me?

But maybe he did.

It was a chilling thought.

When he'd finished the checks, Quinn grinned at Tamsyn. She got the impression that he'd used that smile on his share of women.

"You're well in wiv your inspector, aincha?" he said.

"What?"

"Hear you're a bit of a legend down your way, at the seaside, Devon or whatever."

"Cornwall. Not Devon."

"It's all the same, innit?" he smirked.

Tamsyn turned her head towards him slowly.

"Quinn?"

His grin widened, his chest puffing out.

"That's right, darlin'. But you can call me Joe."

"Well, Joe, why don't you just Fuck Right Off."

To her surprise, he threw back his head and laughed.

"Blimey, officer! You're my kind of girl!" His smile softened. "Don't you worry about nothing. I'll be right outside all night so you can get some shut-eye."

Then he winked at her.

She stared, unsure what to make of him, her brain still reeling from everything Rego had said.

"D'you know a bloke called Jason Johnson? I heard he's in the job down your way."

Her brain felt foggy and it took her a moment to recalibrate her thoughts.

"Yes, he's on E-Team with me," she said hoarsely. "We started the same day. How do you know him?"

"We was in the Marines together, Alpha Company 40 Commando. How is ole JJ?"

Before Tamsyn could answer, a nurse came into the room with the nighttime meds, turned off the TV, and shooed Quinn away.

Before the painkillers began to kick in, Tamsyn made a short call to her grandparents, her words slurred as she assured them again that she was okay and they didn't need to come up.

That drained the last of her strength, and she fell into an uneasy sleep, her dreams dark and troubling. Her breathing escalated and she felt her lungs being crushed, the weight on her chest unbearable. A scream tore from her throat as she thrashed against the sheets that imprisoned her.

Two armed officers burst into the room.

Joe Quinn's face was fierce as he checked every corner, high points and low points, pivoting into the bathroom, then slowly relaxing when he was certain there was no intruder.

He jerked his head at his colleague who nodded and stationed himself outside the room again.

Tamsyn was still gasping for breath and bathed in sweat.

"Cor dear, that took ten years off me life," Joe said with a reassuring grin. "You're alright. No one will get to you, not while I'm on watch. I got your back, Cornwall."

And for some reason, Tamsyn believed him.

He closed the door quietly behind him, and at last, she slept.

When she woke the next morning, she was ready to go home.

CHAPTER 3

Rego's phone rang again as he climbed into a black cab taking him to his hotel near Waterloo station. His finger hovered over the 'reject' button, but he'd already sent three of his mother's calls to voicemail, and he knew he had to speak to her sooner rather than later.

"Hi, Mum."

"My bwoy!" she choked out. "My brave, handsome bwoy!"

Then she sobbed into the phone for the next minute. It was a FaceTime call, but she hadn't realised, so Rego got a close up of her left ear. He decided to wait until she'd stopped crying. And waited. And waited.

"Mum," he said helplessly, "I'm fine. I'm okay. Really. Mum, take the phone away from your ear; this is a video call."

He saw her stare at her phone screen in surprise.

"Robert! There you are! I telled all me friends that you was on the telly," she said, blowing her nose so loudly that he had to hold his phone further away. "You looked so handsome, Robert. But very scruffy! Why were you wearing that awful jacket? Why didn't they let you say anything? Why did that Indian woman do all the talking? She wasn't even there!"

Her voice was so indignant that Rego smiled.

"She's an Assistant Commissioner, Mum. She outranks me quite a lot."

"Humph!"

"Anyway, how are you feeling, Mum?"

"Better now I's talking to you," she sniffed, dabbing at her eyes.

"You're not feeling too sick from the chemo? Cassie said ... well, just one more treatment to go now."

"I'm fine," she said, waving away his concern and adjusting the colourful silk headscarf that hid her thinning hair. "When are you coming home?"

He'd begun to consider his cottage in Newlyn as home, but he knew that wasn't what she meant.

"Tomorrow evening or the day after," he said. "Then I'll have a few days off."

"I should think so!" she snorted. "Are they giving you a medal, Robert? They should give you a medal! My bwoy is a hero!"

The conversation would have continued all the way to the hotel, so Rego was relieved when he saw an incoming call that he needed to take.

"Sorry, Mum, I've got to go, it's work. I'll phone you tomorrow and see you in a couple of days. Look after yourself."

"Robert, don't you..."

He winced as he cut her off, then answered his next call from a former colleague.

"Vik, how are you?"

"I should be asking you that," Vikram laughed, his

Brummie accent as rich as ever. "Saw you on the 6 o'clock news looking very *GQ*, or so Kam says."

"Sod off," Rego laughed. "It's good to hear your voice. How's life at the circus?"

"Full of clowns," Vikram replied.

The 'circus' was a nickname for MI6 where Vikram had been seconded from the National Crime Agency, although it seemed to be becoming permanent. The man was a genius, and he was also a good friend.

"I hope you're not just calling to tell me that your wife fancies me, 'cos I already knew."

"Nah, Kamla has better taste than that!" Vikram paused, his voice becoming serious. "Look, I've been in touch with some friends I still have at the NCA and, so far, they're not finding any trail for Domi."

"Well, it's a bit soon for that," Rego said cautiously.

"Maybe, but usually we'd have heard something by now."

"A confidential informant?"

Vikram didn't answer.

"Well, what have you heard?"

"Not much, and that's the worry. But there is one bit of good news."

"Thank God for that!"

"Yeah," Vikram agreed. "Domi's mum has got a big birthday on Friday. He never misses going to see his old mum, take her flowers and that. We've got eyes on the old dear, so by Friday at the latest, we could know for sure if he's left the UK."

It was longer than Rego wanted to wait for news, but he had no choice.

"I heard the barrister died," Vikram said. "Maybe a murder charge?"

"Maybe, but I'm not going to second-guess what the Crown Prosecution Service will go for."

"Yeah, CPS are a law unto themselves," Vikram agreed.

"Tamsyn really was cut up about it after everything she did to get Sloane out," Rego sighed. "But I won't lie, it'll help the case when we catch up with Domi. Because the evidence to get him on Saemira Ruci's murder ... well, let's just say I wasn't too optimistic about that. And the evidence for George Mason's murder was circumstantial at best. The file of evidence put through to the Crown Prosecution Service bounced back and forward a few times until the burden of evidence gave us a realistic chance of a conviction. It was touch and go, but the CPS were persuaded in the end." He rubbed his eyes tiredly. "Well, Domi is a bit fucked now. He's the most wanted man in the country..."

"And there was me thinking it was you now that your ugly mug has been on TV. I bet your mum liked that, didn't she?"

Vikram had met Rego's mum so he knew what he was talking about.

Rego laughed.

"Yeah, yeah, leave it out. Look, I wanted to ask you something ... one thing that's puzzling me is why Domi went back into the court and shot the place up? The explosion caused enough confusion for him to escape, but he still went back in and sprayed the place with 9mm rounds."

"Maybe it was him being billy bollocks? You know, making a huge statement?" Vikram suggested without much interest. "Anyway, don't worry about it. If they put up a cash reward and it's enough, someone will give him up."

Rego wasn't convinced but let it go. The Hellbanianz

paid gang members well for their loyalty – and were ruthless to those who betrayed them.

"Vik, I'm going to bore you shitless now."

"When haven't you?"

Rego ignored the jibe.

"Article 6 of the European convention..."

Vik groaned. "Yeah, yeah: it protects everyone's right to a fair trial, presumption of innocence, access to a lawyer, yada yada yada."

"All those meetings with CPS sorting out the extradition file, I got to be an expert on Albanian extradition. It was a lucky break that the government entered into the agreement with the Albanian authorities that waives each state's right under Article 6."

"It certainly helps speed things up," said Vik. "Some of these extradition cases can spin on for years."

"Yeah, well this one was quite swift. Our Ministry of Justice and the Albanian General Prosecutions Office got their heads together and sorted all the paperwork."

Vikram yawned.

"Rob, I'm falling asleep already, what's your point?"

"The Albanians couldn't get rid of Domi fast enough. Do you think that was deliberate, because the Hellbanianz already had the Old Bailey plan in place? It could even have been prepped for Domi senior, the older brother that I put in prison a year ago. Either way, there must have been some team behind it to organise that scale of escape."

"Oh, definitely. And I can tell you that he's pushed our buttons. Don't repeat this, but MI6 are on his case as well, and the Prime Minister is asking what the fuck's going on. Whoever gets Domi will get a medal. There'll be a bun fight between Devon & Cornwall Police and the Met as to who gets their hands on him first. That's why your Assistant

Chief Constable was at the press briefing: it's all pissing politics. The Met will want the kudos and probably tell you jack shit about what they're doing." He sighed again. "Do you remember the kidnap case, the estate agent from Brum? When the Regional Crime Squad were looking for her kidnapper and they identified him through *Crimewatch* by playing an audio recording of his voice on TV, West Yorkshire Police beat them to the arrest. I don't think the RCS ever forgave them."

He gave a dry laugh, then his voice became serious.

"But I've got to agree with you, Rob, I'm definitely hearing chatter about Domi senior. There was some sort of celebration from him and the other prisoners on his cell's wing when little brother skipped the Old Bailey." He paused. "Word is that he's making it personal. Watch your back."

Rego's thoughts immediately went to his family. He decided to ask his old colleagues at Greater Manchester Police to keep an eye on them and send regular patrol past the house.

"How did your Tamsyn do on the stand?" Vikram asked.

"It wasn't the best start to her first time in court," Rego admitted, "and that was before the bomb went off, but she wasn't a complete pushover either."

"No one wins an argument with a barrister," said Vikram.

"The exact words I told her," Rego agreed. "Of course, everything that happened after didn't help..."

The conversation reached a hiatus, the easy friendship between them harder now that Vikram moved in the shadowy circles of MI6 and they no longer shared the same national security clearance level.

"Let me know if you hear anything else," Rego said at last. "Thanks for the call."

The taxi pulled up at the wide steps and curving frontage of the Union Jack Club where Rego's team were staying during the trial. He paid the fare then waited while the driver scribbled a receipt.

He was surprised and pleased to see Detective Sergeant Tom Stevens when he stepped into the bar.

"Tom!" he said, walking towards him with his hand outstretched. "Did I know you were coming up?"

"Depends on whether you've checked your emails in the last few hours, boss. I came up with ACC Gray because I thought you could use some help," Stevens smiled, shaking his hand heartily. "Didn't he tell you?"

Rego felt his smile stiffen.

"Must have slipped his mind."

Which was typical of the man.

Stevens didn't seem to notice Rego's change in tone.

"How's young Tamsyn?" he asked.

"Coughing like she smokes two packs a day, but otherwise okay."

Stevens glanced down at Rego's threadbare grey tracksuit.

"You look snazzy, boss," he sniggered. "Did you go to court dressed like that?"

Rego laughed and held his hands out from his sides, showing off the baggy, ill-fitting outfit.

"I know I look like a twat, but I had no choice. They took my trousers and jacket for trace evidence, and gave me *this* to wear. I had to borrow a jacket for the press briefing."

Stevens was still laughing at his own joke.

"I've never been subject of a Post Incident Management

debrief but if the PIM team give me clothes like that afterwards, I don't think I want to."

Rego sighed.

"I was wearing my favourite suit to court, but the bomb detonation is the Met's investigation now, and they need to secure best evidence, so yeah…"

He'd have to put in a claim for his best suit that he'd never see again now that forensics had got their grubby mitts on it.

"Probably best not to ask where they borrowed the jacket from," Stevens added with a big smile. "Did you check it for … stains?"

Rego cringed at the thought.

"The PIM team took Tamsyn's uniform as well. One of us will need to clear out her room here and get some clothes over to her."

"Leave it to me. I'll get Mimi to pack Tamsyn's things and take them to her first thing in the morning."

"Thanks, Tom."

"Mimi said the Met's PIM team were on the ball."

"Yeah, the Met get a lot of criticism but they seemed to swing into action seamlessly. We were all whipped away from the scene in separate vehicles. Tamsyn went straight to hospital, but someone from their PIM team was there when I saw her."

"What were they like?"

"Yeah, okay. Sid, Mimi and me were taken to some building, God knows where, but it was comfortable. They had a load of drinks and snacks laid out for us, so Sid was happy. They asked us again if we needed any medical attention, then separated us for interviews. There's going to be an immediate referral to the IOPC."

Stevens raised an eyebrow. The Independent Office for

Police Conduct investigated the most serious complaints and conduct matters involving the police.

"Yeah, I know," said Rego. "They'll be looking for any police negligence that led up to this, or asking if it could have been prevented. They'll want to blame someone," he shook his head tiredly. "Anyway, I was allocated a DI for the interview and he was fair. He also asked if there were any additional resources I needed, any welfare, operational or technical support as far as our investigation was concerned."

"Blimey, if they're that good, you'll be joining the Met next," said Stevens, only half joking.

Rego was too tired to notice.

"I suppose the only other thing you can say is that at least we don't have to deal with the DSI, because the Death or Serious Injury occurred in London and not on our patch. Anyway," he paused, trying to get his thoughts in order, "I wanted to put a plan in place to make sure that Tamsyn was getting the appropriate medical attention and I asked if she could have armed protection. With Domi still at large and carrying a big fucking gun, I felt she was still at risk. Their DI agreed with me and made a phone call there and then and it was sorted. I couldn't believe it! If it was Greater Manchester Police or our lot, I suspect it would've taken at least 24 hours to put in place." He pulled a face. "And if ACC Gray was asked to make a decision, probably a week, and all he'd want is an entry in the accident book!"

Stevens nodded as if in agreement, but he was surprised, too. It wasn't like Inspector Rego to criticise a superior officer in front of him.

"We may not be as shiny as the Met, boss, but the team are already putting better locks and deadbolts around the Poldhu property."

Rego blinked slowly, then nodded.

"I'm sorry, Tom. I didn't mean to rubbish the team's efforts. Forget I said anything."

Stevens' gaze drifted to the sticking plaster on Rego's forehead and the shadows under his eyes.

"No problem, boss. None of us love the red tape."

They walked towards the back of the room and found an empty table near the bar. Rego slumped into a chair, exhaustion washing over him.

"Tamsyn is really lucky not to have been seriously injured or killed by either the blast or Domi taking her out. She must have someone looking after her up there." He rubbed his eyes. "I told the DI who was interviewing me that Tamsyn is really young in service and when she's discharged from hospital, it would be better to get her back home as quickly as possible. She'll need time to understand the enormity of what's happened and to get a proper psychological assessment. Our PIM team needs to debrief her, as well."

Tom nodded.

"I think we should get someone from the nick to keep an eye on her, just not Chloe Rogers."

"Chloe? Is there a problem there that I should know about?" asked Stevens.

"I've seen some friction between them. They were at school together..."

"What about PC Flowers then?"

"I don't think I know him," said Rego.

"Her. Jasmine Flowers, but she's known as Rosie."

Rego smiled at the bizarre form police humour sometimes took.

"What's she like?"

"A few years older than Tamsyn, solid, a good officer;

well liked on C-team, and about four or five years in the job."

Rego nodded. "Fine, brief her with Bryn Terwillis. He's Tamsyn's tutor."

Stevens made a note in his pocketbook.

"But the first priority," Rego continued, "is to thoroughly assess the risk to her. I don't want Tamsyn's identity in the media; they've already got her picture, but she doesn't need her name being bandied about, because before you know it *Sky News* will have a big van parked outside her house."

He massaged his aching head.

"I need to start a policy book, as well. I know it's more bureaucracy, but when there's a public enquiry, and there will be, I want to make sure that we've thought of everything, most importantly, all welfare issues. If there's anything you think I should be doing, I want to hear it." He gave his sergeant a tired smile. "My ears are still ringing, and you have a clear head. God, what else do I need to tell you? Oh yes, the grandparents refused to move to a hotel."

"I heard. Do you really think Domi is going to come after her again? Or them?"

"I hope not," Rego said fervently. "But I'm not taking any bets on what that psycho does next."

Stevens nodded sombrely.

"I've had a chat with Mimi and Sid – they're a bit shaken up but seem okay. Sid just about chewed my ear off with his moaning, so I know he's alright."

"Talk of the devil," Rego said, nodding his head towards the lifts where Mimi and Sid had just emerged.

Detective Constable Mimi Eagling looked at him with red-rimmed eyes.

"Boss! How's Tamsyn?"

"She's going to be fine. They're treating her for smoke inhalation, but it looks like she'll be discharged tomorrow or the day after."

"Thank God!" she said, closing her eyes, her words heartfelt. Then she gave him a strained smile. "And the paperwork from court?"

"Scene of crime officers are on site, and all the paperwork will be collected by a specialist team and returned to us at a later date. It's all in hand."

"Huh, they always say that," Sid griped, "and it's always a bloody mess."

DC Sid Molloy was the Disclosure Officer assigned from Exeter HQ to work with them on the Domi case. He'd moaned like hell about the assignment, grumbling about having to take over someone else's work, which everyone already knew was the shitty end of a stick – and complaining about life in general. Sunshine in a bottle he was not.

The scruffy, overweight, miserable git always had his shirt hanging out of his trousers and his builder's bum arsecrack on display. His only tie was wrinkled and coffee-stained, and his fingers were yellowed with nicotine. Despite appearances, he'd done a thorough, professional job, and Rego had quickly learned to ignore the moans.

"How are you doing, Sid?"

"Bloody nightmare, boss. May as well put a match to the paperwork and forget about it."

Rego smiled wryly.

"Right, looks like beer o'clock to me: my shout."

The four of them trooped tiredly towards the bar.

The Union Jack Club was for members-only, and reserved exclusively for serving and veteran enlisted members of His Majesty's Armed Forces. Various police forces also used it for their accommodation needs when in London.

For Rego and his team, it felt like a place where they didn't have to look over their shoulders, somewhere they could relax. They needed that tonight. They'd nearly lost one of their own.

Rego bought the first round of drinks, and Mimi ordered the 'buffet', depositing four packets of crisps, a bag of Quavers, some dry roasted peanuts and, of course, a packet of pork scratchings onto the small table.

"You're spoiling us, Mimi," grinned Stevens. "Or shall I just call you 'Nigella'?"

"Call me what you like, but the Quavers are mine!" she said ripping open the packet and stuffing them in her mouth.

One dropped into her cleavage and they were all in fits of laughter as she picked it out and popped it into her mouth with a cheeky smile.

It was a proper icebreaker after a shitty day.

Rego was proud of his team, and he couldn't ask for a better one.

They settled down to decompress over a few beers, talking about the Domi case, the trial and about Tamsyn, all thankful that she'd be going home soon.

"How was she when you saw her, boss?" Mimi asked. "Apart from the smoke inhalation. Did she say much?"

"Not much. She was pretty out of it." Rego studied the nearly empty pint of beer in his hand. "She's got two firearms officers at the hospital so she's scared. Pissed off, too."

They sat in silent understanding.

"There'll be mandatory counselling," Rego added, draining his glass and standing up.

He didn't want to talk about that right now: alcoholic therapy was the only one he was interested in tonight.

"Okay, who's up for another round?"

At that moment, Mimi's phone rang and her face lit up.

"Not a sales call then," Stevens said drily.

Mimi's cheeks flushed as she walked away and Rego heard her say, "Hi, Luka," in the soft voice that people reserved for lovers.

Sid declined another drink, saying he was knackered, then muttered something about having to phone his mother. If she was anything like Rego's, he had every sympathy for the man.

"Tom, same again?"

Stevens guzzled the rest of his beer and nodded.

"Thought you'd never ask."

The plan was for Mimi and Sid to drive back with Tamsyn and an armed escort sent up from Devon & Cornwall Police, assuming she was given the all-clear and released the following day.

Rego and Stevens would take the train first thing in the morning, so neither of them had to worry about having a few drinks. And several pints later, Rego was feeling mellow.

"You happy working at Penzance nick?" he asked his sergeant.

Stevens gave him a surprised look.

"Yeah, sure. Have I done anything to make you think I'm not?"

"No, nothing like that, Tom. I was just wondering why you haven't..." Rego waved his hand in the air, "...moved up the ladder."

Stevens raised his eyebrows and gave a wry smile.

"Well, a few reasons. I took my inspectors exams a couple of times but failed, and I couldn't be bothered to put myself through that again. But ... I don't know ... I didn't fancy stepping away from a role I enjoy to one that's more managerial either. I couldn't see myself going to all those strategy and budget meetings you go to." He nodded to himself. "And promotion meant that I'd have to move away from West Cornwall. The kids were happy in school, love their surfing ... the wife didn't want to move either." He shrugged. "What about you, boss? Why did you come to sleepy old Cornwall?"

They shared amused smiles. The small county had proven to be anything but 'sleepy' in the seven months that Rego had worked there.

"Promotion," Rego said succinctly. "I was told that if I wanted to get promoted faster, I needed a wider range of experience than just being in GMP in Manchester, and I really wanted to have a more strategic role."

His eyes dropped to his beer.

"I was at the Manchester Arena bombing the day after," he said quietly. "Casualty bureau."

"Bloody hell, boss! I didn't know you were there. That was a bad one."

The American pop star Ariana Grande had been on tour, and a suicide bomber who was an ISIS extremist had packed a rucksack with scrap metal and enough explosives to kill everyone within a 20-metre radius.

"Yeah, it was ... bad. I can still see it, smell it. I can't believe it was seven years ago." He paused. "The report later said that there were security guards for people going *in* to the concert, but none in the foyer as people were coming out, so the bomber was able to just walk in." Rego stared into his pint, as if it contained the answer to such insanity.

"He walked in and killed 22 people including ten kids; more than a thousand injured."

Rego chugged half his glass and wiped his mouth on the back of his hand.

"I knew then that I wanted to change the way things were done, to make it safer; so that little kids going to a pop concert weren't going to be blown apart by a nail bomb." He rubbed his hands over his short hair. "My son was six at the time – he wanted to go to that concert and I would have let him, but Cassie said he was too young. Christ! I could have lost him, Tom."

Stevens was silent, a mix of understanding and anger in his expression.

Rego finished his pint.

"And strategic decisions on policing are made by senior ranks." He raised his eyebrows. "I've got a long way to go yet."

"I'll drink to that," said Stevens.

CHAPTER 4

"Any chance I could get your phone number, Tam?"

Tamsyn glanced across to where a tired-looking Joe Quinn was leaning against the wall watching her pack.

Her body was stiff and sore, her brain foggy, and everything sounded like it was underwater. But her blood-oxygen levels were nearly normal and she was being released. Mimi and Sid were waiting outside for the firearms officers to drive them all back to Cornwall.

Joe had stayed with her all night and the following morning, and it appeared that the armed guard was a door-to-door service.

"Go on, say yes," Joe smiled. "You know you want to."

Tamsyn didn't reply, concentrating on shoving her clothes into her hold-all. She wondered if and when she'd get her uniform back from the Met's evidence lockers.

"'Cause, ya know," Joe continued cheerfully, "in case you don't believe in love at first sight, I'll come to Cornwall so I can walk past you again."

"Dude, you need a better line," Tamsyn finally replied.

"Is that a 'yes'?"

She hesitated.

"Aw, come on, what can it hurt?"

She was too tired to argue, and also suitably flattered that he was being so persistent.

"Give me your number," she said, caving in just a little, "and then I'll decide whether or not I want to call you."

"Final offer?"

"Yep."

"You drive a hard bargain," said Joe, "and I ain't braggin', but so do I."

Tamsyn rolled her eyes, but she was smiling.

The doctor had finally finished his morning rounds, arriving at her room just before lunchtime. She was relieved that he agreed to discharge her. She wasn't used to lying around in bed doing nothing. She had her phone but there was only so many times you could send the same 'I'm okay' message to colleagues, and she hated being the centre of attention.

Joe was a nice respite though. She enjoyed his company, and the rubbish he talked made her laugh (and cough).

Besides, he'd told her that they would have to wait a few hours for the Armed Response Vehicle to arrive from Exeter, but she was happy to have the time to shower and wash the stink of smoke out of her hair. Mimi had brought her clothes from the hotel, and getting dressed made Tamsyn feel normal, or close to it.

She wasn't averse to having a cup of coffee with Joe while they waited.

"So, what's the plan?" she asked, trying not to yawn over the takeout cup he handed to her.

"Your lot will be here in an hour or so, depending how bad the traffic is on the Westway. There'll be an armed driver to take your CID car back to Cornwall with one of your ARVs shadowing them."

She gave him a frustrated look, but for once, he didn't laugh or make a joke.

"It's not a job where we take chances, is it?"

She looked down at her cooling coffee. He was right, but she felt like a fraud.

Joe took the hint and changed the subject, so the time passed quickly, perhaps too quickly, and the conversation had been easy.

"...and there was this one time where I was chasing a couple of toe-rags on foot across the Kidbrooke Estate, which wasn't one of my best ideas because that place is rougher than a badger's arse. Anyway, I'd torn my keks on something, couldn't say what, so there I was, in the middle of the day, with my trousers ripped and my arse hanging out," he paused for the punchline, "and I get a round of applause from a group of mums in the playground."

Suddenly, his expression changed, and she saw him tap the Press-To-Talk button on his cargo vest, knowing he'd just received a message via his earpiece.

"Roger that." Then he looked up at Tamsyn, all business now. "Your car's here, but we're not taking any chances even here in hospital. My colleague will lead the way, then you, and I'll be right behind. We're going out the back way to avoid the journalists."

"What?"

"Yeah, you're a bit famous. Don't worry, they don't know your name." Then he muttered quietly. "Yet."

Tamsyn's pulse jumped but Joe's calm demeanour and quiet confidence seemed to transmit itself to her. She nodded and took a deep breath.

As she picked up her bags, Joe's colleague was waiting

outside the door. Joe put his hand on Tamsyn's shoulder, partly to reassure her, partly to control her movement. She felt alert but not anxious.

They escorted her to an area at the rear of the hospital to avoid anyone who might be waiting for her, not just the media.

Joe shook hands with his counterpart from Devon & Cornwall Police.

"Over to you then, fella. Drop me a line, Tam."

Tamsyn didn't want him to go, but he'd already taken up position to cover the hand-over as she was ushered across the ambulance drop-off area which wasn't accessible to the public. She saw that Mimi and Sid were already in the CID car, with a marked BMW X5 parked behind them. The two uniformed officers in the X5 were standing by the vehicle's open doors, one scanning the front and the other the rear.

Tamsyn was ushered to the back seat of the CID car and sat next to Sid who winked at her. Mimi turned around and gave her a tight smile.

"It's so good to see you, Tamsyn. We were all worried about you."

"Thank you," she said, feeling worse by the second because of all the effort and cost just for her.

The driver slid into his seat, his eyes meeting Tamsyn's in the rearview mirror.

"My name's Fergus. We'll have a hot briefing and get on our way. The plan is to take you back home. If anything happens *en route* we'll deal with it. If we're forced to stop, under no circumstances get out of the vehicle unless instructed by me or the two officers in the shadow vehicle."

Tamsyn nodded but felt as if she'd fallen down the rabbit hole.

"We can be tracked on our Airwave personal radios,

and we have an intelligence team back at HQ monitoring our journey. Both of our police vehicles have been hot listed on the Automatic Number Plate Recognition system, so they'll ping up when we hit an ANPR camera. We'll pull off the motorway at two consecutive motorway services. It sounds odd, but it'll allow intel to do some convoy analysis and tell us if we're being followed. If we went straight back to HQ, there's a chance that an innocent vehicle could be following in the same direction as us, but the chances of an innocent vehicle coming off at two service stations is very unlikely."

He gave her a brief glance over his shoulder and smiled.

"You can do loads of stuff with the ANPR; identifying vehicles in convoy over distances is one of the features. If we identify a vehicle that's obviously following us, we'll arrange for armed interdiction on that vehicle or vehicles."

He gave her another quick, reassuring smile.

" 'It's as cunning as a fox what used to be professor of cunning at Oxford University'."

Tamsyn blinked and Sid snorted loudly. "I love *Blackadder*," he said and Fergus grinned in appreciation.

"So, if everyone's okay, we'll crack on."

Even though they'd taken steps to minimise Tamsyn's exposure, there had been a barrage of camera flashes as they left the hospital.

"Those reporters were probably tipped off by a member of staff at the hospital," Sid said knowingly. "It happens all the time."

But no one had followed them and there'd been nothing noteworthy since.

Perhaps the miserable weather had helped to deter some of the journalists. Hail rattled against the car windows as they crawled their way through heavy London traffic. The A40 Westway was gridlocked, and they crept along at less than 10mph, gradually inching their way out of the capital. Sid had already fallen asleep, Mimi had her earbuds in and was listening to something on her phone, and Fergus hadn't spoken again.

The raised dual carriageway was a ribbon of concrete that perched perilously close to the tower blocks and grey slabs of office buildings on either side. It was dreary and drab, the sheen of sleet doing nothing to prettify London's underbelly. Even the thin strings of early Halloween lights did little to dispel the autumnal gloom. Tamsyn longed for Cornwall with its towering skies and roaring seas, and she wondered how people could live in such a confined urban area. She longed for the wind in her face, the taste of salt-spray on her lips, and the wide, wintry beaches, temporarily free of tourists.

She felt a fierce and overwhelming desire to live, to live her life, to no longer be a spectator. She would not let criminals like Domi dictate how she lived. She refused to give in to the fear that whispered inside her.

With that thought front of mind, she pulled out her phone, but was stunned to see that she had over 100 missed calls since that morning, and even more texts and emails.

As she scrolled through, she realised that both her inbox and voicemail were filled with messages from people she hadn't heard from since she'd left school, and more than a dozen journalists had contacted her, a couple offering substantial amounts of money for her 'inside' story.

She pulled up the BBC News page on her browser to see what they were saying about the Old Bailey bomb. She paled when she saw a photograph of herself outside the court wearing her blood-spattered uniform. She looked haunted: there was no other word for it.

And, apparently famous.

The news sites had published her name.

"Shit!"

Fergus immediately met her gaze in the rearview mirror.

"Problem?"

"The online news sites have printed my name."

His lips thinned.

"Call your press office. They need to put a rocket up those reporters' arses."

Tamsyn's mouth felt dry.

"Can they stop them? I mean, they have my name now. Oh my God, what about my grandparents? They'll find out where they live. You don't think the reporters would go there, do you?"

"Tamsyn, breathe. It's going to be okay," Mimi said calmly. "I'll call our press office and see what can be done. They'll let the reporters know that it isn't helpful releasing an officer's name. But I'm guessing that they're already on the case and will be sending out an immediate press release. The main thing is not to respond."

"What? Say nothing?"

"That's exactly what I'm saying. The fastest way to kill a story is to cut off the oxygen; if we say nothing, they have nothing to report. Look, I'll call them now."

Tamsyn could see Fergus nodding with approval.

She didn't like the idea of saying nothing, but if that's what worked...

She glanced through her messages, but they all said pretty much the same thing: *Saw you on the telly!* The only texts she answered were from her best friend Jess, her grandmother, and colleagues from Penzance. The rest, she deleted.

Her fingers hovered over her contacts list for several seconds, then she made a decision and tapped Joe Quinn's number. She debated what to say, but in the end, she kept it simple.

> Thank you

He texted back immediately.

When Rego's phone alarm had gone off at 7am, he'd only been in bed a couple of hours and was still wearing yesterday's clothes.

Badly hungover, he'd managed to drag himself into the shower, but hadn't had the coordination to either shave or put his tie on, so it was screwed up in his pocket. He wasn't even sure he was wearing shoes that matched. He'd only meant to have a swift one with Tom Stevens, but two pints became five, followed by a couple or six of Captain Morgan's spiced rum. It had seemed like a good idea at the time.

Whilst most detectives favoured whiskey, Rego's tipple was rum. He'd been introduced to it by his mother from a very early age. She would tell him that, *a little drop in milk never hurt anyone.* Rego was convinced she used to put it in his bottle when he was a baby. Maybe it was a Bermudian thing. His mum used to drink Wray and Nephew Overproof, which was pretty much rocket fuel. But once his dad had headed down the one-way slope of the long-term alcoholic, rum and everything else had been banned from the house, along with his father.

At 4am, Stevens had bought him a Pusser's Gunpowder Royal Navy Rum, 54.5% proof, to finish off the night, but then it had finished Rego off instead. He had no idea how he'd managed to get back to his room, and suspected that his sergeant might have had to help him.

But this morning, hungover and running late, he hadn't even had time for a cup of coffee, which made the tube journey to Paddington that much more torturous. He would have paid a lot of money for a big, greasy breakfast to settle his stomach, but at least the train sold over-priced bacon baps, and their coffee was strong and hot.

Six hours later, as they trudged uphill from Penzance train station, all Rego was left with was breath that could stun a seagull at a hundred paces and a pounding headache. Stevens looked slightly better off, but not by much.

The bite of a brisk southwesterly felt good, clearing his dehydrated brain just a little. He'd always thought of himself as a city man, but this small town perched on Britain's most westerly peninsula had seeped into his skin.

They were nearly at the squat, concrete building that made up the police station when Stevens whispered urgently, "Boss!"

Rego had spotted the reporters at the same time. Half-a-dozen journalists were huddled together by the low wall in front of the station's car park.

They looked half-frozen, and were sucking on take-away coffees and stamping their feet to keep warm.

"Bugger," Rego said softly.

He knew that they were here for both him and Tamsyn, and either one of them would do.

"Tom, you go and distract them and I'll nip around the back."

"Will do, boss. I'll tell them I'm just coming on duty and don't know anything. It's mostly true," he grinned.

"Thanks, Tom. I'll stick the kettle on and see you in the CID office in a couple of minutes."

Stevens yawned and nodded, running a hand over the stubble on his chin.

"Coffee for me, boss! Two sugars."

Rego threw a quick smile at his sergeant, waited until the reporters were distracted, then darted through the back of the car park like a criminal, using his entry fob at the rear door of the nick. He felt absolutely shite.

The Criminal Investigation Department was Rego's territory, and he hoped he'd be able to spend a quiet couple of hours catching up on the case before going home and crashing out.

As Rego walked past Inspector Walters' office, the door was open, and she was seated at her desk, her uniform tidy, her boots bulled, short hair shiny.

Walters was in charge of Penzance police station and its uniformed staff, but Rego was a Detective Inspector and in charge of CID in the same building. They were equals in rank but had differing priorities, and sometimes that led to tensions: like right now.

She looked up as he passed, and Rego managed to give a brief wave with his left hand; he definitely wasn't in the mood for chit chat.

"Rob, can I have a quick word?"

Damn it.

Rego stopped in his tracks, spun round, bumping into an admin officer that he hadn't known was walking right behind him.

"Sorry," he mumbled.

The young woman gave him a wide berth, as much as the narrow corridor allowed, no doubt because he smelt like a brewery and looked like he had been dragged through a hedge backwards at least twice.

Rego stood at the entrance to Walters' office with his hands on either side of the doorframe, hoping that she would be quick. He needed at least another gallon of coffee.

But he was out of luck.

"Please come in, Rob, and close the door. Take a seat."

She gestured to a small seating area by the side of her desk, which consisted of four low chairs and a scarred coffee table.

Rego sighed. Walters obviously had something important to say, so he shuffled inside and slumped into a seat.

There was no coffee on the coffee table.

Walters sat opposite Rego and leaned forward with her elbows on her knees, her polite smile gone.

"What the fuck are you doing with PC Poldhu?"

Rego didn't know what he'd expected, but it wasn't this. He frowned and sat up straighter.

"You'll have to be more specific, Maura," he said, his voice several degrees cooler.

"She seems to spend more time with you than she does with the rest of her team, and since she started, she's been kidnapped, arrested, blown up, and the target of this Hellbanianz crime gang." Her eyes narrowed. "And I'm told that she had the room next to yours at the Union Jack Club. So, I think, 'What the fuck is going on?' is a fair question."

Rego's defence mechanism kicked in immediately. He liked to think that he was normally an easy-going guy, but his fight or flight instinct had been triggered and he was going to come out fighting.

The fuzzy head vanished and he focused his thoughts.

Inwardly, he told himself to keep calm, remembering the conflict resolution strategy he should pursue: *don't raise your voice, be professional, don't lower yourself to the behaviour of the aggressor.*

But what came out was, "Who the fuck do you think you are, talking to me like that?"

Walters' eyebrows snapped up, and she opened her mouth to speak, but Rego was on a roll.

"If you want me to stay where we can have a civil conversation, lower your tone and apologise for that insinuation, otherwise I'm going, and we can have the Superintendent referee this for us."

Rego didn't blink as he met her astonished gaze. Walters sat upright, taken aback by Rego's response.

"Rob, I'm sorry, I've had a bad morning trying to manage the media now that they've got hold of Tamsyn's name. I've had local reporters camped out here all morning. I had to go to the expense of putting extra officers on duty at the Poldhus' house, as well as taking officers off frontline duty. Frankly, I have better things to do with my time."

Rego leaned closer, his eyes flashing with anger.

"You were bang out of order, Maura. There was no need for that. And don't you think my week has been pretty fucking bad? I was there when the incendiary device was initiated; I carried the judge out of that courtroom, wondering if *our officer* was going to make it out with me, then finding out that Domi went back to kill her, and now that murdering bastard is on the loose. So, if your bad morning consists of a nasty paper cut from updating the nick's budget report, don't take it out on me."

He took a deep breath, folding his anger and fear into a small box hidden deep inside himself.

"Shall we start again?" he said in a more reasonable tone.

Walters was more cautious now, and trying to claw back some dignity and control of the meeting.

"I'm only looking after the welfare and best interests of my young constable. She has been exposed to as much in the first few months as some officers have seen in their entire service. She needs to spend time on the shift; she needs to get to grips with her bread-and-butter core duties, rather than running around with CID."

She steepled her fingers together like a headmistress with an errant pupil, and that sent Rego's blood pressure rocketing again.

"Tamsyn is well liked, and she's a popular member of her shift, but sooner or later tongues will start wagging ... about where her loyalties lie," said Walters, accusation glinting in her eyes.

Nope. Rego wasn't having that.

"It's not my fault that the level of criminality she has been exposed to is off the scale. Trouble is not following her around, nor is she going out of her way to invite trouble: it's what happens when this type of crim finds an area where they think they can operate with impunity. Well, they're wrong, because we'll be all over them like a rash."

He kept his eyes pinned to Walters.

"Things will calm down when Domi is returned to prison. Look, Maura, Tamsyn is a good kid, a good officer, tougher than you might think. She'll be back to work soon, but there are going to be some bits and pieces she'll need to top and tail with CID, and I may have to call on her to help if this investigation progresses. All I can say is that I'll come to you first: it was remiss of me not speaking to you before, perhaps I should have done, and I apologise for that." He leaned towards her. "But if you *ever* insinuate that there is something inappropriate going on between me and PC Poldhu again, then I don't see how you and I can have a constructive relationship."

He stood up.

"I hope this has cleared the air between us."

Walters' lips were tight with annoyance.

"I would be grateful if you could let me know if and when you need Tamsyn," she said tightly. "She can work alongside you as long as it doesn't interfere with her days off or courses she has to complete."

There was every chance that any future encounter with the Hellbanianz would interfere with Walters' rotas and days off, but Rego didn't say that.

This meeting had been the perfect antidote to his alcohol-induced bad head. Nothing like a shot of adrenaline to clear a hangover.

"Maura."

"Rob."

He walked out of the office, pulling the door closed behind him.

With renewed energy, he climbed the stairs to his office.

CID's door was not accessed by a key fob, although it had been when he'd arrived at Penzance. He'd had the lock removed because he wanted to encourage uniformed officers to drop in whenever they wanted to discuss cases or pass on information that had come their way.

There was a separate briefing room that was swipe-controlled when he needed to limit confidential intel.

Besides, it was policy to keep a 'clean desk' with no paperwork left lying about; everything was supposed to be locked up when away from your desk. It didn't always happen. DC Jen Bolitho was the worst offender. On a good day, her desk looked like someone had dumped an entire filing cabinet on it from a great height.

At the far end of the CID office was a door leading to the toilet. But when Rego pushed it open, Tom Stevens was standing at the sink in his underpants, shaving, with his stubble dropping into the dirty cups and mugs stacked up beneath the mirror. His crumpled suit and shirt had been tossed over the back of the toilet door.

Rego's day hadn't been improved by seeing his sergeant's hairy back and sweaty pits.

"Bloody hell, Tom!"

"Sorry, boss!" Stevens said cheerfully. "Kettle's on."

Rego disappeared into his office and shut the door.

CHAPTER 5

Rego's run-in with Inspector Walters was pushed to the back of his mind but not forgotten. He was finalising the plan being put in place to protect Tamsyn before he went on a few days' well-earned leave to see his family.

Then he called the press office at HQ to make sure that they'd briefed Tamsyn's grandparents.

The press officer gave a strained laugh.

"They're already camped on PC Poldhu's doorstep," she said tiredly. "I had to tell Mr Poldhu that setting the dog on them or drenching them with a hosepipe wasn't in anyone's best interests. But Mrs Poldhu, well, I got the impression that she was dying to talk to the reporters about her granddaughter. She seemed to think that she should be making tea and sandwiches for them all."

Rego could imagine that. Tamsyn's grandmother was the complete opposite of her grumpy and cantankerous husband, and she loved to feed people.

"Well, thanks for the update," Rego said, smiling to himself. "And I've been informed that there are a couple of uniforms at the Poldhus' residence to keep the journalists away from the cottage."

Rego glanced at his wristwatch, amazed that it was nearly 4pm, and he still had a five-hour drive ahead of him.

He yawned and stretched, glancing over to where Stevens was still at his desk, eyes glued to his monitor. He was grateful to have someone with his experience and competence to act up as Temporary Inspector while he was away.

Once he'd handed over the policy book that he'd started for the Domi incident and emailed his sergeant the firearms risk assessment, there was nothing more he could do. Still, he felt uneasy leaving. But he also knew that you had to be able to leave the job behind at the end of the day or you'd burn out completely.

"Over to you, Tom," he said, as he reached for his coat.

"Yeah, no problem, boss. See you in a few days."

Rego drew in a deep breath, relieved he had a safe pair of hands to take over.

Stevens endorsed the policy book and risk assessment that he was now temporarily in charge. He was more than capable of making critical decisions.

Once Rego had left the office, Stevens scanned through the details of Tamsyn's transfer. His Airwave radio had been changed onto the dedicated radio folder that Firearms were using for her escorted journey back to Cornwall, so he could listen in to their communications.

He had plenty to do while he followed the progress of Tamsyn's armed escort as it headed southwest. The paperwork for another recent case had to be archived, documents boxed and catalogued, exhibits had to be returned, although he'd get some of his team to do the running around with those; and electronic documents, and emails had to be sorted out so that if the investigation reared its head again in the future, it would be in a good order to review.

The incident room was unusually quiet, and Tom was concentrating so hard on his computer screen that when his desk phone rang, it startled him.

"DS Stevens, can I help you?"

"Ah, Sergeant Stevens. This is Assistant Chief Constable Gray. I've been trying to contact Inspector Rego."

Tom looked away from the computer screen, surprised to receive a call from the second in command of Devon & Cornwall Police.

"Good afternoon, sir. DI Rego has just left on leave for a few days, and I'm temporarily taking over his duties," he said politely. "What can I do for you?"

"Yes, well, you'll have to do."

Stevens could hear the annoyance in the man's voice.

"I've just come from the senior officers daily briefing and learned that we've sent armed officers to London! I'll come straight to the point: who authorised an armed escort for PC Poldhu from London back to Cornwall?"

Stevens knew that Rego had put it in place because he didn't have the time for HQ to make a decision. He liked Rego and thought he was a good boss, so there was no way he was going to grass him up or tell ACC Gray the real reason he'd been bypassed was so Rego could just get on with it.

"Sir, I think it was a joint decision following a comprehensive risk assessment being made about the risk to PC Poldhu's life. I have the RA if you would like me to send it to you."

"I'm not happy, sergeant! Not happy at all! Firstly, I

don't believe there is any risk to the officer's life, and my experience tells me that the shooters are long gone. Do you know how much this is *costing?*" Gray said, emphasising the word.

Stevens raised his eyebrows but responded calmly.

"Well, with respect, sir, there isn't any intelligence to suggest that Domi has gone to ground, and..."

But before he could continue, Gray interrupted curtly.

"Who is in fucking charge here! Certainly not you or Rego, and to go behind my back! I understand that we've already gone to considerable expense with locks and a panic alarm at Poldhu's house. Well, as soon as the armed officers get back to Cornwall, they're to take PC Poldhu home and then resume normal duties. This outrageous abuse of your rank and authority will *not* continue."

Stevens held the receiver away from his ear.

"Okay, sir, if you could send me an email to that effect, I can update the Risk Assessment."

"Sergeant Stevens, I haven't got the time to send you anything. I'm already late for a dinner at New County Hall in Truro with the Lord Lieutenant of the county. I expect my orders to be acted on immediately."

At which, the call was terminated.

"Prick!" Stevens muttered under his breath, then checked that the call really had been ended and he hadn't just insulted his boss's boss's boss.

He replaced the receiver quietly when he really wanted to smash it into the cradle. He rubbed both hands over his face and headed to the kitchen to make himself a strong cup of coffee.

He was standing in the kitchen, lost in thought, when Sergeant Bryn Terwillis walked in, his uniform still immaculate despite it being at the end of his shift.

"Everything okay, Tom?"

Stevens shook his head, sighing.

"Rego is going to blow a fucking fuse. That idiot ACC Gray, has decided that Devon & Cornwall Police won't be providing any additional protection for Tamsyn. He's made a unilateral decision to pull the plug and won't confirm his decision by email. All I can do is document the phone conversation. I just have this feeling that it's not ended yet, and when it goes wrong, that the shit will roll downhill and stop at my feet." He took a gulp of his coffee then winced as he burned his mouth. "I've watched that Gray for years now. Do you remember him as a sergeant?"

Terwillis shook his head.

"He was a sergeant at Tavistock, gets himself promoted after three years, then flies through to Inspector by counting paper clips. Then he disappears into HQ, before rearing his head as an ACC. How many good people has he trampled over climbing that greasy pole? I'm not telling Rob about anything, but I'll have to tell Walters, if she doesn't already know."

They shared a look.

"She'll have to cease the patrols outside the Poldhu residence. Anyway, there's nothing Rego can do from home and I'm not spoiling his leave." Stevens grimaced. "He'll be pissed off that I didn't tell him, but he'll just have to find out when he gets back. I think that this is Gray's way of getting back at Rob, you know, after all that funny business in the summer."

Terwillis looked thoughtful.

"When he and Tamsyn were arrested then released later and we were told it was 'a training exercise'? Yeah, I don't think anyone believed that at the time. But I heard from a friend at HQ that there was some James Bond type involved and Gray didn't like it."

"MI6? Why haven't I heard that rumour?"

"Dunno, mate," Terwillis grinned. "I thought you were supposed to be a detective and you don't even know what's being gossiped about on the rumour-mill."

Stevens didn't smile.

"And now the Hellbanianz are gunning for Tamsyn? What else don't I know? What the hell is going on?"

Joe Quinn had continued to text Tamsyn on the long journey back to Cornwall. It had been so easy to talk to him because she didn't have to edit everything she said or felt, and somehow, he'd made everything a little more ... normal.

She told him that she lived with her grandparents less than a mile from Penzance, and that her grandfather was a fisherman and crabber. He told her that he lived with his sister and her two boys. He was 28 and had joined the police at 24 after six years in the Royal Marines. As a kid, he'd hoped to make it as a professional footballer and he was a huge West Ham fan. He'd been a firearms officer for two years and thought it was the best job in the Met.

He was intrigued to hear that she surfed and asked if she had any photos. She sent him several that a friend had taken of her getting barrelled at Gwithian. Joe was impressed.

But after an hour of texting, he had to admit that he was nodding off after nearly two days without sleep. He ended his message with a question:

> I have some leave coming up. Me and a mate from my team were thinking about doing something away from the city – maybe we should check out the surf in Cornwall?

Tamsyn only hesitated for a second.

> You should definitely try it. Can't wait to see you wipeout!

> Deal! Night, Cornwall ZZZ

At Exeter, she was escorted to the canteen and sat with the ARV crew while Mimi and Sid unloaded some evidence boxes from the car into Sid's office to be checked and sorted over the next few days. He moaned and groaned about the size of the job ahead, but by now Tamsyn knew that complaining was just his default setting. They had a quick cup of coffee together, then she and Mimi continued heading west with Fergus driving, still shadowed by the ARV and firearms officers.

"How are you really doing, Tamsyn?" Mimi asked as she pulled out her earbuds.

"I'm okay."

Mimi shook her head disbelievingly.

"I'm not okay and I wasn't even in the courtroom."

Tamsyn glanced at her briefly then stared out at the dark, rain-slick road.

"I don't know how I feel," she said at last. "Everyone's telling me that I have to talk about it, but I just want to forget it and put it all behind me. I don't see what's wrong with that."

"There's nothing *wrong* with it," Mimi said slowly,

implying that there was everything wrong with it. "No one can tell you how to feel…"

"But that's exactly what they're doing," Tamsyn said defensively.

Mimi hesitated.

"Well, you'll have to do the mandatory counselling, but if you just want to *talk*, colleague to colleague, give me a call, okay?"

"Thanks. I appreciate it." There was a short silence. "Mimi, can I ask why you decided to go into CID?"

Mimi perked up and smiled.

"I think it's different for everyone, but I spent four years on Response: I'd go out on a call and I'd be there to help people and I'd be invested in them when things were sometimes at their worst, but I didn't get to be involved in the outcomes that much. I wanted to be able to follow an investigation through from the start to the end. I suppose, I wanted that closure." She shrugged and gave a wry smile. "I don't always get it, but that's what I'm aiming for."

And for the next hour, Mimi told her about the long and irregular hours, the days, weeks, or even months when a case seemed to stall, knowing that the file would stay on her desk until she did something about it, the eye-watering amounts of paperwork, the software that she used as an analyst to control the flow of data coming in on complex cases, and the rare and wonderful days when a case came to fruition.

It wouldn't be an easy road or a quick one to CID, the average career path taking between five and eight years to becoming a police detective, but Tamsyn was intrigued.

It was only as they came off the A30 and turned into the tiny lane for Gulval village that Tamsyn's worries came flooding back.

The narrow road was crammed with cars and Tamsyn could see a news van with a satellite feed on the roof.

"Bloody hell," Fergus sighed, seeming more annoyed than worried.

A patrol car was parked next to Tamsyn's battered Fiat and she wondered which of her colleagues was on duty for this shit-fest.

"Is there a way in around the back?" Fergus asked grimly.

"Yes," Tamsyn whispered as adrenaline pumped through her. "Turn left here."

Fergus turned the ARV into an unpaved lane that ran behind the row of cottages.

Even with all the extra protection and the crowd of journalists at the front of the cottage, Tamsyn glanced about her uneasily, wondering who or what might be waiting for her, concealed in the shadows.

"Stay in the car until they've checked the property," Fergus ordered.

Tamsyn saw the dark figures of the other two firearms officers scanning the lane, then they disappeared through the gate in the fence at the back of the Poldhus' cottage.

When they gave the all clear, Fergus contacted the officer inside so there would be no waiting around.

"Do you want me to come in with you?" Mimi asked. "I could talk to your grandparents, if you like?"

"No, it'll be fine, but thank you," Tamsyn said with a smile that took more effort than she'd have liked.

"Okay, well, take it easy, and I'll see you soon ... but not too soon, okay? Remember, you're on sick leave."

Fergus was out of the car first, then indicated for Tamsyn to follow him. Taking a deep breath, she climbed out of the back seat and was bustled through the small garden.

The kitchen door opened, spilling a pool of yellow light into the patch of grass, and a ball of fur shot out of the door, the small, hairy dog dancing around Tamsyn's legs, overcome with joy and demanding to be picked up.

"Morwenna!"

Tamsyn scooped the little dog into her arms and buried her face in Morwenna's thick fur as she squirmed and wriggled, trying to reach Tamsyn's cheek to lick her.

Fergus bundled her inside, then Tamsyn's grandmother was there, tears slipping from her bright blue eyes as her white candyfloss hair glowed like a halo in the kitchen light.

And her grandfather, who disliked displays of emotion, swallowed several times, nodding slowly.

"Tammy," he said. "Tammy."

And his strong arms surrounded her. She breathed in the scent of pipe tobacco, diesel and fish, the scent of home.

They walked into the tiny living room together and Tamsyn saw her colleague and friend PC Jasmine 'Rosie' Flowers.

"Glad to have you back in one piece, Tamsyn," she said, giving her a quick hug. "Really glad."

"Thank you so much for being here with my grandparents. It's great to be home."

Fergus did a quick check through of the cottage under the baleful watch of Tamsyn's grandfather. Then he introduced himself to Rosie and went through the protocols for the third time.

"Tamsyn, I know you've heard it all before, but I'm going to say it again – and your grandparents need to hear this, too. If you're going out, check around your car and when driving, keep your car doors locked; don't use the same route every day; be aware of your surroundings; don't go out when it's dark and always keep a torch with you, just in case; tell people where you're going and check in regularly, more regularly than usual; be wary of new people that try to befriend you..."

Tamsyn saw the shock on her grandmother's face and squeezed her hand, knowing how extraordinary and far-fetched this seemed, but knowing Fergus's advice could save her life.

"And if you're sitting in a pub or café," he went on, "plan out your escape route; watch the doors, and keep your back to a wall."

"Got it," said Tamsyn, glancing at her grandfather's stony face.

Fergus took a call on his radio and stepped into the hallway for some privacy. He was only gone a minute, but when he walked back into the living room, he was frowning.

"I don't know what's going on, but we've all been ordered to stand-down. The order came from ACC Gray."

"That's ridiculous," said Rosie, her eyes flashing to Tamsyn. "I thought we were..."

"Me, too," said Fergus shortly. "But I'm going to have to leave with the team, and you should, as well."

"I'll stay for a bit," said Rosie. "My shift is ending soon anyway."

When Tamsyn's grandmother offered, Fergus politely declined a coffee, saying that he had to take the CID car to Penzance, then he'd join the ARV team and head back to Exeter. He didn't say that he'd been ordered to leave.

"Look after yourself, Tamsyn," he said, shaking her hand. "Follow the protocols. I mean it; don't take your eye off the ball until Domi has been apprehended."

"Thank you," she said, for the hundredth, heartfelt time. "I don't know ... I..."

He smiled and nodded at her. "No worries."

"I'll stay with you," said Rosie, casting an eye at Fergus.

"No, that's okay. You've done enough."

"Are you sure? Because I'm happy to stay, Tamsyn."

"Really. I'll be fine now."

"Okay, well, any problems, you know what to do."

"Thank you so much."

"Talk to you soon." Rosie gave her a hug. "How's my makeup? I want to look my best if I have to face the paparazzi."

Tamsyn gave her a weak smile.

"You look hot – knock 'em dead," then she winced when she realised what she'd said.

Rosie just winked at her then saw herself out.

The volume of noise increased the moment Rosie stepped out of the door, and even through the closed curtains, Tamsyn could see starbursts of camera flashes. She shivered, remembering the minutes after the bomb had gone off and the reporter who'd taken pictures but not stopped to help her.

She heard the reporters shouting questions, and something else...

"Is that Miss Nellie? What's she doing?"

She peeped through the curtains, giggling in disbelief as their elderly neighbour faced down the mass of journalists, berating them loudly and brandishing her walking stick at them.

Tamsyn's grandmother joined her at the window.

"Bleddy greet tuss!" bellowed the tiny, shrunken old woman, tottering forwards, her walking stick swinging wildly, hacking at shins which made the journalists hop out of her way, backing off rapidly.

"Looks like Miss Nellie is giving them what for!" laughed Andrea Poldhu.

"Grandad!"

They both saw her grandfather putting on his coat, ready to go on the attack with Miss Nellie.

"Ozzie!" her grandmother scolded. "'Ell-ya-doin-of! We'ns told not to go out!"

And she marched him into the kitchen.

Tamsyn raised her eyebrows; her grandmother rarely raised her voice but right now, she was giving her grandfather his character with no holds barred.

The hullabaloo outside seemed to have calmed down. Tamsyn peeped through the curtains again and saw Rosie escorting Miss Nellie inside, and the reporters being 'encouraged' to leave the street by other neighbours who weren't happy about all the noise.

God, it's good to be home.

Tamsyn decided that she'd find some way to thank all their neighbours, especially Miss Nellie.

Then her smile slipped. What if Besnik Domi really was out there, waiting for the chance he'd missed in London.

She shivered at the thought.

The kitchen was quieter too, the angry voices dropped to a familiar murmur. Tamsyn gave her grandparents another minute to calm down, then risked going to see if there was anything to eat. She knew there would be.

But when the kitchen door opened, all was calm, as if nothing had ever ruffled the smooth surface of her grandparents' long marriage.

Her grandfather reappeared in the living room, settling into his usual armchair.

Tamsyn sat opposite him with little Mo on her knee, the fire crackling in the grate between them.

"Are you okay, Grandad?"

"Shouldn't I be asking you that, maid?"

"I'm fine. Honestly. How's Gran?"

"Been worried about you."

"I know, I'm sorry."

He nodded, his unlit pipe clamped between his teeth.

She waited until her grandmother returned from the kitchen carrying a tray crowded with teacups, a jug of milk, a heavy teapot, and a plate piled with thick slabs of saffron cake that caught Mo's attention.

A pot of tea and a plate of food was her grandmother's response to every moment of drama or high emotion.

"That nice Mr Rego sent some men to fit extra locks and a button that links us dreckly to the police station."

That wasn't all: Tamsyn could see that her grandmother had been busy putting protection symbols over the doors and windows. She doubted it would help, but she respected her grandmother's Wiccan beliefs. More practically, perhaps, her grandfather had put a shovel by the back door and a boat hook at the front. And he wouldn't think twice about using them if he needed to protect his family.

"Yes, he told me the same thing, Gran. I'm glad they've done it."

"Are they going to come after you, angel?"

Her grandmother's face stiffened with fear, and her grandfather's weathered frown creased even more deeply.

Tamsyn kept her body angled away from her grandmother, unable to meet her anxious gaze. Dread uncoiled like a snake in her belly.

"No, Gran," she said with a certainty that she didn't feel. "DI Rego says they're business men and reprisals against police are bad for business."

The answer didn't satisfy either of her grandparents but it was the best she could do. And she couldn't tell them the rest – she simply wouldn't add to their worries that way.

"Then why did they want us to go to a hotel? Why do we have to have all this security? I had to go next door and tell Miss Nellie to lock her back door. She's never locked her back door in her life! What's happening, Tammy?"

She couldn't tell them that Domi had come back to kill her. She couldn't tell them anything.

"It's just a precaution. They want to make completely sure that he— that the criminal has left the country." She wouldn't say his full name, not in this house, not in her home. "It's just routine."

"I don't understand. How does he know where you live? How does he know about me and your grandfather?"

"Like I said, it's just a precaution."

She wasn't sure they believed her, but there was an unspoken agreement to be complicit in the lie, because how else did you go on with your life if you were paralysed by fear, by things that might never come to pass?

"All the neighbours been asking after you, Tammy," her grandmother said with pride trembling in her voice. "I been stopped in the street more times, I kent membr. Like a celebrity, I was!" She crossed her arms. "I wanted to tell those reporters that my granddaughter was a hero, but your police people said I mustn't talk to them."

"It's better that you don't, Gran," she said. "The less we say, the sooner they'll leave us alone."

Her grandfather grunted in agreement.

Tamsyn smiled then turned to watch the flames

throwing shadows onto the cottage's granite walls and felt as if she was letting out the breath that she'd been holding since she first went to London.

She was home, and all would be well.

She didn't comment as her grandfather checked all the new deadlocks on the windows and bolts on the doors, and she pretended she didn't see her grandmother peering anxiously out of the window. Instead, she took the sleeping pill that the doctor had prescribed, and curled up in her own bed with Mo nestled beside her.

The cottage settled into silence and Tamsyn's mind began to drift, but the soft snores of the small dog beside her took Tamsyn's dreams to a lighter place.

CHAPTER 6

Tamsyn stirred slowly the next day. She'd been vaguely aware of her grandfather leaving for the harbour in the small hours. He might have brought his crab pots in for the winter, but a lifetime of rising before dawn couldn't be changed, and there were always nets and pots to be mended.

But her grandmother must have decided to stay home, because Tamsyn could hear the low murmur of the radio in the kitchen.

She only managed to drag herself out of bed and into the shower a few minutes before noon, and was still sitting in the kitchen in her dressing gown when she got a text from Jess to say that she was on her way over.

Her grandmother opened the door when they heard Jess's car pull up.

The patrol cars had gone but two, lonely-looking reporters were still waiting outside. They stirred to life when they saw where Jess was going and pelted her with questions.

She ignored them except for sticking her middle finger up at them.

That was so like Jess.

Her grandmother opened the front door a crack and Jess darted inside. After a short conversation that Tamsyn couldn't hear, Jess walked into the kitchen. She didn't say a word, but hugged Tamsyn tightly. Then Jess's shoulders began to shake, and she sobbed into Tamsyn's wet hair.

"Aw, shit," she sniffed after a minute. "I promised myself that I wasn't going to do that. Oh my God, I'm such a dumb-ass! You're the one who got blown up. What if you'd died? Then what would I do for a best friend?"

Tamsyn didn't know what to say to that.

Then Jess seemed to recover herself.

"I had reporters round at my house, too. I don't know how they found out that we're friends. Well, maybe I do. Some of our friends have big mouths. Oh, don't worry, I didn't say anything except to tell them to fuck off," Jess said proudly. "I told them that if they didn't stop ringing our doorbell, I'd set my nan on them."

"No one sane would want that," Tamsyn agreed. "By the way, you should have seen Miss Nellie last night! She charged at the reporters with her walking stick!"

"No way!"

"I know, right? It was great! I'll have to go over and thank her – when there's no one around."

She drew in a deep breath, wondering how soon it would be before she was old news, to the reporters, at least.

Jess picked up Morwenna and stroked her wiry fur. Then she glanced surreptitiously at Tamsyn's grandmother who tactfully left the kitchen and began hanging up washing on a clothesline in the back garden, because life went on, and laundry needed washing, and daylight made the threats a little less terrifying.

"Were you scared?"

Tamsyn stared into her cup of tea.

"Yes."

Jess reached across and squeezed her hand.

"I froze," Tamsyn admitted. "I thought I was going to die. I thought of you," and she gave Jess a small smile.

"Of course you did," Jess half-laughed, half-cried.

"I thought of all the things I haven't done. I want to try everything, Jess."

Jess sniffed again. "Yeah, like what?"

"All sorts of things. I've never been anywhere. I want to travel the world; I want to see everything and do everything!" Tamsyn laughed wildly. "I want to jump out of aeroplanes!" Then her voice sobered. "I've lived in this village my whole life, and I love it, but I want to try other things, too. I want *more.*"

Jess cocked her head on one side. "Do you mean that?"

"God, yes!"

"Because I've had an idea! We could get a flat together. Just us, doing our thing. I even know the perfect place! There's a new rental that'll be coming on the market in six to eight weeks: completely done up, new furniture, WiFi. A two-bed unit above the Turkish barbers in Penzance. Oh, go on, Tam, say yes! It'll be awesome!"

Tamsyn could picture it: movie nights with her bestie; the unspeakable luxury of having her own space; a double bed, not the narrow single that she'd slept on forever. Her mind drifted to Joe Quinn.

"Yes! Hell, yes! Let's do it!"

"Really?"

"Really!"

"Oh my God, Tam! We are so getting our fun on! It's going to be frickin' awesome! I won't even have to list it. We'll have first dibs. Let me just find out exactly how much rent they want, and then I'll talk them into knocking a bit off," and she giggled. "Perks of being an estate agent!"

Jess couldn't stay long after that, but doing something positive and new felt wonderful to Tamsyn after the last few days.

She made a sudden decision to go to the station, just to show her face. It might get weird if she left it too long. Officially, she was on sick leave for the next two weeks, but she'd rather get back to work sooner. Besides, she was still a probationer, and she didn't want anyone to think she was slacking.

But when she slipped into the station from the rear entrance, unobserved by the waiting press, everything was quiet. She knew that DI Rego had gone to see his wife and children in Manchester, and Mimi had said that she'd be spending the next couple of weeks working from Exeter.

She wanted to find out if there was any news about Domi, but she knew they'd have told her if there'd been a sighting, and Tamsyn couldn't think of another reason to go into CID.

Instead, she wandered aimlessly into the main workspace which was stuffed with computers, happy to find that she wasn't completely alone.

Rosie glanced up from her computer screen and smiled when she saw Tamsyn.

"Hey, you! You're not supposed to be here, but it's good to see you."

And she stood up and gave her a big hug.

"How are you? Did you sleep well?"

Tamsyn shrugged. "Yeah, I'm okay."

"Got a lot to process, right?" Rosie said with understanding in her eyes. "You're in all the newspapers, although they spelled your name wrong. Does the sarge know you're here?"

"No, I just came in to see who was around. I thought C-Team were on lates?"

"Yeah, but your lot are short at the moment because Carl and Jethro are on a course, and Ky is off sick, so I've moved over to cover for a couple of weeks."

Which basically meant that Rosie was doing Tamsyn's job. She immediately felt guilty.

"Look, we should go out for a drink some time," said Rosie. "I don't know how you survived so long on E-team with just the boys."

Tamsyn smiled. "I know, right? Yeah, I'd like that."

And then the last person that Tamsyn wanted to see sauntered into the room.

Chloe's dislike of Tamsyn hadn't lessened, and it was mutual. But Tamsyn tried to ignore her because Chloe loved drama and to be the centre of attention. Today was no exception.

"I'm surprised you've bothered to slum it back here," Chloe said snidely. "I thought you'd be off talking to your agent. I hear Hollywood's been calling you. B-movies aren't what they used to be."

"Chloe, why don't you go and take a job with sex and travel," Tamsyn said, her tone flat.

"What?"

"I think Tamsyn just told you to fuck off," Rosie said with a wide smile.

Chloe glared from one to the other, snarled, "Cunts!" under her breath, but turned and left.

"Do you think she doesn't like us?" Rosie laughed. "Right, where were we? Yeah, let's arrange a time to go out."

But before they could make a date, Sergeant Terwillis walked into the room, did a doubletake when he saw Tamsyn, and immediately summoned her to his office.

Rosie mimed calling her and Tamsyn nodded.

"It's good to see you, Tamsyn," said Sergeant Terwillis, pointing to a chair opposite his desk. "Although I'm surprised. I was told you'd be off for the next couple of weeks. How are you? Everything okay at home?"

Tamsyn was slightly puzzled by his question.

"You mean the journalists? There were only two and I went out through the backdoor."

He gave her a searching look.

"You haven't seen *The Sun* then?

Tamsyn was taken aback.

"No, why?"

Sergeant Terwillis sighed and passed her the tabloid newspaper with its lurid headline:

My daughter – the Old Bailey hero!

Beneath was a large picture of an attractive, middle-aged woman, with blonde hair and blood-red fingernails an inch long, holding a faded photograph of Tamsyn as a child.

She didn't recognise the woman, but she knew that picture: there was a copy of it in her grandparents' bedroom.

Tamsyn hadn't seen her mother since she was five years old, and felt no connection with the woman in the newspaper. Even so, she could see the similarities between them: the same nose, the same eyebrows, the same oval face, but not the eyes; her blue eyes came from the Poldhus.

The woman was a stranger, and Tamsyn's heart sank as she read the story that was one part truth and ninety-nine parts fabrication; how her mother was so heartbroken by her husband's death that she'd had to leave Cornwall 'to find myself'.

The truth was that Tamsyn's father had died five years *after* her mother had left.

The story went on to say how she'd been kept from her daughter for all these years.

In fact, Tamsyn hadn't received anything except a single postcard since her mother had disappeared from her life. She'd had no idea where or how the woman was living. Until now.

She was always so brave, even as a child. She had no fear. I'm not surprised she's a hero. I'm so proud of her.

Tamsyn felt sick, angry, frustrated and completely blindsided.

"Did you know your mother was giving an interview," Sergeant Terwillis asked carefully.

"No! God, no! She left 16 years ago and this is the first I've heard of her except for one lousy postcard. I can't believe she'd do this! She had 16 years to get in touch with me, but because I'm in the frickin' newspaper, she thinks she has the right to..."

Fuming, Tamsyn started to close the newspaper.

"I'm afraid there's more," said Sergeant Terwillis gently, his expression sympathetic. "Turn to page 13."

A source close to Police Constable Tamsyn Poldhu told this Sun *reporter exclusively that the young officer is a risk-taker!*

"She's only been in the job a really short time so it's not like she really knows much, but she's always getting herself into these situations. I'm not sure that she's really cut out to be a police officer."

Tamsyn was horrified.

"A close friend? Who the hell would say those things about me?"

But one name came to mind instantly.

"Are you okay, Tamsyn?" asked Sergeant Terwillis. "I know this attention is a lot to take in. I'll just say this once, and then we'll drop it: ignore it."

"What?"

"Ignore it. We both know it's rubbish. This is what happens when you get a little bit of fame," and he gave her a wry smile. "All the cockroaches come out of the woodwork. It's just the way it is, but don't let it get to you. So, like I said, ignore it. And if you see any more journalists, just say, 'No comment', right?"

"Okay."

"Tamsyn..."

"I'm fine, sarge, really. And ... I'd just like to get back to work."

Sergeant Terwillis pressed his lips together and leaned back in his chair.

"That's not going to happen, Tamsyn. Look, you've been through a lot and I know for a fact that the doctors in London said you needed at least a week to rest, followed by another week of light exercise. Have you been to see your GP yet?"

Tamsyn shook her head reluctantly.

"Then that's your first step. You'll get signed off for a few weeks so take some time out to compose yourself. I also want you to look at all the resources you can access online from the College of Policing: employee support and trauma support, the mental and emotional wellbeing team, PTSD support. And take a look at the Oscar Kilo website, too. You can get four counselling sessions for free, as well as dedicated support for up to nine months, and a plan to return to work." He glanced up at her. "I would have sent you all this information in a few days, but ... here you are."

Tamsyn's head was spinning. *Months?* Was Sergeant Terwillis saying that she should be off work for *months?* No, she *needed* to work, she needed to feel normal.

"Sarge, I really appreciate it and I–"

He cut off anything else that she might have said.

"It's non-negotiable, Tamsyn. You might think you're fine, but take it from an old warhorse like me. You need to process everything that's happened, otherwise it's a slow poison working inside you. Being in the job, it's a marathon, not a sprint. The ones who make it are the ones who know how to pace themselves, otherwise you'll be burnt out within the first few years. You've got the potential to go all the way ... so take the time, take the counselling, and then use everything you've learned to take you forwards in the job."

Tamsyn felt defeated. She also knew for a fact that DI Rego would be back at work after just a few days with his family. No one was forcing him to do counselling, as far as she knew.

Terwillis gave her an understanding smile.

"I know that you want to show us how tough you are, especially as you're a probationer, but trust me, you need to take the time off." Then he paused. "But don't forget you're a police officer. Besnik Domi might be on the run, but he didn't escape by himself, so keep your eyes peeled."

"The firearms officer told me to keep changing my routes, keep my car doors locked, and all that."

"Good advice."

"Have there been any sightings of Domi?"

"You'd be informed if there had been, I can promise you that. Is there anything else?"

Tamsyn recognised that she was being dismissed, and stood up.

"No, that's it. Thank you, sarge."

She pulled up the hood on her sweatshirt as she left the police station, sneaking out through the Fire Exit to avoid the lone reporter who waited doggedly at the front.

Keeping her head down, she jogged towards Penlee Gardens before she pulled out her phone.

"Hi, Gran. Look, have you seen today's edition of *The Sun*...?"

Rego had enjoyed his three bonus days with his family. As well as doing the school run, he'd been able to take his mother to her final chemotherapy session.

Patricia Rego was an emotional woman, so Rego had been surprised and touched by her stoical acceptance of the treatment, and it was clear that the oncology team had a soft spot for her. It had made him feel guilty, again, for being down in Cornwall when she clearly needed him. Having his family 350 miles away was tearing him in two. And it was exhausting.

But he'd be home for Christmas which was only eight weeks away.

As he headed southwest yet again, the darkness of dawn sped away from him. Rego was in a good mood, relaxed after his R&R, and the fiasco of the Old Bailey in the past.

He had about ten seconds left to enjoy his complacency.

For the moment, he was singing along to the old Specials song, *Ghost Town*:

***This town, is coming like a
ghost town
Bands won't play no more
Too much fighting on the
dance floor..."***

You couldn't beat Rico Rodriguez on the trombone, and this song always reminded him of home.

His phone rang, the music cutting out, and Vikram's name showed on the in-car infotainment screen.

"Hiya, Vik! How's it going, mate?"

"Not good, Rob."

"Why? What's happened?"

"Domi never turned up for his mum's birthday yesterday."

"Shit," Rego said softly.

"Yeah," Vikram agreed. "I'm sorry, Rob, but the thinking is that Domi is still in the UK but gone to ground. We don't know for sure, but he hasn't turned up in any of the usual places. At this point, we can't rule out that he's making his way to your neck of the woods."

That was not the news Rego wanted to hear, so by the time the second call came to disrupt his peace of mind, he was not happy.

"Morning, boss!" said Tom Stevens. "Are you on your way back now?"

"Yes, I'm nearing Bristol, so I'll be with you in about three hours. Everything okay?"

There was a long, pregnant pause. Coming after Vikram's news, Rego was already tense.

"Tom?" Rego said sharply.

"Sorry, boss. It's just, I didn't want to tell you while you were on leave, but ACC Gray cancelled the firearms officers protecting Tamsyn."

"WHAT? Why?"

"ACC Gray said..."

"I can guess what he said."

Rego's words were clipped, and he swore bitterly under his breath, knowing that because the order had come from a senior manager, there was nothing he could do about it. It was part of a pattern too, where Gray consistently and deliberately undermined him. More importantly, did this leave Tamsyn exposed?

It even made him wonder if transferring to Devon & Cornwall Police had been the right thing to do. Would this have happened if he'd stayed with Greater Manchester Police? And going forwards, how would this affect him when making critical decisions in the future, knowing that there was at least one senior manager who didn't support him? Would he be second-guessing what ACC Gray would agree to or countermand?

He shook his head. No, he wasn't going to make decisions that way.

"What about the media? Are they still outside Tamsyn's grandparents' house?"

"Most of them have gone. It's just a local reporter now."

"Is it a problem?"

"I don't think the local bloke is, no. But did you read what the *The Sun* printed about Tamsyn and her mum?"

Rego grimaced.

"Yes, and three different people sent me links to the articles. Do we know who this 'close friend' is? Because I'm tempted to have a word."

"I don't think that would help, boss," said Stevens, his

tone carefully neutral. "The damage is already done, but we can keep an eye open."

Rego sighed.

"I know. You're right. Please tell me there's some good news – anything at all?"

"We've kept up some patrols past her grandparents' place on the QT, and every snitch and contact has been asked about gangs moving into the area or anything unusual. But nothing has come in, so there's been nothing to investigate. Just a fat lot of nothing!"

Stevens' own frustration showed through, so Rego made an attempt to rein in his own disappointment.

"Have you seen Tamsyn?"

"No, boss. But I know that Bryn Terwillis has talked to her. She'll be on sick leave for another ten days or so."

"So, that's it? Nothing else to report?"

"No, boss."

"Well, I have news. I've just been told that Besnik Domi didn't return to Albania for his mother's birthday yesterday, a date he's never missed before, apparently. At this point, we have to assume he's still in the UK."

"Oh, shit," said Stevens.

Rego didn't disagree.

"I'm going to HQ on my way back. I don't know how long I'll be," he said, biting out the words.

He really wanted to see ACC Gray face-to-face, even if that might not be a good career move.

Rego contemplated whether to try and make an appointment to see Gray or simply to turn up. He'd prefer to show up unexpectedly but he knew that the chances were that Gray would be out of the office or in a meeting: such was the life of an Assistant Chief Constable.

In the end, he rang Gray's PA to find out where he was. He had a plan.

She answered immediately.

"Good morning, this is Detective Inspector Rego. I was wondering if I could get a meeting with ACC Gray as soon as possible."

"Oh, I'm sorry, Inspector, his diary is pretty full this week."

"It's just that I'll be passing by Middlemoor shortly and I think he'd want to hear my update on the crime statistics for West Cornwall. I know he likes to keep abreast of those."

"Well..." she hesitated. "I'm sure we can squeeze you in. Shall I tell him you're coming or will you just turn up?"

"I can be there in 20 minutes," Rego offered helpfully.

"Let me see ... yes, that should be alright. We'll see you then, Inspector."

Rego ended that call then rang Tom Stevens.

"Tom, I need the latest crime stats on car theft in West Cornwall, and email me the report on the initiatives we were discussing."

"Do you need them now, boss?" Stevens asked, sounding puzzled.

"Yes, please. I have an appointment with ACC Gray on the pretext of talking about crime stats but while I'm there, I'll have another go at trying to persuade him that Domi is in all probability still in the UK."

"Right, gotcha," said Stevens, his tone amused.

Rego's voice hardened.

"I have to try, Tom. I have to try and get Gray to reverse his decision about security for Tamsyn."

"I guess it's worth a go, boss," Stevens replied dubiously.

ACC Gray was not known for his ... flexibility.

"I know it's a long shot," Rego admitted, "but the decision to withdraw additional protection grates on me."

Surely anyone with a shred of common sense could see that that the threat risk was through the roof? And if Tamsyn or a member of her family got injured or killed – well, he didn't want to think about that. Besides, the shit that would follow would be severe. People would lose their jobs or even go to jail over it. And if anything happened to the Poldhus because of this stupidity, a prison sentence would be bloody well deserved.

Rego arrived at Middlemoor, Devon & Cornwall Police HQ with the devious plan in mind. He was canny enough to realise that going in all guns blazing wouldn't get him what he wanted, and it definitely wouldn't be helpful to his career. He'd been in the job long enough to know how to play a senior officer, even one as difficult as Gray. Besides, he had no choice but to make the best of a bad situation.

He checked his phone and read through the email that Stevens had sent, then headed up to where the senior managers lurked.

"Inspector Rego, right on time," Gray's PA smiled at him. "He's waiting for you, do go on through. Can I bring you a coffee?"

Rego thanked her, knocked briskly on the door then walked inside when he heard Gray's curt, "Enter."

"I only have five minutes, Rego," he said, frowning. "I have an important meeting with the MP for Plymouth Sutton and Devonport, who as you know is the Parliamentary Under-Secretary of State in the Ministry of Defence."

Rego was vaguely aware of the politician in question but also recognised that Gray was employing his favourite habit of name-dropping all the important people he knew.

"I won't take up much of your time, sir," said Rego. "I just want to update you with the latest crime stats for West Cornwall and the initiatives I want to put in place to reduce car theft and increase detections. I've emailed the preliminary ideas to you."

Gray turned to his email and opened up the document, scanning it quickly, nodding to himself.

While Gray was occupied, Rego's phone appeared to ping with a text message, but it was really the timer going off.

"Sir, I've just had an intel update on the Besnik Domi case. It appears that he didn't return to Albania for his mother's birthday this week, and he's *never* missed her birthday before. The belief is that he's still in the UK. I have to say, sir, that I'm concerned for PC Poldhu's safety, as I'm sure you are."

Gray frowned and looked up.

"What's the source of this intelligence?"

"I can assure you, sir, it's a tested source."

Gray waved his hand in the air dismissively and Rego's heart sank.

"Unless you have evidence, *actual evidence*, that he's been positively identified in this country, my view is that he doesn't pose a threat. Rego, you have to learn to prioritise resources. This is why I've been making these decisions..."

Rego had already tuned out, knowing that he wouldn't be getting any extra resources to protect Tamsyn.

He wondered if could get Inspector Walters on his side. Maybe she'd view cooperation between uniform and CID as a peace-offering after their argument. It wouldn't hurt to sound her out about keeping up a visible presence around the Poldhus' cottage.

The other person to try and win over would be DCI

Finch. Rego knew that he'd have to work out where Finch's allegiances sat, but his instinct told him that his immediate superior was a career detective, and not someone flitting between roles and departments. Besides, there was already a certain level of trust between them.

Although that had been somewhat strained by an incident last summer which had brought MI6 to Cornwall: Rego had known what was going on but hadn't been permitted to tell DCI Finch.

Rego sighed.

This wasn't going to be easy.

CHAPTER 7

Tamsyn's surfboard was old and battered, an unfashionable swallowtail thruster. The V-shaped tail gave her more control and fast movements out of turns which meant more drive to get over fat sections of the wave. It was a style that had been popular in the nineties. These days, most surfers preferred round tails for greater stability. But she'd learned to surf on the swallowtail and she loved it.

It had belonged to her father.

Just after lunchtime, she was standing on Fistral Beach in Newquay, Cornwall's surf capital, gazing out at even sets of three-foot waves rolling up the wide sands.

The weather was a sunny 12°C, with a light offshore breeze: perfect conditions for learning to surf.

"Why are our surfboards the size of small tankers and yours isn't much bigger than a skateboard?"

Calvin Adade stood 6' 4" and towered over Tamsyn, his muscles straining the seams of his rented wetsuit.

"'Cause we're beginners, you muppet!" said Joe Quinn, eyeing his friend in amazement.

Calvin scowled, leaving creases in the mahogany skin

across his forehead, his almond-shaped eyes narrowed in irritation. He'd been smiling since Tamsyn had met him an hour earlier, but now his lips were pursed, eyeing Joe as if he was something unpleasant that he'd found on his shoe.

Tamsyn laughed, not bothering to point out that Cal also weighed at least double her 130 pounds and needed something the size of a small barge to support his weight in the water, and even Joe was several stone heavier than her.

"Spongies are really stable and work on small waves, so they're good to learn on," she said reassuringly. "Once you can pop up and catch a wave each time, you can use a lighter, faster, fibreglass board."

Cal didn't look convinced, examining the 12-foot foam surfboard with distrust.

Tamsyn pointed to her own board.

"See, on bigger waves, the key is to take turns slowly, so when you called your board a tanker, you were kind of right. Swallowtails like mine don't really allow that. But on small waves, you can rip and shred, cut back, and jump rails better without sacrificing your planing speed."

"I've no idea what you just said, Tam," Joe laughed, "but you sounded fuckin' hot saying it!"

Surprised and pleased she grinned at him, and their eyes locked, the shared gaze intense.

"Feeling like a third wheel here," Cal griped. "What's this popping-up lark all about then?"

Joe winked at Tamsyn, but she took Cal's hint, demonstrating how to 'pop up', going from a prone position on the board to standing, in one smooth move.

Both men were fit because with jobs as firearms officers, their lives depended on it, so it didn't take them long to get the idea. Of course, doing it on a moving wave would be a different matter.

For two years after she'd left school, Tamsyn had been a lifeguard and also taught surfing to small groups in the summer, so it was easy for her to slip back into that other persona, the person she'd been before she'd joined the police, before an armed criminal tried to gun her down.

No, Besnik Domi is not going to spoil today. He's not going to take this from me, too.

The cloudless sky and near-empty beach lifted her spirits. She laughed as the guys fell off time after time, swallowing water and wiping out on foot-high waves that were barely more than ripples. She shouted encouragement as they took off on a wave together. They both jumped to their feet but Joe fell off immediately, and only Cal managed to wobble his way to the shore on a small wave.

"Joe, your weight is too far back!" she called. "You'll catch more waves if you keep a bit further up the board."

"I'm catching plenty of waves in my face!" he yelled back.

Tamsyn laughed out loud, feeling light, the weight of worry falling away from her. She grabbed her board and paddled out towards the other surfers who were heading for the line-up, just beyond where the waves broke. A flock of them bobbed on the water, waiting for their wave. One by one, they peeled off, paddling for their breaker and riding it down the line, or missing it and heading back to wait for the next one.

"I can see why you like this," said Joe, as they bobbed up and down astride their boards, the black wetsuits making them look like seals in the sea, the weak winter sun on their faces.

They faced out toward the far horizon, because you never turned your back on the sea.

"It's a pretty amazing feeling when you catch a wave and stand up on the board."

"Not sure how you'd know," Cal laughed. "I haven't seen you stand up yet!"

"That's 'cos you weren't looking at the right time!" Joe complained.

"I don't have a crystal ball to look into the future," Cal said sardonically.

Joe leaned across to push him off his surfboard. Then ignoring his spluttering friend, he held out his hand to Tamsyn.

"Thanks for this, Tam," he said. "It's good to get away and out of the city sometimes."

Tamsyn hadn't held hands with a guy like this in forever, maybe since she was 15. Just the sun and the sea, not talking, just being. It felt odd, but in a good way. She liked that Joe seemed so open with his feelings – certainly more open than she knew how to be.

Then she saw a bigger set rising up.

"Go for it, Tam!" said Joe. "Show us how it's really done."

She threw him a quick smile, then spun her board around, paddling hard as the wave lifted her up and began to break over her head. With two more long strokes, she sprang to her feet, racing down the front of the wave, cutting in deep and ripping back, arms outstretched, shifting her weight, keeping her balance, utterly focussed and in tune with the wave, one entity, pumping the board, working it until its energy began to die, then she dug in hard, sending the board shooting over the back of the wave, catching air high above the water's surface, flying, free, weightless, then crashing down the other side.

Joe and Cal were whooping and cheering as she paddled back towards them.

"That was epic!" Joe laughed, shaking his head, his eyes wide and bright as he gave her a round of applause. "Fuck me!"

Tamsyn was thinking about it.

"What can I get you?" the bartender yelled, leaning across the polished teak as the noise behind them escalated.

"Three Dirty Pirates!" Jess shouted back.

A shot of rum in Bailey's with a splash of coke was Jess's new favourite drink, and had a helluva kick. Jess loved ordering them because the name made her laugh.

Tamsyn smiled as Rosie threw her an amused look.

Jess and Rosie had both been eager for a night out in Newquay, and were meeting each other for the first time. Tamsyn felt slightly awkward as her old life nudged against her new one, but Rosie and Jess were getting along fine. Which was just as well because the three of them were sharing a room at one of the cheap surf lodges that proliferated in Newquay's back streets.

The room was small, cleanish and cheap, but perfect from Tamsyn's point of view as it also came with an outdoor shower in the back garden where she could rinse the salt from her wetsuit, plus a secure surfboard storage area.

The guys had booked a room at the same place but seemed to be taking a lot longer than Tamsyn and her friends to pretty themselves up for a night out.

"Liquid courage for when Mr Hottie-Armed-Policeman arrives," Jess leered, picking up her glass.

"Keep your voice down," Tamsyn said, although the chances of being overheard were minimal.

"Right, sorry," Jess said, pulling a face.

"Is that them?" Rosie asked. "It must be because that's Jason with them."

Tamsyn's colleague on E-team had been eager to meet up with his old buddy from the Royal Marines, but hadn't been sure if he'd be able to make it. It seemed he'd managed it after all.

Jess ogled the trio and licked her lips.

"Lush," she said huskily.

Tamsyn didn't know which of the guys she was referring to; maybe all of them.

She introduced everyone while Jess ordered more cocktails.

"Are you two sisters?" Calvin asked, his gaze flicking between Tamsyn and Rosie, who were both tall, slim, blondes.

Rosie smiled at him.

"Sisters by way of the uniform."

"Gotcha. What about you, Jess?" asked Calvin. "You in the job?"

"God, no! I'm an estate agent."

"Someone who's normal!" Jason grinned at her.

Jess looked as though she didn't know whether to be offended or not.

"What's it like living at the seaside all year round?" Cal asked, his question aimed at no one in particular. "In the winter, like this time of year."

"Newly-weds and nearly-deads," Jess sang out, making them all laugh. "That's what we call the out of season holidaymakers. It'll get busy two days before Christmas until the first week of January, then dead as a dodo until Easter. It's when locals get to enjoy the place."

Cal shot her a look, and Rosie smirked at him.

"It's okay. You're invited so that makes you practically a local."

He grinned at her and moved his bar stool next to hers.

They drank, they danced, and for one night, they had no worries. Tonight, they were just another group of twenty-somethings having a night on the town. Even though five of them were police officers, contending with high-stress work conditions, and shift patterns that made personal relationships difficult.

They dealt with emergencies regularly, even at the cost of their own lives, and the statistics said that as first responders, they were three-times more likely to be high-alcohol consumers than the rest of the population.

Tonight, they didn't care.

Jess and Jason seemed to have hit it off and were working up a sweat on the dancefloor at Walkabout, the Australian-themed bar that had once been Newquay's old cinema. Cal and Rosie were sitting with their heads together, having a deep and meaningful conversation.

Which left Tamsyn and Joe.

"Has there been any word on that lowlife toe-rag?" he asked.

Tamsyn blinked, slightly thrown by the serious subject, not that she had many moments where Besnik Domi was far from her mind.

"No credible sightings, but they don't think he's gone back to Albania either."

Joe frowned. "Why's that then?"

"He missed his mother's birthday and apparently that's a really big deal."

Joe scowled. "A crim who loves his dear old mum: bleedin' stereotypes."

"I won't be allowed back on frontline duties until they know where he is," Tamsyn seethed. "It really pisses me off that he's *still* controlling my life and he's not even in Cornwall!"

"What do you mean?"

"I'm on medical leave for another week, and even when they *finally* let me go back, I won't be back with my team on Response, but no one will tell me how long that will be for."

He looked at her with understanding but didn't say anything.

"Can we talk about something else? I don't want to spoil this, too."

Joe nodded and raised his hand to tuck a stray lock of hair behind her ear. It wasn't an original move, but it made her blood sing.

She hoped he'd kiss her, but he leaned back, his expression serious.

"Are you in touch with your mum? I saw that article in *The Sun*."

"No!" Tamsyn said hotly. "I haven't seen her since I was five frickin' years old! I don't know how the reporters even found her. I haven't got a clue where she lives and, apparently, she's just remembered that I'm her daughter."

"Maybe she found them."

"What do you mean?"

Joe looked sympathetic, and then the penny dropped.

"Oh," said Tamsyn. "Oh, right. You think she went to them and they paid her for her so-called story."

"The world's a shitty place sometimes," Joe said quietly, his voice barely audible above the noise."

"Tell me about it," Tamsyn said bitterly.

"I'd rather tell you how hot you look ... and that I've been wanting to do this all night."

Joe leaned forward, his lips brushing hers, the lightest of touches.

But then he moved away again and Tamsyn was left disappointed and frustrated.

"I wish I didn't have to go home tomorrow," he said, putting his arm around her shoulders so she could lean against him. "I'm only just getting to know you. And learning to surf."

"And your surfing still sucks," she murmured. "You'll have to come back."

"Is that an invitation?"

She sat up straight and met his gaze, his eyes twinkling with a smile that didn't always reach his face.

"Maybe. You could meet my grandparents."

"Bloody hell, Tam! From what you've told me about your grandad, he'd take me out in his boat and make me walk the plank just for looking at you!"

Tamsyn laughed out loud.

"Probably, yeah. You worried?"

"Not if you promise to protect me. Us Celts have to stick together."

"Celts?" she said, wrinkling her nose.

"Well, yeah. You're Cornish and my dad's Irish, not that I've seen the old bastard since he walked out on us."

Tamsyn looked down at her drink, her expression unreadable, and Joe's smile drooped at the edges.

"I'd like to say yes, Joe, but how would it work? You're in London, I'm down here..."

"Yeah, I know," he grinned. "Two of us in the job, shift work, knackered all the time – dating each other is a terrible idea. So, do you want to go out sometime, like a proper date, just the two of us?"

His smile was infectious and Tamsyn found herself smiling back at him.

"With an offer like that, how could I possibly say no?"

"You tried pretty hard."

"I could have tried harder."

"So, is that a yes?"

She studied his hopeful expression.

"Yeah, that's a yes."

He leaned forwards and Tamsyn only hesitated for a second as his lips met hers. She wrapped her arms around his neck, pulling him closer, his body heated and hard against her.

"Hell yeah, it's a yes," he breathed, and this time, he kissed her again.

CHAPTER 8

Rego had not had the best of times since he'd come back from leave.

ACC Gray had point blank refused to reinstate protection for Tamsyn. The fact that Domi hadn't been seen was proof enough for Gray that it was an unnecessary expense.

Maura Walters had rather grudgingly allowed her officers to do drive-bys through Gulval village at the start and end of their shifts, but that was all she'd conceded.

The Met were working with various police forces across the UK to follow up all the credible 'sightings' of Domi, but the results had been disappointing, and the intel from the various agencies involved only reinforced how well planned Domi's flight from justice had been. Or as Stevens had said to him, so far, the investigation had found a whole lot of nothing.

And two weeks since their 'lively debate', relations between Rego and Walters didn't seem as if they were thawing either.

"I'm not sure this is appropriate," Inspector Maura Walters said with her usual air of irritation.

Rego withheld his own annoyance and simply nodded to acknowledge that she'd spoken, then took a seat in her office without comment.

In truth, she'd given him less than ten minutes' notice that the meeting was taking place, clearly hoping that he wouldn't be able to make it.

"Thank you, Maura," he said, his voice neutral. "I appreciate you inviting me to this meeting, but given the cross-over with CID's ongoing investigation..."

He didn't need to finish the sentence. In the days following the Old Bailey incident, half the world had seen the photographs of what had happened: they'd seen the smoke and flames billowing from the iconic Edwardian building; seen the cement truck that had blocked the street in front, slowing the response of the fire brigade, police and paramedics; and they'd seen the front-page photograph of the young police officer, blood on her face and an expression of such anguish that it moved even hardest of hearts.

At least the press was leaving the Poldhu family alone now. With none of them or their neighbours giving interviews, the assembled journalists had soon lost interest, having to make do with a handful of interviews from Tamsyn's 'close friends', even though she hadn't spoken to any of the ones they'd found since she left school nearly three years earlier.

Jess had consistently told the journalists to do something which was anatomically impossible, and that just made Tamsyn love her even more.

It had certainly shown her which people she could trust, and if the price were right, who would sell their own mother. Or daughter.

Sir Malcolm's widow was a more interesting target for the reporters, particularly as she had been scathing about the lack of progress in finding out how a bomb had been smuggled into the Old Bailey, even though her late husband had been defending the man who benefitted from the attack. But none of the newspapers were willing to put that in anything but small print: the wife was the innocent victim, after all.

In fact, Rego had a report on his desk that showed the investigation had uncovered quite a lot of new information.

Rego had received a nice letter from Judge Whittaker, filled with long sentences of gratitude, thanking Rego for carrying him from the courtroom, concluding with the words:

> *I'll be corresponding with the Chief Constable about your heroic actions in challenging circumstances.*

Tamsyn hadn't heard anything from the Sloane family.

"I understand that you disagreed with ACC Gray about removing Tamsyn's armed protection," said Walters.

Rego calculated his response carefully.

He wasn't going to risk slagging off Gray to Walters because he didn't trust her and wasn't sure if she wouldn't stab him in the back given the opportunity; and if not that, he was convinced that someone at the nick was reporting back to HQ about him; whether that was to do with him being a transferee from GMP, or even that he was the first biracial inspector in Cornwall, or simply that he was an unknown quantity. Whichever it was, Rego was careful what he said and who he said it to.

"Yes," he said, at last. "I think the decision was…"

There was a firm knock on the door, drawing the gaze of both inspectors.

"Come in," Walters called out, clearly annoyed that Rego hadn't finished his comment on ACC Gray's decision.

The door opened and Tamsyn walked into the room, her confident step slowing just a fraction when she saw Rego.

"Ma'am, sir," she said formally as Rego gave her a reassuring smile.

"Thank you for coming in, Tamsyn," said Walters. "Please have a seat."

Tamsyn sat opposite Walters and to one side of Rego, looking alert and composed, but to Rego's mind, as if she was acting a part.

"How are you, Tamsyn?"

"I'm fine, ma'am. Ready to come back to work," Tamsyn replied firmly.

Walters glanced down at the file on her desk before speaking.

"I've had an email from your coach on the Learning and Development Team and I've spoken to Sergeant Terwillis," Walters continued, but didn't disclose what either had said. "You took advantage of the occupational health referral to see a counsellor, I believe."

"Yes, ma'am."

"How was that?"

"Very useful, ma'am. Four sessions on Zoom and she gave me the link for PTSD Support."

"And the TP, the TRiM Practitioner at Middlemoor?"

"Yes, ma'am. I picked up some useful techniques."

TRiM was the acronym for trauma risk management, first trialled by the British Military during the War in

Afghanistan, and unlike some other projects designed to improve mental well-being, this actually seemed to work; TPs were valued members of staff.

Walters leaned back in her seat.

"You're ticking all the boxes, Tamsyn, but my concern is that this has been a lot to take in and that you haven't properly had time to process it. I can't put an officer on the streets under those circumstances."

Tamsyn glanced at Rego whom she knew had been back at work almost immediately, only taking off enough time to spend a long weekend with his family.

She also knew that if she admitted to having flashbacks and nightmares that she wouldn't be allowed back on duty. She'd already had two weeks off and she was ready to work; she needed to work. She needed something to occupy her mind so she could stop being inside her head all the time. Mindfulness could just fuck off. Surfing was the only thing that helped, but now there was a band of high-pressure hanging over the Atlantic coast, and the waves had gone, leaving the sea as flat as a millpond.

"I'm really keen to get back to work, ma'am," Tamsyn said, looking directly at Walters who gave a brief nod of approval.

"Sergeant Terwillis has suggested a few weeks of recuperative duties where you won't be deployed; you'll work from the station, catch up on your paperwork and make a fresh start in the New Year."

Tamsyn wasn't sure what a 'fresh start' would look like or how it would help her, and weeks of paperwork and desk duty was not what she'd hoped for. But at least she'd be back in uniform. She'd missed it more than she'd ever have thought possible.

Even so, paperwork was the bane of a police officer's life, and that multiplied significantly for a student officer who was also trying to complete her Police Constable Degree Apprenticeship. At least she could use the time to get ahead on her coursework.

Inspector Walters' offer was less than Tamsyn wanted, but she was sure that she could convince them that she was fine if she could just rejoin her team.

She assumed that the interview was over and started to stand, but Rego looked at her thoughtfully.

"I've had dreams about that day," he said, his voice pensive as she sank back into her chair reluctantly. "Well, nightmares."

Walters cut him a look.

"When I started in the job, there were still some old-school coppers who thought the less you said, the sooner you got over something. But that's not always the case, is it?"

He waited for someone to fill the space he'd left, but neither Walters nor Tamsyn spoke.

"I've found talking to the TP has helped," he said at last, looking directly at Tamsyn.

She was taken aback, having assumed that he'd gone straight back to work with no repercussions.

"It's helped a lot," Rego continued, "and I wasn't the one who had a gun pointed at my head."

Tamsyn looked down. The only reason that she wasn't dead was because Domi's machine pistol had either jammed or was out of bullets. She didn't know which. She didn't want to know. All that mattered was she'd survived.

"Can I ask you something, sir?" she said, her voice clear and strong.

"Of course."

"Have there been any sightings of Domi?"

That wasn't the question Rego had been expecting and he had to reorder his thoughts quickly.

"Yes and no," he said tiredly. "He's been seen everywhere from Buckingham Palace to the Taj Mahal. It's often the way that we get a shed load of false sightings, and/or false reporting to us or through Crimestoppers. The more credible ones are followed immediately, but eventually, every single one will be looked into, but that takes time."

He didn't add that the Met were all over Domi's associates and they'd even interviewed the brother in HMP Manchester. Search warrants had been executed at a number of Hellbanianz associates and the houses of family members. Basically, the Met were making a nuisance of themselves, hoping to get lucky, or just hoping that someone would give them names of anyone involved.

"There's a lot happening behind the scenes, and sometimes it's just a bit of luck as well as hard work that brings benefits rather than relying on intelligence." He paused. "I will say that he couldn't travel on any of the travel documents in his name or his known aliases. He's wanted on an Interpol Red Notice; and on Border Force's Watchlist, which flags people travelling on airlines. He's probably in hiding while he has people working to get new ID."

Tamsyn looked as frustrated as Rego felt.

"It's also possible that he's travelling on a fraudulently obtained genuine passport. Other than facial recognition, fingerprints, or someone recognising him, an individual can travel relatively freely without coming to the attention of law enforcement."

He didn't mention that he'd also flagged Domi on the Police National Computer, so anyone searching the database for him would automatically alert Rego and Devon & Cornwall Police.

"Albanian officials are on the alert for him, too, so he won't be able to just take up where he left off. We'll get him, Tamsyn, but it's going to take some time."

The silence stretched out until Walters decided that the meeting was over, gathered her papers and shuffled them into a stack.

"Any further questions?" she asked crisply.

Tamsyn shook her head.

"No, ma'am."

"Then we'll see you on Monday." She stood to shake hands. "Good to have you back, Tamsyn."

"Thank you, ma'am." She glanced briefly at Rego. "Sir."

And she left the room.

As soon as the door closed, Rego turned to Walters.

"She's not ready to come back, Maura."

Walters sighed. "Her TP thinks she's doing well."

"She's hiding something; she's saying what she thinks we want to hear."

Walters closed her eyes briefly and massaged her temples.

"Bryn Terwillis agrees with you."

"He does?" Rego asked with surprise.

"For God's sake, Rob," Walters said impatiently, "you're not the only one who's invested in Tamsyn's well-being, but it's clear that she wants to come back to work, and if she's on restricted duties ... oh God, what's the new terminology again? You know ... recuperative duties. We'll be able to keep an eye on her."

Rego nodded. "Good point."

Walters looked at him.

"Did you just make up that about nightmares for Tamsyn's benefit?"

Rego stood up to leave.

"No," he said. "I didn't."

He headed back to his office deep in thought. He was worried about Tamsyn for several reasons, but when he sat at his desk eyeing the Everest of paperwork, he put those concerns to one side, and started ploughing through reports and case files, analysing performance data and information against team objectives to feed into programs that told the Chief Constable how well his team were doing. It was tedious, but apparently necessary. It was part of an inspector's job, and the part he liked the least.

Rego rolled up his sleeves and got stuck in.

Hours later, just as he'd decided to call it a day and head home, DS Tom Stevens tapped on Rego's office door.

"You alright, boss?"

Rego stretched his arms over his head and gave his detective sergeant a wry smile.

"I feel like ten kinds of shit, Tom. So, no change there."

Tom grinned, then his smile faded.

"Heard you saw young Tamsyn earlier. How's she doing?"

"She says she's fine. But I don't think anyone can be fine two weeks after a bomb, a fire, a madman with a Mac 10, and a defence barrister bleeding to death all over them."

"Ah well, you know what they call a hundred lawyers at the bottom of the sea?" Tom Stevens paused for the punchline. "A good start!"

Rego raised his eyebrows. Not many police liked defence lawyers, but still...

"Yeah, I know," Stevens sighed, feigning contrition. "I'll

have to write myself up for another political correctness course."

"Better yet, I need a volunteer to attend the next diversity, equality and inclusion strategy planning meeting. Cheers, Tom!"

Stevens looked at him askance. "Fair do's, boss!"

"It'll be good for you," said Rego, trying not to smile at his sergeant's woebegone expression.

Stevens muttered something under his breath that Rego chose not to hear.

"Any news on Domi?" Stevens asked. "What did the PIMs team find out?"

Rego's frown reappeared and he pushed the folder across his desk containing the Met's Post Incident Management report.

"You know that they debriefed me with Sid and Mimi, then Tamsyn at the hospital; well, it turns out that by then they already knew about the hijacked lorry with the ready-mix concrete, and the escape on a motorbike."

"Bastards!" Stevens said with feeling.

"Since then, investigators focussed on a cleaner at the courtroom who didn't show up for work the following day," Rego continued. "Apparently, he was a member of the Hellbanianz. The cleaning company who hired him are in the firing line; apparently, they're 'reviewing' their security-vetting of personnel, but they've already lost their contract with Central Criminal Court. As for the, 'cleaner', investigators think he used a 'dropper' – malicious malware that bypassed the security system at court to control electronic door-locking systems. That gave him access, and he wore a fake security guard uniform so he wasn't challenged. Cameras were disabled, so with a distraction, Domi could just walk out." He paused. "I'd say they planned for Domi to abscond with maximum confusion but minimum casualties."

"I don't think poor old Sir Malcolm would agree with that, would he?" Stevens snorted with disgust.

"No," Rego admitted. "But the thinking is that the cleaner managed to slip a small incendiary device into Sir Malcolm's briefcase, not into his robes. It was just bad luck that Sir Malcolm was too close when the device initiated. The gang member had also sprayed the courtroom with an accelerant, a version of RDX. It's colourless and odourless, stable at room temperature, and it's a key ingredient in Semtex."

"Bloody hell!"

"Yep, but the version he used is some sort of pesticide used for killing rats and available relatively easily."

"So, no records of purchase."

"Exactly."

"Which meant that Domi was able to make a run for it during the chaos?"

"Chaos for us, not so much for him: it was a well-planned op. He was behind reinforced glass so he knew that he wouldn't be injured by the explosion. He was waiting for it, and as soon as the incendiary device detonated, he clobbered the prison guards and stole their key."

"And then he just ran out through the front door," Stevens concluded.

Rego was silent.

"Boss?"

"He should have," Rego said thoughtfully. "That's what anyone else would have done, but instead he grabbed the Mac 10 from his buddy and ran back inside a burning building. Why did he do that, Tom?"

Stevens shrugged. "He wanted to finish off Sir Malcolm?"

Rego shook his head. "Surely, he'd go for the prosecution team, not his own brief? But my gut is telling me something else."

Stevens eyed him warily. "Such as?"

"Tamsyn."

"Boss?"

"I think he went back for Tamsyn."

Steven's eyebrows would have hit his hairline if he wasn't already as bald as a billiard ball.

"Are you saying he went back to kill Tamsyn for giving evidence against him? That seems..." Stevens was at a loss for words.

"I don't know the reason he went back in, Tom. He could have killed dozens of people, but instead he sprayed the ceiling and walls with bullets. Why bother? He'd already terrorised everyone with the explosion and fire. He went back for another reason."

Stevens rubbed his hand over his bristly chin.

"Tamsyn said that his gun jammed or was out of bullets."

"Yes, that's what Tamsyn said." Rego paused. "A Mac 10 machine pistol has 32 9mm rounds: 27 bullets and 26 casings have been recovered so far..."

Stevens nodded, not following where Rego was going with this.

"Sounds like a jam or maybe just not a full magazine."

"But if he intended to kill Tamsyn and he'd run out of bullets, he could have just clubbed her with the barrel; he could have stamped on her head and crushed her skull. She was stuck under Sir Malcolm so she wasn't going anywhere."

"Maybe Domi ran out of time."

Rego wasn't buying that.

"No. He's already escaped the building, but then he grabs a gun from his accomplice, runs back into a burning building, searches for Tamsyn but doesn't kill her when he finds her?"

Stevens scratched his head.

"So, if his intent wasn't to kill Tamsyn, or the judge or jurors or whoever was around, then what was it?"

"That, Tom, is the six-million-dollar question." Rego stood up and reached for his coat. "Read the report tomorrow. Right now, there's a pint waiting for you at Wetherspoons. I'm buying."

"Cheers, boss!" Stevens said, his face brightening.

Rego switched off the light in his office as they headed out into the November evening, the prevailing south-westerly wind slicing the frigid air forced them to walk with their heads bowed and their shoulders hunched.

Rego was happy to leave the office but his mind was whirring.

There were two things that he couldn't tell his sergeant:

Firstly, that the Prime Minister was taking a personal interest in the investigation because he'd gone to school with Sir Malcolm. And as Domi hadn't contacted his mother in Tirana on her birthday or in the weeks since then, the assumption was that Domi hadn't fled the UK after all. Secondly, the NCA suspected that there was another reason why Domi might have run back into the Old Bailey that day, one that Rego only knew about because MI6, and therefore Vikram, were keeping their fingers on the pulse of this case at the Prime Minister's very express order.

This so-called reason hadn't made it into the official PIMs report. In fact, Rego was aware that the National

Crime Agency and the Secret Intelligence Service knew far more about Domi and the Hellbanianz case than they were sharing with Devon & Cornwall Police.

Vikram had told him something which had shocked him to his core.

The NCA was working on the theory that Domi had run back into the building not to kill Tamsyn ... but to save her.

CHAPTER 9

Rego slept badly.

He'd been unable to reconcile what he'd learned from Vikram's classified intelligence with Tamsyn, a young officer that he'd come to know pretty well. He couldn't believe that she'd fooled him so comprehensively and was involved with Besnik Domi; or rather, he didn't want to believe that could be the case.

But the National Crime Agency was adamant that someone else in Cornwall was running Domi's operations for the Hellbanianz. The drug smuggling business had apparently managed to survive the murder of their main distributors, Saemira Ruçi and George Mason, and the arrest of several members of its network, not least Domi himself, and was still active.

Rego wasn't sure when Tamsyn had become a person of interest to the NCA, possibly about the time that Domi had failed to kill her at the Old Bailey. If his best friend Vikram had still been at the NCA, he would have had a chance of persuading them that Tamsyn had nothing to do with any of this, but Vikram had been seconded to MI6 and was working in the grey world of spooks and spies. Rego's new NCA contacts hadn't come up through the ranks with him like Vik had, so when he said that Tamsyn was innocent, that simply made them question his judgement.

They also questioned Tamsyn's account that Domi had pulled the trigger. Even Rego's own sergeant had asked why Domi hadn't bludgeoned her to death if indeed the Mac 10 had failed. But neither Tamsyn's statement nor the NCA's theories answered the question of why: why had Domi run back into the burning building and then left her there?

But Rego knew Tamsyn. He'd seen her devastation when she realised that George Mason was not the family friend that she'd believed him to be, that he was, in fact, a key player in the Hellbanianz drug smuggling business. That was real – it must be real. No one was that good an actor.

Besides, Tamsyn had nearly died that night after jumping from Mason's boat into the sea to escape Domi. She'd been almost two miles from land, fully dressed, and the sea temperature had been 10°C. She couldn't have known that she'd be saved and she very nearly wasn't. So, the National Crime Agency's interest in her didn't make sense to Rego. But he'd been made aware that his own objectivity was being questioned by the NCA. Hell, Rego's own wife had warned him that Tamsyn had a crush on him, even if it wasn't reciprocated. Although, he did have a soft spot for her, which meant that he had to be on guard in case he was wrong about Tamsyn ... and about how well he really knew her.

And that pissed him off.

The NCA was seriously considering that Domi was still in the UK. Having kept a very close eye on all ports of entry and exit, they could find no evidence that he'd travelled abroad by car, train or plane. They'd also followed up every report of a sighting, no matter how spurious, but there had been no credible intelligence and simply no trace of him. The Hellbanianz had powerbases in East London, Liverpool and Manchester, so it was possible, likely even, that Domi had gone to ground. But what about Cornwall? Had elements of his southwest drug distribution network survived the multiple arrests earlier in the year? If so, it was possible that Domi would once again attempt to leave the mainland by yacht as he had, successfully, the previous March.

Unable to lie in bed questioning himself any longer, Rego crawled from under the duvet and into a sweatshirt and pants, then laced up his Nikes.

It was still an hour before sunrise and Rego shivered in the freshening breeze that swept across the harbour. He adjusted his head torch and set off at a slow jog past the bronze-and-granite Fisherman's Memorial, then picking up his pace as he hit the long, straight stretch of promenade all the way to the seawater lido, the Jubilee Pool, in Penzance.

At this time of the morning, he was the only runner on the prom, but there was a steady flow of road traffic, and Newlyn Harbour was a refuge port, which meant it was open 24 hours a day, 365 days a year.

His footsteps pounded out his frustration. *We work best when we work as a team.*

He'd said those words on his first day at Penzance and he still held them to be a fundamental truth, so having one of the officers under a cloud, it wasn't good for anyone.

He decided that he'd make some casual enquiries of his own.

Rego didn't want to go up the line and ask around at Exeter; he preferred to keep this more informal until he could be convinced that Tamsyn had something to hide. So, he started with his premier source of all local knowledge: his Detective Sergeant.

"Tom, do we have any firearms trained officers at this nick?"

Stevens started to shake his head then paused.

"No, boss, but there's one of the newer recruits on E-team who was a Royal Marine. He'd probably know a thing or two: PC Jason Johnson."

Stevens was clearly waiting for a reason for the question, but Rego ducked back inside his office and left a message for Johnson to contact him when he came off shift that afternoon.

Rego would have pegged PC Jason Johnson as a Bootneck before he'd even introduced himself: hair buzzed, frame bulky, demeanour calm and confident.

"You wanted to see me, sir?"

"Yes, thanks for coming. Take a seat. I'm told you're the man to talk to about guns and I have a question about semi-automatics. Is that in your wheelhouse?"

Johnson nodded.

"I know a bit, sir. I spent three months deployed to Kenya for weapons training and there wasn't much to do except eat, sleep, work, repeat." He shrugged. "And I was a boring, work-obsessed nerd anyway. Was there something specific you wanted to know?"

"I know that 9mm bullets are not that easy to come by and criminal armourers are very inventive. So, start with the less legit end of the market and assume I know nothing."

Johnson raised his eyebrows and took a moment to order his thoughts.

"Okay, well, when we were training the Kenya Marine Commando Unit, most of the weapons we took from al-

Shabaab pirates were using re-loads. That's where the brass, the spent cases, are reloaded. Gunpowder is quite easy to come by, and there's a specific 'reload' machine you can buy. In this country, you can get quite a sophisticated kit for as little as £200. The gunpowder is weighed and poured into the case and the lead bullet pressed into place. Anyone with a bit of technical knowledge could make a 9mm mould and make their own bullets by pouring molten lead and maybe doing a bit of reshaping after."

None of this was good news.

"What about automatic weapons jamming?" Rego asked.

"Pretty common with firearms that crims use. Auto and semi-auto weapons rely on a cycle where the fired bullet is ejected by the top slide being thrown backwards either by a small amount of gas, which is siphoned from a tiny hole in the barrel, pushing back the top slide, or recoil pushing a spring to move the top slide. Jams are quite frequent because crims don't know how to clean the weapons properly or don't care, so there's powder-fouling, which is a build-up of burnt gunpowder residue. That can cause a weapon to malfunction. Or you might get a worn ejector which doesn't throw out the brass so it stays in the breach. Then reloaded bullets can get misshapen cases, especially the more times they're used. And the cyclic rate – that's the rate of fire – is so high, the breach and barrel get really hot, which also affects reloads."

Johnson was on a roll, but Rego had heard enough: jams were common, especially when bullets were homemade and weapons were badly maintained, which meant that Tamsyn could well have been telling the truth about Domi's gun jamming.

"The only type of gun that doesn't jam is a revolver,"

Johson continued, and Rego thought his description as a gun nerd was spot on. "All that can happen is a misfire and..."

"Okay, thank you, Jason. That's really useful. I appreciate you taking the time at the end of your shift."

Johnson looked disappointed that the conversation was over, but stood up immediately.

"Happy to help, sir," and he left Rego's office almost marching from the room.

It wasn't much to prove Tamsyn's innocence, but it was a start.

Rego tapped his fingers on the desk. There must be more he could do. But what?

CHAPTER 10

It had been another long, boring day for Tamsyn.

For most of her shifts over the past few weeks, she'd been doing paperwork, coursework, and busy-work until she was cross-eyed and climbing the walls in frustration. Not forgetting trying to avoid/ignore/blank Chloe's bitchy comments.

Once word had gone round that Tamsyn was on desk duties, Bitchtits had been in her element, thinking it made Tamsyn a sitting target. But instead, Tamsyn had taken a leaf out of Rosie's playbook and annoyed the hell out of Chloe by giving her huge smiles and the most insincere compliments known to woman. Today's verbal smack-down had been a zinger.

"I love that colour on you, it makes you look less washed-out than normal."

Chloe had given her usual, crude reply, but left the room, which was the result Tamsyn wanted.

Besides, she wasn't ready to forgive Chloe for spreading lies to the media about her. It was one thing to be a bitch in person, it was very different to smear her publicly, maybe even damage her career in the police force.

Of course, Chloe hadn't admitted it, but Tamsyn knew: the wording sounded just like Chloe, and she'd also made the comment about 'Hollywood' before Tamsyn had known anything about the story in the *The Sun*.

Telling her grandparents had been awful. Her grandmother promised that karma would find Alex Poldhu, or whatever she was calling herself these days; her grandfather had stamped around the cottage in silent fury, and the few brave souls at the harbour who remembered Alex and dared to mention her, soon wished they hadn't.

Tamsyn half expected her mother to get in touch with her, but after 16 years of silence, a few more weeks weren't a complete surprise either.

Tamsyn wished that she could stop thinking about her, but the memory was there, a splinter of unresolved resentment that kept her awake at night.

There had been a brief reprieve from the tedium of desk duties in the shape of three days and six primary schools while she shadowed an officer from Community Policing. They'd been speaking to kids aged from five to eleven about the role of the police in the community, as a way of extending the perception that the police just caught burglars and 'bad people'. Equipped with a copy of the children's book, *PC Ben*, that her colleague had nabbed from Thames Valley Police, the initiative was designed to explain the varied nature of modern police and their role within the community, as well as building trust and confidence with the pupils.

Tamsyn liked little kids so she didn't mind, and it had been a welcome change to get out of the station even if she had fielded a surprising number of questions from Year 6 girls who wanted to know about her uniform, hair and makeup. One had even asked if she could run in high heels, and Tamsyn had patiently explained that she wore boots with steel toecaps, rolling up a trouser leg to show off her Altberg Peacekeepers to prove it.

Apparently, the boots were "well cool", and she received an invitation to a sleepover with a group of eight-year-old girls.

Her mentor on the project, PC Jake Weston, had given her such a glowing report that Sergeant Terwillis suggested Tamsyn should contact the head teacher at her former secondary school to set up giving a talk there, too. Humphry Davy School had been named for the man who invented the miners' safety lamp a couple of hundred years ago, and the pupils were aged 11 to 16. Tamsyn thought that she'd need more than *PC Ben* to take on a room full of teenagers. Although, she could always practise on Chloe: the woman had the mentality of a sulky thirteen-year-old.

Sergeant Terwillis popped his head into the room.

"Ah, Tamsyn, you're here."

Where else would I be? She thought.

"Come into my office for a moment, would you?"

She followed him into the tiny office crammed with filing cabinets, and squeezed into a chair, her heart racing, wondering if he had news of Besnik Domi.

"I've got some good news for you," he said, leaning back and looking pleased. "We've managed to get you on your blue-light training, starting on Monday."

Tamsyn was delighted. Two weeks out of the station! Two weeks to get certified for her blues-and-twos.

"You'll report to the Bodmin training centre, and for the next fortnight, you'll be learning to drive safely at speed, practise in different environments from built-up areas to country lanes." He smiled at her. "Hopefully, after you pass the test, you'll be certified to drive a ton-up, lights on and sirens blaring."

"Wow! That's great! Thank you, sarge. I can't wait."

"I know it's been pretty boring stuck here, so it'll be good to get this for your portfolio and ticked off the list."

Tamsyn nodded, still grinning as she left his office.

The timing was interesting though: the blue-light training course was extremely desirable and Tamsyn knew several other PCs who'd waited nearly two years to get their chance; only 55% of officers had completed the course across the whole of Devon & Cornwall Police.

Even though there had been no news of Domi, she suspected that her superiors were trying to find other training areas where she wouldn't be frontline. Thank God, they hadn't sent her to work at the custody suite again – dealing with the nightly collection of drunks, drugs, shit, blood and vomit was not on her to-do list. Besides, last time she'd worked there, she'd broken two ribs on a man whilst doing CPR. She'd also saved his life, but still…

As she walked past the lockers, she saw her sometime friend, PC Jamie Smith. At least, he'd been friendly towards her until he'd started dating Chloe. But now he was staring into space, a lost expression on his face.

"Alright, Jamie," Tamsyn said, not planning to stop.

He grunted something but it didn't sound particularly friendly.

Tamsyn headed to her own locker, her nose wrinkling as a pungent odour assaulted her.

"What the hell?"

She yanked open her locker door, revolted to see a pile of stinking fish heads piled on top of her coat.

Chloe just happened to saunter into the locker room, watching her, a malicious smile on her face.

"What's the matter with you?" Tamsyn yelled, throwing the fish heads at Chloe's feet.

She recoiled and turned her hate-filled face towards Tamsyn.

"That isn't anything to do with me, you freak!"

Tamsyn was too angry to listen.

"I've got a fucking gang-banger murderer after my family! Isn't that enough without your pathetic games?"

"Maybe you're just not as popular as you think you are!"

Chloe turned on her heel.

"Oi, that was bang out of order, Tam!" Jamie said angrily. "She's never done anything to you!"

"Really?" Tamsyn snarled. "You can actually say that with a straight face? Funny how my car was vandalised after Chloe met that druggie Ollie Garrett for a drink, and funny that you're here *and* you're the only other person who's ever broken into my locker!"

She regretted the words as soon as she'd said them: Jamie had only been in her locker once to fetch her clean clothes when she'd been taken to hospital last Easter. But it was too late.

His face reddened.

"Fuck off! Chloe was right about you!"

He threw her a disgusted look and headed out after his girlfriend.

Tamsyn was furious, with herself as much as with Chloe. Once again, she'd let the woman get the better of her causing her to lash out at Jamie.

She truly doubted that he'd have had anything to do with Chloe's prank, but it rankled that he wouldn't believe the bitch-on-wheels was capable of it either. Although, he wouldn't be the first man to be led around by his dick.

Tamsyn found a dustpan and brush to clear the fish heads into a bin bag which she left outside the station, but other than spraying her locker with half a litre of bleach and wrapping her coat in another bin bag until she could wash it a dozen times, there was nothing she could do about the stench.

She thought about reporting it because it was undoubtedly bullying and harassment, but she didn't want to be thought of the officer who always ran to the boss and the first sign of trouble, the officer who brought the drama.

But what could she do about Chloe?

CHAPTER 11

Tamsyn was in a better mood when she went into work the following morning. Being given the blue-light training, she no longer felt like she was at the bottom of the pile, even though she was the youngest officer on the shift. This felt like she was making some progress in her career.

The different teams always seemed to be having some sort of drama of one kind or another, although no one was mentioning fish heads, for which she was eternally grateful. The general gossip was that more changes were on the way, including another round of budget cuts and a shake-up of backroom staff; police officers who had not walked the streets for years were going to be identified and reassigned to frontline work.

She'd heard that two officers from B-team were leaving, not just Penzance station, but leaving the police. Both had applied for jobs as train drivers with more money, better hours and a lot less stress.

That was bad for B-team and bad for morale, but Tamsyn was keen not to be the newbie, so if she had some courses under her belt, the additional new staff, if they ever emerged ... well, they might be asking her advice one day.

Of course, she had to pass the blue-light course first.

Tamsyn's team were on nights, so she sat alone doing paperwork until boredom and the need to stretch her legs sent her up to the break room.

She'd just made herself a cup of tea when a Traffic Officer she knew by reputation breezed into the room and helped himself to a drink.

Charlie Matthews was more than a legend in his own lunchtime; he was a *bona fide* highly-decorated officer, one of the last of the old-school coppers, and a petrol head from the tip of his shiny bulled boots to the top of his hat, the peak slashed and almost touching the bridge of his nose.

Tamsyn could hear the click of his shoes on the tiled floor, and she thought he must have segs in the heels of his shoes. He even had creases sewn into his trousers.

"Are you Tamsyn? I was told I could find you here. I'm Charlie Matthews."

He held out his hand and shook Tamsyn's firmly, clearly a man who took no prisoners.

"I've been asked to come and have a chat with you about your blue-light training next week."

"Oh, thank you..." Tamsyn paused, surprised and slightly intimidated by the force of nature that was Charlie Matthews.

"So, what can I tell you about patrol cars?"

She'd heard that he had petrol instead of blood running through his veins.

"Wear shoes, not boots: you need to *feel* the pedals under your feet; you need to be responsive to them."

Charlie drew out the 'feel' as if he had intimate

relationships with his cars. If the rumours were true, he probably did. But still, Tamsyn made a note to wear shoes on Monday and take her Altberg's with her, just in case. She'd learned a belt-and-braces approach from her grandfather: *better to have it and not need it, than need it and not have it.*

A couple more officers came into the break room and Charlie clearly enjoyed having an audience. He started to really swing the lamp about the olden days.

"When I started in the job and dinosaurs still roamed the planet, new Women Police Constables, our lovely WPCs, had their bare bums stamped with the nick's stamp. Hard to imagine now, but people had a sense of humour in those days, and it was just a bit of banter."

Tamsyn had never heard that story and was disgusted that it had ever gone on.

"Did they do it to the men, as well?"

Charlie paused.

"Now and then. Of course, women wore box skirts for early-worms and late-turns well into the 1980s, but you could wear trousers on nights in case you had to go climbing over fences after a crim."

Tamsyn's eyebrows lifted higher.

"And you try controlling a car with your knees together in a bloody skirt. The instructors would tell them to hitch their skirt up to their thighs. One instructor would pinch the inside of your leg if you missed a gear or couldn't recall the previous road sign. Mind you, that wasn't just the girls, the lads had the same treatment as well."

No one is touching the inside of my leg unless I want them to, Tamsyn thought, her mind wandering in the direction of Joe Quinn while Charlie rambled on.

Attitudes towards women officers were changing and these days they made up around 40% of all the officers at Penzance. The public perception was changing too, especially with people her age, but she remembered before she'd joined the job that one of her grandfather's fishing cronies had said to her, "Tamsyn, I hear you are going to be one of those lady policemen."

Charlie nudged her arm, sensing that her mind had drifted.

"The two books you'll need are *The Highway Code* and *Roadcraft*. Know them inside out. Oh, and have these as well."

Charlie turned over his cap and pulled back the clear cellophane inside the top. There were two pieces of paper that looked as though they'd been typed with a manual typewriter. In fact, they were so old that Tamsyn wondered if they'd been typed on parchment. One was headed *Cockpit Drill* and the other *The System*.

"You can keep those," said Charlie. "I have copies. Put them in the top of your bowler."

Tamsyn scanned the text.

Handbrake on
Check handbrake/footbrake operation
Gear lever in neutral
Seat and mirrors adjusted
Doors secure
Familiar with controls
Depress clutch
Switch on ignition
Note warning lights
Start engine (choke to be used as required)
Slowly release clutch

Check instrument readings.

Tamsyn read the list, most of which she already did every time she climbed into a patrol car, although not even Tamsyn's knackered old Fiat had a choke and she only had a vague idea what one did. But none of the patrols had them, so she could cross that off the list ... just not while Charlie was watching her with narrowed eyes.

"You'll be expected to do all this before you start driving, not just chuck your bag in the car and drive off."

"Yeah, thanks," said Tamsyn, trying to sound sincere.

There was nothing on Charlie's list about seat belts or automatic gearboxes. But Charlie was in his element, talking about a subject that had been his life and his whole career for 40+ years. She didn't know if that was amazing or kind of sad.

"Before getting in the car, have a look round it for any damage, and check that the tyres, have sufficient tread or any side wall damage."

"Okay."

"During your blue-light training, every day will start with the group doing all the checks: oil and water levels, of course; also, that brake lights and indicators are working; and oh, check that the blue lights are working. There's nothing worse than finding a fuse has blown in your blues." He peered at Tamsyn. "Read *The System*, go on."

1. Course: the driver having seen the hazard decides on the correct line of approach. He looks in his mirrors and if it is necessary to change position to obtain the correct course, he considers a deviation signal.
2. Mirrors, signal and speed: the mirrors are again used and if the intention is to turn right or left at

the hazard, consideration must be given to a deviation signal, any reduction in speed for the hazard will be accomplished at this stage, preceded by a slowing down signal, if appropriate.
3. Gear: the correct gear is selected for the speed of the vehicle following application of the second feature.
4. Mirrors and signal: it is essential to look in the mirrors again and to consider a signal to deviate, if not previously given, or to emphasise an existing deviation signal.
5. Horn: sound the horn if necessary.
6. Acceleration: the correct degree of acceleration is applied to leave the hazard safely.

Charlie chipped in while Tamsyn was still reading.

"That's your driving bible. Don't leave home without it."

Tamsyn finished reading the faded type, and out of courtesy said, "Thank you."

She wondered how old these pieces of paper were. Should they be in a police archive or museum? How many caps had they been in? What cars were around when this system was implemented?

"Of course," said Charlie, "reading about it on paper isn't the same as doing it in real life. I can take you out for a spin if you like and show you the system."

"That sounds great," Tamsyn said politely, "but I don't think Inspector Walters would approve of me leaving the station."

She hated to admit to the tough-as-old-boots Charlie that she was on recuperative duties only.

"What wouldn't Inspector Walters' approve of?"

The woman herself walked past just as Tamsyn finished speaking. Her frown faded when she saw who Tamsyn was talking to.

"Charlie! How are you? I haven't seen you since I did a refresher course two years ago."

"Hi Maur— ma'am. Good to see you, and I think it was three years ago. I've just offered to take your officer out for a spin for half an hour to show her the system."

Inspector Walters smiled and nodded.

"That's fine by me, just bring her back in one piece. Good to see you, Charlie," and she walked off.

"Taught her everything she knows," Charlie said, tapping his nose.

He was on his feet straightaway, picking up his cap between his thumb and middle finger, obviously being careful not to leave a finger smudge on the peak. He strode out towards the rear car park, his shoes clicking on the polished linoleum.

Tamsyn hurried to follow him, passing Chloe as she did so.

"Maybe if you blow him, he'll give you a pass on the test."

"Stupidity isn't a crime, so you're free to fuck off," Tamsyn replied as she breezed past.

In the rear car park, Charlie was standing next to a gleaming Audi Q6. Tamsyn wondered if he was checking the paintwork for finger marks, but as she walked towards the passenger side of the vehicle, she could see that the boot was crammed with cones and yellow Peli cases, presumably full of tools and other equipment.

Charlie jumped in and clipped his seat belt on, pulling up the slack so it was tight. Tamsyn copied him, wondering what sort of lesson she was in for. But if he tried to touch her thigh, he'd regret it to his dying day.

"I'll drive, you scribe," he said, grinning at her.

"Sorry, what?"

"In the old days, we'd rush to grab the car keys because it was the passenger's job to do all the paperwork." He let out a sigh. "Half the fun has gone out of driving now we have automatics: double declutching, selecting the right gear. Those were proper skills."

The Audi roared to life, and Tamsyn watched as Charlie push-pulled on the steering wheel, keeping his hands at 10-to-2 as he manoeuvred around the car park. Tamsyn had learned the technique of both hands on one side of the steering wheel, hand over hand, as if she was pulling in an anchor rope, and letting it slip through her hands as the car straightened up.

Charlie drove smoothly up Alverton Road towards Wherrytown, his eyes darting from the rearview mirror to the side mirrors as he stopped at a roundabout, waiting for a gap to merge into the traffic. An old lady jammed on the brakes of her old Fiesta, flashing her lights to let the police vehicle out.

Charlie shook his head slightly but moved forward slowly, his right indicator still illuminated. He looked directly at the nice old lady and snapped his right hand from the steering wheel into a half salute, looking like he was going to karate chop the side window, before returning it to the steering wheel.

"Always acknowledge a nice driver that lets you out, even if they don't know what they're doing."

Or I could just nod and smile as usual, Tamsyn thought.

Charlie glided effortlessly through the traffic, silky smooth driving, making ground where he could. Then he started a commentary about the road conditions, the weather, light conditions, then commentating about what he could see: pedestrians, cyclists, road signs, bus stops, junctions.

He started to overtake a bus at a bus stop, then slowed just as a passenger walked into the road right in front of the bus. Charlie sounded his horn and came to a halt. The man jerked back in shock, retreating to the pavement, putting his hand up as if to say, *sorry*. Charlie snapped another right-hand salute acknowledgement before slowly driving away.

"Anticipation," he said. "I saw that fella walking down the length of the bus so I was prepared in case he tried to cross in front of me. It's not just what you see happen, Tamsyn, it's what *might* happen."

He continued to describe everything he saw, and within a few minutes, Tamsyn could also see what Charlie was seeing. Her opinion of him gradually began to soften and she realised that she was learning a lot.

And the man loved to chat, talking about his long career.

"Of course, there's nowhere to hide now."

"What do you mean?"

"Well, these cars are fitted with trackers, so the control room can see where we are at all times." He gave a wistful smile. "We used to be able to slip off our patch and have a blast down the A30 to Hayle to get a napalm-hot Philp's pasty. No chance of that now, although..."

He winked at her, then blasted them up the A30, almost launching Tamsyn from her seat as he took off at speed, startling a surprised laugh out of her as she grabbed the *oh-shit* handle.

Trees whizzed past, yet the car felt very stable, and not

for a second did she doubt Charlie's skill. He slowed almost as quickly as he'd sped off.

"That was amazing!" she laughed, and a slow smile stretched his leathery skin.

"You'll be doing that soon," he said. "If you're a good shot, you'll be good at driving at speed."

"I've never shot a gun," she replied. "But I've driven a boat at speed."

"Have you?" he asked, his eyebrows rising with interest. "You'll have to tell me about that."

She remembered just in time that racing a friend's dive boat near the Manacles rocks off Lizard Point had been part of a classified op, and she'd never be able to tell Charlie Matthews about it, no matter how much she would like to.

Luckily for Tamsyn, Charlie was distracted by a call-out: a Road Traffic Collision with injured drivers near Buryas Bridge.

"Sorry, Tamsyn. Injury RTC. Duty calls!"

And before she knew it, she was back at Penzance police station.

She'd barely closed the passenger door when Charlie spun the car around, illuminating the blue lights, with the scream of the sirens echoing off the walls.

Tamsyn arrived at the Bodmin training centre at 7.45am the following Monday, and was met by her instructor, Karen Vyvyan, and two other officers: Dave and Emily. Both had been in the job 18 months.

Once again, Tamsyn was the youngest and the newest.

The first few days were desk-bound, including the formalities of checking driving licences, eyesight, and a

Highway Code test. Failing the Highway Code test meant the long highway home.

"Right," said Karen, "so far so good. This unit assesses the skills, knowledge and understanding required to prepare, manoeuvre and drive emergency vehicles implementing the police system of car control which you'll have heard referred to as 'Roadcraft', including pre-driving checks and managing factors relevant to safe driving."

Dave turned and whispered to Tamsyn.

"Heard you met Charlie Matthews. That guy is a *legend*."

"Yeah," Emily agreed. "I heard he got up to 160mph on the A30 near Truro!"

"I'd appreciate your *full* attention," Karen said with irritation, and they all gave a guilty start.

Each day, for the next fortnight, the three of them were worked hard, driving in urban environments with single- and dual-carriageways, making ground through traffic whilst staying within speed limits; and rural environments, which meant muddy or sandy tracks, gravelled areas and some off-roading, all while being watched and commented on by Karen and the two other officers.

On the final day before the test, they worked a late shift so that all three had an hour's driving in the dark. It was chucking it down as well, which reduced visibility and made the roads slick.

Tamsyn couldn't help thinking that one day this would be for real: her ability to get somewhere fast could be the difference between life and death. Maybe saving a life, maybe prevent a death. And maybe, just maybe, it would be the day when she finally brought Besnik Domi to justice.

She broke out in a cold sweat just thinking about facing him again. But that was the job. That was what she'd signed up for. So, she hoped she was up to it, because her life – or someone else's – might depend on it. She wanted to feel brave enough to run towards danger, not run from it.

Tamsyn barely slept on the night before her final test. She'd stayed up late re-reading all her notes and revising hard. Sleep continued to be elusive, as possible test scenarios played in her mind.

When she heard her grandfather moving around in the hours before dawn, she got up to join him in the kitchen.

Mo gave her an aggrieved look, then moved into the warm spot in the middle of the bed which Tamsyn had vacated.

"There's loyalty for you," Tamsyn muttered as she yawned widely.

When she trudged into the kitchen, her grandfather looked up, no surprise on his face.

"Kettle's on," he said. "You were late last night. Piddle down, didda?"

"Yes, it was pretty heavy rain most of the day, but it was good practice."

He was silent for several seconds, then he stood up, rinsing his tea cup in the sink.

"Don't you be standing in your own light today," he said gruffly. "You show 'em what a Poldhu is made of!"

"I will. Thanks, Grandad."

Tamsyn smiled to herself as he took his pack of sandwiches and headed out the door into the night.

It wasn't worth going back to bed, so Tamsyn went through her notes again, took a reluctant Mo for a walk in the dark and mizzle, then climbed into her ancient Fiat and was the first to arrive at Bodmin test centre, with time to drink half a flask of coffee.

Emily and Dave arrived, looking eager and tense.

"Good morning, everyone," said Karen with a smile. "Glad to see you all came back."

They laughed nervously.

"We're going to draw straws to see the order in which you'll be tested."

Tamsyn drew the short straw.

"Looks like you're first."

Tamsyn gave a weak smile.

"And I see that your examiner has just arrived."

The examiner was a tall, lean, humourless man in his forties.

"PC Poldhu, come with me please."

Tamsyn was bricking it, but Emily and Dave gave her big smiles and thumbs up. It helped that they were all in it together, but now it was make or break.

"Don't forget your glasses," Dave whispered.

"I don't wear glasses!"

"You should!" he teased.

She was taken to a BMW X3. She'd driven this car before and liked it. It was a higher driving position, giving her a better view of the road.

She checked around the car as she'd been taught, trying to ignore the examiner who was writing on a notepad.

Then she climbed into the vehicle and again went through the cockpit drill. She gave her seat belt a final tug to tighten it, thinking briefly of Charlie Matthews, and sat there with the engine running and her hands at the ten-to-two position on the steering wheel, conscious that she had a vice like grip, her knuckles turning white.

She glanced across at the examiner as he looked up from his notepad. Tamsyn forced herself to relax, her grip loosening, allowing her body to blend into the seat. She was going to smash this.

"I'm here to check that you've taken on board everything you've been taught and that you have reached the necessary standard for me to authorise you to use blue lights and sirens," said the examiner. "I'm not going to intervene or speak other than to give you directions, so please don't take my not speaking as anything you may have done wrong. The test will be between 40 to 45 minutes."

"Okay," Tamsyn nodded, her throat dry.

"Right, let's get under way when you're ready."

Tamsyn put her right foot on the brake, and drew the auto gear control to the drive position. She made it obvious that she was checking her rearview mirror, then nearside and offside mirrors, before pulling slowly into the morning traffic.

They moved easily through the commuter traffic around Bodmin, but as soon as they hit an empty stretch of the A30, he told her to hit the lights and sirens all the way to a small private airfield five miles outside the town.

Her pulse jumped and her focus sharpened.

A thousand things ran through Tamsyn's head: the best route to the 'incident', reading the road ahead to pick the quickest line, maximise visibility, identify hazards, avoiding sudden acceleration or braking wherever possible, ensuring that members of the public didn't feel intimidated, judging when to apply sirens.

She gripped the wheel, racing around cars that parted like the Red Sea, hitting 110mph on the A30.

Her breathing evened out as time seemed to slow down. It was like the moment where she paddled for a wave three times her height, threatening to crush her if she timed it wrong, *feeling* the road surface under her wheels, *seeing* the road, knowing the exact moment to nudge the steering wheel, that incredible split second where she caught the wave and she was completely in sync with it.

She didn't remember much after that and was driving back into the test centre's car park after what seemed like a few minutes, not forty: it had all been a bit of a blur.

Tamsyn parked in a designated driving school parking space, pushed the gear into 'park', switching the engine off, keeping her hands on the steering wheel.

"Test conditions are over now, Tamsyn. I'm happy to tell you that I'm satisfied you've reached the necessary driving standard and you have passed. In fact, you had a really good drive. On your report, I'll recommend that you come back for a full advanced driving course, when one becomes available."

"Thank you!" she said, genuinely surprised.

The tester gave her a rare smile as he turned away to await the next candidate.

Tamsyn's legs felt rubbery as she walked back into the classroom, and she was trying to hide a big smile, knowing that she'd passed.

Dave was up next, looking slightly green, and she whispered, "Good luck!"

Emily had her head bent over her books, her mouth moving silently as she revised her notes.

Tamsyn made herself a cup of coffee then messaged Jess but didn't get a reply, which probably meant she was with clients.

She decided to tell her grandparents in person; maybe cook them a special meal to make up for being so short-tempered recently.

The only other person she wanted to message was Joe.

He texted back immediately.

> Knew you'd smash it, Cornwall!

His reply made her smile.

At the end of the day, all three of them had passed their blue-light training. Their celebration included cleaning the test car inside and out before they were all sent on their way home.

CHAPTER 12

There were only thirteen days before Christmas and Tamsyn hadn't started her shopping. Not that she had much to get: Angler's Dream pipe tobacco for her grandfather, scented candles for her grandmother (Wiccan approved), a secret Santa for E-team, and a stocking full of small gifts for Jess. So far, all she'd bought her was a startling lime green nail varnish and some glow-in-the-dark condoms. They'd begun the tradition of small 'smile' gifts when they were nine and it was too much fun to bin now that they were older.

Tamsyn didn't have much in the way of family. There was Edern, her second cousin, and his son Jago who lived on Bryher, the fifth largest of the Isles of Scilly (half a square mile, population 84), but they weren't close. She hadn't seen them since she'd joined the police nine months ago and had only received one reply to a text message she'd sent. They wouldn't be swapping presents.

In fact, she doubted whether she'd see her cousins this side of New Year unless they came to the heaving metropolis of Penzance to do some Christmas shopping. Unlikely.

There had been one piece of news from the cousins this summer: Jago had finally, finally received permission from the Duchy who owned the island, and had done so since the 14th century, to build a house on his father's acreage.

Tamsyn wondered if she'd enjoy a posting to the islands. The crime rate was low, with June having been the busiest month that year: eleven crimes reported.

But Tamsyn was well aware that the islands were also used as a staging post for the influx of drugs to the UK. Nowhere was free of the insidious presence of the drug trade, and even this far-flung outpost of the British Isles wasn't entirely what it seemed.

The Isles of Scilly had a small police force with one DS, two PCs, a community support constable, and one special – a volunteer – stationed on St Mary's, the largest of the islands. And because there were only two custody suites, if the island police found themselves with three detained persons, two constables from the mainland had to attend and bring one of the prisoners back to Camborne.

There was one other member of Tamsyn's family: her mother. But she didn't count.

Her thoughts returned to Joe again, something that seemed to be happening more frequently, and she mused whether it was too early in their friendship to buy him a gift. Or was it a relationship? She wasn't sure, but she definitely didn't want to come over as desperate or a level-5 clinger. So, what type of present said: *I don't know you all that well but I like you and I think I might like you a lot.*

They were planning to get together after Christmas; maybe meet halfway, somewhere like Bristol. The details hadn't been worked out yet because Joe had volunteered to cover the festive season for colleagues who had families, and Tamsyn didn't know when she'd be back on shift and allowed to return to frontline duties.

They texted every day and had managed some short conversations on the evenings Tamsyn was doing her blue-light training. Joe had done the course a couple of years back and had made her laugh with some of his shenanigans.

She'd finished the training on a high, so it irritated her that she felt slightly anxious to be back at Penzance station. The incident with the fish had messed with her head – she knew it was stupid, but she couldn't help it.

Unfortunately, when she walked inside, it was like a re-run of the last time with Jamie standing at his locker again.

He glanced up and saw her, slamming shut his locker door violently.

Tamsyn raised an eyebrow, unwilling to be intimidated by him, but her guard was well in place. She was hesitant to speak to him, then decided that saying nothing wouldn't be helpful to their professional working relationship either.

"Are you okay?" she asked after a short pause.

"Yeah, everything's great," he said bitterly.

He leaned his head against his locker and Tamsyn realised that his anger wasn't directed at her. She felt her guard slipping. He looked so miserable. Sometimes the job got to you.

"Do you want to talk about it?" she asked cautiously.

He shook his head so Tamsyn turned to walk away.

"She dumped me," Jamie said.

Tamsyn turned to look at him.

"Chloe?"

"Yeah. Found herself some rich bloke." He gave a sour

laugh. "She wanted me to take her to the *Ugly Butterfly* in Carbis Bay. Do you know what their menu costs? One-hundred-and-eighty-five quid per person, for fuck's sake. And that's without the wine. Apparently, you don't just go for a meal, you go for 'an experience'. A PC's salary doesn't cut it."

Tamsyn thought he'd had a lucky escape both from the restaurant and the relationship, but knew that now wasn't the time to say it.

"I'm sorry you're upset."

"Yeah, sure you are. You can't stand her!"

"No, I can't. But you and me – we're friends and colleagues, Jamie."

He nodded slowly. "Yeah, sorry. Thanks, Tam."

"Okay, well ... if you do feel like talking..."

He didn't reply.

Then Sergeant Terwillis spotted her.

"Tamsyn, congratulations on passing your blue-light training. I've read the report, so, well done. We'll get you on that advanced course when you've got some experience under your belt."

She smiled with pleasure at the compliment, and it felt like another step forward.

"Thank you, sarge. I'm looking forward to being on Response again."

He nodded slowly.

"We're all hoping that will be in the New Year."

Tamsyn tried to hide her disappointment. She'd hoped that her days of being office-bound were over.

Sighing, she heaved up her backpack of textbooks and made her way to an empty desk.

The rest of the day passed without incident as she churned her way through the paperwork she'd missed during the last two weeks. After a third cup of coffee, she started reading her coursework on how the police dealt with residential burglary:

- *bring offenders to justice*
- *reduce the fear of burglary*
- *ensure that victims receive a professional response*
- *prevent offences taking place.*

Even where it is not possible to identify a suspect, victims want to know the crime has been taken seriously, and that police have taken all reasonable steps to identify and arrest the perpetrator and recover any stolen property.

She closed the folder and stretched her arms above her head. She knew all too well that sometimes all you could do was log the crime and give the victim telephone numbers for local jewellery shops, pawn shops, and auction houses.

As Tamsyn left the station that afternoon, the wintry sun had long since started its descent towards the sea, and Tamsyn knew that she had less than an hour before it disappeared behind the granite cliffs of Land's End. She planned to take Mo for a walk along Penzance promenade to see the Christmas lights illuminated in the black water as the day settled into night. The little dog loved being out after dark and always had an extra spring in her step: tail up, nose down.

Tamsyn was surprised to see Mo curled up on the doorstep when she reached the patch of grass in front of the cottage, light spilling from behind the curtains.

"What are you doing, Morwenna? How did you get out here? Did you get locked out?"

But little Mo didn't look up or wag her tail, and when

Tamsyn reached down to stroke her, the dog was rigid and ice cold.

Tamsyn recoiled with a soft cry, her heart slamming against her ribs. She crouched down, reaching for Morwenna with shaking hands. Then she peered closer.

No, that's not right.

The shade of tan was wrong, the tail too thin, and it was a male.

Not Morwenna.

But even as relief rushed through her, she knew exactly what this poor creature was: a message.

She stood up, looking around her fearfully, hating that she was afraid, but the street was still and silent.

"What do you want from me?" she screamed as if Besnik Domi could hear her. "What do you want me to do?"

The only reply echoed in her mind.

Die.

Five miles north of Manchester, Maisie Rego was waiting for her grandmother to meet her from school. She was late. Grandma Pat had been late a lot since she'd started having the chemo; she said it made her memory 'dusty'. So, Maisie had become used to waiting, but she wished that Grandma Pat would hurry up. She was cold and it was getting dark. All her friends had already been picked up.

Maisie glanced back towards her brightly lit primary school, wondering whether to go inside and tell her teacher that she was still waiting.

But before she could decide what to do, a man in a hoodie crossed the road, scanning the street in both directions.

"You're Maisie, aren't you? Your mom told me that you were pretty. I'm her new friend. I've got a message for your daddy."

Maisie's hair stood on end as the man smiled at her.

"I'm waiting for my grandma," she said in a small voice.

"Your grandma isn't feeling well. She sent me to pick you up."

He took a step towards her, still smiling, his hand held out.

Maisie took a step backwards, pressing herself against the playground's railings.

The man's smile grew wider and he made a lunge for her, grabbing at the handle of her school bag.

"No!" Maisie yelled, letting the bag slip off her shoulder. "Help! Stranger! Help! HELP!"

The man's eyes darted left and right, and he swore in a foreign language, trying to grab her hair.

"Get your hands off her!" shrieked Patricia Rego, charging up the street and brandishing her handbag like a weapon.

She swung it at the man's face, screaming a war cry.

The man deflected the blow easily, knocking Patricia to the ground, then casually kicking her in the ribs twice.

He sprinted back across the street and disappeared into the gathering darkness.

Patricia was on the ground, moaning softly, and Maisie was sobbing, snot and tears covering her face.

People ran towards them from all directions, talking over each other, asking questions, phoning the police, and more than one was filming Patricia and Maisie lying on the cold pavement.

Rego's phone rang just as he was packing up for the day.

"Sir, it's Tamsyn," she said, her voice urgent. "I think Besnik Domi is back in Cornwall."

CHAPTER 13

Rego was caught between family and duty, a rock and a hard place.

He'd been on the phone to Maura Walters, trying to impress upon her the implied threat of Tamsyn finding a dead dog on her doorstep. Not just any dog, but one that bore a striking resemblance to Morwenna. Or, more likely, someone had thought the poor creature was Tamsyn's dog.

Walters had been inclined to dismiss it as nothing more than an unhappy coincidence. Rego had no idea how she had reached the rank of inspector and still believed in coincidences like this. He'd had the poor creature scanned for a microchip but none was found, so that was a dead end, no pun intended.

Tom Stevens had also mentioned the interesting titbit that Walters had gone up to Middlemoor to a meeting with ACC Gray, which meant that there was a strong possibility he'd recruited her to the 'Rego is paranoid' campaign.

Rego smiled to himself ruefully, thinking of the adage: *just because you're paranoid doesn't mean they aren't after you.*

He'd be watching his step around her.

Nevertheless, he'd insisted that the threat level be taken seriously, and she hadn't liked anyone telling her how to do her job either. While he was arguing with her, Rego had sent three calls from his wife and mother to voicemail before it occurred to him that there was an unusual urgency about the coordinated calls.

Cold clawed at his gut while he waited for his wife to answer her phone.

"Rob," she said, her voice hoarse. "Thank God! You have to come home straightaway. We need you."

He listened with mounting horror and fury as she described the attempted abduction of Maisie and the attack on his mother.

"Where are you now? Are you safe?"

"We're at the hospital with Patricia. They think she's okay," Cassie said hastily, "but they wanted to give her an X-ray, just in case. Chemo can contribute to bone loss," she added in a hollow voice.

"Where's Max?"

"I asked Kamla to take him home with her. He's safe."

Then she started to cry, the sound muffled at first. Rego felt sick, helpless to offer her any immediate comfort except to drive to Manchester as fast as possible.

"Cassie, luv ... Cassie?"

He grabbed his coat, trying to put it on with one hand as he held the phone to his ear with the other. He had an arm in the sleeve when he heard rustling through the phone, then his daughter's voice.

"Hi, Daddy."

"Maisie! Thank God!"

"Mum can't come to the phone right now," she said, so young, so serious.

"Are you okay, May Day? Did that man hurt you?"

"Nah," she said. "Grandma Pat scared him away. It was brilliant, Dad! She gave him a right clout with her handbag. He pushed her over, and that made me angry, but she says she's okay."

Rego couldn't tell if Maisie was in shock, or denial, or genuinely bouncing back in the way that children sometimes could.

"Are you coming home, Daddy? Mummy won't stop crying."

"I'm getting in the car now, May Day," he said. "I'll be with you in a few hours. I love you so much, baby girl. Mum said you screamed really loudly. I'm so proud of you!"

"We did stuff about strangers at school," she said calmly. "So, I knew what to do. And you've told me and Max like a million billion trillion times."

"You did really well. Really well. I can't wait to see you."

"Me too, Daddy. Can we get a dog?"

"Get a what?"

"A puppy."

That's what he thought she'd said, but it had thrown him, coming out of the blue.

"I don't think..."

"It could be our guard dog and bark at the bad man."

"I ... Mummy and I will have to talk about it, but now isn't the time, May Day."

She sighed heavily, the world-weary super-sigh of a thwarted child.

"But a dog would scare away burglars too, and he could sleep in my bed and I'd walk him after school. Pleeeeease, Daddy."

"I'll think about it."

"Okay!" she said happily.

Rego's throat closed up and his head was filled with terrifying what ifs: *what if Patricia had been a minute later? What if the man had been with an accomplice? What if his mother had been seriously hurt?* He felt sick at the thought and he had to swallow several times before he could speak again.

"Can you give the phone to Mummy for a second?"

"Okay. Bye, Daddy. See you later! I'll save some pictures of dogs for you."

His wife came back on the phone sounding slightly more in control.

"Cass, I'm in the car now and I'll be home in four or five hours; six, if the traffic is bad. Look, this is important: don't go home, even if they discharge Mum, okay? I'm going to send Vik to pick up you and Maisie, and I want you to go back with him. Just him – nobody else. No one, even if they say I sent you, okay?"

He knew she must be really scared when she didn't even try to argue.

"What about my mum?" she asked shakily.

Cassie's mother lived in Macclesfield, a small town in the hills 20 miles south of Manchester. She'd probably be okay, but Rego wasn't in the business of taking chances.

"Call her and tell her to go to a friend, and the further away from her own house, the better."

"Okay, I'll do that now. Please hurry."

"I'm on my way, baby. Just hold on. I love you."

"Just get here, Ace Boy," she said, using a familiar Bermudian nickname. "Just get here."

His next call was to Max who was his usual monosyllabic, teenage self, and clearly annoyed at having missed all the excitement.

"Can I go home and get my X-box?" he asked. "It's boring here. Aunty Kam doesn't even have Netflix."

Rego felt the top of his head come off.

"No! You cannot go home, Max! You'll stay exactly where you are so Kamla can keep an eye on you until Vik gets there. You will not move a muscle! Got it?"

"Wow, take a chill pill, Dad," Max yawned.

Rego clenched his teeth.

"This is serious, Max. Very serious. If Maisie..."

His words dried as he tried very hard *not* to think again of all the ugly scenarios that Domi and his thugs might have dreamed up.

Max's voice changed, becoming more like the sweet kid he used to be, before hormones and secondary school got a grip on him.

"I know, Dad. But I spoke to her, and she's okay."

Rego's death-grip eased on the steering wheel.

"Yeah, I know. I spoke to her, too. Look, I'm on my way home now. I'll be with you in a few hours. Just do what Vik and Kam say: stay inside, don't answer the door, even with a chain on it. I don't care if it's a police officer or Taylor Swift driving a Ferrari. No one! Do you understand?"

"Yeah, Dad!"

"Say it!"

"Don't answer the door to anyone except you or Uncle Vik."

Rego let out a long breath.

"Okay, that's good. Just ... stay safe. I love you, kiddo."

It felt important to say it even though he wasn't expecting the sentiment to be returned. But Max surprised him.

"Yeah. Me, too."

As Rego headed north, he made call after call to his

former colleagues at Greater Manchester Police, ensuring that security was in place with frequent patrols past his home and Patricia's house; then he found someone to talk to at Cheshire Constabulary who could do the same for Cassie's mother's house.

There was no way of knowing how far the Hellbanianz reach extended, or whether this was the work of the Domi in prison or the one on the loose. Either way, this was not a time when Rego was prepared to take chances.

He sent a rocket up Maisie's headteacher, letting her know what he thought of a school that allowed a not-quite-nine-year-old girl to wait in the near dark by herself. She'd protested that Maisie knew she was supposed to wait in the playground or alert a teacher if her pickup was late. With gritted teeth, he reminded her that Maisie was a child, and children didn't always make good choices.

The conversation ended on a stalemate as Rego punched the 'end call' button with more force than necessary.

It frustrated the hell out of him to be 350 miles away and unable to coordinate efforts beyond what he'd already done or to be there in person.

Colleagues at Greater Manchester Police agreed to increase the security of his house: reinforce doors, put in CCTV, pressure pads around the house, all within the next 48 hours, and there'd been an offer to escort the kids to and from school for the next week. One week: that's all that had been promised. And Rego knew that the powers-that-be would be thinking about balancing costs against perceived threat. He couldn't help thinking, *do I trust them?*

Devon & Cornwall Police seemed to be leaking like a sieve, and he didn't expect GMP to be much better. He wanted to trust them, but the concerns played on his mind:

right now, the only people he completely trusted were Vik and his wife, Kamla.

He was 100% sure that this had to do with Domi although he had no proof. He wondered how long the Hellbanianz had been stalking his family. He shuddered at the thought. It was his crazy mother's bravery and some insane luck that had saved the day. He couldn't risk there being a second attempt with a different outcome.

He also felt guilty for leaving Tamsyn to cope by herself with the lukewarm efforts of Inspector Walters. He thought he'd detected a thawing in the inspector's attitude when he informed her that a man had tried to take Maisie, and that he felt sure it was connected to Domi, although she'd also asked about other criminals who might have a grudge against him and his family. Yeah, hundreds, but only one of them had recently escaped from custody. And he definitely saw a pattern with the coordinated 'messages' to both him and Tamsyn. The Domi case was the only one that they'd worked on together: it *had* to be connected.

His emotions were at war with his professional duty, but right now he couldn't see how he could do any of his jobs well: father, husband or police officer.

Vikram phoned as Rego approached Birmingham.

"I've picked up Cassie and Maisie from the hospital. They want to keep your mother in for the night just to make sure she doesn't have a concussion. They're putting her in a private room and GMP have an officer outside her door. I'll go back in the morning when she's discharged. I'll do it myself. No one else, just me."

"Thank you. I ... thank you."

"I got your back, brother." He paused. "You think this is Domi?"

"It's got to be, Vik, especially as Tamsyn was targeted at

her family home the exact same time: maximum fear, maximum disruption. There's no way it's a coincidence. No way."

There was a long pause and Rego's innate detective heard what Vikram *wasn't* saying.

"The NCA aren't buying it?"

He heard Vikram's sigh.

"The attack on your family, yes; the fact that the dog wasn't Tamsyn's makes it suspicious in their eyes. If her own dog had been killed, yeah, they'd be more inclined to believe her, but a decoy dog? Come on, Rob. Even you must agree that's one hell of a coincidence."

Rego's frustration returned full force.

"Who's 'they', Vik? Who's putting this spin on Tamsyn?"

"You know what," Vikram said after another pause, "that's a good question. I've just been passing on feedback, but I'm not in that department anymore, so I don't know which analyst has been doing the work. Let me ask a few questions ... if you're sure about Tamsyn."

"Jesus! I'm sure!"

"Okay, okay. I'll ask around. Discreetly."

"Thank you."

"So, what are you going to do next?" Vikram asked.

"I haven't told Cass yet, but I'm going to send them away – somewhere safe until Domi is caught."

"Where have you got in mind? Your mother-in-law's place? Do you think Kenise lives far enough away?"

"No. I told Cassie to get Kenise to go to a friend's house. But you're right, it's not far enough." An idea sprang to his mind. "I'm going to send them to Bermuda to stay with my Auntie Barbara."

"I like it," said Vik. "But it's Christmas soon. Will you able to get flights for them at short notice?"

"I don't know," Rego said grimly. "If you've got a better idea, I want to hear it."

"Not better," Vikram said thoughtfully, "but I have a contact at the Protected Persons Service. I could make a call…"

"Do it, in case I can't get them on a flight for a couple of days."

"You got it." Vikram hesitated. "Do you have enough moolah to buy tickets to Bermuda for the whole family, because they'll cost an arm and a leg and at least one kidney at this time of year … I'm good for a loan, if you need it, brother."

Rego swallowed hard.

"I appreciate that more than you know, Vik, but I'm good for now. I won't forget it."

"Yeah, you will," Vikram said cheerfully. "You still owe me a fiver from when you cheated at our last poker evening."

That was true.

CHAPTER 14

"Gran, talk some sense into him! Please!"

Tamsyn was frustrated. Her stubborn, difficult, hard-headed grandfather was refusing to leave the cottage.

"I don't know, Tammy..." said her grandmother, wringing her hands.

Her grandfather sat in front of the fire, frowning at *The Cornishman* newspaper. Tamsyn doubted he'd read a single word.

"You're not *safe* here!" She smacked her hand on the arm of his chair. "Grandad!"

He snapped the paper shut and glared at her.

"Stop your nagging! I won't be chased out of my own home by some bastard wrong 'un."

"This man is dangerous! He sent someone to kidnap Maisie Rego! He killed that poor dog! He probably thought it was Morwenna."

Little Mo looked up when she heard her name, a worried frown on her furry face as she gazed from Tamsyn to her grandfather and back again. Then tucking her nose under her tail, she curled up tightly in her bed by the fire, her dark eyes watching everything as the humans she loved most in the world shouted at each other.

"And where would I go, miss?" he growled. "Where else do we belong to?"

"Anywhere!" Tamsyn yelled. "Away from here!"

"No!" roared her grandfather, as he started to rise. "No, I..."

But her grandmother pushed him down into his chair.

"Ozzie! You're like a pig with one ear! Listen to what our Tammy is saying!"

The fire crackled in the grate as they all took a breath.

"What do you want us to do, Tammy?" her grandmother asked, still resting her hand on Ozzie's shoulder.

"I want you to go to Edern and Jago's place on Bryher, just for a few ... weeks."

"Weeks!" Ozzie roared again. "Did you hear what the *cheel* said? Weeks! No!"

Andrea Poldhu gazed at Tamsyn with a faint smile.

"I think that's a good idea," she said as Ozzie's mouth dropped open in surprise. "Don't you argue with me, Oswald Poldhu." She stared him down. "And it's time you saw your nephew and his boy. We'll mebbe take 'em some lobster if anyone's hauled one up?" When Ozzie didn't reply, she gave him a look and crossed her arms. "I expect Harvey's will have a couple in their tanks."

Ozzie stomped into the kitchen, muttering to himself, and Tamsyn drooped with relief.

Her grandmother wrapped her in a warm hug and whispered conspiratorially, "You can lead a Cornishman but he wa'ent be drove," and the two women smiled at each other.

The fear-fuelled adrenaline that had stoked Rego during the long journey had drained away. He was exhausted, driving on nerves and caffeine.

He still had another hour to go when his phone rang, making his pulse leap.

"Vik!"

"It's okay, Rob. Everyone's fine. I've just got an intel update for you."

Rego's heart was still hammering.

"Let's hear it," he wheezed.

"First off, this part of our conversation never happened, agreed?"

"Okay," Rego said cautiously.

"The intel I'm going to give you is about Tamsyn, and it's been graded at E4."

The source evaluation E-grade meant that it came from an untested source, one grade *below* unreliable; the level-4 handling code meant that it could only be disseminated within the originating agency. Officially, the intel could not be given to anyone else, which meant Vikram was breaking a boat-load of rules even by telling Rego about it.

"That's odd. Why wouldn't they want to share it? Because they think it's shady?"

Vikram didn't reply immediately which told Rego a lot.

"I'm sorry, Rob, but there's no smoke without fire."

Rego shook his head automatically.

Where on earth had they got this intelligence from? A source used and *accepted* by the National Crime Agency indicated a link between Tamsyn and the Hellbanianz. Rego simply didn't believe it.

But he *did* believe in a detective's gut instinct. And

since Vikram had told him that Domi senior in HM Prison Manchester could well be pulling the strings to make the puppets dance, it could mean that intel had been leaked into the system by the Hellbanianz.

Dritan Domi was a bastard, but a clever one, and definitely devious enough to disrupt an investigation into his younger brother's whereabouts by sowing fake news.

Besnik was the enforcer, vicious, but not as smart as his big brother.

Something else to consider was that if Vikram knew this intelligence, it was possible that someone else with connections much higher up the food chain within Devon & Cornwall Police would also know; someone who spent a lot of time networking. It would be interesting to see what decision would be made about Tamsyn's return to work. If she was kept 'offside', then there could be some credibility to Rego's theory. Or maybe the thinking was to bring Tamsyn back to work, then let her hang herself during a covert investigation, and at the same time catch Domi and make a big play with the media that Devon & Cornwall Police wouldn't tolerate corruption.

Rego knew that he had to keep an open mind, and tread carefully.

His head throbbed as he tried to piece all the parts together. What value was Tamsyn to Domi? She was the main witness against him and her evidence could get him life imprisonment. So, why would he want to keep her alive?

"What else?" Rego said stiffly. "What's the intel *exactly?*"

"Don't shoot the messenger," said Vikram.

"Jesus, Vik! Just tell me!"

"Okay, keep your hair on, Rob! A phone attributable to

Domi senior was found at the prison – not in his cell, but they still suspected that it belonged to Dritan Domi. Anyhow, it's taken the technical department until now to unlock the pin to get into the phone. We found WhatsApp messages that we believe are from Domi junior, bragging that he'd escaped. More damning, there were details about the murders of Saemira Ruçi and George Mason that only the murderer would have known."

"And they're sure about the attribution of the phone to Domi senior?" Rego asked.

"Yes, it's rock solid. In contacts, there was a phone number listed as 'home' which goes to the mother in Albania; there were also other numbers which were attributable as family; a few selfie pictures of both brothers with various girlfriends..."

Vikram paused, and Rego sensed this was the climax of his story.

"And another number led to a burner that was bought in Cornwall but went offline at the time of Besnik Domi's escape."

"Shit!"

"Yep. And the last message sent from that burner to big brother Domi said, 'looking after your family'. You can decide for yourself what it means."

Rego was silent, processing everything Vikram had said.

"All that tells me is that the dealer network that Ruçi developed is still in place," he said slowly. "There's nothing in what you've said that implicates Tamsyn directly, unless you're telling me that her phone number was in Domi's contacts?"

"No," Vikram said, his tone guarded. "Look, Rob, I don't like it any more than you do, but at this point we have to consider Tamsyn as a suspect."

"I don't believe this!" Rego cried in frustration.

"All I can tell you is that a plan is being put in place that will either exonerate her or catch her red-handed."

"Anything else?" Rego asked tightly.

"One thing: a colleague at the Protected Persons Service got back to me – he's found a place in Wales for Cassie and the kids; Patricia, too, if she wants to go and if you can't get tickets for them to Bermuda."

Rego felt like a shit for having taken out his frustration on his friend. Vikram never failed to come through for him.

"Thanks, man. I really appreciate that. As soon as I've seen them with my own eyes, I'll be checking flights to Bermuda. If I can't get them on one tomorrow, I'll take you up on that." His breath hitched. "If anything happened to them..."

"I know, brother. I'll keep them safe."

Rego cleared his throat.

"Thank you ... and I'll let you know about the safe house."

Rego's brain churned all the way to Vikram's house. He wanted details: of the intelligence and its source, and of the plan that would make Tamsyn sink or swim. And his mind wouldn't stop replaying the news that the older Domi was back in the game.

Most of all, he wanted his family safe.

HM Prison Service did their best to keep mobile phones out of British prisons, but it was an endless cycle of searches and confiscations, rinse and repeat. Prisoners were allowed to have limited access to phones for legal or medical reasons, but that required explicit authorisation and was strictly monitored. Other phones were smuggled in by visitors, tossed over walls, hidden in packages, brought in by corrupt staff, and more recently drones had been used to fly them in.

It was frustrating as hell to consider the possibility, even the likelihood, that Dritan Domi was doing everything in his power to misdirect the search for his brother.

When Rego was two minutes from Vikram's house, he phoned to say he'd be at the door shortly and to keep an eye out for him. He drove up and down the street in both directions, as if looking for a house number in the dark, but really, he was looking for any suspicious activity such as occupants sitting in a parked car, people loitering on a cold winter's evening, but all was still and silent.

He saw Vikram's silhouette behind the front door, then it was opened a crack and Rego slipped inside.

The two men shook hands and Rego gripped Vikram's shoulder.

"Thank you for looking after my family."

Vikram smiled. "Anytime, brother. Anytime."

When he walked into the living room, all peace was at an end.

"Daddy!" yelled Maisie, launching herself at him and talking nineteen-to-the-dozen.

Cassie joined in the hug-a-thon, trying and failing not to cry, and Max looked up from his phone with a laconic, "Hey, Dad."

Once he'd seen that his family were well with his own eyes, Rego felt like he could breathe again.

When he'd joined the police, he'd never considered that it could put his family in harm's way; if anything, he'd thought there'd be a built-in network of safety and support for them.

Thank God for Vik and Kamla.

"Are you hungry, Rob?" Kamla asked.

"We saved you some rice pudding, Daddy," said Maisie. "It's really good."

Kamla's rice pudding was legendary and Rego's stomach growled enthusiastically.

He and Cassie made no attempt to tell the kids that it was past their bedtime. Tonight, they needed to be together.

It was only when they were alone in the spare room that Rego told his wife what he'd planned.

"Bermuda?" she said, confused and surprised.

"I want you somewhere out of the way," he said, "somewhere safe. You can stay with my Auntie Barbara and I want you to take my mum with you as soon as she's cleared to fly. If you want Kenise to go as well, that's fine."

Cassie raised her eyebrows.

"What about you?"

"I'll join you when I can."

"Rob!"

"I promise you that I'll fly out on Christmas Eve at the latest. I promise, Cassie."

He hoped he'd be keeping that promise.

"Can we afford this?"

Rego pulled her into his arms, feeling the warm weight of her body against his chest.

"My family is the most precious thing I have, Cass. Yes, we can afford it."

She tilted her head up to look at him, questions in her eyes that he couldn't answer.

By late-afternoon the following day, Patricia had been released from hospital and Rego had packed off his entire family, including his mother-in-law, to Bermuda for a three-week holiday that was burning through two credit cards. Despite the cost, it was a better offer than the basic amenities provided by a safe-house in Wales.

Maisie was upset to miss her last week of school, or rather her class's Christmas disco. Max was just as happy to miss as many days as he could, although he was his usual surly self, so it was hard to tell.

Patricia was tearful when she found out that Rego wouldn't be travelling with them, but at least she and Cassie's mother were polite to each other, which wasn't always a given.

"Come as soon as you can, Ace Boy," Cassie said to Rego as he escorted them to the security line.

"I will, I promise. I'll call you every evening." He paused. "It might not always be in time to talk to the kids, but I'll call."

"Okay," she said, tears making her eyes glassy. "I love you."

And then Rego watched as his family prepared to travel more than 3,000 miles away from him.

Once they'd cleared security, Cassie and his mother waved, then disappeared into the airport.

With a heavy heart, Rego walked back to the short-stay car park, climbed into the driver's seat, and headed back to Cornwall. Again.

CHAPTER 15

Tamsyn was staying at Rosie's house.

It was a new-build on a development of joint ownership properties for essential workers, and Rosie had moved in just four months previously. It was cosy and colourful, reflecting Rosie's outgoing personality.

Tamsyn studied the photographs on the walls and a child's drawings stuck all over the fridge.

"My little sister, Karenza," said Rosie. "She's a great kid but I can't say it's not amazing having my own space. Anyway, you'll probably meet her soon."

Tamsyn had thought a lot about sharing a flat with Jess, and she had to admit that having somewhere she could call her own was appealing.

Built behind Penzance Fire Station and near to West Cornwall Hospital, Rosie's house was only ten minutes' walk from the town centre. The whole development was full of nurses, firefighters, police and paramedics. Which made it a good place to be if you had a fire or medical emergency.

Rosie and Tamsyn had been put on the same shift so

they could travel to work together. They weren't allowed to walk, even though it was so close to the police station; not until Tamsyn's situation was resolved, one way or another.

Morwenna had gone to stay on Bryher with Tamsyn's grandparents and the cousins. Tamsyn missed the little fur ball, missed coming home to her grandmother's cooking, and hated feeling so uncertain all the time.

Rosie was great, but Tamsyn felt adrift, a ship without a sail, lost and untethered.

Jess called her every evening, but Tamsyn thought it would be safer if she didn't see her for now. Jess said that she understood, but Tamsyn could hear the hurt in her voice.

The only person who seemed to understand how she was really feeling was Joe.

"You gotta hang on in there, Tam," he said as they FaceTimed before work. "They'll catch the bastard."

"I hate feeling so useless, and I hate that it's affecting everyone around me."

Joe sighed. "I wish I could be there but..."

"I know," said Tamsyn with a hollow laugh. "Duty calls."

He didn't return her laugh.

"As soon as I get some leave, I'll be down. You can bet on it, Cornwall." Then he made a deliberate effort to lighten the conversation. "Did you know that Cal has been talking to Rosie?"

Tamsyn smiled.

"Yeah, they really hit it off when we were at Newquay, and I know that she's met him in Bristol since."

"Cal says they're planning to meet up again in the New Year, as well," Joe said, something wistful in his tone.

"They're moving pretty fast," Tamsyn agreed.

"There's a lot of that going on," Joe smiled. "Must be something in all that water you have down there."

"Maybe!"

He was silent for several seconds.

"Look, Tam, when this is all over..."

"Yes?"

"We should really try and make this work, you know?"

"Okay," she said softly.

"Really?" he sounded surprised.

"Yes, really."

"Okay," he echoed. "Okay. Look, I gotta get my arse moving now but ... stay safe, yeah?"

"I will. You, too."

Rosie walked into the kitchen swinging her car keys.

"Was that Joe?" she asked.

"Yep, he's on earlies, too."

"He really likes you. And he's frickin' hot!"

Tamsyn grinned. "So's Cal."

"Hell, yeah!" Rosie smiled, fanning her face. "The trouble is, they both know it." Her eyes slid to Tamsyn. "I really like him. I know it's early days and all that, but ... well, I *really* like him."

"Aw, you're blushing," Tamsyn laughed. "How cute is that?"

"Yeah, alright," Rosie laughed, her cheeks still pink. "You ready to head out?"

Tamsyn nodded and picked up her go-bag containing all the extras an officer might need on shift, including spare uniform shirt and trousers in case she was bled on, puked on, or got covered in cow shit, and if she was really unlucky, all three at the same time: it had happened before. Although the chances of that happening at her desk were slim.

Rosie parked at the back of the station as close to the

staff entrance as she could, and both women looked about them carefully before exiting the vehicle.

Tamsyn was expecting to be on desk duty again, but before she even made it to the locker room, she was intercepted by DI Rego.

"Join me in CID's briefing room, Tamsyn," he said without a smile or even a greeting.

"Uh, okay. Sure."

She sketched a wave at Rosie then hurried up the stairs after him.

Rego was shocked when he saw Tamsyn. In the last couple of weeks, she'd lost weight that she couldn't afford to lose, looking almost gaunt and several years older. Her obvious vulnerability at a time when she was under investigation was a concern in so many ways, and it pissed him off that he was being forced to question where her true loyalties lay.

So, he said only what had to be said and kept his feelings tightly in check. The truth was, Rego was furious but trying hard to control his temper.

Vikram had passed him intel about a covert operation that the National Crime Agency had been conducting in Cornwall. Right on his doorstep! And he'd only found out because of Vikram.

He paced the room, quietly fuming, ignoring Tamsyn who was perched on the edge of a chair. The door to the briefing room opened and DS Stevens walked in, casting a surprised glance at Tamsyn then at Rego.

"Boss?"

"Take a seat, Tom," said Rego. "I've just been informed that the National Crime Agency has traced a phone used by an associate of the Hellbanianz to a north Cornwall address, close to Saltash."

Tamsyn sucked in a shocked breath and Stevens looked equally surprised.

"That's not all." He ran his hands over his cropped hair, forcing himself to speak calmly. "Some months ago, I flagged Domi on the NCD while he was being extradited and going through the court process, and I kept it on after his escape."

Stevens nodded but Tamsyn had no idea what this meant and she raised a hand cautiously.

"I'm sorry, sir, but what's the NCD?"

Rego looked frustrated but didn't want to take it out on a student officer. This fuck up wasn't her fault.

"We have a system to try and prevent 'Blue on Blue' contact – operations against the same suspect by different law enforcement agencies. It's called the National Compromise Database."

Tamsyn nodded and pulled out her pocketbook.

"So," Rego continued, "protracted covert operations should be flagged and their details checked against the NCD. If you get a message saying 'no trace', then no other officer or agency has registered an interest in that subject and you flag them to yourself, meaning that if anyone else tries to investigate the same subject at a later date, you'll receive an automatic alert. And vice versa, so if you're looking at a crim who's already being watched or investigated by another officer or law enforcement agency, you won't be told who logged the flag, but the system will alert the owner of the flag that someone is checking their nominal – the named subject. That way we avoid compromising another agency's investigation."

Tamsyn's pencil was whizzing across the page but Stevens was twitching, waiting for Rego to get to the point.

"If you're not the owner of the nominal, you can't do

any investigations into that individual until you've been contacted by the owner of the flag. Usually," said Rego, biting out the word, "usually, the intelligence officers talk to each other, and any person making an enquiry should disclose their interest and have a grown-up conversation. If the enquirer's investigation is deemed to be more important, the flag can be transferred."

He paused.

"National Security nominals are similarly flagged, but that triggers a silent alert to the flagging agency. That's what *should* happen, but I didn't have the names of Domi's known associates, so couldn't add them to our investigation." He rubbed a hand over his head. "And as the NCA appear not to have tried to flag Domi, the compromise system wasn't implemented."

Tamsyn wanted to ask a question but Rego had already moved on.

"The NCA can investigate any of Domi's associates and not breach any protocols. What's interesting is that the NCA have beaten the Metropolitan Police to flagging these people."

Rego was being economical with the truth, because he didn't believe for a single second that the NCA weren't aware of him having flagged Domi. What he didn't say to Tamsyn was that his suspicion was that someone higher up in Devon & Cornwall Police *had* given permission to the NCA to investigate and *not* to tell Rego. He suspected ACC Gray, but had no evidence of that. He'd have to play his cards close to his chest and avoid putting Vikram in the frame.

"It was sheer chance that I learned of the covert operation they're conducting."

"Why wouldn't they tell you?" Tamsyn asked.

Sometimes her naivety was breathtaking, but Rego wasn't going to be the one to alter her rosy view of interagency cooperation.

"It's possible that they've only recently checked the database," Stevens said stoically. "The identification process can take some time."

"They probed the subject's car, Tom," Rego said testily. "And you know that can take a couple of weeks to prepare." He glanced at Tamsyn. "The term 'probing' means placing a listening device in the subject's car."

Her eyes widened comically.

"This is what I know so far," said Rego. "The NCA has been investigating the Hellbanianz for some time, and one of the subjects whose car has been probed was involved with helping Domi escape from London immediately after they dumped the stolen motorbike. There were three subjects in the car: the driver, Domi, and an unknown person, and their conversation was recorded." Rego's face had a sour expression. "Apparently, Domi was laughing and providing vivid descriptions of the murder of Saemira Ruçi and George Mason, as well as other criminal activity. However, as the conversations were in Albanian and needed translating, there was a delay in identifying Domi who, as we know, subsequently disappeared."

Stevens swore under his breath.

"But there is one piece of positive news," said Rego, his eyes on Tamsyn. "The investigation team is part of a joint initiative from the NCA's Exeter office and the Met's Organised Crime Partnership, and they have a photograph of the subject who was driving Domi. This person is believed to be living in a rented house at Saltash."

A third man entered the room, nodding at Rego and Stevens, but ignoring Tamsyn. It was becoming a theme.

He had short grey hair, a grey goatee beard and hard grey eyes. Technically, he was in plain clothes, but his waistcoat was so garish, it could probably be seen from Devon.

"Tamsyn, this is an investigator from the NCA and he would like to show you some surveillance video to see if you recognise anyone."

The man, whom Rego had not named, set up a laptop on the table, then pressed 'play'.

The video showed a group of men standing in front of a café by a Mercedes car.

"That street looks familiar. Is it Plymouth?" she asked. "Recently?"

Rego glanced at the NCA investigator, then gave a curt nod. Tamsyn closed her eyes briefly, wondering just how recently Domi had been 90 minutes from her. Was he closer now? Had he killed that poor dog? Was he watching the station now?

"I've been in that Costa coffee shop," she said quietly.

She swallowed, her gaze darting between the three men, then her eyes returned to the laptop as she concentrated on the other figures.

The initial sequence was wide-angle video, and she couldn't see their faces clearly. Then the camera zoomed in, focusing on each of the man for several seconds.

"No..."

She shook her head as the camera panned past the second, third and fourth man.

"No ... no ... no..." then there he was.

The blood drained from her face as she stared at the dark figure from her nightmares: Besnik Domi, having a casual chat as if he hadn't just escaped from the Old Bailey, as if he hadn't just pointed a gun in her face.

The NCA investigator had paused the video, so it seemed as if Domi was staring back at her.

"Tamsyn?" Rego said, then raising his voice a little. "Tamsyn!"

She jerked in her chair, licking her lips several times before she answered.

"Yes," she said huskily. "That's Besnik Domi."

The three men in the room exchanged glances, and the NCA investigator let the video run through its sequence, focusing on the faces of a few other men. Tamsyn didn't recognise any of the others.

Once the video had ended, the NCA investigator brought out a folder containing still images of all the men.

The first image was headed *Subject 12*, and underneath was an exhibit reference number, initials and a date. It was different from the format she was used to, and Tamsyn guessed the initials were those of the investigator taking the image plus the date it was taken.

The rest of the photographs were headed *unknown associate*, each with a sequential number.

Tamsyn stared at the faces, trying to commit them to memory, but then the NCA investigator snapped the laptop shut, slid all the photographs back into the folder, nodded at Rego, and left the office.

"He doesn't talk much, does he?" said Stevens, watching as the door closed behind the man.

Rego didn't answer, not feeling in the mood for banter.

"I take it we won't be picking up the suspect then, boss," Stevens said more formally, and Tamsyn's head swivelled so fast, Rego almost smiled.

"No, not yet, but I've invited myself to a surveillance briefing with the NCA team from Exeter," said Rego. "And I'll be taking Tamsyn with me ... for the experience."

Stevens' face tightened.

"Could I have a word in private, boss?"

"Of course," said Rego, having expected this response from his sergeant. "Tamsyn, wait in my office, please."

"Yes, sir."

She stood up hastily, snatched her go-bag from the floor and fled the room.

Rego could see that Stevens was seething.

"I know what you're going to say, Tom..."

"She's a student officer! She's not trained for this sort of operation!"

"I know you're pissed off, Tom, but it's not up for discussion. Understood?"

Stevens nodded, but his expression was still furious.

"Yes, sir," he said tightly, then turned on his heel.

Rego scrubbed his hands over his face.

He'd just criticised the NCA and the Met for not sharing intel in a timely manner, but he was doing exactly the same thing to his sergeant, a man he'd come to respect and trust.

The reason Tamsyn was going to be included on the surveillance team was so that the NCA operatives could keep an eye on her and prevent her from communicating with anyone in the Hellbanianz. Tamsyn would be under surveillance, too; she just didn't know it.

And Rego couldn't tell his sergeant that.

CHAPTER 16

The National Crime Agency surveillance team was made up of investigators from Exeter, Bristol and Bridgend with assistance from a dedicated covert listening unit who recorded everything.

They'd gathered to discuss the surveillance of a known Hellbanianz associate, and this was the meeting that Rego had been invited to, somewhat belatedly.

The NCA building was located at a site surrounded by a high security fence on a bland, featureless industrial estate. Rego stopped at the gate, identified himself at the intercom and followed directions to the parking area.

There were several cars already there but no one was in sight.

Rego climbed out of his car, his expression masking his real thoughts as he walked towards the building and pressed another intercom.

Tamsyn followed him, wishing he'd talk to her, wishing he'd say something. There was a time when she'd enjoyed his ease with silence: this wasn't one of them. It almost felt as if she'd done something wrong, but she had no idea what it could be.

She wouldn't have admitted it to another living soul, not even Joe, but right now, she needed some reassurance.

The door buzzed as it was unlocked and they walked into a small reception area where they were greeted by a uniformed security guard who asked to look at their IDs. The guard studied them for several seconds before handing them back.

"Phones, laptops, tablets in here, please," he said, holding out a plastic tray for them. "Are either of you wearing a Smart watch?"

Tamsyn threw a surprised look at Rego. He simply shook his head and handed over his personal mobile and work phone without further comment, and Tamsyn did the same.

"This is a Strap environment," said Rego, glancing at Tamsyn.

"I ... I think I remember learning about that," she said hesitantly. "It's, like, a secure place?"

"That's right: Strap is a codeword not an acronym and it denotes an environment where information or intelligence is sensitive. Usually, a person working within that environment requires higher levels of vetting."

Tamsyn looked intrigued.

"So, it's kind of an honour to be allowed in here?"

Rego ignored her excitement and simply continued speaking.

"Phones, Smart watches, tablets and laptops aren't allowed in these spaces: they have to be secured, because Smart devices are hackable."

Tamsyn nodded earnestly.

But the truth was that Vikram had already given Rego

a heads-up: under normal circumstances, the NCA wouldn't want Tamsyn within a million miles of their facility, and the only reason that she'd been allowed in was because they planned to download her personal phone. Rego guessed that an NCA tech would be getting to work on it within minutes to access the information, or even put a Trojan on it. It was entirely possible, likely even, that they'd be doing the same to his. All police work phones were already subject to lawful monitoring, in conjunction with Devon & Cornwall's Counter Corruption Unit. The only thing the NCA couldn't do was listen to conversations, because that required sign-off by the Home Secretary, as well as a bloody good reason for doing so. As far as Rego was aware, they hadn't reached anywhere near that threshold.

The whole scenario pissed him off, but if it helped exonerate Tamsyn, he'd put up with the invasion of his privacy.

"Wait over there, please," the security guard said, pointing to the sort of plastic chairs that you'd find in a school. "Someone will be along to collect you shortly."

He handed them each a pass with the words *escorted visitor*.

A door at the end of the corridor opened and a woman in jeans and a sweatshirt propped it open with her foot.

"DI Rego, PC Poldhu, thank you for joining us. The briefing will start in a few minutes. We're through here."

"What do we call you?" Rego asked, his voice neutral.

She threw him an amused look.

"H," she said simply.

She swiped them into a large, open-plan office. The front part was a breakout area with a flatscreen TV where *Sky News* played silently. There was also a small kitchen unit with a microwave, and a sink stacked with dirty bowls, mugs, and plates.

Tamsyn raised her eyebrows: so, it wasn't only Penzance where everyone seemed to be too important to wash their own dishes.

H saw the direction of her gaze.

"Tea? Coffee?" They both declined and she grinned. "Don't blame you. I just think of it as boosting my immune system."

The main office area had five rows of desks, each with two monitors. The desks were devoid of paperwork, but some had photographs of children, and several other work spaces were plastered with yellow Post-it notes stuck up haphazardly. The entire room was lined with tall filing cabinets, each piled high with old folders, empty mugs, tins of food, and several odd items including an electric fan with the front safety-guard missing and an antique-looking police helmet in the Custodian style.

H led them through the office to a closed door with a privacy sign which indicated that the room was occupied.

"Briefing room," she muttered, ushering them inside.

The room was windowless, stuffy, and smelled stale. There were more men than women crammed around the large table in the middle of the room, none in uniform and none wearing the usual police lanyard to identify them.

Rego glanced around, but every seat was occupied and there was nowhere for him and Tamsyn to sit.

He didn't know if this was a powerplay or simply that they'd run out of chairs. He leaned against the wall and folded his arms. Tamsyn watched him out of the corner of her eye and copied his stance.

The last time Rego had been involved in such a large-scale orchestrated surveillance, he'd still been a Detective

Sergeant with Greater Manchester Police. Even so, as he listened to the briefing, it felt like familiar territory.

Tamsyn, on the other hand, looked overwhelmed.

A man wearing a baseball cap rapped his knuckles on the table.

"Right, you lot, listen in. Thank you for getting up so early. For those of you who don't know me, I'm Rick O'Donnell. I'll be conducting a surveillance briefing; the firearms briefing will be held separately."

He looked around the table, making sure that everyone was listening.

"We have two guests today from Devon & Cornwall Police: DI Rob Rego and PC Tamsyn Poldhu."

One investigator, who was dressed in paint-spattered overalls, gave a murmur of appreciation, then grinned and winked at Tamsyn.

Even though she felt every eye on her, she met the man's gaze without flinching and without smiling. O'Donnell shot the man an annoyed look.

The door to the briefing room opened again, taking the spotlight off her. The new arrival was wearing biker leathers on his bottom half and a scruffy Metallica t-shirt on the top. The braces from his salopettes hung loose as he pushed and squeaked his way to the far end of the briefing room. His braces caught on the back of a chair which jolted the occupant, spilling hot tea into their lap.

"Sorry I'm a bit late, boss. I've just had to drop the kids off."

There were sniggers from several of the team, and a man with a shaved head held his nose.

"That's funny, cos I thought you was in the bog when I walked past – it sounded like you were giving birth. Cor dear, what a pen and ink!"

Too much information, thought Tamsyn. But that's how it was with a group of people who worked closely together doing a dangerous job. And she'd heard far worse from the guys on E-team.

O'Donnell ignored the byplay and continued.

"DI Rego is the Officer in Charge investigating two murders in Cornwall. He was also at the Old Bailey when explosives were used to facilitate the escape of the suspect, an Albanian national named Besnik Domi. I'm sure you've all read the report and seen the pictures in the newspapers."

He glanced at Tamsyn.

"Domi is also accused of the murder of Sir Malcolm Sloane KC and the attempted murder of Judge Donald Whittaker, barristers and other court staff, together with conspiracy to cause an explosion and escaping from lawful custody, which I suppose is the least of his worries."

A faint ripple of amusement ran through the room.

"PC Poldhu has looked at some of the video you took last week," he said, glancing at an older man with a long, grey ponytail. "She identified the escaper, Domi, and he's associated to Subject 12 from Op Blue Lagoon, which all of you have worked on over the last few weeks."

Tamsyn was taking notes so fast, she wondered whether she'd be able to read her own handwriting.

"Anyway, let's crack on: I'll go through the dispo first. Right, the runners and riders: 10 is Grandad, Slinky and Berlin. They'll have the drone and CROPS capability. I'll come onto their terms of deployment during the briefing."

What the hell were 'crops'?

O'Donnell continued rapidly and no one else seemed confused. Tamsyn started to make a note to Google it later, when Rego held his notebook in front of her. Written in capital letters was: *COVERT RURAL OBSERVATION POST*.

She nodded her thanks as she made a note, but the briefing hadn't paused for a second.

"Pansy is 11, he's the Ops comm today, and his driver is Dinky. Skippy is 13; Jonah is 14; Rooster is 15; Sweetpea is 18; Kate, 21; Granty, 22; and Angel is 28. Tactical Support Desk today is Bats with Geeta doing the intel, and the log keeper is Amy."

He peered at a small woman who seemed so mild-mannered that no one would ever guess she was a top-notch investigator of organised crime gangs.

"Amy, come and see me if you need some more log books. Everyone okay with that? All cars and bikes, okay? Give Bats up-to-date ISSI numbers for your radios: all cars have to be seen on the tracking. If not, you'll have to change your car. We might get an aerial platform from the Met, but the cloud cover is low, so I'm not banking on their support."

Tamsyn had no idea that so many people were needed to do surveillance. She only had the vaguest idea what everyone's jobs were.

O'Donnell stared around the table.

"I don't need to remind you that these are very dangerous people."

The mood in the room became sombre.

"D&C Police will provide arrest teams which DI Rego is organising." He nodded at Rego. "I'll give you a couple of drivers who are surveillance trained."

Then he turned back to his team.

"Bats, H will be one of the drivers. When I know who the other is, I'll let you know and the vehicles they're in. I'll be in the TSD, with Silver Commander from our Armed Operations Unit. Ultimately, Silver has overall control of today's surveillance which may go into tomorrow, depending on how it pans out. Be prepared for a couple of long days."

Several of them groaned but most nodded as if that was the norm.

"Skippy has put together a PowerPoint briefing which I'd hoped to put on the Smartboard, but some thieving git has nicked the HDMI lead; I suspect the firearms threat desk because they were in here last, the thieving toe-rags. But we haven't got time to mount a counter raid of their office, so we've printed off the briefings. And for God's sake, don't take them out with you; we can't afford a compromise if one gets lost. I'll get Bats to send a copy to your tablets."

He passed around a pile of documents so everyone had a copy.

"Information: Subject 12 vehicle is probed..." O'Donnell glanced at Tamsyn. "An audio listening device has been attached to the car, and it's also been fitted with a VTD, a vehicle tracking device."

Tamsyn's cheeks were red, knowing that she was the only person in the room who didn't know all these terms. She nodded, keeping her eyes down as she jotted a few lines in her notebook.

O'Donnell continued.

"Subject 12 is likely to be collecting Albanian national Besnik Domi, known as Subject 66 during the course of the next two days. Subject 66 escaped from custody with a very complex and well co-ordinated distraction plan by blocking the entrance to the local nick and using a concrete mixer to discharge concrete across the escape route. We have intelligence that his group are very surveillance aware, even more so now that Subject 66 knows he's wanted. There are no known community issues around the local area, however, if the surveillance drifts into other areas we'll make dynamic assessments."

He lifted his eyes from the briefing sheet and looked around the room.

"Subject 66 is armed, very dangerous, and discharged an automatic weapon when he absconded from the Old Bailey. Under no circumstances is he to be approached by unarmed officers."

The room was silent, the seriousness of the situation apparent to everyone.

"Intent: the intention is to conduct conventional surveillance, with the conventional team supported by a bolt-on MAST team."

There were so many acronyms that Tamsyn was completely lost. Rego saw her confusion and leaned closer to whisper.

"Mobile Armed Surveillance Team, okay?"

She nodded and made another note. She wished someone had given her a crib sheet before the meeting, then she wouldn't feel so stupid.

"Surveillance will be conducted against Subject 12 from his home address. As soon as he is identified, surveillance will be handed over to Bats in the TSD who'll be managing the tracker on Subject Vehicle 12. Subject 12 will be the focus of the surveillance and we'll go wherever he goes, even if he switches vehicles. Slinky and Grandad will have spare tracking devices in that event, but will only deploy when supported by an armed officer and at a place dictated by Silver."

Both men nodded in acknowledgement.

"Intel supports the scenario that Subject 12 will lead us to Subject 66. The sole intention is to arrest Domi, and this investigation supersedes ours. When we have Domi, we need two independent identifications. Silver will dictate the time and place of our armed interdiction. Whoever has the eyeball when State Amber is called will provide an enhanced commentary."

He raised his eyes from the briefing paper.

"You've all trained for this, so you know what's expected, but Silver will need a word-picture of the surroundings – shops, pedestrians, schools – before he'll call State Red."

Tamsyn made notes on the document.

"Write it in your pocketbook, Tamsyn," said Rego. "You can't take this briefing sheet from the room."

Tamsyn withheld a sigh. It was almost as if they didn't trust her not to screw up.

"Method," O'Donnell said, moving to the next item on the briefing. "Bats checked the tracker this morning: it's still at the home address and hasn't moved all night. We'll have a visual on Subject Premises 12, and will need to identify Subject 12 getting into the vehicle which will be tracked electronically until it stops. We'll need to get an eyeball on the vehicle at all stops, but it's imperative that no one deploys on foot without the express authority of Silver, *and* will be supported by an armed officer. We don't know where Domi is residing, so he could get picked up from anywhere, but again, when he is identified and we have our two separate positive identifications, Silver will call the armed team to effect the arrest. It goes without saying that we need as many photographs as possible; you don't have to ask permission, just take them when it's covert to do so.

"When Subject 66 has been detained, the conventional team will put a cordon around the stop. No person or vehicle will be allowed into that cordon under any circumstances. Once the situation is contained, DI Rego and his team will effect the arrest and arrange transport. If there are more than two prisoners, we may have to use a couple of surveillance vehicles to convey prisoners into custody. Subject 12's vehicle will be preserved for evidence and forensically lifted to a secure garage.

"Everyone will then return to the branch office for a full debrief and standby in the event that DI Rego needs our help."

He glanced around the room.

"Next, administration: we have a RIPA authority in place..."

"Regulation of Investigator Powers Act," Rego whispered, but Tamsyn already knew that one.

"The RIPA authority was amended yesterday to include Besnik Domi. I have it here if anyone wants to read it. There is also a risk assessment which has been updated in view of the danger." He looked up to underline his words. "Your safety and safety of members of the public is of paramount importance. We also have a duty of care for the subjects of this operation."

A duty of care for a murderer: the irony was not lost on Tamsyn.

"Communications will be on folder Exeter 1 for cars and body-sets. You'll need your mobile phone, and if tasked to undertake a role away from your vehicle, you'll need to carry two forms of communication. Pansy will ensure that a sequential comms check is conducted for car and personals.

"Humanitarian Issues: I bring to your attention ECHR Articles 6 (right to a fair trial), and Article 8 (respect for family and private life). The rationale for this operation is based on what a reasonable person would expect law enforcement to do if they were aware of the circumstances: this has been assessed to be the arrest and detention of

Domi. Finally, I have made it clear that Silver Command has control of the tactics."

O'Donnell looked around the room.

"Any questions?"

Tamsyn had a thousand but stayed silent. She wasn't sure what her role was here, but DI Rego seemed to understand. For now, she'd go with the flow.

O'Donnell slapped his hands on the desk in front of him.

"Bats, fire up the tracker and locate the vehicle. Let's go."

There was an exodus from the briefing room, all the NCA investigators chatting or cracking jokes. The energy was palpable. They hoped that today would be a win for the good guys.

The only people left in the room were O'Donnell, Rego and Tamsyn.

"You seemed a bit lost there, Tamsyn," O'Donnell said kindly.

"It's a lot to take in," she admitted. "But I've got the gist of it. Thank you, sir."

"Rego, a word," O'Donnell said, looking at him meaningfully.

Taking the hint, Tamsyn wandered into the main area, startled to see two men standing in their underpants and strapping radio harnesses to their legs whilst they discussed the briefing. Nobody else batted an eyelid, so Tamsyn pretended to read her notes.

Five minutes later, Rego walked from the briefing room.

"Thanks for coming," O'Donnell said, shaking hands with Rego and Tamsyn. "We'll be over to your Middlemoor office shortly to collect your arrest teams."

Then H handed back their mobile phones and escorted them from the building.

Despite only having half the picture, Tamsyn was bubbling with excitement. It felt real, like it could all be over soon. Everyone was intent on catching Domi and locking him up for good.

"Right, next stop Exeter nick," said Rego. "We'll meet up with the others from the arrest team I brought up from Penzance. You'll know most of them."

He glanced at Tamsyn.

"The arrest team are the people who escort detained suspects away, but they're not necessarily the ones who make the arrest. It's going to be a dynamic situation, and whichever way it goes, the decision will be made for operational reasons."

Tamsyn nodded but didn't say anything.

"So, what did you think?" Rego asked after a short pause.

"Are the NCA police officers?"

"No, technically, they're Civil Servants; police officers are Crown Agents. And we get paid more. They don't have the same day-to-day risk that uniform officers have, but they're up against some really nasty people."

Tamsyn was thoughtful.

"Why am I here, sir? I don't know anything about any of this." She gave a self-deprecating laugh. "I don't think you could find anyone who knows less!"

Rego paused before he replied.

"You've met Domi face to face."

It was the only answer he could give her.

CHAPTER 17

Tamsyn was relieved to see DC Jen Bolitho's friendly face as they rolled into Exeter Police station's private car park, because Rego had hardly said a word to her.

He had only spoken to phone ahead, ensuring that the arrest team from Penzance was already kitted up and ready to go as soon as the NCA drivers arrived.

"How'd it go?" Jen whispered to Tamsyn.

"My head is spinning," Tamsyn admitted. "There's so much to remember, and I only understood about half of it to begin with."

Jen gave her an understanding smile. "You'll get there."

Tamsyn recognised the other detectives John Frith and Jack Forshaw, and of course, DS Stevens. He didn't look pleased to see her, and Tamsyn wondered why he hadn't been at the briefing instead of her.

Rego had just finished briefing the arrest teams and checking they all had the correct Personal Protection Equipment for the op. PPE kit today included incapacitant spray, baton, handcuffs, and covert body armour. It was designed to fit under normal clothing but was famously uncomfortable, especially for women.

The Penzance team had only just finished their checks when H swept through the electronic gate into the yard. She was driving a VW Tiguan SUV, and was followed by a Skoda estate driven by a female investigator who had been at the NCA briefing.

H didn't bother parking or turning off the engine; she simply rolled down the car window:

"Three in with me, and three in with Jo."

Tamsyn ended up in H's car with Rego and Jack Forshaw.

Then both NCA vehicles swung out of the car park at speed.

"When we get nearer to Subject 12's dwelling, I'll park up and see what today brings," H said. "If you need a pee or anything, don't sit there wetting yourself, we can always find you a hedge."

Tamsyn hoped she was joking.

H drove fast and efficiently, weaving her way through the traffic, followed by the Skoda, and 45 hair-raising minutes later, they were at Waitrose's car park in Saltash.

The car radio, which had been quiet, burst into life.

"From 11: permission TSD."

"TSD 11: no change, tracker is alive. Subject Vehicle 12 remains in the vicinity of Subject Premises 12, go ahead."

"From 11: I need a visual on Subject Premises 12."

"13 will do that."

"Obliged, Skippy. When you get into position, you'll have primacy. Received, TSD?"

"TSD: yes, yes."

"Skippy: TSD, I'm already there. I'll take primacy."

"Over to you then."

"13 has a visual on both Subject Premises 12 and Subject Vehicle 12, and will be able to ID."

"From 11: all understood. Permission then 13, to plot and then a sequential vehicle check."

"From 13: go ahead."

The other vehicles were then directed to locations around Saltash so whichever route the vehicle took when it drove away from the house, it would always pass a surveillance vehicle. Then everyone had to confirm they were receiving radio comms, which led to a flurry of responses, "Yes, yes."

And then ... nothing.

H locked the doors, lowered her seat and immediately seemed to fall into a deep sleep.

Tamsyn was hot and uncomfortable, her legs cramped and her neck aching from her headrest that was pushed too far forwards. She glanced at Jack who shared the backseat with her, and he shrugged his shoulders, then went back to reading something on his tablet.

She wished she could listen to some music but she hadn't brought her ear-buds with her.

Rego was making notes in his blue book, still in no mood to chat, so Tamsyn checked her emails and looked at TikTok videos while they waited.

The ordinary car radio played quietly in the background, but other than that, there was silence. Every half hour, the radio communications reported, "No change, no change," with 11 acknowledging.

Four hours later, they were still sitting there and nothing seemed to be happening. Tamsyn's phone battery was down to 24% and she was bored.

H opened her eyes and raised her seat to the upright position.

"Right, I'm off for a wee. I've put the car radio on 'loops' but I've got my personal radio so I can hear if anything happens. If anyone else wants a loo break, I'll lock the car up."

Rego, Tamsyn and Jack all got out, grateful to stretch their legs and use the facilities.

The four of them walked towards Waitrose supermarket, Tamsyn and H turning off to the ladies together.

"Is it like this all the time?" Tamsyn asked.

H gave her an amused look.

"Not exciting enough for you? You've just got to get on with it. But no, we're investigators as well, so there's the usual paperwork, and I bet you already know what that's like."

They'd only been back in the car a matter of minutes when the radio came to life.

"Standby, standby, standby!"

H was awake and ready. Tamsyn tensed, her pulse quickening.

"From 13: positive ID of Subject 12, from Subject Premises 12. He is wearing blue skinny ripped jeans and a black hoodie with a gold-coloured motif on the front. His hood is down and he is good for his photo. He is with a female, early twenties, very slim, also wearing blue skinny jeans and a pink hoodie. Neither are carrying anything. No comms for a sec while I take some photos."

In the background, the mic was still open and Tamsyn could hear a camera shutter taking multiple shots.

"From 13: Subject 12 and the female are walking along

the pavement to Subject Vehicle 12. CMU are you getting this?"

"From CMU: yes, yes, and the audio in the vehicle had been activated."

"From 13: Subject 12 into the driver's seat of Subject Vehicle 12; female in the front passenger seat. Standby ... engine alive ... brake lights illuminated ... it's off off off, original, out of my view and over to the team."

"From the TSD: tracker is activated. Subject Vehicle 12 north on Callington Road. Towards you, Jonah."

"From 14: yes, yes ... waiting ... eyeball ... confirmation ID Subject 12 driving, female is still in the passenger seat. Subject Vehicle 12 goes left, left, left onto A38. Are you happy to have it, TSD?"

"TSD: yes, yes."

Tamsyn listened intently to the radio commentary and how the vehicles switched between themselves, interacting with the Tactical Support Desk, all while keeping the Mercedes in view. The convoy of vehicles headed further west, and Tamsyn had the uncomfortable feeling that they were heading toward Penzance. The longer they drove, the more certain that feeling became.

"From 21: I have the eyeball," the woman's voice over the radio was clear and calm as she commentated on the position of the Mercedes.

The TSD piped up. "21, you're generally towards the A30 major trunk road."

"From 21: obliged TSD. I have four for cover on the approach to a traffic light controlled junction, lights are currently on green in our favour ... bikers make ground."

The two operatives on bikes, 18 and 28, had anticipated the potential problem if the traffic lights suddenly turned to red, leaving 21 stranded.

In the distance, Tamsyn could see a set of traffic lights which were on green, then amber, then the lights went to red.

"From 21: bikers come through."

In unison, 18 and 28 said, "Yes, yes, we're with you."

Years of experience from both bikers meant that they had pre-read the situation, and both had started to come through the surveillance convoy without being asked.

Tamsyn could see H's eyes in the rearview mirror scanning the driver's wing mirror as well as behind her. For a second, her eyes locked with Tamsyn's.

"Our motorbikes are really vulnerable, coming through at speed," she said. "One silly move and we could knock them off. It's happened before, so I need to be able to see them."

The two motorcycles roared up, overtaking on the inside, speeding towards the traffic lights.

"From 21: Subject Vehicle 12 is through the lights. I'm held at pole. There's a good view back."

H said to Tamsyn, "Kate can't go through the red light in view of the Mercedes because they might see her, which could compromise the op. The bikes will try and get through."

Tamsyn was transfixed by the skills of the motorcyclists as both mounted the nearside pavement when close to the traffic lights, much to the annoyance of some motorists who were unknowingly within the surveillance convoy. Both bikes bounced down the kerb and went through the red light, accelerating hard. Subject 12 driving the Mercedes hadn't seen a thing. And they knew that, because the listening device in his car would have picked up any concern.

A few seconds later the radio crackled.

"From 28: eyeball, no deviation; speed, four-zero; three for cover. 18 is your back up."

H nodded to herself.

"The bikes have got the Mercedes in view."

Tamsyn sucked in a startled breath when a black VW Golf GTI shot down the outside of the road, just missing the wing mirrors of the queuing cars as it overtook the convoy. She could have sworn that the driver of the Golf grinned at her as he sped past.

"Is that a surveillance car?" Tamsyn asked.

"Yeah," H sighed. "That's 22, Granty. He's always doing that – he's a bugger!" She paused. "He's a great driver, though."

Tamsyn watched the Golf's tail lights disappear into the distance and she smiled to herself. She remembered the adrenaline rush as she'd charged up the A30, blue lights on, siren wailing.

Then her smile slipped. These guys had to race at speed in unmarked cars with no expectation that other traffic would get out of their way. It was dangerous.

The Mercedes continued along the A30, obeying the speed limits.

The familiar placenames all led further west: Goss Moor, Indian Queens, Penhale, Zelah, Marazanvose, Redruth, Rose-an-Grouse.

As they crested the hill, it was the first sight of the sea, the Atlantic Ocean, grey and wintry today, a flat slab of lead on the horizon. Penzance was just a few miles away and Tamsyn shivered. Had Domi been hiding just a few miles from her all this time? Had he stood outside her grandparents' cottage and killed that poor little dog? She clenched her fists, wishing him all the darkness that he deserved. If she followed her grandmother's beliefs, she'd call down the fury of the four winds to tear him limb from limb.

"From 22: Subject Vehicle 12 is on the approach to a roundabout with the A30; speed three-zero at the roundabout, and on the roundabout: not one, not one; not two, not two; takes the third, the third onto Varfell Lane. TSD are you happy to have primacy?"

The TSD responded that they were, and continued to track the Mercedes electronically.

The road was very familiar to Tamsyn – her grandfather sold his crab to the Cornish Crab Company on the industrial estate; she took Morwenna to the beach at Longrock.

The surveillance team were working hard, the eyeball changing at regular intervals. H and Jo kept at the back of the surveillance convoy, the vehicles yo-yoing their speed, sometimes even stopping if they thought they had got too close.

Tamsyn wondered how much further they were going, she was hungry and thirsty, wishing she had bought some water from Waitrose.

As they approached Morrison's roundabout, 14 took another exit off the roundabout, leaving 13 to take over the eyeball, but his first words were, "loss of sighting on Subject Vehicle 12!"

Tamsyn knew that this roundabout had Morrisons off to the left, McDonald's and a petrol station to the right, as well as multiple business units.

Rego looked at H, then over his shoulder at Tamsyn sitting in the back. His frustration seemed to say: *how can they lose the Mercedes at this critical point?*

H was calm.

"Don't worry, guys, we'll get it back."

The Covert Monitoring Unit interjected: "Subject Vehicle 12 has stopped. There is conversation, but it's not clear because they're listening to music."

"From 10: they're at McDonald's. CCTV black spot, no external cameras. Reckon they've done this before."

Tamsyn wondered how he could be so sure. The choice of parking spot could be a coincidence, couldn't it? But no one else seemed to doubt was happening.

"The Mini is nose-out," Rego said quietly, as if he was reading her mind. "That gives them sight of any suspicious vehicles – us – or a rival gang looking to rob them."

Tamsyn nodded, but no one was paying attention to her.

The 10 team of Berlin, Slinky and Grandad parked their van, and Berlin got out, walking towards McDonald's, hands in his pockets, looking for all the world like a surfer dude, tall and gangly with long swept-back hair. Grandad and Slinky had crawled over the back seats of the van: Grandad with a camera, and Slinky providing the commentary.

"10 has the eyeball. Subject Vehicle 12 has stopped alongside a blue Mini, driver's door to driver's door; both drivers' windows are down. I can see it's a female in the driver's seat of the Mini and there is a male in the passenger seat. A blue plastic carrier bag has been passed from the Mercedes into the Mini. Stand by, stand by. The Mercedes is manoeuvring, the Mini's engine remains alive – the brake lights are illuminated against the fence. Subject Vehicle 12 is off off off. What do you want us to do?"

The meeting between the two vehicles was an unexpected development; decisions had to be made quickly.

"From 11: let it run, just push it out of the plot. Bats, if you can monitor the tracker to make sure it doesn't double back on us; CMU, keep the audio running to gather all the evidence we can. CMU, have you an update?"

"From CMU: the translator is going through it now live-time."

That just left the Mini in the car park.

"Okay from 11: the subject now is switched to the Mini and its occupants."

Rego knew that the phone line would still be open, informing the ever-revolving circle of decision making: gather information and intelligence; assess risks, and develop a working strategy; consider powers, policies and procedures; identify options and contingencies; take action and review what happens.

At all stages, the centre of the decision-circle was about saving lives and reducing harm: the thought-processes and assessments, all done in seconds.

Tamsyn could hear Grandad's camera shutter taking multiple photographs, while the numberplate of the Mini was passed over the radio.

"Holy shit!"

Rego's eyes snapped to Tamsyn's.

"What? What is it?"

Tamsyn couldn't get her words out, trying to compute what was happening.

"For fuck's sake, what's happening?" he snapped.

"That's Chloe's car! Chloe Rogers."

"Who's Chloe Rogers?" H asked sharply.

"She's a civilian investigator working at Camborne nick and often at Penzance," Rego said, his voice iced over with rage.

He had not anticipated this outcome.

"From 10: male has dark hair, mid- to-late thirties – fits Subject 66's description. Can we get ID?"

"Slinky: I'll get the quick deployment drone."

Within less than a minute, a mini drone was deployed from the side door of the NCA's van and was airborne, live-streaming into Chloe's Mini.

"Grandad: looks like they're counting money from the plastic bag that was thrown into the car. The man looks like Subject 66 but I cannot make a positive ID."

Everyone was on high alert and Tamsyn's heart was thundering. She'd broken out into a cold sweat at the thought that she was so close to the man who had twice tried to kill her. And she couldn't get her head around the fact that Chloe was with him. She hated Chloe and thought she was a skank, but not this ... never this...

"Streaming now," said H. "Do we have identification?"

Tamsyn leaned over the seat as Rego studied the video.

"Yes," said Rego, "that's him. That's Besnik Domi."

"Tamsyn?" H asked, but Tamsyn was frowning at the video and didn't reply.

"Tamsyn!" she said again, her voice sharper.

Tamsyn's head shot up, doubt in her eyes.

"I ... I don't know ... I'm not sure..."

Rego was 99% certain that the man was Domi: same strong jaw; same cold, dark eyes – it was definitely him. And the fact that Tamsyn refused to ID him filled him with disappointment, with anger. He'd been so sure that the NCA were wrong about her. Vikram had texted him that not a single piece of incriminating evidence had been found in the six hours that they'd been analysing Tamsyn's data on her personal phone, and he'd felt vindicated. Of course, the NCA could argue that just meant she knew what IT forensic officers were capable of, and the importance of having a burner phone.

"It's definitely him," Rego said, his voice loud in the car.

H turned to Tamsyn again. "We need a second positive ID, Tamsyn."

"I ... I don't know! I'm sorry, I can't tell. I don't think ... I can't be sure..."

In the rearview mirror, Rego's eyes met with Tamsyn's.

H's lips pressed together and she glanced at Rego. She compared the headshot of Domi that had been given to the newspapers with the man on the video.

"I'm happy it's a positive identification of Domi," she said, then turned to Rego. "We have to assume he's armed, but there's nobody else in the car park. The car is nose in to a fence with spaces near-side and off-side, and the rear is free. There's no one walking about. This will be an armed intervention."

O'Donnell's voice came over the radio.

"It looks like we have two positive ID's on Domi. Right, let's arrest them."

"From Silver Commander: State Red, State Red, State Red. Block them in and take them out through the windows."

It could have been a scene out of a Hollywood movie as three, armed response vehicles screamed past them, lights blazing and sirens shrieking, pinning the Mini in place, virtually touching the doors so that the suspects inside couldn't exit in any direction.

The attack team stormed from their cars, weapons raised.

"Armed police! Show your hands! Show your hands!"

A second team were racing to put out a cordon so no civilians could stumble onto the scene.

The suspects didn't stand a chance.

The attack team smashed the Mini's side windows on

both sides, slicing through the suspects' seatbelts and dragging them out through the windows.

Within seconds, they were on the ground and handcuffed, a cursory search finding a knife on the male suspect but no gun.

Jo walked over to the suspects and said in her broad Sheffield accent,

"Aright love, don't worry, we ain't mugging you. We're from the National Crime Agency, and you and your friend are under arrest."

She held her warrant card for Chloe to see.

"You've been arrested on suspicion of conspiracy to murder, assisting an offender, and misconduct in a public office. We believe you have been providing information to an offender who has escaped from custody, and you have provided information to him which led to the murder of Saemira Ruçi and George Mason, and of taking bribes from a criminal gang. The arrest is necessary for a prompt and effective investigation of the offence, and to obtain evidence by questioning," she paused. "But I'm sure you already know this."

Chloe was breathing hard, and Tamsyn saw her feet rise off the ground in pain as the handcuffs were double-locked to prevent them tightening on her wrists later.

Jo gave a similar speech to the male suspect. Then she stopped, frowned, and took a tentative sniff, wrinkling her nose in Chloe's direction.

"Oh, my God! What's that smell? Has she shit herself?"

H pulled a face.

"I think she's got dog shit in her hair."

Jo and H looked at each other, then at a squashed dog turd on the ground, and smiled.

Tamsyn heard all this from the car's radio. She still couldn't quite believe it.

Rego hadn't spoken to her and she felt as if he was blaming her for something. He moved into the driver's seat, driving the NCA vehicle towards the arresting officers and spoke quietly.

"Look, H, we can't take them to Camborne until we know if anyone else was involved."

She nodded grimly. "Newquay nick it is then."

John Frith was instructed to drive Chloe's Mini to Newquay where it would be searched, and the suspects were bundled into separate cars. He pulled on a pair of latex gloves before he touched any part of Chloe's Mini.

Everyone left the car park quietly, without any fuss; holidaymakers and locals were none the wiser about the drama that had taken place. It was a text book arrest.

Tamsyn took a deep breath and climbed out of the car with shaking legs. She peered into the back seat of the second arrest vehicle and the man stared back at her coldly, his face impassive.

"Sir," she said to Rego, wringing her hands. "Sir ... that's not Besnik Domi."

CHAPTER 18

Rego was furious. He'd been led up the garden path by the National Crime Agency and then made a fool of himself. He should have trusted Tamsyn; he should have trusted the gut instincts that had kept him alive this long.

But the truth was he'd *wanted* it to be Domi, *needed* it, because then his family would be safe and his private hell would be over. He'd seen what he wanted to see, but Tamsyn hadn't wavered, even with all eyes on her, telling her to make a positive ID. He admired that, and he felt ashamed of his own reaction.

As soon as he could get some privacy, he called Vikram and told him about the arrest and subsequent fuckup.

Vikram listened in silence.

"I've been doing some digging, Rob, just for curiosity's sake. I kept thinking that the NCA would have to have some compelling intelligence that Tamsyn was providing the Hellbanianz with intelligence. And it got me wondering about that confidential informant which you didn't hear about from me."

"Go on."

"We know Domi senior has some reach, and the fact that your civilian investigator, Rogers, is complicit, it makes me wonder if Domi has other informants in Devon & Cornwall Police and elsewhere. What if ... what if the Hellbanianz have a CHIS with the NCA." Vikram sighed. "Do you remember when we used to call Covert Human Intelligence Sources 'informants'?"

Rego ignored that comment.

"You mean that the CHIS has been feeding false intel to their NCA handler?"

"It wouldn't be the first time," Vikram agreed. "Possibly giving some low-level intelligence about a rival Albanian group or even someone within their own group that they wanted out of the way, hoping that law enforcement would do their dirty work for them, and all authorised by the Domi brothers. And I'm also hearing rumours of a power struggle within the Hellbanianz: there's been something of a vacuum since big brother Domi was put away, and little brother isn't cutting it. Word is that Dritan is looking to replace his brother. Besnik is vicious as hell, but a hothead: definitely not a thinker and a planner. Putting a target on Tamsyn and sending him off on a hunt would just be a nice little side line which keeps Besnik out of the way while a replacement is found."

"You think Domi senior would do that to his own brother?"

"That's the intel we're getting. He wants business as usual, not vendettas with police officers. If Besnik kills a police officer, then he'll be a marked man and finished as acting head of the Hellbanianz."

Rego was chilled by the casual way Vikram talked about Tamsyn being murdered.

"But a double-bluff that makes it look like Tamsyn is

corrupt works for them, too," Vikram continued. "Imagine if she ended up in prison."

Rego felt all the frustration of this tangled and complex case.

"NCA have done some surveillance work on Tamsyn, as well."

He gave a dry laugh.

"Well, they've wasted their time, Vik. I'm more convinced than ever. As far as I'm concerned, if there's an intelligence leak other than Chloe, then it's not Tamsyn."

"I thought you'd say that," said Vikram. "But would you stake your career on it?"

"I don't have to," Rego answered. "The NCA's covert investigation will do it for me – and Tamsyn will be exonerated."

With the call ending somewhat uncomfortably, Rego sat in silence, brooding on the enormity of his mistake.

The NCA team had handed over all the evidence and driven back to their branch office, while Rego had attended a meeting with the counter corruption unit.

ACC Gray had already taken pleasure in leaving a message on Rego's phone demanding that Rego go straight to HQ at the earliest opportunity for a full debrief. The message ended on a petulant note:

"Why have you called an armed intervention on two unarmed people? Have you even considered the reputational damage? And what has this farce cost?"

Rego decided that 'earliest opportunity' gave him some leeway, so instead, he ignored ACC Gray's message and headed back to Newquay to listen in to the four interviews: Subject 12 and his girlfriend who'd been picked up near Redruth; then Chloe and the male suspect in the Mini, who claimed to be Janusz Broź, a Polish national, and Chloe's boyfriend – simply in the wrong place at the wrong time and who had no idea why he'd been arrested.

It was the man's bad luck that an officer at Newquay's custody suite had a Polish wife and could say for certain that the man was not Polish and had certainly never been to Łódź, where he had told them he was from. After that, he'd given a 'no comment' interview. They strongly suspected he was a member of the Hellbanianz and hoped that analysis of his phone would give them the evidence; his fingerprints were already on the way to the authorities in Albania.

Until he'd been positively identified, their hopes were pinned on getting Chloe Rogers to talk.

Rego was sitting with DI Frank Morton in one of the custody suite's viewing rooms at Newquay police station. Neither man spoke and the atmosphere was tense.

Morton had interviewed Tamsyn under caution earlier in the year on an unrelated case, and Rego was feeling vindicated in holding a grudge against the man. He knew that was unfair, but this whole op had been a shit fest.

Without attempting conversation, Morton pushed a piece of paper across to Rego, listing the questions that he intended to ask Chloe. There was nothing that Rego could add or disagree with, and that irritated him even more.

"Fine," he said tersely.

Morton gave him a considering look, but simply nodded then rose and left the viewing room.

The custody suite was sparsely furnished with a plastic chair for the suspect and a plain, white table – both secured to the floor. Three other seats were moveable: one was for the suspect's legal representative, and two for the interviewing officers, DI Morton and his sergeant, DS Phil Brown.

In the centre of the table was the digital recorder for making an audio copy of the interview.

Rego watched Chloe as she entered the interview room. The first time he met her seven months ago, she'd been heavily made-up with her dark hair shiny, her clothes smart and professional, although her attractiveness had been marred by an air of arrogance and superiority that was unappealing. But his lasting impression was of venomous spite towards Tamsyn, especially when Chloe had called her 'Tampax', and made other snide remarks on Tamsyn's first day at Penzance.

It had been Rego's first day, too, and his negative opinion of Chloe had stuck. She was reasonably competent at her job, but not well liked.

Today, her eyes were red, her skin blotchy, and it was clear that she'd been crying. She wore a grey tracksuit supplied by the custody officer, too large for her small frame.

At least she'd washed the dog shit out of her hair, the problem being that the custody suite had run out of shampoo, so the only option was to use washing up liquid. And because the custody suite didn't run to conditioner either, Chloe's hair was dull and lifeless. With her borrowed and ill-fitting clothes, pasty complexion, and limp hair, she looked dreadful.

She also looked scared. But then she lifted her chin, looking directly towards the camera pointing at her.

As this was going to be a criminal interview, Chloe was allowed to be legally represented by a trained lawyer; if it had simply been a disciplinary offence, she could have been represented by a friend or union rep.

Following her into the interview room was the duty brief, Maurice Springfield, a thin wiry man in his 50s.

Springfield was bald, with an unkempt beard, and a moustache that was yellowing through years of smoking. His index and middle fingers on his right hand were similarly discoloured.

Springfield was profoundly short-sighted, his soft-boiled eyes peering at the world through John Lennon glasses that constantly slipped down his nose due to weight of the thick lenses. Every few seconds, he pushed them back into place.

Springfield was well known to most of the detectives, and Rego had met him enough times to dislike him.

The man was forthright, bordering on obstructive. No one had ever seen him crack a smile, his drooping lips barely visible behind the tobacco-stained moustache. His monotone voice lacked any colour and sounded as if he was from Essex, although Rego had been told that he was born and bred a Cornishman.

DI Morton and DS Brown were clearly both very experienced, and Rego suspected that they'd come across Springfield before, although probably not while he was representing an employee of Devon & Cornwall Police.

The initial pre-interview formalities were gone through: names, where the interview was taking place, date, time.

Often, the aim with interview questions was to catch the suspect in a provable lie.

"Chloe, you have been arrested on suspicion of conspiracy to murder Saemira Ruçi and George Mason; conspiracy to kidnap Maisie Rego, aged nine years old..."

"What? Who?" said Chloe, glancing at her brief who put his finger to his mouth in a shushing motion. "Do you mean Rego's kid?"

"...assisting an offender unlawfully at large, namely Besnik Domi; and misconduct in a public office. You are further under arrest for the murder of Sir Malcolm Sloane..."

Again, Chloe looked like she wanted to interrupt but managed to keep her thoughts to herself, even if her expression was easy to read.

"...and conspiracy to murder PC Tamsyn Poldhu."

Chloe bristled, completely unable to shut her mouth.

"Tamsyn? What's this got to do with her? What's that bitch been saying? Is this about the fish heads? Did she set me up?"

"Chloe!" Springfield hissed. "Leave this to me."

Rego frowned, wondering what the comment about the fish heads was, and making a note to find out.

Chloe clamped her lips together in a thin line, but her hasty words would go a long way to exonerate Tamsyn.

Rego could argue that it proved Tamsyn wasn't involved with Chloe in any way – he'd never believed that she was.

From the viewing room, he gave a grim smile, and DS Brown continued reading from the written disclosure. Chloe was handed a copy but her eyes couldn't seem to take in what she was seeing.

"There will no doubt be a number of separate offences under that heading, but we suspect that you have been unlawfully passing on police intelligence to a crime group and receiving substantial remuneration for doing so," said DS Brown as Morton pretended to go through a thick pile of documents.

If Chloe was shocked or surprised by anything that had been said subsequent to her outburst, she didn't show it. She sat with her arms crossed, her face stony.

DS Brown went on to read out the caution.

"You do not have to say anything. But it may harm your defence if you do not mention when questioned something which you later rely on in court. Anything you do say may be given in evidence."

Chloe didn't react.

Before DS Brown could ask a single question, Springfield leaned forward, pushing his glasses up his nose.

"My client, Miss Rogers, will decline to answer your questions. I don't think for one moment you have made adequate disclosure for us even to consider the possibility of Miss Rogers being able to answer your questions appropriately; but, in order not to appear obstructive, she has made a prepared statement about the allegations. Here is the signed original, and I have a copy."

The lawyer handed over a single sheet of paper.

DS Brown looked at the A4 sheet, his eyebrows rising.

"Chloe, can I confirm that this is your signature at the end of the text?"

Springfield frowned and insisted on replying for her.

"Yes, it is. I told you that Miss Rogers will not be saying anything."

DS Brown gave a professional smile.

"I did hear you, but Chloe is an adult and can answer that simple question for herself."

Springfield snorted. "Well, my instructions are clear and she has been advised not to say a word."

DS Brown shook his head but continued.

"Okay then, Mr Springfield, for the purpose of this part of the interview, I will read Chloe's prepared statement so that it's recorded, then this part of the interview will be concluded. Chloe will go back to her cell, so that we can go away and consider the contents of this document."

He picked up the piece of paper and read it aloud.

"I am Chloe Rogers. This is a statement of truth. I have no knowledge of nor am I involved in any way of conspiring

to murder Saemira Ruçi and George Mason. I have not leaked any information to any criminals and I do not know Besnik Domi. I have not assisted him in any way. I do know this man's name because he was involved in a criminal investigation by Devon & Cornwall Police. I am a civilian investigator where part of my lawful duties included having access to information about this man, as his name was on numerous intelligence briefings that I, and many other officers, had lawful access to. I did not pass any of this information to anyone who should not have access to it. I haven't done any of the things you've alleged. You have the wrong person."

DS Brown paused and looked at Chloe, but she simply stared at the table, her arms folded, so he continued reading out loud.

"In relation to the money: I have no knowledge of this money. It is not mine. I was sitting in my car in McDonald's car park in Long Rock with my boyfriend, Janusz Broź. We were waiting for his friends because we were going to the Peak Fitness gym where I am a member. I don't know their full names because they were just introduced to me as Aleksy and Emil. They have helped me at the gym, and have 'spotted' for me several times since. Sometimes we have a coffee or a burger afterwards. We usually meet at McDonald's car park then drive in our respective vehicles to the gym together. When I was waiting for them, a car, whose occupants I did not know, drew alongside me and threw a bag into my car which landed on my lap. Then it drove off. We were shocked. I looked into the bag and saw it contained a lot of cash. I was going to count the money, but in shock, I forgot about forensic evidence. My intention was to take it straight to the police station, and hand it in and speak to CID. Before I could do so, I was arrested."

DS Brown looked up.

"It's signed *Chloe Rogers* and has today's date." He looked directly at Chloe. "Is this a statement of truth?"

Springfield didn't look up from his notepad, grunting, "It says so, doesn't it?"

DS Brown shrugged.

"Okay, this part of the interview is terminated and Chloe will be returned to her cell while we consider the detail contained in your prepared statement."

"Is that necessary?" Springfield frowned.

"Yes, it is," said DI Morton. "We need to talk about this because we planned our interview before we were made aware of Chloe's statement."

Chloe looked less assured now as she stared at Springfield wide-eyed.

He put his finger to his lips and shook his head.

DI Morton turned off the recorder and DS Brown gathered up the file of papers as they prepared to leave the interview room.

Rego knew that the last piece of phased disclosure would be the set of statements from witnesses at Chloe's gym, and fingerprint evidence from the cash and envelope. The DNA evidence would come later, if necessary.

He leaned towards the one-way glass dividing them, staring at Chloe, willing her to talk.

CHAPTER 19

As the two detectives stood up to leave, Springfield gave a reptilian grimace which may or may not have been a smile, satisfied that he'd won the opening gambit.

"I'm quite happy to wait here, Detective Inspector Morton. It would be far more convenient and comfortable," he said expansively, settling his backside more comfortably in his seat as if he were in Costa not a custody suite.

Morton frowned but it was his sergeant who replied.

"I'm sure it would be, Mr Springfield," said DS Brown, completely unmoved. "But custody blocks are busy places and this room will be required, so Chloe *is* going back to her cell. And it's up to you if you decide to wait for her or return to the comforts of your office."

Springfield looked annoyed.

"In that case, it would probably be more convenient if I waited in your canteen where I can get a drink. Other officers have obliged me previously," and he stood up as if his request was bound to be granted.

DS Brown shook his head.

"Again, sorry to disappoint you. We'll happily provide you with a hot drink, but you would have to wait in the public area."

DI Morton took over smoothly.

"This is a very busy working police station where sensitive matters may be discussed, so that option for any legal representative stops today. And while this recording continues, I can perhaps provide you with a bit more disclosure for Chloe to consider ... while you wait in your cell."

This got Chloe's attention, her worried gaze darting between DI Morton and DS Brown.

"Firstly," Morton continued, "your home is being searched under the provisions of section 18 of PACE; your car has been seized and will also be searched; we have already identified a gym locker key on your car keys and this has been searched with the consent of the owners of the gym. We have recovered a pay-as-you-go phone, with three SIM cards, evidence of internet banking, and some Devon & Cornwall Police intelligence reports."

Chloe's face drained of any remaining colour.

"Further, we have seized the CCTV covering the gym locker area, where we will establish if you have sole control over it or if it's being used as a dead-drop. I can also tell you that the occupants of the car seen to deliver the money to you have been arrested by our law enforcement partners. It's our understanding that there is some technical equipment in the car which may have captured conversations. Your former boyfriend PC James Smith is being interviewed under caution to establish if he has had any involvement. We will be looking at any searches both of you have made on our intelligence systems. From your entry fob, we know the times and dates you have entered any Devon & Cornwall Police establishment on- and off-duty, and we will be interviewing everyone on duty during those times to establish what contact they had with you. Lastly, the whole matter has been referred to Scotland Yard's Counter Terrorist Command to establish if the enquiry is upgraded to a terrorist incident," he leaned into Chloe's space, his expression hard. "And that could mean your stay with us will be under the Terrorism legislation. Again, you will know that could be days rather than hours, although we hope we'll get the answer shortly."

DI Morton turned his attention to the lawyer.

"Hopefully, Mr Springfield, that is sufficient disclosure for Chloe to consider and instruct you on when we next interview her." He glanced down at his wristwatch. "The time is now 19:07."

Chloe looked like she had been run over by a bus and turned to Springfield who gave a brief shake of his head.

Even so, before the recording was switched off, she mumbled, "it's not a solicitor I need, it's a frickin' miracle."

Chloe was placed back in her cell, and Springfield was escorted from the custody block into the public waiting area. He'd be waiting a long time for his cup of tea.

Rego had watched the whole interview and was pleased that Morton and Brown were really going to town on Chloe. They hadn't conceded an inch, despite Springfield's best efforts to throw them off with the pre-prepared statement.

Rego leaned back in the uncomfortable chair, stretching out his cramped muscles. He'd been working the last 15 hours and didn't see his day ending anytime soon. At least Tamsyn had been debriefed and driven back to Penzance now she was no longer deemed useful to the investigation. It was probably just as well. She didn't need to know what was going on in Chloe's life, although Rego couldn't help thinking there was something karmic about it.

"A time will come in your life when some people will regret that they treated you wrongly."

PC Winston Deleon had said those words to Rego before he'd joined the police, before he'd realised that being a bad lad and hanging out with sketchy 'mates' was not a good move for a young man who wanted to make something of himself.

Rego's mind went back to that first morning at Penzance nick, both he and Tamsyn new to the station. Chloe was condescending, deeply unpleasant and unprofessional. Now the tables were turned. The game that Chloe was playing was dangerous, and it had well and truly come back to bite her.

And he thought about Besnik Domi. His circle of trusted lieutenants had been smashed today, and he no longer had Chloe as a police insider tipping him off. And if he didn't know by now, he soon would, that another two of his trusted associates had been nicked, including the gang member who'd driven him out of London.

Despite what ACC Gray had said to Rego, and despite the fact that they hadn't found Domi yet, there was satisfaction in having picked up the not-so-fab four, currently under lock and key in Newquay's custody suite.

Domi himself would be looking over his shoulder, wondering if he was next. But a cornered rat could be even more dangerous, and Rego knew that the man had already tried to murder the one person whose evidence would get him a life sentence in prison.

The threat risk against Tamsyn had gone up another

notch. Rego needed to put in place a protection plan for Tamsyn until Domi was in custody again ... and do it without ACC Gray's support. He'd have to go directly to the Chief Constable.

Having made that decision, he called Middlemoor, not expecting to be put through immediately, but then the Chief Constable was on the line.

Rego hoped his luck was changing.

"I've got five minutes before my next meeting, Robert, so make it quick," said Evans in his usual brisk tone.

"Boss, in my opinion, there's an obvious and serious risk to PC Poldhu's life."

And he filled in what had happened with Chloe Rogers and the enmity between the two women.

Chief Constable Evans listened without interrupting.

Finally, he said, "Do what you think is necessary, Robert. You have my full support. Just make sure that you document everything."

Rego was so surprised that he nearly dropped his phone. After all his tussles with ACC Gray, this seemed too good to be true.

He was just about to phone Tom Stevens to discuss their next steps, when both DI Morton and DS Brown returned to the viewing room.

"Rob, there's been a development," said DI Morton. "Chloe wants to see us urgently without her brief."

They all knew that this could be the moment they'd been waiting for.

"She's been taken from her cell to the custody officer where her request has been recorded on the sheet, and it's on audio in the cell block, as well. It appears the Custody Inspector was there when she made the request, and Chloe was explicitly informed that this was unusual as she'd previously been represented by Springfield. But she's adamant that she wants to speak with us. I haven't got a clue what it's about, although I know what we're all hoping for."

Yes, they were all hoping this case would crack wide open and she'd hand over Domi with a pretty red bow on top.

Morton gave a thin smile.

"She can stew for a bit or else it makes us look too keen to see her."

When Chloe was brought back into the interview room 45 minutes later, Rego knew that DI Morton was right: she was going to spill everything.

"Chloe, I need to remind you that you're still under caution, do you understand?"

She looked up at DI Morton, then once again into the camera pointed at her, giving Rego the eerie feeling that she knew he was watching her.

"Yes."

Chloe's gaze seemed far away as she stared down at her hands. Several of her nails had been broken from being pulled through her car's window and then handcuffed on the ground.

DI Morton leaned forward.

"Chloe, I have to remind you that you're entitled to be legally represented, and that would be in your best interests. Do you understand?"

She closed her eyes briefly then sat up straighter.

"No, I want to continue."

DI Morton didn't look happy, and Rego knew why. If she changed her story later, she could say that she hadn't been given legal advice. Morton was getting it on tape, which was definitely the smart thing to do.

Morton tapped his fingers on the desk.

"I'd like to ask you the reason why you didn't want a solicitor?"

Chloe smirked, something of her old cockiness returning.

"I don't need a solicitor if I'm going to tell you the truth, do I? It's all recorded what I'm going to say and everything that happens in this room. I'm an adult and can make my own decisions." She slumped back in her chair. "And I'm a trained investigator, aren't I?"

She lifted her eyes, her gaze dull, the sudden spark extinguished as quickly as it had come.

"I've sat on your side of the table hundreds of times, DI Morton. I'll know if I don't think a line of questioning is correct."

"Okay, Chloe," Morton replied. "And I'm going to ask if anyone has influenced your decision since your initial interview?"

"No, no one. Everyone has been ... very professional." She blinked rapidly, her composure crumbling. "I'll tell you everything and ... and I hope that ... that ... the judge will give me a reduction in sentence," she said, her voice cracking with emotion.

"It's in your best interests to tell us everything," Morton replied, "but I can't promise you anything. This is the way it works: under Section 73, Serious Organised Crime and Police Act 2005, agreements for plea and reduction in sentence are most commonly used and relate to cooperating defendants who do not benefit from immunity. This means that a defendant enters into a written agreement with the prosecutor and is then eligible to receive a reduction in sentence after entering a guilty plea."

When Chloe heard the words 'guilty plea', her head

dropped into her hands, the enormity and seriousness of the situation breaking through her final defences.

"It will be up to the judge to decide how much reduction in sentence he or she is willing to give you."

Rego knew that there was every chance that Chloe would be charged with malfeasance in a public office, and there was little doubt that she'd be going to jail: she'd provided information to a criminal gang, and that had benefitted a man wanted for murder, a known international drug dealer.

"But you will get some discount for seeing the error of your ways. So, instead of three to five years..." Morton continued.

Chloe let out a soft whimper.

"It's possible that will be reduced to two years, although I make no promises. That's it. That's the deal."

"I don't know ... I'm really scared."

"You came to us, Chloe. I think you want to do the right thing now, and we can protect you."

She took a deep, shuddering breath.

"Okay, okay. I'll tell you everything."

She wiped her sleeve across her face then started speaking, her eyes still fixed on the table.

"I started dating Jamie, PC James Smith, just before Easter. He doesn't have anything to do with this and he doesn't know anything either."

"Noted," said DI Morton.

"Okay, then," she swallowed. "About three months ago, I met Janusz at the gym, like I said. He was hot and he drove a new BMW, so when he asked me to meet him for a drink, I didn't see the harm," and she gave a strangled laugh. "He took me to these really expensive hotels and he bought me clothes and jewellery. I thought he really liked me. But he didn't want me to break it off with Jamie which seemed weird at the time, but I did anyway. I'm not a slut," she said defiantly.

No one commented on that, and eventually she continued.

"Anyway, then Janusz told me about a friend of his who'd got caught with some weed on him and could I see what they had about him on the Police National Database, if there was any soft intel. I didn't want to do it, but he kept asking me and I knew we were changing over to the Law Enforcement Database..." she paused and her pasty cheeks turned red. "I didn't think anyone would notice, or they'd think it was a computer glitch," she whispered. "That's what I was going to say if anyone asked me. But they didn't." She looked up. "I was so relieved."

DI Morton pushed a paper cup of water towards her and she took a long drink. She had to use both hands because they were shaking so badly. When it seemed as if she didn't know where or how to start again, he prompted her.

"Did Janusz ask you to do anything else?"

Chloe nodded.

"For the tape please, Chloe."

"Yes," she said, clearing her throat twice. "Yes, he asked me to look up other things."

"Such as?"

"He wanted to know which officers would be at the Old Bailey ... and ... and he wanted to know where they live."

"Did he mention any names in particular?"

She nodded.

"For the tape, Chloe."

"Yes, he wanted to know where Detective Inspector Rego lives."

DI Morton exchanged a look with DS Brown and couldn't help glancing up at the video camera. In the interviewing room, Rego's fury reached boiling point.

His children, his wife, his mother: they'd all been put in danger because Chloe was stupid and greedy and weak.

"Did you give him DI Rego's address?" Morton asked.

"Yes," she whispered. "But it was the one in Manchester so I didn't think that would matter because he wasn't there anymore. I couldn't find where he lives in Penzance. Janusz was angry, really angry. He hit me and said..." her words trembled. "He said I had to try harder or I'd be sorry. I didn't want to do it," she said again.

"Detective Inspector Rego's family live in Manchester, and because of the information you gave to your boyfriend, there was an attempt to abduct his nine-year-old daughter. Nine years old, Chloe."

"I didn't know! I didn't know what he was going to do!" she cried. "I didn't want to help Janusz anymore."

"But you did," said Morton. "Didn't you, Chloe?"

"He made me! He had me driving him around and ... and I was so scared! I didn't know what to do..."

She broke down crying.

Rego gave zero fucks for little Chloe Rogers. She'd risked his whole family to save her own neck.

When the interview resumed a few minutes later, Chloe gave them everything she knew, every tiny little grim and mundane detail of her three-month relationship with the man who claimed to be Janusz Broź.

Unfortunately, that information didn't include Domi's whereabouts, and she adamantly denied that she had either seen him, spoken to him, or heard his name mentioned by Janusz or his friends. Clearly, they hadn't fully trusted her.

But there was one other question that Rego wanted

answered, to satisfy his own curiosity if nothing else. He scribbled a note and had a PC take it to Morton in the interviewing room.

DI Morton glanced at it and nodded.

"Chloe, you also mentioned something about PC Poldhu and fish heads. What were you referring to?"

"Oh, that," she said, exhaustion making her shoulders sag. "I told Janusz that I hated her. She was always so fucking smug and superior." Chloe's lip curled as her voice became hard. "She was like that at school, as well. Anyway, Janusz said I should put something gross in Tamsyn's locker to let her know."

"To let her know what?"

Chloe shrugged.

"That anyone could get to her."

It was a chilling comment, although Rego doubted that Chloe meant it quite that way; he suspected that the real message came from the man she knew as Janusz.

"Were you involved in killing a dog that you believed belonged to PC Poldhu?" asked DI Morton.

Chloe looked startled.

"No! I wouldn't kill a dog! That's just sick!"

Rego rubbed his eyes tiredly, urging his brain to think logically and not emotionally. Chloe had been played by an expert, but he doubted she'd known what was really going on. Still, she'd known enough to ensure she received a custodial sentence.

When Rego's phone rang, he assumed it would be ACC Gray, in which case he'd ignore it, but instead it was Vikram.

"Rob, how are you, mate? Heard you got a good collar today?"

"Yes, it's looking promising. How did you hear about it?"

"Are you kidding me? I told you that the Prime Minister and Home Secretary have eyeballs on this case and anything to do with the Old Bailey bomber, so a little bit of positive news after the last few weeks has got them turning cartwheels."

Rego sighed.

"It's too soon to know what we've got; definitely too soon to think that we'll have Domi in custody in the near future." He paused. "I doubt you're calling just to give me a pat on the back."

"Well, that as well," said Vikram. "But I've heard some more chatter that Domi senior isn't happy with his little brother. We know that big brother is the brains in their operation, and Besnik is the brawn, but it looks like there's recently been a major shift in the balance of power."

"Meaning?"

"Domi junior is losing the plot. He's not stable ... if he ever was. He's furious that his bribes to the Albanian authorities didn't stop him from being extradited. And he's got a helluva lot of resentment against the people who brought him back, specifically *you*. Domi senior isn't happy with his little brother putting them in the spotlight again. I told you that there were rumours of a power struggle going on within the Hellbanianz, well, Besnik has stopped taking orders from anyone. Without his brother's restraining hand, he's starting to unravel, and he's making more impulsive decisions."

Rego was thoughtful.

"Dritan Domi is ruthless, but he's always put business first, even ahead of his family. You're saying that Besnik Domi is coming for me after failing to kidnap Maisie?

What? It's some sort of revenge for getting caught in the first place? That sounds crazy even for that bastard."

"Yeah, that's my point, Rob. Although I think it started when you banged up his big brother. Don't forget, he killed Tamsyn's dog, or thought he had. The guy is a few sandwiches short of a picnic. If there's a spectrum for psychopaths, he'd be at the top of it. You need to be careful."

CHAPTER 20

Tamsyn slid into the passenger seat of Rosie's car, shivering as the cold of the vinyl seats seeped through her jeans.

Even after Rosie started the engine and turned the heaters up full blast, it took several minutes for any warmth to come through.

"What a crazy frickin' day," said Rosie. "I still can't believe it about Chloe. We all knew she was a bitch but..." she put the car into gear and pulled out of the car park. "Did you know that the Counter Corruption Unit from Exeter interviewed Jamie, as well?"

"Yeah, I did," Tamsyn said tiredly. "But I heard that Chloe told them he didn't have anything to do with it."

"He had a lucky escape," Rosie said, shaking her head. "You don't want something like that on your record. People will always think there's no smoke without fire."

Tamsyn thought she was probably right and wondered if her own dream of progressing up the ranks was already damaged. But she didn't say any of that to Rosie.

"Sergeant Carter says that they'll interview everyone

she worked with eventually, here and at Camborne, as well as looking at every case she ever worked on."

"Wow, that's going to take weeks!"

"Months," said Rosie glumly. "Or longer."

"I still can't believe she'd be so stupid! I mean, she must have known she'd be caught. Maybe not like that, but they check to see what databases we're logging into. God, poor Jamie," said Tamsyn. "He must be worried."

"I bet it's a while before he thinks about dating again."

"If ever," said Tamsyn.

"Preach," Rosie agreed, sighing heavily.

"Do you think the magistrates will keep Chloe in custody?"

Rosie nodded.

"Oh, definitely, because she's connected to an organised crime group. The Counter Corruption Unit would be worried that she'd abscond to Albania, if she has contacts there. And the severity of the offence – she's going to get a significant custodial sentence, which is another reason that makes her a flight risk. Anyway," she said grimly, "she'll be safer in custody than on the streets."

Tamsyn wasn't so sure. Domi had proved that he had a long reach, even before he'd escaped.

"Was it exciting being part of the National Crime Agency team?" Rosie asked.

"The first four hours were so boring, just sitting there with nothing to do. H, the woman driving the car I was in, she put the seat back and went to sleep. I couldn't move my legs at all; I thought I was going to go mad. But then it all kicked off big time!"

"I'm mega jealous!" said Rosie. "You're so lucky that you've got DI Rego looking out for you."

"What's that supposed to mean?" Tamsyn bristled.

"Down, girl!" Rosie laughed, side-eyeing Tamsyn. "I wasn't implying anything, even if he is lush. I just mean that no one else got asked to be part of a surveillance and spook squad stuff! He must like you."

"It's because I could identify Domi," Tamsyn said stiffly. "That's all."

"Let's not talk about work," Rosie yawned. "God, I'm knackered. How does a takeaway, Netflix, and Häagen-Dazs salted caramel ice cream sound?"

"Perfect," Tamsyn smiled, relieved that Rosie had changed the subject. "Chinese or Indian?"

"You choose. But I get to pick the film."

As they approached Rosie's small house, the security lights blazed brightly, and they both took a few extra seconds to check behind them as well as the neighbours' driveways. Then they hurried inside out of the cold.

Rosie's house was much warmer than the 200-year-old cottage where Tamsyn had been brought up. The radiators kicked out real heat, and there were carpets and laminate flooring instead of flagstones, rugs and hot water bottles.

Tamsyn turned the radio on in the kitchen as she rummaged through a drawer for the takeaway menus, gazing longingly at the can of Rattler that Rosie had in her fridge. But she didn't want to outstay her welcome by drinking her host's only cider. She made a note on her phone to buy some more the following day then slumped on Rosie's settee to order from the Chinese at the end of the road: preferably enough chow mien and Kung Po bean curds to last for two, if not three days.

Tamsyn had just placed the order when a video-call from Joe came in. She couldn't help smiling

"Hey you! I was just thinking about you," she said.

"Dirty thoughts?" he grinned.

"Ha ha, you wish!"

"I do," he laughed. "Every friggin' day."

Tamsyn's heart fluttered.

"What are you up to?"

"Just ordering takeout from the Chinese and wondering if I've ordered enough. That's what made me think of you," she teased.

He held his hand to his chest as if in pain.

"Are you calling me a pig?"

"If the helmet fits," she replied.

He burst out laughing.

"Why'd I have to fall for a woman 300 miles away?"

"Have you?" Tamsyn asked almost shyly.

"Have I what?"

"Fallen for me?"

"Yeah, from the first time you told me to fuck off," he grinned. "I knew then you were the one for me."

Tamsyn didn't know what to say. She wasn't used to being with a man who was so open with his feelings, and she didn't know whether to trust her own emotions, but for these seconds, this precious moment stolen from time, everything was perfect.

"Miss your face," he said quietly.

"Yeah," she said lamely. "I ... why are you still in uniform? I thought you were on earlies?"

"Yeah, it's been a long day," he said, stifling a yawn. "What about you?"

She pulled a face. "It's been ... interesting."

As she told him everything about Chloe Rogers, his expression grew grim.

"You've got to be careful with that terrorist running around, Tam. Christ, I wish I could come down there!"

"I am being careful," she said. "I told you that my

grandparents have gone over to Bryher to stay with my cousins, and I'm still at Rosie's. We drive to work every day and I'll be back on desk duty."

Rosie walked into the room wearing pyjamas with little unicorns on them. They were at odds with the tough exterior she wore when she was at work.

"Is that Joe?" she asked, gesturing to the phone.

Tamsyn nodded.

"Tell him hi."

"Tell him yourself," Tamsyn smiled.

"Hi, Joe!" Rosie waved. "Tell Cal to answer his bloody phone! It's been off all day and he promised me phone sex tonight."

Joe laughed as Tamsyn lunged to grab her phone from Rosie.

Then the doorbell rang.

"That must be the Chinese I ordered," Tamsyn said, still holding the phone out of Rosie's reach.

"I'll go," Rosie called over her shoulder.

"Saved by the bell," Joe snickered.

Rosie stuck up her middle finger, which made Joe laugh.

"Have you got any pound coins for a tip?"

She was still rifling through her shoulder bag as she headed to the front door, glancing quickly through the peephole.

Joe started telling Tamsyn about his day when she heard a strange sound and a thud at the front door.

"Rosie? Rosie? Hang on a minute, Joe…"

Tamsyn walked into the hallway and gasped.

The front door was wide open and Rosie was lying on her back, blood spilling from a gash across her neck. The unicorn pyjamas were dyed red.

Tamsyn dropped the phone as she skidded in Rosie's blood, clasping her hands around her friend's neck, trying to staunch the blood as it pumped from the wound, ever more slowly.

"No!" Tamsyn screamed. "No!"

A light breeze made the blue and white police tape flutter. When Rego arrived, it was already strung across the front of Rosie's house, and the delivery boy from the Chinese takeaway was being treated for shock by paramedics.

Jasmine, her name was Jasmine Flowers. Rego had seen her around Penzance station; one of those people who always seemed upbeat and made being in the job a little easier.

He showed his ID to the officer with the scene log and stepped out of his car, cramming his six-foot frame into a fresh forensic suit from the go-bag in his boot.

Crime scene officers were on their hands and knees crawling across the driveway, the thin drizzle making the work even more miserable. Rego doubted that there would be much of forensic significance to find, but they had to look.

He recognised Tamsyn's beat up Fiat parked on the road nearby but he couldn't see her. He'd view the crime scene first then go and find her.

Lights still blazed in the small new-build house, and the front door was wide open but screened from any reporters or members of the public. No one needed to see this, especially not Rosie's family. Rego had checked her file and saw that she had a younger sister who was the same age as

Maisie. The girl's name was Karenza, and she was now an only child.

Looking at the file, it struck him how alike Rosie and Tamsyn were in looks and build. He could picture the assailant seeing two young blonde women enter the house, then wait a few minutes before ringing the bell. Maybe he'd waited for them to be more relaxed, off-guard; maybe a neighbour coming home from work had made him cautious; or maybe he'd followed them from the nick and had parked his car nearby. All those scenarios were possible.

Rosie's body had already been removed and Rego was thankful for small mercies.

He stepped past the screen, his face impassive as he stared down at the dark blood pooled in the hallway.

"Anything?" he asked the nearest tech working in the entrance.

The man shook his head.

"Nothing so far," he said. "The bastard."

Rego nodded. "We'll get him."

The technician turned away, neither agreeing nor disagreeing.

Rego poked his head into the lounge, studying the pile of presents under Rosie's Christmas tree, presents that she would now never give to her friends or family, presents she would never open herself. The small sofa was crowded with cushions and a thick blanket. The whole house was warm and feminine, and Rego had the strong sense of a life suspended, as if someone had pressed the *pause* button, and any second Rosie would walk back in and re-start her life.

He could hear Christmas music still playing from the radio in the kitchen, and he wished someone would turn it off.

He'd seen enough. Abruptly, he left the small house,

peeling off his forensic suit and dumping it in the black bin bag provided by the crime scene techs.

Two senior officers had arrived while Rego had been inside. The murder of one of their own deserved nothing less, but Rego was relieved that it wasn't ACC Gray. He would have struggled not to tell him what he thought of him when his own emotions were so worn down.

Instead, he saw Detective Chief Superintendent Nathan Richards talking to ACC Sue Nash. She was a new hire, only weeks in the job, and an unknown quantity as far as Rego was concerned, although he'd heard good things about her. DCS Richards he knew only slightly better, but liked him and respected him.

"Rego," said DCS Richards, shaking his hand. "It's a bad business. Have you met ACC Nash?"

"No, I haven't. Good to meet you, ma'am."

"Not how I'd hoped to meet you, Robert," she said, offering her hand. "I'm not here to interfere, but if there's anything you need, keep me updated daily. Anything of significance, my phone is on any time of the day or night."

"Thank you, ma'am."

"What do we know so far? Any leads?"

"Too early to say, ma'am."

"Of course. I've already contacted Dr Manners, the pathologist. We'll get the *post mortem* fast-tracked, top of the list."

She paused, knowing that there was nothing she could do to help PC Rosie Flowers now, but her family would be another matter. Speeding up the *post mortem* was one small thing that they could do. She glanced down at her watch.

"Let me know when you're seeing the family, I want to come with you."

"Thank you, ma'am."

"Anything to add, Nathan?"

DCS Richards turned to Rego.

"Do you need anything else? Any extra resources?"

"I don't think so, sir, ma'am, not at this point."

"Well, keep us informed," said ACC Nash. "We'll let you get on."

As they walked away, Rego overheard them discussing the press release that would need to go out.

He watched them leave, then went to find Tamsyn.

She was sitting alone in the back of an ambulance, a blanket around her shoulders, shadows under her eyes and in the hollows of her cheeks. Her clothes were stiff with blood and there was a dark smear across her cheek.

Rego felt renewed fury at the way this case had been handled from the start. This *must* be connected to Domi, it *must* be; he just had to prove it.

"Tamsyn, how're you doing?"

She blinked several times before she seemed to understand his words.

"I didn't even see him." Her voice was hesitant, haunted. "It was supposed to be me, wasn't it?"

Rego looked at her thoughtfully.

"We're keeping an open mind. There have been several robberies and a mugging in the area..."

Her eyes shot up to his as she blinked in disbelief.

"You don't believe that, do you, sir?"

He shook his head.

"No, I don't."

He climbed into the ambulance and sat facing her.

"Look, I think you should go to your grandparents on Bryher."

"And put them in danger, the way I did Rosie?"

Her voice hardened, almost a snarl, like a dog who mistrusts you and is getting ready to bite.

"I can contact the Protected Persons Service instead if you prefer, but you said that Bryher is a small island where a stranger will stand out."

She wouldn't look at him.

"You are *not* responsible for Rosie's death, Tamsyn. The man who murdered her is responsible."

"Besnik Domi."

"Or someone Domi sent, yes."

"Why won't anyone believe it then?" she asked, her voice rising in anger.

"I'm dealing with that issue," Rego said, being economical with the truth. "But I can't tell you everything, you know that. Look, can you get over to the Scillies? I'll contact the island nick on St Mary's; they'll help you. When is the next *Scillonian* sailing?"

"March," she said dully.

"What?"

She ran her fingers through her tangled hair, giving up when the knots defeated her, and let out a long sigh.

"The ferry is seasonal. It's flat-bottomed, so it's not good in winter with the big swells because it rolls too much and they have to wash vomit off the deck."

"Damn," he said softly. "I thought we might be able to avoid a paper trail that way. It won't be possible if you're catching a flight, but..."

"I can still sail there," she said tiredly.

"On your grandfather's boat? I thought that's how he'd got there himself?"

She gave him a look that said he didn't know what he was talking about.

"For a punt like Grandad's to get to the off-islands,

you'd need a break in the weather and flat calm for a couple of days. But we've had all these weather-systems coming in, so that's not going to happen anytime soon."

"What did you have in mind then?"

She shrugged.

"I could ask one of the local trawlermen to drop me over there." Her mouth twisted. "What about Rosie's funeral?" She stumbled over the word. "I don't want to miss it. I can't miss it."

"I don't know if it'll be before Christmas now."

"Oh, yeah. Christmas."

She looked down.

"Tamsyn," Rego said gently. "I know this is hard, but we *will* get him. We caught him before and we'll catch him again."

"Maybe," she said, her voice distant. "But who else will get killed before that happens?" She met his gaze. "What about your family, sir? I heard he went after Maisie."

Rego's lips thinned.

"Yes, one of his minions. I've sent them all to Bermuda."

"An island," she said, nodding to herself. "Like Bryher."

"Well, a bit bigger than Bryher and a lot sunnier, but yes."

"Why? What makes you think they'll be safe there?"

He pursed his lips, not wanting to tell her that it was gut instinct to get them as far away as possible.

"Two reasons: they've gone to my aunt so they'll be with family. And where they're staying, my aunt knows a lot of people, so there's a built-in neighbourhood-watch network. Any shady white guys will stand out like a sore thumb."

A ghost of a smile crossed Tamsyn's lips.

"And the second reason? You said there were two reasons."

"The Hellbanianz have a long reach, but it's not infinite. They don't have penetration into the Caribbean drug markets."

That was dominated by the cartels of South America.

Tamsyn nodded but still seemed listless and disconnected, her mind elsewhere, which could be a symptom of shock, although she didn't seem disorientated.

"And we've done untold damage to Domi's network down here. Chloe Rogers has given us a lot of intel, and they're still interviewing the other three people who were arrested at the same time. We're going to break this ring, I promise."

She shrugged.

"It won't help Rosie."

"No, but bringing her murderer to justice will help her family. *This* is why we do the job, Tamsyn."

Her head drooped.

"I'm sorry. I just..."

"I know..." he regrouped quickly. "Look, there's still an all-ports alert out on Domi, so getting a flight to the islands will be nearly impossible for him, and I've personally contacted the Port Authority at St Mary's so they'll be scrutinising every yacht, boat, ship, ocean liner, paddle-steamer and canoe in the area."

"Yeah, I guess."

"Good. Because I want you to leave as soon as you can."

"There's only two more days of the neap tides," she said.

Rego nodded. He'd been in Cornwall long enough to know what that meant: the two weeks a month when small fishing boats went to sea, the time of the month when there was the least difference between high tides and low tides and therefore less volume of water moving about which could damage fishing gear.

"Then you'd better get going."

He gave her over to the care of DS Stevens.

"Tom, take her wherever she says," said Rego. "And get an initial account from her." He turned to Tamsyn. "I'll arrange for Sergeant Hutton from the island police to take your statement. That'll be a more detailed account: what you've done during the day, if you saw anyone, noticed anyone unusual; all the events leading up to this. I know you're still in shock," he said gently. "So, you need to think about this rather than rushing into it. But let's keep it between you, me, and Sergeant Hutton, okay?"

He glanced towards Stevens.

"Tamsyn will tell you where to go."

Stevens nodded, his expression bleak as he escorted Tamsyn away from the scene. She cast one long look over her shoulder, meeting Rego's eyes, then her gaze dropped to the ground again.

Rego watched them drive away, Tamsyn too quiet and too still, feeling like he'd failed her and Rosie.

His thoughts darkened as he remembered all the times he'd try to get ACC Gray to engage with how dangerous and volatile Domi was, and the violence of which he was capable. He blamed Gray for undermining him and underestimating the threat Domi posed.

And he blamed himself.

I should have done more. I should have pushed harder.

He turned back to the crime scene: he still had a job to do.

He decided to bypass ACC Gray and go to Sue Nash, hoping she'd back up her words from earlier with actions.

And she did, but not in the way he'd imagined.

"Rob, you know that you're too close to this case, so I'm

bringing in an SIO from Camborne who has an excellent record."

"Ma'am, I'd really like to be the Senior Investigating Officer on this case because..."

She interrupted him brusquely.

"No, we don't want this investigation influenced by your involvement with Domi and everything that's happened since the Old Bailey."

"Ma'am..."

"We've got to do this case right, Rob, and we will. You have my word on it. Now go home. You're officially off the case and on leave."

She turned and walked away from him.

CHAPTER 21

Rego waited until ACC Nash was out of sight. The SIO from Camborne hadn't yet arrived, so he'd continue to work the case until she did.

He went to speak to the officer who held the scene log, noting comings and goings.

"Who's the PolSA?" he asked.

"PC Teague, sir."

The officer pointed towards a short brunette who was the designated Police Search Advisor.

"Thanks."

Rego introduced himself and asked her to run through what she'd already actioned.

"Uniform are on door-to-door; we haven't located any CCTV but a lot of residents have door-bell cameras, including the victim."

She paused, her expression filled with the anger and grief he saw on all the officers' faces.

"Did you know PC Flowers?" Rego asked gently.

"Not well, but we'd met." She shrugged uncomfortably. "She was a good officer; a nice person."

Rego waited a moment to see if PC Teague wanted to say anything else.

She lifted her chin and continued with her list of actions.

"PC Flowers' door-bell cam showed a man of medium height and build, wearing dark clothing, and a hoodie hiding his face."

"White?" Rego asked.

"I'd say so, sir, yes. We'll use door cams from the neighbours to try and map his escape route. I've got a search team checking the surrounding roads and lifting drain covers in case he got rid of the knife. PC Flowers' phone and laptop have been sent to the IT techs to see if there were any online threats from boyfriends or ex-boyfriends. PC Poldhu told me that Rosie ... that the victim ... that she'd recently started seeing a firearms officer from the Met, Calvin Adade, so his whereabouts should be straightforward to ascertain. The neighbours are being interviewed and then we'll work outwards." She glanced at Rego. "PC Flowers' parents have been notified and they've been assigned a dedicated family liaison officer."

"Is the family local?"

"Yes, sir. They're from Pendeen, just a few miles away."

"Okay, I'll speak to them as soon as possible, and we'll probably have a press conference asking if anyone has seen anything suspicious, or got anything on dash cam footage. Has the HOLMES incident room been set up?"

"I was told they're doing that at Camborne, sir. They're pulling in staff from all over the county."

Rego nodded.

"Right, I'll let you get on, PC Teague. Thank you."

She hadn't mentioned the South West Regional Organised Crime Unit, but Rego was determined that all stops would be pulled out for PC Rosie Flowers, and ACC Gray could go fuck himself.

Rego's phone rang. Speak of the devil...

"Ah, Mr Rego, it's ACC Gray."

The familiar, patronising tone came loud and clear over Rego's mobile.

Rego's eyes rolled back, and his heart sank, as if every part of his body was trying to shrink away from the Assistant Chief Cockwomble and his irritating, nasal voice. This conversation was just what he didn't need right now.

"Yes, sir, I think I know why you're calling."

"I thought you might. I'm not happy that you didn't respond to my earlier message."

"I'm at PC Flowers' house now. Scene of Crime techs are here and..."

"Who is PC Flowers?" ACC Gray interrupted testily. "I'm talking about the business from this morning."

"The young officer who's been murdered, sir!" said Rego, his voice rising with disbelief.

There was a long pause and Rego sensed that Gray was scrambling to retain his dignity and find the correct script.

"Yes, of course. A tragic loss and a terrible situation, losing a young officer this way."

"I strongly suspect she was killed by Besnik Domi or one of his gang members," said Rego, "which means that..."

Gray interrupted again.

"You seem to see conspiracies everywhere, Rego, but it's clear to me that she was simply in the wrong place at the wrong time. We know that there's been a spate of robberies in this area, and on one occasion, a woman was followed home and mugged at her front door."

"But, sir! PC Poldhu was living here with..."

"Poldhu again!" Gray snapped impatiently. "You're

obsessed with this case, Rego. You've lost all perspective and I'm considering replacing you. I'm seriously questioning your judgement."

Rego's jaw was clenched so hard, he was in danger of cracking a tooth. How could this idiot be so blinkered? He was sick of senior managers who hadn't earned their stripes on the streets.

But before Rego had a chance to speak or make the fool see reason, ACC Gray was talking again.

"I need to see you at the earliest opportunity, Rego, for a debrief about this morning's complete fuckup."

"Do I need to put a book down my trousers for a spanking, sir?"

"Stop being flippant!" ACC Gray bleated. "You've dug a big hole for yourself already. My advice is to stop digging and get over here to see me."

Rego pressed the red 'end' button on his phone without another word, sticking his middle finger up at the device for good measure. It was unprofessional and childish, but it made him feel a bit better.

Rego knew his summoning to see Gray at HQ, aka 'the dream factory', was about the misidentification of the man who was going by the name of Janusz Broź, and his subsequent arrest. He knew that Gray wasn't going to congratulate him; more likely he'd be getting a verbal beatdown.

Rego always knew that making dynamic decisions on the hoof carried risks, but better to make a decision than sit twiddling your thumbs, and not make one. No officer had the benefit of knowing the end result beforehand, and then analysing what should happen. Did Gray really think that Rego and the team had wanted to arrest the wrong man?

Besides, it was a good collar, and when it came to intel, pretty damn close to winning the lottery.

As a kid, Rego had watched re-runs of TV programmes like *The Sweeney*. What he'd give for a DCI like Frank Haskins now. No matter what Regan and Carter did, Haskins always had their backs, and was the buffer between the sharp end of policing and Scotland Yard.

Although to be fair, Rego's immediate boss, DCI Finch, was a decent bloke, but even he had to answer to a muppet like ACC Gray.

Unlike his name, the man saw policing matters in black and white, with all answers to all problems being contained in *Blackstone's Police* manuals, the only manuals endorsed by the College of Policing. He seemed unable to make any sort of decision in the grey areas which occurred in every investigation. Instead, he sat on the fence, let someone else make a decision, then jumped on the back of the best one. Rego doubted that Gray had ever had a 'fuck it' moment, one of those 'shit or bust, let's go with my gut, let's take a risk' moments: hadn't had them and didn't understand them.

When Rego had been a young, wet-behind-the-ears copper, he'd learned his trade from all the old sweats who had thirty-plus years of experience apiece. But the implementation of police regulation A19 in March 2011 had bollocksed the police service big time. The newspapers had dubbed them 'the austerity years', but government cutbacks had led to the sudden retirement of thousands of very experienced police officers, right up to the rank of Superintendent, all at the stroke of a pen, all just to save a few quid.

Fast forward to the tail end of 2024 and millions were being spent on recruitment, but there were as many officers leaving as joining, and retention was crap. A lot of young officers just wanted a cheap way to earn a degree, and Rego couldn't blame them. No, he blamed the politicians: you reap what you sow.

Two hours later, having clocked up a lot of miles in the last 16 hours, Rego was standing outside Gray's office making small talk with his Personal Assistant who looked flustered.

Rego was beyond pissed off that the man was keeping him waiting while there was the murder of an officer to investigate.

When the PA's phone finally rang, she glanced up at Rego with something like relief.

"I'll send him in now."

Gray didn't even glance up from his desk as he barked, "Come in and sit down."

After half a minute had passed in silence, Gray looked up at Rego.

"Another gargantuan cockup on your part, which I have to explain away, and I hear that young Poldhu was with you," he sneered, "again."

By now, Rego knew how Gray's mind worked, so he knew what was coming. The College of Policing approach went straight out of the window. Instead, Gray's formula for dealing with issues was: load, fire, aim. The man regularly blasted his mouth off, then when he realised he might have made a mistake, he tried to make his decisions fit the events, then hide behind layers of bureaucracy while he waited to see which way the fall-out would go.

Rego had met other senior officers like Gray, but none quite so talented at covering their arses. Was the man made of Teflon?

Rego managed to stay professional instead of saying

what he thought of Gray. He simply described all the circumstances leading up to the 'strike' by the NCA team in some detail.

"I have to support PC Poldhu, sir. She was there at the request of the NCA to identify Domi, and she didn't think it was him. She was right and I was wrong. But there is a massive plus here. We've identified and arrested a corrupt officer whose damage to Devon & Cornwall Police has yet to be established."

Gray leaned back in his chair and steepled his fingers.

"The problem with you, Inspector, is your thought process. You might think it's tactical, but I would call it cavalier; you consistently fail to consider the bigger picture. My operational approach to this would have been strategic. All you have done is to open up a media frenzy where we'll have every major news organisation camped outside demanding an explanation. What you should have done was to observe the woman, what's her name? Yes, Charlotte Rogers..."

Rego interrupted.

"Chloe Rogers, sir."

"The point is, you should have followed her home, then waited for her to turn up at work the following day and arrest her then. A softly-softly approach would have meant no fuss, no press, enabling us to keep it all in-house until the investigation process was complete. But no, you blundered in, as usual, and now it's up to me and the Chief to sort the shit out."

He glared at Rego.

"You should be focussing on catching the perpetrator of the opportunistic attacks that led to the death of a young officer. The women of West Cornwall need to know that we're taking this seriously. Now, I have to go and speak to the press about it." He shuffled the papers on his desk. "That's all."

Rego stood swiftly without saying a word, but inside, he was seething. Although as far as Gray could tell, Rego had taken the dressing down without blinking, which had annoyed the Assistant Chief Constable even more.

There was no point to any of the meeting, except for Gray to throw his weight around. Rego hadn't even bothered to point out that the male suspect at McDonald's had been armed with a vicious-looking knife.

What a fucking waste of time.

Rego needed coffee after an 18-hour day. Lots of coffee. And cake. Any sort of food, but preferably cake.

He headed to the canteen to calm down. He hadn't spent much time at HQ since his arrival, so he knew very few officers. At least that meant he could sit and contemplate his next steps in solitude.

Rego sat in the corner on his own, with a mug of strong black coffee and a slice of double-chocolate cake the size of a brick.

He was reading a text from Tamsyn to say that she'd be able to get one of her grandfather's friends to take her to Bryher in a few hours, and that she'd be safe at the harbour with him until then. So, he didn't notice that the canteen door had opened or who was walking towards him.

Heads swivelled as the Chief Constable walked through the room, and every conversation stopped, underlining how unusual it was to see the top man down with the rank and file.

The Chief strode towards him and all Rego could think was that Gray had dobbed him in and he was heading for another smackdown.

Then the Chief smiled.

"Ah, you're still here, Rob, I'm glad I've caught you. Can I have a quick word in my office? I'm sorry to disturb you, I know it's been a long day. Please do bring your coffee and cake with you ... in fact, that cake looks good. I think I'll have a slice myself as we're celebrating."

He strode over to the serving hatch and was supplied immediately.

Somewhat bemused, Rego followed the Chief back to his very plush office. Waiting for them was the Police and Crime Commissioner, a press officer, and the Chief's staff officer, all seated on comfy chairs around a low coffee table.

"Have ACC Gray join us, please, John," he said to his staff officer.

Then he smiled at the others.

"Don't mind us, this cake is excellent, isn't it, Rego?"

Rego wondered if he should tell the Chief that he had chocolate on his chin, but decided to keep his mouth shut. For once.

ACC Gray stalked into the office, glaring at Rego in confusion.

The Chief continued.

"Rob, I must congratulate you and your team for the tremendous work you've done in identifying and arresting a corrupt member of staff, a civilian investigator, correct?"

"Yes, sir."

"Exactly the right call! It'll enable us to demonstrate that we actively investigate corruption and deal with it immediately."

He beamed at everyone in the room.

"This is huge for us. We can go to town with a press release, and if there's sufficient interest, we can call a press conference and broadcast that corruption will not be tolerated. The Police and Crime Commissioners are over the moon, and so am I! This dynamic arrest sends out a significant message to all our staff that if you're corrupt, there's nowhere to hide. I'm sure that we'll be seeing some very positive messages on social media once we release footage of the arrest. I'm going to ask ACC Gray to put together a press briefing which will be released as soon as we can." Then he frowned. "Of course, there's the terrible news of the murder of a young officer. So, it'll be very welcome to have some good news, as well."

Rego inhaled sharply, internally modifying his response.

"Thank you, sir. I know you'll have considered this, but perhaps hold back on the press release until at least any house searches have been completed. We don't want anyone from the crime group clearing up following the arrests."

"Yes, of course."

ACC Gray cleared his throat.

"Ah, I've already sent out a press release, Stephen. We needed to get ahead of the story."

Rego clamped his mouth shut to stop the words he was dying to say.

The Chief frowned, then moved the conversation on without commenting.

"These Albanians appear to have been relying on intelligence from Rogers, so with her out of the picture, we're part way to cutting off the snake's head; we're actually on the front foot now."

He turned to ACC Gray with an assessing look.

"I know you managed to speak with Rob before me, so you got in first to congratulate him. You always were quick off the mark."

A muscle twitched behind Gray's left eye, but otherwise, he was the picture of composure.

"Yes, sir," he said smoothly. "I knew the significance of this arrest and wanted to be the first to speak with ... Rob."

Rego was enjoying having a grandstand view while Gray squirmed. The man was a bare-faced liar with the survival instincts of a rat.

"Yes, sir," Rego couldn't help saying, "the ACC and I had a meaningful chat, and I'm pleased that a corrupt member of staff has been nicked ... but the hard work starts now. And I must add, sir, that it's my belief that the murder of PC Flowers is linked to Domi."

"Oh?" said the Chief, frowning at Gray. "What evidence is there for that and why haven't I been told about it?"

"Because there is no evidence!" Gray said at the same time as Rego spoke over him.

"Circumstantial evidence, but my instincts tell me it's connected. There are too many coincidences otherwise."

"You think this is connected with the conversation we had earlier?" the Chief asked, causing Gray's eyes to narrow further as he stared at Rego. "Tell me more."

So, Rego did.

He'd given up trying to convince ACC Gray that Rosie's attack was the work of Domi. The man refused to see what was obvious to Rego, proving that he was as stubborn as he was stupid.

Rego had lost any respect he might have had for the pompous dickhead some time ago, but now Gray was risking lives, just so he could prove Rego wrong.

The Chief, however, was listening.

CHAPTER 22

Only five of the islands that made up the Isles of Scilly were inhabited, and Bryher was one of the smallest: one mile north to south, half a mile east to west, and fewer than a hundred souls living there all year round. It was ringed by hills and fringed by narrow inlets and sandy beaches, climate change threatening to swamp parts of the island forever. Some archaeologists thought the 140 islands that made up the Isles of Scilly might have been a single landmass in pre-Roman times, but the sea was slowly reclaiming the land.

Bryher had a hotel, a pub, and a shop with a post office: one church, two quays, a growing number of Airbnbs, and countless shipwrecks at Hell Bay, full fathom five.

Three days before Christmas and an hour after highwater, Tamsyn arrived at Church Quay.

The four-hour voyage had seemed longer, and even though one of the beam trawler's crew had offered her his cot-side bunk, she hadn't slept because although she'd closed her eyes, horrific images kept her wide awake.

The seas had grown wilder, and the boat had dipped, rolled and plunged as it chugged through the water.

When she finally arrived at Bryher, she was exhausted, angry, depressed and worried. With too many volatile emotions fighting for space inside her, she was sick at heart and overwhelmed. The stench of fish and diesel didn't help, even though she'd grown up with both.

She thanked the trawlerman for going out of his way to bring her to Bryher.

He waved away her thanks and nodded toward the west.

"Storm's coming sou'-sou'-west. Regards to Ozzie."

"I'll tell him. Thank you for everything. Fair winds!"

He grunted.

"Smooth seas never made a skilled sailor."

Tamsyn smiled and scrambled from the trawler to the quay, waving goodbye as the boat put out to sea again.

There was no one to meet her because no one was expecting her. Even if she'd tried to let her family know that she was coming, mobile reception was spotty on the island, especially in stormy weather, and if you wanted a good signal, your best bet was to climb to the top of a hill. The island did have broadband, with free WiFi at the pub, hotel and shop, although that wasn't completely reliable either. Besides, neither of her grandparents owned a Smartphone.

Electricity came via an undersea cable from the mainland but a few years earlier that had failed, leaving the small population reliant on generators for nearly two weeks until it could be repaired.

Islanders were a tough, self-reliant breed.

Tamsyn felt strange being alone after having been so watched over, ever since the bomb at the Old Bailey. She wanted to enjoy the peace and quiet but it had come at too high a price.

Rosie.

Rosie who had been kind to her on her first day.

Rosie who had laughed and teased, shared drinks and jokes, and had danced herself dizzy.

Rosie who had opened her home to Tamsyn.

Rosie who had her whole life ahead of her.

Tamsyn's brain told her that only the murderer was responsible for stealing the life Rosie should have had, but it didn't feel like that. She felt guilty, she felt dirty, as if she could still feel the stickiness of Rosie's blood on her hands and clothes.

She closed her eyes, pushing the images away. She had to trust that they'd catch the man who did this ... catch him again.

Other than the lights from Church Quay, Tamsyn walked in a world full of shadows. There were no streetlights on Bryher, no roads and no cars, only the cry of gulls and the restless sea broke the silence: the island seemed to be sleeping.

It had been six years since Tamsyn was last here, but when she saw its stark beauty anew, she wondered why she'd left it so long to visit. It was wilder and harsher than Tresco, it's more manicured neighbour.

Joe would like it here. For all his London ways, he loved wide open spaces and big skies.

She'd spoken to him briefly since ... since...

No, I won't think about it.

Joe had been shocked and afraid for her, announcing he'd drive from London to be with her; he'd abandon his post and his duty to be with her.

She'd told him no. No, no, no. She wouldn't be so selfish; she wouldn't let him do that.

He'd begged, he'd pleaded, he'd tried to order her, but she'd told him she was going away, and that she'd be safe.

"I'll see you in the New Year," she'd said. "After... after..."

He'd tried to argue.

"Calvin will need you," she'd said, and that had silenced him.

Cal and Rosie, Rosie and Cal...

I won't think about it.

She walked slowly, her footsteps crunching on the rough track that led to her cousin's cottage. She wasn't close to Edern and Jago, barely knew them from their brief and awkward annual trips to Penzance. Other than the time Jago had appendicitis, father and son rarely visited the mainland.

Tamsyn's grandmother phoned them on their birthdays, but they were always busy. During the summer, Edern and Jago took tourists out on their boat, cleaned holiday cottages, mowed lawns and did gardening, and Jago took a few shifts in the pub in the evenings, as well; during the winter, they did repair work and odd jobs, anything to make a penny and save a pound.

Edern was the son of Ozzie Poldhu's brother who'd died from a heart attack years before Tamsyn was born. Edern had married young, divorced young, and his son, Jago, who was 15 years older than Tamsyn had chosen to stay with him. Both men were useless at keeping in touch, so it was left to Tamsyn to put the odd post in the family WhatsApp group, and occasionally Edern or Jago would respond.

Occasionally.

Reception was poor.

That was the excuse she'd use, too. Tamsyn hadn't called her grandparents because she didn't have it in her to tell them that Rosie was dead. Not there and then. Not like that, not when Rosie's blood was on her clothes. Although her jeans and jumper were evidence now and had been taken away by forensics techs. Again.

She cursed the tears that threatened, angrily wiping them away and taking a steadying breath. But the tears came faster: tears of regret and rage, tears of loss and love, darkened by promises of retribution and revenge.

Tamsyn stared up at the endless skies as the stars winked out one by one with the coming of dawn. Maybe if she looked long enough, she'd see a shooting star and seal the promise she'd made.

Down at the quay below, she heard the unmistakeable sound of a diesel engine, and knew that morning had come and the island was waking up.

Her moment of weakness was over. No one had seen her, no one had heard her, so maybe she hadn't broken down on one of the longest nights of the year.

She took a moment to get her bearings although not much had changed in six years. Her cousins shared a cottage two minutes from Church Quay, and Jago was building his own place where their old garage used to be.

She turned and looked behind her where the sun was still below the horizon, painting the clouds a deep coral.

Slowly, feeling old beyond her years, she trudged up the slope behind the bakery to her cousin's cottage. As she approached the door, lights appeared in the upstairs rooms, and she heard the soft sound of water rushing through old pipes.

She waited until she could hear the heavy tread of her

grandfather coming down the stairs before knocking on the door.

His eyes were narrowed with suspicion when he opened the door a crack, but widened quickly as he took in her careworn expression.

"Rosie's dead."

She hadn't planned to start like that, but the words tumbled out as he drew her inside, his blue eyes darting toward the empty path behind her.

Morwenna charged down the stairs at the sound of Tamsyn's voice, dancing around her ankles and demanding to be picked up.

The simple joy and pure love of the small dog brought tears to Tamsyn's eyes yet again, tears that she was fighting so hard to keep at bay.

Ozzie ushered her into the kitchen, pushing a mug of tea toward her, and when her grandmother rushed down the stairs followed by her two Poldhu cousins, Tamsyn told her story again, with Morwenna refusing to leave her lap as the tea cooled in front of her.

Her cousins swapped dubious glances, but when she told them with faltering words how she'd tried to stop the blood leaving Rosie's body, they grew still, watching her face and hanging on every syllable.

"Are 'em coming after you?"

Edern asked the question they all wanted answered.

"I don't know," she said quietly. "But I think so, yes."

"Are 'em coming here?"

Tamsyn looked up. "I don't see how Domi could know I was here. Only my boss knows where I am, Detective Inspector Rego."

"And who would 'ee tell?"

Tamsyn started to deny that Rego would tell anyone anything, but she thought of his last words.

"He was going to contact the island police and the Port Authority on St Mary's."

Jago groaned. "The Main Island! Biggest bunch of gossips out there!"

"Surely they wouldn't," Tamsyn began.

But she knew how quickly news spread across the small islands. Fishermen always shared news when they met another ship on the water. Hadn't Penzance known before London that Horatio Nelson was dead after the Battle of Trafalgar?

Sometimes Tamsyn wondered at the random rubbish that ran through her mind when she was stressed.

"It's just for a few days," she said, but really, she had no idea how long her isolation would continue.

"We'll look after you, cuz," Jago said confidently.

The trawlerman had been right about the storm coming in. The brief moment of sun dissolved into grey, and the skies darkened throughout the morning. The locals took their boats to the east of the island where they would be sheltered, because when a storm raged from the west, the fetch of the waves could be 2,000 miles, crashing on the reefs and rocks of Bryher's rugged coast. Hell Bay would live up to its name, facing the full strength of the storm and becoming a boiling cauldron of spume and spray.

It was as bleak as it was beautiful, but Tamsyn struggled to keep her feet against the force of the wind, her hair flying in every direction as she helped Jago tie down tarpaulins over the building materials strewn across the site of his new house.

He laughed at her.

"Mainlanders are soft!"

Morwenna had been sent wild by the blustery weather, hurtling in all directions, turning somersaults and charging around in circles chasing her tail.

"I love it here!" Tamsyn shouted into the wind. "I love it!"

And then guilt filled her. How could she feel happy when Rosie was lying in a cooled storage drawer at Truro's mortuary?

Her smile slipped away and Jago saw her mood change.

"Come on, cuz. I'll buy you a drink at the pub. I'll introduce you to everyone so they'll know to look out for you."

"I don't want anyone approaching this man," she warned him.

He shrugged, his expression stern.

"We look after our own."

Tendrils of unease wound through her belly. Had she put the islanders in danger by coming here?

CHAPTER 23

Rego was beyond frustrated.

He'd thought that after everything Chief Constable Evans had said about the success of the NCA surveillance and subsequent arrests that he'd be open to considering a connection to the murder of PC Flowers. But instead, the Chief had backtracked, urging caution and further investigation.

Gray had been smug, insinuating that Rego was 'too tired and too closely involved' to be objective, and backing ACC Nash's appointment of a different SIO to look into Rosie's murder.

The Chief had listened and agreed with Gray, telling Rego to go on leave and be with his family.

The only consolation he had was that as he'd left the meeting, the Chief had turned to Gray with a cold expression on his face.

"Ian, can you stay behind after Rob's gone. We need to talk in private."

Even as he closed the door behind him, Rego had heard

Gray getting his arse kicked for sending out the press release before the house searches had been done.

He suspected that Gray would blame him for that, too.

Seriously disappointed with the way the meeting had gone, he'd ignored both men and driven back to Penzance to catch up on a few hours' sleep before heading into the station early the next morning to check on the current state of the investigation.

Rosie's doorbell camera footage had been forensically examined, and as Rego had been told, it showed a nondescript white male who'd concealed his face by wearing a hoodie. The only new information was that he'd worn gloves during the ten seconds it had taken for him to ring the doorbell, wait for the door to be opened, stab Rosie in the neck, and get away without anyone seeing anything. It had definitely been planned.

But there had been some progress in the investigation: door-to-door had generated more door-cam footage of a man running away and disappearing into a wooded area behind the housing estate. From there, with a bit of a climb and a scramble, he could access the playing fields of a local nursery school, and then get to the A30.

Unfortunately, there were no traffic cameras on that stretch of the road. They had no sightings, no forensics and no clues. But maybe a press conference would prompt someone to come forward with dash-cam footage. They could only hope. But even so, that wouldn't be until the following day.

Time was slipping away, and each moment gave the perpetrator more distance to run – if indeed that was his plan, which Rego doubted.

He'd also met with Rosie's parents and little sister. It was the worst part of the job, dealing with other people's grief. He hadn't even been able to let them have her body because it was part of an ongoing investigation and the *post mortem* had not yet taken place, despite ACC Nash's insistence that it was fast-tracked.

Rego's phone rang.

"I hope it's good news, Tom," he said to his sergeant, "because I could really use some."

"Ask and ye shall receive!" Stevens said happily. "One of the house searches in Saltash has turned up a Mac 10 machine pistol. And get this – it's got a broken firing pin. We'll get ballistics to check, but it's looking like the weapon used at the Old Bailey shooting."

"Hallelujah!" Rego said softly.

Surely, this new information would prove to the NCA that Tamsyn had been telling the truth about what had happened: a broken firing pin had saved her life.

"Thanks, Tom. I'm calling DCI Finch now."

Less than a minute later, Rego was talking to his immediate boss.

"Sir, house searches have found the weapon that is looking like a good match for the one used by Domi in the Old Bailey incident."

"Finally, some positive news! Good work, Rob. I'll be happy to give this news to the Superintendent and ACC Gray." He paused. "How did it go with PC Flowers' family?"

"Pretty grim," Rego said honestly.

Finch summed it up.

"You've just given the family of an officer the worst news they'll ever have. There's no good part of it, Rob. But I have to agree with you that the murder is almost certainly planned and not opportunistic. I know you think that he's likely to stay in the area, and that means we've got a bloody good chance of apprehending him. Between you and me, I think it's likely that it's linked to Domi but we have to keep an open mind. Major Crime from Camborne is dealing with it now and they'll liaise with Tom Stevens in your absence."

Rego was sure that he felt the cold, clammy touch of ACC Gray in Finch's words and the fact that the case was being taken from his hands.

"But, sir...!"

"For now," DCI Finch continued, "I want you to go to your family and enjoy your Christmas. Come back in a week refreshed and ready for the chase, because right now, there's bugger all you can do." He paused. "And orders are orders."

Once the call ended, Rego stared down at the paperwork stacked up on his desk and found he had no appetite for starting on any of it. The files would still be there when he came back.

Deciding to follow his DCI's advice to the letter, he logged out of his computer, shoved the files in a desk drawer without looking at them, locked it, then grabbed his coat.

"Right, Tom," he said to DS Stevens. "I'm heading to sunnier climes, but I want to be kept informed on progress into PC Flowers' murder, as well as the Domi case."

"Will do, boss," said Stevens, looking up as he endorsed the policy book and risk assessment that he was now temporarily in charge. "Even on Christmas Day?"

"Even then. Jack is covering Christmas Day and Jen's doing Boxing Day, right?"

"Yep, and John is on for Tom Bawcock's Eve tonight."

"I know you're speaking Cornish," Rego said with a wry smile, "so you're going to have to explain that one."

"Ah, well," said Tom, leaning back in his chair, always ready to tell a good story. "A long time ago, there was hardship and famine in Mousehole, so a rare gentleman of the name Tom Bawcock, headed out to sea to try and catch some fish so the people wouldn't starve. A great storm swept up from the west and poor ole Tom thought he would die for sure, but instead, the fish fair leaped into his nets and he came back to Mousehole a hero. They invented Stargazy Pie in his honour."

"I'm almost afraid to ask," said Rego.

"You must have seen it, boss!" said Stevens, aghast. "Boiled eggs and potatoes with pilchards baked into it, their heads sticking out of the pastry as if they're gazing up at the stars."

Rego's stomach lurched.

"Right. Good to know. And what happens in Mousehole tonight?"

"Oh, right," said Stevens with a grin. "Lantern procession and a couple of hundred Cornishmen singing sea shanties and getting pissed, not necessarily in that order. There's not usually much trouble."

"Okay, in that case, I'm off. I'll see you in a week, Tom. Merry Christmas."

"Cheers, boss. Don't forget your secret Santa!" and he pointed at the sad little CID office Christmas tree with a small pile of badly wrapped presents beneath it.

Rego found the one with his name and shoved it in his messenger bag.

"Can't wait to open that," he muttered to himself.

He'd been driving less than 20 minutes when he got a call.

"Inspector Rego, this is Hervey Jenkin from the Port Authority on St Mary's. It's probably nothing..."

Rego felt a swift sense of foreboding.

"Go on, Mr Jenkin."

"Well, as I said, it's probably nothing, we've had a lot of rough weather ... but we've been tracking a yacht out of Portugal that took cover east of St Martin's and was last seen by a couple of local fishermen passing north of Round Island Lighthouse..."

"Yes?"

"You said you were looking for anything unusual ... and now it's disappeared, sudden like: no AIS, that's the Automatic Identification System, the transponder."

Rego sucked in a breath. It had been the same thing back in March when Domi had escaped the UK by arranging for a pickup from a yacht out of Biscay.

"Have you tried to raise them on the radio?"

"Of course," said Jenkin, sounding affronted. "And so has Falmouth Coastguard, but there's been no response."

"And that isn't normally cause for concern?"

"Usually, yes. But earlier in the day, the Coastguard radioed them and the captain confirmed that he was okay and hadn't realised that the AIS was down but would seek to find the problem and rectify it. He informed the Coastguard that he was putting in to Tresco to effect repairs and would wait till the stormfront had passed over. They were last seen sailing past Gimble Porth on Tresco so it was assumed all was okay," he said defensively. "But there's been no sign of them since and they didn't make enquiries about repairs anywhere. I've called every marine mechanic on here and on the off-islands, which is why there was a delay in getting in touch with you."

"Have you informed Sergeant Hutton?"

"Yes, he knows as much as we know."

"Good, thank you. And if you could send everything you know about the yacht to Detective Sergeant Tom Stevens at Penzance police station, as well: the yacht's registration, where it had been before it disappeared, any communications at all, and any more sightings by local fishermen. Thank you, Mr Jenkin."

Rego sped around the first roundabout he came to and headed south again. His wife was going to kill him.

His first call was to the island police on St Mary's.

"Sergeant Hutton, this is DI Rego from Penzance. I believe Mr Jenkin from St Mary's Port Authority has alerted you to this mystery yacht and discussed the situation with you?"

"Yes, sir. Hervey called me this morning to say that it had disappeared from radar."

Rego was taken aback by the man's casual tone and the fact that he didn't appear to think it important.

"This morning? It's 2.30pm? Why the hell wasn't I informed earlier?"

"I didn't think..."

"Didn't think *what?*" Rego snapped. "I specifically told you to look out for this sort of unexplained event."

The sergeant fell silent.

"What time *exactly* did the yacht disappear from radar?"

"Eleven-seventeen, sir," the man replied promptly.

Three hours ago!

"And what is the maximum distance it could have sailed in three hours?"

Hutton cleared his throat.

"Anywhere up to 30 or 40 miles. Sir."

Rego swore bitterly. The yacht could have even reached the mainland by now.

"And there's no way to trace him?"

"No, sir. But there are innocent reasons that the Automatic Identification System could be lost: weak signals, spotty satellite reception, and interference can all cause gaps in AIS tracks."

This didn't feel like an innocent situation; it felt like one of the ominous coincidences Rego didn't believe in.

"And, uh, sometimes fishermen turn off their AIS to keep fishing grounds secret from competitors."

"That's not the case here though, is it?" Rego responded tersely. "I want you to call PC Poldhu immediately and give her this information. Tell her she's to stay indoors until you can reach her."

Hutton cleared his throat, a precursor to giving bad news.

"I'm afraid comms are down on some of the islands, sir, since the last storm. The mobile masts are often affected, but this time the power is out, too. They'll be down to using generators by now."

"Then how the hell am I managing to speak to you?" Rego asked, frustration evidence in his clipped tone.

"Bryher is the most westerly of the isles, the most remote, so the storms hit it hardest."

"I thought the islands had 4G!"

"They do. Most of the time."

Rego was silent, thinking of possible solutions.

"Can you raise her by radio?" he asked. "Use the VHF Marine Radio channel?"

"No, sir. That works on line-of-sight and Bryher is hilly. Besides, the winds like we have now affect the aerials."

"Then you'll have to go to her, Sergeant," Rego said shortly, losing his patience. "I'd be happier with a police presence on Bryher anyway, given the circumstances."

This time, Hutton's pause was even longer.

"Sir, there's no way we can get across to Bryher today. We don't have our own boat and have to share with the local doc if we're going off-island, but the swell is growing all the time and our craft isn't equipped for that. I'll keep trying to raise PC Poldhu; sometimes comms come and go, so it's worth trying."

"Do it now and get back to me."

"Yes, sir."

Just in case, Rego called Tamsyn's phone himself, but it went straight to voicemail. He left a message to call him immediately she received the message.

Hutton called him back as soon as he hit 'end call'.

"No luck, sir," he said. "No one can get through."

Rego grimaced.

"So, there's no way to contact PC Poldhu? Email? Carrier pigeon? Anything?"

"Not at the moment, sir."

"For God's sake! It's the 21st century! I can FaceTime my friend in Brisbane, and we've got Russian underwater drones listening to communication cables under the sea but you're telling me I can't call a number 40 miles from the Cornish coast?"

"Not at the moment, sir," Sergeant Hutton said cautiously.

"Can you get the lifeboat out to her with a message?"

"Sir, may I speak freely?"

Rego's eyebrows shot up.

"Go ahead."

"We don't know if the yacht is anything to do with the criminal you're tracking, but if it is, the lifeboat boys are all volunteers: they're trained to assist vessels in distress not approach criminals who may be armed."

It was a fair point, and one that Rego knew he should have considered.

"And anyway," Hutton continued, "unless it's a life-or-death emergency, I wouldn't want to call out the lifeboat. The seas are pretty lively now and the weather is deteriorating with fifty-knot gusts being forecast." He paused. "Even if the crims are out there, they'll be facing rough weather themselves. If they have any sense, they'll make a run for the nearest harbour."

"And where would that be?" Rego asked, his voice tight.

"Old Grimsby Quay on Tresco, sir ... or Church Quay on Bryher."

Shit.

Tamsyn would be completely blindsided. Rego rearranged his priorities rapidly.

"Thank you for being so candid, Sergeant. Keep trying every avenue of communication to get a message through to PC Poldhu and keep me updated."

Rego slammed the heel of his hand on the steering wheel, then touched the accelerator, making the powerful car leap forwards.

He'd known that there would be logistical difference between policing in Manchester and policing in Cornwall, but he'd never thought that simply being able to *talk* to an officer would be so impossible.

It crossed Rego's mind that he was doing exactly what Gray had accused him of: seeing conspiracies where none existed. There was no evidence whatsoever that the missing yacht had anything to do with Domi.

His mind whirred. He was still searching for an answer when DS Stevens phoned back.

"Boss, I just spoke to Nigel Hutton at St Mary's police station and he told me of your concerns, but I've got news."

"Yes?"

"There's been a sighting of Besnik Domi."

"Where?"

"Liverpool."

Rego was stunned.

"Liverpool? Are you sure?"

"Yes, boss. I just took a call from your friend Rick O'Donnell at the National Crime Agency: there was a sighting of Domi in Liverpool."

Rego wasn't convinced. The timing was too perfect.

Still, Gray's words rang in his ears, and he flexed his fingers on the steering wheel.

"Well ... that's good," Rego said, his tone unconvincing.

"Yes, but the source evaluation is E-grade."

Rego's expression became grim.

"Tom, I don't like it. Twice, Domi's tried to kill Tamsyn; there's this mystery yacht far too bloody close to her; and suddenly there's a sighting of Domi 300 miles away, but it's from an untested source, one grade *below* unreliable. I don't like those odds."

"I know, boss."

Rego's expression was grim.

"I need to make a call. I'll get back to you," and he rang off.

His next call was to Vikram.

"I thought you might be calling me, Rob. So, you've heard then?"

"About Domi being sighted in Liverpool, yes, but from an untested informant. Do *you* think it's credible?"

"We're trying to verify that. All I can tell you at the moment is that there's 'chatter' from Albanian authorities into MI6 suggesting that Domi is in Liverpool."

"They're sure?" Rego asked, his tone urgent.

"No, mate: I said it was 'chatter' for a reason. Look, our authorities are pulling out all the stops and connecting with anyone who might help. MI6 are actively tasking our informants to verify the intelligence. All of that has been shared with the Met and your lot. And I've got to tell you, the Met has been putting some pressure on Devon & Cornwall Police, saying that they're the lead on the investigation and not to do anything rash."

"What the hell is that supposed to mean?" Rego fumed.

"It means that they're sending staff to Merseyside to support the hunt for Domi – they're taking the intelligence seriously."

"Come on, Vik! Domi senior has put the word out that his brother is in Liverpool when he's really down here having killed one of my officers and hunting another. Are they waiting for Tamsyn to be murdered, too, before they get off their incompetent arses and *do* something?"

"Rob..."

"I'm telling you, Vik, Domi is setting us up!"

"Alright, keep your hair on! I do have one piece of intel that supports that theory..."

"Why didn't you start with that?" Rego all but yelled.

"Because," Vikram said patiently, "because I want to give you the full picture."

"Which is?"

"We've got the transcript from the probe in the Mercedes, or rather the Met did, but I've been keeping an eye on the case. Someone in the Merc mentioned a word in Albanian that was translated as 'boss' or 'leader'. You know what it's like, you never ever get a word for word transcript from a probe, and it's always very broken, with some words and even whole sentences written up as 'inaudible'..."

"I know that! So?"

"So ... sometimes the full context of a conversation is either missed or not interpreted correctly. And sometimes an Albanian interpreter might interpret a word or phrase in a different context, or it doesn't have an exact English equivalent."

"Vik! For fuck's sake! What was the word?"

"Skipper. The word was skipper. They assumed it meant 'boss' but what if it's not?"

Rego's breath caught in his throat.

"The thing is, it's a slang word in Albanian with many meanings, so we can't be sure of the context."

"It's a boat! It's a fucking boat! We need to get the Coastguard's Search and Rescue helicopter over to Bryher to evacuate the Poldhu family immediately."

"Who would authorise that, boss?" Vik asked cautiously.

Rego groaned.

"I'll speak to DCI Finch. Give me five minutes, and I'll call you back."

But Finch wouldn't authorise calling out the Coastguard's SAR helicopter.

"I'm sorry, Rob, but with a credible sighting of Domi in Liverpool..." he let the words hang there.

"You're not going to call out the Coastguard, sir?"

"No, Rob, I'm not. I'm not convinced there's a need at this point in time, and neither is ACC Gray. I want you to do what I told you an hour ago: leave it. Go on holiday, take a break, clear your head. This has been a bloody awful business and I wouldn't blame you for losing perspective."

"But, sir! ACC Nash thought that there was a credible link, and the Chief Constable said..."

"The SIO from Camborne is the lead on the murder of PC Flowers, not you: and for very good reasons which I know ACC Nash has discussed with you, Rob. No, you can't speak to her, she's gone on leave for her daughter's wedding."

"The Chief..."

"...is halfway to Chamonix as we speak; ACC Gray is holding the fort, as usual." He sighed. "It's the holidays, Rob, and you're officially on leave. So, that's the end of it. Enjoy your holiday. Merry Christmas."

Rego knew that if he pursued this, he was putting his career on the line, and not for the first time. But possibly for the last time.

Maybe he was wrong. Maybe he was losing the plot, but he needed to be sure.

And then he had a brainwave.

His next call was to the Bronze Commander at RNAS Culdrose, Sergeant Ed Bladen.

When he answered his phone immediately, Rego sent up a swift prayer of thanks.

"Rob, how are you? Is this a social call?" Bladen asked, his tone dry.

"'Fraid not, Ed. I've got a situation over on Bryher, and I need one of your helicopters to take me over there. Today. Now, if possible..."

"You want me to do *what?*" Bladen's tone was incredulous, clearly thinking that Rego wasn't playing with a full deck.

Rego ploughed on, explaining about Domi and Tamsyn and Rosie.

"Why aren't your own people on this?" Bladen asked.

It was a perfectly reasonable question, but one that Rego had hoped to avoid.

"Because my boss's boss's boss is a knob who doesn't know his arse from his elbow."

And he went on to explain the opposing theories of Domi's whereabouts.

"But I know I'm right about this, Ed..."

"You *think* you're right, Rob, but at this point, I've got to agree with your boss's boss's boss ... even if he is a knob."

"Have you never just trusted your gut, Ed?" Rego asked tightly.

There was a long pause.

"I'm sorry about the death of your officer, Rob," said Bladen, sincerity ringing in his voice. "That's never easy. And I'd like to help, but I can't authorise it, no way. These birds cost north of £14,000 an hour just to get them in the air. I'd lose my job, and probably end up in the brig."

"Ed, I need to get to Bryher. Please."

His request was met with an uncomfortably long silence.

Finally, Bladen replied.

"You're asking a lot, Rob," Bladen said honestly. "I can't authorise putting up a helo and I'd have to clear it with Captain Hall," he continued, naming the Commander of the Royal Naval Air Station base.

"My gut is telling me this mystery yacht is important; plus, it's how Besnik Domi escaped last time. It's got to be him again, Ed. It's got to be."

"You're fishing, my friend. Look," he sighed, "after what happened this summer with the Jameson situation, we owe you, I know that."

They were both silent and Rego knew that they were thinking of the Russian spy ring that Rego and Tamsyn had helped uncover at the naval base.

"Leave it with me," Bladen said at last, "and I'll see what I can do."

Rego drummed his fingers on the steering wheel as he tried Tamsyn's phone, but once again it went to voicemail. He left another message telling her about the mystery yacht and that she was to stay indoors, away from windows, and not to allow anyone in her family to answer the door.

As he approached Camborne, he made a decision to head straight to Culdrose. Maybe a face-to-face meeting would persuade Bladen to help.

The light was failing as he cut through the back lanes, his headlights finding few vehicles on the narrow roads. He could feel gusts of wind rocking the car and his concern for reaching Bryher grew.

When he reached the A394 and Bladen still hadn't called him back, the tension made his head throb and the muscles in his neck tightened minute by minute.

What the hell was he trying to prove by riding to Tamsyn's rescue? Domi was armed and he wasn't. He didn't even know for sure that it was Domi in that yacht, although it would explain why they hadn't been able to find him. The transponder being turned off and the yacht becoming invisible to radar was too much of a coincidence: it *had* to be Domi. But ACC Gray's words insinuated themselves into his mind, undermining his own confidence in himself. What if he was seeing Hellbanianz where it was just street scrotes and crises where it was coincidences?

But then he thought of PC Flowers: her murder was too calculated, too planned. The murderer hadn't hesitated, hadn't been concerned, and hadn't stopped at any other doors in the area. Nor had he been found.

If Domi was on Bryher, Tamsyn would be 40-plus miles from anyone who could help her. Unless Bladen could get Rego to the tiny island.

Rego phoned DS Tom Stevens to take his mind off the insanity he was proposing.

"Please tell me you're halfway to Exeter, boss," Stevens said as he answered the phone.

"Nope, I'm on my way to Culdrose."

He filled his DS in on the latest developments.

"Boss..." Stevens said, clearly at a loss for words. "If it is Domi, we know for a fact that he's armed with a submachine gun. Have you even got Captor spray with you?"

"I never leave home without it," Rego joked.

Even though Rego was CID and not Response, he'd never got out of the habit of keeping incapacitant spray in the boot of his car, locked in a gas box which was wired into the car's alarm.

But Stevens wasn't laughing.

"I know," Rego said, serious now, "but I can't sit on my hands and do nothing. If I can't get a ride with the fly-boys, I'm out of ideas. I just wanted to give you a heads up. I hope I'll be seeing Bladen in about 20 minutes. If not ... well, either way, I'll let you know."

"Good luck, boss."

"I'll need it."

CHAPTER 24

Ed Bladen was already shaking his head as soon as Rego walked into his office.

He wasn't alone either. Rego was surprised to see Corporal Campbell from Culdrose's Defence Serious Crime Unit. The three of them had worked together on a case of espionage last summer, albeit briefly, and the dour Scot had barely spoken a word to Rego and had zero sense of humour.

Bladen spoke immediately.

"I'm sorry, Rob. I got my backside handed to me just for making that request. Captain Hall won't go against your Assistant Chief Constable. There's no way I can get a helo for you. I'm really sorry."

It had been Rego's last stand, and he had nothing left.

There was an uncomfortable silence until the usually saturnine Corporal Campbell spoke.

"Actually, sir," he said, "I think we might be able to help after all."

Rego was surprised. He'd had the distinct impression that Campbell didn't like him.

Bladen looked equally taken aback.

"Well?"

"The Culdrose Christmas Care team are heading out shortly."

"That's today?" said Bladen, sharing a thoughtful expression with Corporal Campbell.

"What's the Christmas Care team?" Rego asked when neither man was more forthcoming.

Bladen gave a quick smile.

"Every Christmas we do a collection asking staff and civilian employees on the base to donate tins of food or dry goods that would make up a Christmas meal: Fray Bentos pies, tinned potatoes and carrots, Christmas pudding, mince pies, that sort of thing, and it goes out to families on Scilly who need a bit of help. Officially, it's a training run, but we've got 150 parcels being flown out there ... well, any minute now."

"Sixteen-hundred hours, sir," said Campbell. "We'll have to hurry. They'll be prepping the helo now."

The three men jogged from Bladen's office and jumped into Corporal Campbell's ATV, speeding over to the hangars and screeching to halt.

Rego jumped out then stumbled to a halt, blinking hard and uncertain what he was seeing. It was a surreal sight as four burly Santas loaded boxes of provisions into the Merlin Mk2, more usually deployed as an anti-submarine helicopter and armed with Stingray torpedoes. But the Mk2 could also be tasked for casualty evacuation, lifting under-slung loads, as well as search and rescue; today, it was standing in for Santa's reindeer.

The four crewmen turned to stare at Rego while Bladen explained the situation.

The biggest of the Santas was the mission commander,

who along with two pilots and an aircrewman, made up the flight team ... or Santa's little helpers, depending on your point of view.

"You sure this man is on Bryher, hunting your officer?"

Rego grimaced.

"No, I'm not sure, but I can't risk it. She'd be completely blindsided. She's 21 and only been in the job a few months. We've already lost one officer this week..."

His words died away as the aircrew stared at him, but their faces showed they knew what he was feeling.

Rego cleared his throat and looked away.

"You armed?" asked the mission commander.

"Yes."

The man nodded, clearly assuming that Rego had something that fired bullets, not just an incapacitant spray. Rego didn't bother to correct him. He'd got this far and he didn't want to give anyone a reason not to let him on the flight.

"You been on a helo before?"

The man might have been smiling, it was hard to tell behind the acrylic beard.

"Just once," Rego nodded.

He wasn't going to admit that it had been more than 15 years ago and a pleasure flight over the Grand Canyon when he and Cassie were on honeymoon.

"This won't be like any other flight you've been on," said the mission commander. "You're not even a dabber and I don't like goofers either."

Rego had no idea what a 'dabber' or a 'goofer' was, but neither sounded complimentary.

"I just..."

"Listen, Inspector Rego," said the mission commander impatiently. "We're tasked to go St Mary's, not Bryher. I don't have authorisation to touch down there and I'm not going to ask for it because the answer will be *hell no*. The windspeed is gusting 45 knots already and is forecast to increase. Yeah, this baby can handle winds up to 90mph, but that's generally considered to be pretty fucking unsafe and not something that everyone can handle. I'm not risking my crew."

Rego closed his eyes in frustration.

"But," said the mission commander, "I am willing to take you to Bryher ... providing we don't touch down."

And he looked at Rego expectantly.

"Sorry, what? Then how..."

"I'll lower you on a winch. Last and final offer."

Rego had been a copper for 17 years and was about to have the third 'fuck it' moment of his career – his second since he'd been in Cornwall.

He was doing this for the right reasons, but it was risky, very risky, possibly foolhardy, definitely dangerous.

If he didn't drown or die from a heart attack, and if Domi didn't shoot him, he'd have to explain to Cassie, and the look on her face when he let her down was scarier than anything.

"Fuck it," Rego breathed. "I'm going to crack on with it and see what shakes out of the tree."

"And you have to wear a Santa suit like the rest of us," said the mission commander, nothing in his expression showing that he might be joking.

"Now you're taking the piss!" said Rego.

"Ho! Ho! Ho!"

Minutes later, Rego was dressed in an enormous Santa suit, complete with vast, rubbery belly and itchy beard.

"Seriously, why the Santa suit?"

"Because a civvy on this flight will stand out like a sore

thumb on a hand cream commercial, but another Santa, they'll just think they counted wrong."

"Do they have black Father Christmas's in Cornwall?" he asked the young aircrewman.

"Dunno, mate. You want to be the first?"

"Jesus," said Rego. "I look like a pint of Guinness wrapped in a red duvet."

He climbed into the helicopter, was told where to sit, how to strap himself in, and to keep his mouth shut. His heart was hammering and his hands were shaking from the adrenaline.

Yeah, definitely adrenaline. Not fear.

What had seemed like a good idea at the time, now seemed like the worst idea he'd ever had, and he'd had a few of those. He fumbled a quick text full of typos to Tom Stevens, telling him what he was doing, and received a text back full of question marks and exclamation marks, which pretty much said it all.

But on the other side of the equation, there'd still been no contact with Tamsyn or anyone else on Bryher. Which meant that Rego was going ahead with his bone-headed idea.

He tucked his Santa hat in his belt and tightened the flight helmet under his chin. At least now he could hear the pilots talking.

"Yeah, it's gonna be a bit dynamic out there ... think the civvy will spew?"

Rego really wished he hadn't heard them after all.

The rotors began their wind up and were soon roaring, although it was more like feeling the noise than hearing it, and the helicopter seemed to quiver with repressed power. Rego squeezed his eyes shut and tried not to think about the single bolt that attached the rotor blades to the fuselage.

God, why didn't the Royal Navy have Chinooks anymore? Or was that the RAF? At least they had two engines and two sets of rotor blades...

The shuddering increased and Rego opened one eye as the ground fell away, not very far at first, as they hovered ten feet above the ground, then twenty, thirty...

The pilot must have received clearance from the tower, because suddenly they rose steeply and Rego hoped his stomach would join him again sometime soon.

It was only minutes later when Rego recognised the jutting peninsula of Lizard Point below and the wide, grey seas beyond, stretching out toward the blurred line of the horizon. From their cruising height, the whitecaps on the waves looked tiny, but the swell was probably twenty feet or more. Rego was very glad he wasn't in a boat on *that* sea.

The flight was short and in under 15 minutes, Rego could see the first of Scilly's islands.

A voice came through the headphones.

"Approaching St Mary's. Bryher e.t.a. three minutes: prep the winch."

All Rego could think about was not puking or pissing himself. He'd rather die than die of embarrassment.

But there was no more time for fear or recriminations because the winchman slapped him on the shoulder.

Oh, shit.

For a second, Rego was confused as the aircrewman pulled him closer, strapping Rego against him. Then relief spread through Rego when he realised that he was going to be winched down attached to someone who knew what the hell they were doing. He'd been panicking that he wouldn't be able to unhook himself from the winch, get dragged by the helicopter and make a fool of himself. Or die.

If anyone had seen it or been there to film them, they'd

have made a fortune from TikTok views: the sight of two Santas, one black, one white, arriving by helicopter on one of the most westerly of England's islands.

Rego could see the imprint of the downdraft as long grasses leaned in all directions away from the powerful rotors. But the steel cable, strong enough to lift 4000kg, was buffeted by the wind, and it felt like being on some crazy fairground ride whilst having his face thrust into another man's chest.

It was several, nauseating seconds before Rego's feet touched down and he seriously thought about copying the Pope and kissing the ground, but instead he was hustled out of his harness and had the helmet yanked off his head. Then the winchman was gone, soaring twenty feet above him.

"Thanks," Rego said to the empty air.

Then he threw up.

CHAPTER 25

> *"A good sword and a trusty hand!*
> *A merry heart and true!*
> *King James's men shall understand*
> *What Cornish lads can do!"*

Tamsyn's grandfather bellowed out the words, determined to prove to the islanders what they were missing by not sharing a Cornishman's love of the anthemic *Trelawny*. Although a good number of residents who were blow-ins from the mainland were happy to join in, the true Scillonian was not a Cornishman, and you had to be born on the islands to earn the title.

> *"And have they fixed the where and*
>   *when?*
> *And shall Trelawny die?*
> *Here's twenty thousand*
>   *Cornish men*
> *Will know the reason why!"*

Ozzie had put away several pints and was in fine voice, and the pub was filled with song as people thumped out *The Song of the Western Men*, Cornwall's unofficial national anthem. It referred to an incident that had happened some 400 years earlier when thousands of Cornishmen had threatened to march on Parliament, demanding the release of Sir John Trelawny from his imprisonment in the Tower of London. Practically, breaking news for the people singing lustily today.

It was a belief that being Cornish or from the islands, these things set a man apart, made him special. As for the *bal* maidens, back when the mines had made Cornwall an industrial land, Cornish wenches wielded sledgehammers, shattering the rocks of ore into smaller pieces. You didn't mess with a Cornishwoman either.

The singers were well oiled, and Tamsyn felt fairly sure that any minute now they'd be breaking out *What Shall We Do with the Drunken Sailor?*

Tamsyn reached for her bottle of Rattler and Jago jogged her elbow deliberately, which earned him a filthy look.

"I could plant potatoes in that frown o' yours," he said. "It's Christmas! Smiling is free, or so they tell me."

"Oh sure, because I've got nothing to worry about," she snapped.

"Oh sure," he mocked her, "because worrying makes it better."

He was right, of course.

"You ever hear from your mum?" he asked out of the blue.

Tamsyn was taken aback.

"No. Why d'you ask?"

"Well, I heard about the article in *The Sun*."

Tamsyn rolled her eyes.

"She probably did it for the money."

"Is that right?"

"I can't think of another reason. And it's definitely not because she cares about me; she hasn't been in touch."

But her curiosity was piqued and she gave Jago an assessing look.

"Did you know her?"

"Met her a few times," he nodded. "She was only seven years older than me."

Tamsyn blinked at him in surprise. She'd forgotten how close they were in age. She leaned forwards, lowering her voice.

"What was she like?"

Jago looked thoughtful.

"She lit up any room she walked into," he said, reflectively. "But she liked to party a bit too much, if you know what I mean." He coughed uncomfortably, clearly wishing he hadn't brought it up. "Your dad, well, he preferred the quiet life, didn't he."

"I don't remember," Tamsyn said wistfully. "It's all ... vague."

"He was a good 'un," Jago nodded. "Sorry I mentioned it, cuz," and he put his arm around her, squeezing her shoulder with his large hand.

She gave him a thin smile, then for the hundredth time, slid her mobile from her pocket to check for a signal. But there was no connectivity whatsoever. Zip, zero, nil, nada. She tried to think what the word was in Cornish.

Her grandmother nudged her, raising her eyebrows at the phone. Tamsyn felt chastised for being caught looking again.

She'd already endured lectures from almost everyone in

the pub about a) "young people today" and, b) "mainlanders".

"Gran, what's the Cornish word for 'nothing'?"

"*Mann.*"

"What? Really?"

Her grandmother winked at her.

"The Cornish for 'nothing' is '*mann*'. Isn't that a coincidence?"

Tamsyn started to smile, then she remembered that Rosie was dead; dead and lying in Treliske's morgue. She had no right to smile.

She lifted Morwenna off her knee, hoping to make a discreet exit, but half the pub turned to look at her.

"Just going to get some air," she said weakly.

"It's roaring like Cudden out there, wadna you!" exclaimed her grandfather.

"Let her go, Ozzie," her grandmother said, hushing her husband.

"Perhaps she's taken up smoking," said Jago, loving to stir the pot.

She gave her cousin a huge, fake smile and leaned down to whisper in his ear.

"Fuck off, Jago."

He smirked back at her.

"Maybe it's them funny fags you like instead, is it?"

Tamsyn wouldn't have minded a spliff right now to take the edge off, but she hadn't indulged since she'd been sworn in as a police officer.

She ignored her cousin's continuing commentary, pulling on a set of heavy oilskins that she'd borrowed from him. She'd packed in such a hurry that she'd forgotten half the things needed for island life in the winter.

"Sure you should be going out by yourself?" Jago asked, real concern replacing the teasing.

Tamsyn hesitated, the ever-present fear pushing to the front of her mind.

"I'll be okay," she said at last. "Morwenna needs a walk. I'll take her up to the top of Watch Hill and see if I can get a signal while I'm there. I won't be long: twenty minutes, tops." She forced a smile so her family wouldn't worry. "It's your turn to get a round in, Jago. I want to see the moths coming out of your wallet when you do."

As she fought to open the pub's door against the near gale, the wind whipped her hair around her face and the oilskins wrapped around her legs, acting like a sail so she staggered slightly.

Pushing her way outside, she did her best not to let the door slam, then tried to tuck her wayward hair inside the oilskins' hood, zipping it up tightly. Then, with Mo at her heels, she began trudging up the footpath that led to the top of the hill, the track overgrown with stalks of brown bracken.

Morwenna trotted ahead, her fur ruffled by the wind and standing on end, her tail at two o'clock, as she investigated potential rabbit holes.

It only took a few minutes to reach the top of Watch Hill, aptly named to view boats coming from the Main Island. But there was still no signal on Tamsyn's phone. Zero bars. Zero anything.

She didn't feel like returning to the pub just yet, instead she watched Morwenna snuffling around while her eyes unseeingly tracked a lone yacht making its way down Tresco Channel, a narrow strip of water between Bryher and its slightly larger neighbour, Tresco. Tamsyn was lost in thought, but she gradually realised that the yacht was struggling. Idiots! Being out in such weather. At least the crew seemed to have had the sense to stow the sails and were coming in under engine power, but Tamsyn could see the craft bucking on the swell even in the sheltered stretch between the two islands.

They were taking a hell of a risk because Tresco Channel was notorious for being shallow with several submerged sandbars, and it could only be safely navigated during the rise two hours after low water for vessels with a draw of up to 1.3 metres and at half flood for those drawing 1.8 metres.

She guessed that the yacht was approximately 12 metres in length, and Tamsyn calculated that they needed at least two metres underneath them or risk being grounded on the underwater sandbar, dangerously close now. She could see a figure at the helm grappling to hold a steady course.

She checked the time on her phone: at least it was still useful for that, if nothing else. It was nearing 4.30pm, so the yacht had very little time before the tide would drop away too much, leaving it stranded. It might already be too late...

Tamsyn saw the exact moment that the yacht foundered on a hidden sandbar, shuddering as its keel grounded. It listed to one side and stopped.

A second man appeared on deck, struggling to stand, slipping and sliding across the deck to the small inflatable at the rear.

So, it was with a sense of disbelief that she saw the two crewmen arguing, almost coming to blows, then only one of them climbed awkwardly into the small RIB, yanked on the outboard motor with difficulty, then fought the heavy swell all the way to the quay.

Tamsyn squinted, peering into the failing light. There

was definitely only one person on the RIB; perhaps the other man had refused to leave the yacht and hoped he'd be able to refloat it. If so, he was taking a huge risk.

She glanced back at the pub, torn on what to do for the best, then decided to head down to the quay, tell them that they were being idiots, and hopefully convince them to secure the yacht properly against the coming storm; and, most importantly, for both of them to come ashore.

She hoped that there was enough time to keep them afloat so the lifeboat from the Main Island didn't have to be called out.

She headed down the hill at a jog, the over-long oilskins hampering her movements, Morwenna loping beside her.

The man in the RIB had just managed to reach the quay but was unable to tie along. Seeing her in the bright orange oilskins, he yelled something at her that was lost in the wind, gesturing at the rope in his hands.

She nodded in understanding, stretching out her arms for the rope, managing to catch the line when he threw it and tied the RIB securely to the quay.

"It's not safe to anchor your yacht here," she began, "because…"

The words dried in her throat as she saw the man's face. For a second, he looked as surprised as Tamsyn, and then he smiled, his shark-like eyes glinting.

Morwenna started to bark, a loud, warning yip, backing away from him, fierce and terrified.

Tamsyn turned and ran, pushing her body against the near gale-force winds, Morwenna racing ahead. She thought she heard a gunshot, but she didn't stop running, almost expecting to feel a bullet slamming into her spine.

I can't lead him to my family!

Even as she had the thought, she stopped so abruptly,

Besnik Domi crashed into her, sending them both tumbling to the ground.

His solid weight landed on top of her, forcing the air from her lungs so she was gasping like a landed fish.

Domi sat up slowly, gripping her chin roughly with his free hand and squeezing her jaw painfully.

"This time, I'll kill you myself," he scowled. "No more mistakes."

"You killed Rosie? By mistake?" she mumbled as his fingers dug into her cheeks.

He shrugged.

"I find you here. I know where you run to. Where's that black man? He's the one I want. My brother is in prison because of that *nënë-qim*. Is he here?"

Tamsyn tried to shake her head, but he was holding her too tightly.

"Where is he?" Domi screamed, dropping his hand from her face and instead pushing the pistol against her forehead.

"He's at Penzance police station!"

"No! I was told he'd gone away. Where is he?"

"I don't know!"

"Tell me or I kill you now."

"I don't know! I don't know! I don't know!"

He pressed the gun against her forehead until it felt as if he'd push it right through her skull.

Suddenly, the pressure was gone from her chest and Domi sat back, his full weight on her legs. He curled his fist and Tamsyn was sure he was going to hit her, but instead he thumped himself in the head over and over again, then screamed loudly, his spittle flying into her face.

He mumbled something in his own language.

"I'll finish this," he snarled in English, but Tamsyn

wasn't sure if he was talking to her or himself. "I finish this and show my brother he's wrong. My own brother doubts me!" and he laughed wildly.

His face contorted, then his voice returned to normal.

"You call that policeman now. He'll come for you."

"I can't!"

"Yes!"

"There's no phone signal here!" she screamed at him desperately. "I don't know anything!"

He pressed the gun barrel against her head again, then seemed to change his mind.

"No matter. I'll find him. I'll find him and kill him. Then I'll find his family and kill them," he said, his voice eerily calm. "But you, you fight so hard to live. Maybe I'll let you live. Maybe I'll take you with me, pretty little policewoman. And there's nowhere left for you to run."

"Nor you."

"What?"

She mumbled a few more words until he lessened his weight on her body.

"Your yacht is grounded on a sandbar, and that RIB won't make it through the swell. You're trapped here," and she started to laugh, the hysteria bubbling up inside her.

He slapped her so hard that her lip split, but that just made her laugh more, blood bubbling up through the crack and leaking down her chin.

Domi frowned, then hit her again, and Tamsyn tasted the blood in her mouth as her laughter died away.

He stood up, then grabbed the front of her oilskins and tugged her into a standing position, struggling to hold on as her knees buckled.

Tamsyn's mind was working at top speed as plans were developed and discarded in an instant. Could she use her wobbly balance to her advantage? Could she trick him in some way? If she could get the gun...

Satisfied that she was sufficiently cowed, Domi half-dragged her along with him, cursing her slowness as she stumbled and staggered, but all the time the gun was pressing against her spine. She expected at any moment that he'd lose patience and shoot her.

At the quay, he prodded her towards the RIB which was lunging against the mooring line and thudding onto the buoys skirting the granite wall.

"Get in!"

"There's no point!" she yelled, flailing a hand towards the yacht. "You're aground! You can't go anywhere!"

He shrugged.

"The skipper says we'll float at higher tide."

"You could be holed under the waterline!"

He pointed the gun at her again.

Without a choice, Tamsyn clambered into the boat, moving as slowly as possible, looking for any possible opportunity, any half-second when he was distracted.

Maybe she could disarm Domi as he jumped down, but he waved the gun at her, telling her to move away to the furthest point she could go. Then he untied the lines and jumped smoothly into the boat.

"Start the engine!" he snarled at her, motioning the pistol toward the pull-start on the outboard motor.

Tamsyn saw her chance.

She pulled weakly, ineffectually, knowing it would really need a sharp tug to start it.

When nothing happened, Domi yelled at her, swore and threatened.

"You'll die like your Uncle George," he screamed. "Like your father! I will find this policeman, Rego, without you."

Pretending to be helpless, she tried again with the same result.

"I think it's the fuel line," she said, not having to fake looking scared.

"Fix it!" he screamed at her. "Or I shoot you like dog!"

Tamsyn's head jerked up. Did that mean he'd shot Morwenna? She remembered hearing a shot...

Her eyes blurred, but Domi screamed at her again, looking so crazed, she was afraid that he'd shoot her on the spot.

She turned back to the outboard motor, her hands shaking as she managed to shut off the fuel line. She hoped that Domi was as inept as he seemed when it came to boats. She hoped he wouldn't notice, because if he did...

Untethered, the RIB had started to drift away from the quay. Tamsyn was playing a dangerous game, one where the loser would end up dead. Maybe even both of them.

Domi didn't seem to have realised that the RIB was in danger of being swept away by the surging currents. He seemed unable to comprehend that he was risking his own life.

All Tamsyn needed was a split second of inattention and she'd jump over the side, leaving Domi to drift towards the open ocean. He couldn't survive long without oars or engine.

Of course, the chances that Tamsyn would survive a swim to the shore were slim, too. But better than nothing. Better than Domi's chances. Definitely better than her chances if he got her to the yacht.

And maybe they'd start to wonder at the pub, wouldn't they? They'd come to look for her, wouldn't they?

Her heart sank. No, it was too dangerous. He'd kill

them. He wouldn't care. He'd empty his gun and wouldn't care.

She tugged again on the pull-start cord as hard as she could. Domi bellowed at her, threatening her every time the outboard failed to catch.

"It won't start!" she screamed. "It won't start!"

Domi pointed the gun at her, but this time, Tamsyn didn't close her eyes.

CHAPTER 26

Rego hadn't recognised Tamsyn in the bright orange oilskins. As he'd made his way down from higher ground where the helicopter had left him, he'd seen two figures running along the street.

Then Tamsyn's dog had sprinted away, and Rego's heartrate exploded as he realised what was happening. Immediately, he recognised the threat implicit in the way the taller figure pointed a gun.

The wind caught in the oilskins, tugging the hood from the figure on the ground. Long, blonde hair spilled out and Rego saw Tamsyn's white skin, ghostly in the twilight.

He couldn't see the man's face, but it was Domi, he was sure of it. The Captor spray in his pocket seemed a poor substitute for the handgun held by a wanted and ruthless criminal.

Rego knew that he'd have to move quickly without being seen: easier said than done in a red and white Santa suit. If it wasn't so serious, he'd die laughing.

But in the failing light and Domi so preoccupied with capturing Tamsyn, Rego saw a thin thread of possibility.

He pulled the Captor spray from where it was hidden inside the suit, then hurried behind the two figures, concerned that Tamsyn appeared to be unsteady, staggering as Domi dragged her along the empty street.

All sensible people were indoors, snug and warm before the winds reached gale-force, and Rego didn't know whether to be relieved that there were no civilians around to be harmed or used as hostages, or disappointed that there was no one to help them.

Instead, he waited for his chance, growing more desperate as Tamsyn was hustled into the small inflatable.

Tamsyn appeared to be trying to start the engine, and the tiniest doubt crept into Rego's mind. She was shouting something angrily, but then Domi pointed the gun at her again, and Tamsyn looked directly at Rego.

Time had run out.

Knowing that twenty feet was too far away for the incapacitant spray to work, especially with Domi facing away from him; in this wind, it was just as likely to blow back in his own face, or in Tamsyn's. He could throw the can, although it didn't weigh much...

Suddenly, Rego sank to his knees, scrabbling on the ground and finding a fist-sized pebble. He lobbed it as hard as he could, suddenly grateful for school summer holidays when he'd spent hours playing street cricket with his mates, in between shop-lifting sprees.

The rock hit Domi square between the shoulders, and he staggered in the bucking boat. Rego could only watch in admiration as Tamsyn tried to bludgeon him with the metal anchor. As she raised it a second time, Domi screamed something, blocking Tamsyn's move with his arm and shoving her backwards.

As she fell, the anchor that she'd used as a weapon sank

into the side of the little boat, hissing loudly as air whistled through a tear in the rubber.

Domi lurched to one side but kept his grip on the gun. He fired a single time in pure rage, the shot going wild. Rego was out of ideas; he had no strategy, but he couldn't watch Domi shoot Tamsyn without trying something. So, he yelled at full volume and sprinted toward the RIB.

"Besnik Domi!"

The man spun around, his eyes pinched in confusion when he saw Father Christmas on the quay, and in that split second of hesitation, Rego took the chance, unleashing a stream of the synthetic pepper spray and leaping across the water.

He didn't make it.

The current caught the RIB, jerking it from the quay, with Rego's rubber belly smacking the side of the boat as he slid into the freezing water.

The weight of the Santa suit tugged at him, the heavy boots pulling him down. He tried to grab the boat's smooth sides, desperately trying to find something to hold onto, but the waterlogged suit dragged him down relentlessly and his mouth filled with seawater.

Coughing and gasping, his arms flailing, Rego surfaced as Domi's red-eyed, demonic face leered down at him, and he pointed the pistol.

Then Tamsyn reared up behind Domi, her eyes flashing with fury. She wrapped the anchor rope around Domi's neck and shoved him into the water.

A second later, he was gone.

She leaned over the side of the RIB, her arm outstretched, hoping that the boat wouldn't sink yet.

"Take my hand!" she shouted. "Take my hand! Rob, take my hand!"

Rego's limbs were numb and he couldn't feel anything. He tried to reach for Tamsyn, but she seemed so far-off.

A wave broke over his head, filling his mouth and nose with water again, and the RIB bobbed further away, out of reach.

He tried to swim, tried to move his arms, but he was being sucked down, following Besnik Domi to the depths.

His last thought was, *How ironic.*

When Rego disappeared beneath the waves, Tamsyn didn't hesitate. She knew that she'd flooded the outboard so it would be impossible to start, and the RIB's oars were missing.

Domi had been a sloppy sailor.

The little boat began taking on water, its buoyancy deflating with every second.

Decision made, Tamsyn yanked off the oilskins and jumped into the water, ignoring the clawing, icy cold, swimming strongly to where Rego had disappeared. She took a deep breath, and dived down, her blind hands fumbling for him. She kicked harder, moving deeper, and her left hand brushed against something.

Her fingers closed around the collar of Rego's Santa suit, the fake white fur almost luminous in the water. He was heavy, so heavy, and her lungs burned, fireworks going off in her vision as her oxygen-deprived heart nearly burst with the effort.

She kicked hard, using all her strength to drag him with her, her head breaking the surface as another wave crashed over them. She nearly lost him, but managed to grip hold of the wide, black, plastic belt that held the fake belly in place.

The current was stronger the further out they were carried, and it took everything in her to inch towards the quay, but she was getting tired now, so tired, and her strength was failing.

"Catch the lifebelt, Tammy!"

Cutting through the roar of the keening wind, she heard her grandfather's voice.

"Catch it, maid!"

She lunged for the lifebelt as he tossed it towards her, tantalisingly close. The rope was slick and cold, her fingers numb and slipping on the rope, but she managed to hook one arm through the lifebelt as her grandfather, Jago and Edern heaved on the rope to land their half-dead catch.

Water sprayed in Tamsyn's face, and she felt rather than heard the downdraft of a helicopter's rotor blades.

Her arm slipped from the lifebelt and the downwash pushed her further away from the quay.

Before another wave broke over them, she saw more faces lining the quay, men and women from the pub, all reaching out to her, all trying to save her.

She twisted her hand in Rego's belt more firmly, kicking and flailing to get closer to the quay. She could hear the helicopter above her but further away now, the pilot using a different angle of the downdraft to push her back towards the quay.

Her grandfather was shouting, throwing the lifebelt to her again, urging her to try, try, try! Try to reach out, try once more, but she knew her strength was almost gone.

She saw Morwenna up on the quay, heard her high-pitched bark, the one that meant she was scared.

Poor Morwenna, she thought. *Who will you snuggle with now?*

And then Jago was in the water, one strong hand grabbing her and pulling her towards him, the other grasping the lifebelt as Ozzie, Edern and half-a-dozen people pulled with all their might on the other end, the crowd on the quay all jostling to help.

Rego was manhandled from the water, his body heavy and limp. Then Jago boosted Tamsyn up, hands grabbing for her and hauling her onto the quay where she lay shivering and gasping for breath. Edern was belly down on the cold granite quay, reaching for Jago, refusing to let the sea take him, holding onto his son, until others came to his aid, heaving the fisherman from the water.

Morwenna wriggled through the legs of the bystanders, licking Tamsyn's face, her whole body shaking as she tried to get closer.

One of the women from the pub galvanised the crowd, turning Rego onto his side. He coughed and spluttered, seawater pouring from his mouth and nose.

His eyes opened and Tamsyn reached out for him, finding his frozen fingers and holding on as if she'd never let go.

He might have smiled, but then his eyes closed again.

"Let's get off the bloody quay, cuz," said Jago, his voice shaking with cold. "My brass monkeys are about froze off."

Edern wrapped his arm around his son's shoulders, helping him to walk, and Tamsyn's grandfather pulled off his own oilskins and bundled her up, his lips pressed together, the words trapped behind his rare show of emotion.

Two men from the crowd carried Rego to the Poldhus' cottage and put him in a chair next to the fire.

Edern helped him pull off the ruined Santa suit, then paused and blinked.

"You're black," he said.

Rego nodded and coughed.

"Don't tell my mum!"

Relieved laughter rippled around the room, then Tamsyn's grandmother swaddled Rego, Tamsyn and Jago in blankets while teams of people were sent to the kitchen to make hot drinks for the bedraggled trio and all the helpers.

"Are you alright, Tammy?" her grandmother asked anxiously, kneeling next to her.

"Y-yes," she stuttered. "C-cold."

Edern stoked up the fire until it was roaring, and everybody else started to sweat in the tiny cottage.

"H-how did you know to come and look for me?" Tamsyn asked as she began to warm up.

"We'n heard little Mo barking outside the pub," said her grandfather.

Morwenna looked up when she heard her name, but refused to move from Tamsyn's lap.

Hot tea was pressed on the three sodden survivors of what would soon be known on the islands as 'the Church Quay killer'.

Questions, opinions, conjectures and wild conspiracies flew around the room: so many questions, so few answers. Finally, Tamsyn's grandmother chased the rescuers, gawkers and bystanders away, so the shivering and exhausted trio could each take their turn in the cottage's tiny shower until the hot water tank ran empty.

Tamsyn knew that she should be worried about Rego and the chance of 'secondary drowning', something she'd learned about during her lifeguard training: water inhaled into the lungs could cause swelling of the tiny air sacs, preventing oxygen from entering the bloodstream. It could happen up to 48 hours after a sudden immersion. She tried to remember the symptoms, but her brain was foggy and her head was nodding.

"You should be in hospital," she said to Rego, her voice husky.

"I'll only need a hospital if I break my promise to my wife and don't make it to her for Christmas," he replied, his eyes twinkling even as exhaustion threatened to overwhelm him.

"The doctor comes to the island every Thursday," said Edern, glancing between his son, Tamsyn and Rego. "But that's after Christmas now."

Tamsyn started to laugh, and once she started, she couldn't stop. Rego was grinning at her like an idiot, wheezing and coughing as he joined in.

Jago's gaze swivelled between the two of them.

"Pair of nutters," he mumbled. "Don't know if it's the seawater or what it takes to be a copper these days."

And that sounded like the funniest thing Tamsyn had ever heard.

CHAPTER 27

The gale blew itself out overnight, and Tamsyn woke to a watery sun and the aroma of bacon and toast.

Her whole body ached. She felt as if her bones had turned to blancmange and her head was stuffed with cotton wool, but somehow weighed a hundred pounds. Moving slowly, she sat up, disturbing little Mo who was curled up by her feet.

"You're such a clever girl," Tamsyn said, stroking her wiry fur. "You went and got help. If it hadn't been for you..."

The dark memories threatened to overwhelm her again, but Tamsyn pushed them away, wondering how many times she could do that before they came thundering back like a winter storm.

All her training as a police officer, the blue-light course, the paperwork, the coursework – and it had all come down to a scrappy fight at a rain-slick quay on an island that few had ever heard of.

So many thoughts had flashed through her mind, fight overcoming the need for flight. She'd tried not to let the panic take her, tried to follow her training and keep a sterile gap between her and Domi.

What would have happened if she hadn't been trained? Would she have had the confidence to fight back. She didn't know what any of it meant.

But that was something to worry about on another day.

She wrapped herself in Jago's dressing gown, a pair of Edern's thick socks on her feet, and she plodded down the stairs.

Rego was sitting at the table, scarfing down a bacon sandwich. He was wearing jeans and a gansey sweater that belonged to her grandfather. Andrea Poldhu had knitted it years ago in the Newlyn pattern. Each fishing village had its own distinct style, and not much had changed in two hundred years or more.

Rego smiled when he saw her.

His feet were bare.

Self-consciously, Tamsyn put a hand to her uncombed hair, then gave up and plonked down into a chair opposite him.

"Morning," said Rego, his voice a little hoarse, the only sign of what he'd endured the evening before. "How are you feeling?"

"Like I've been run over by a truck," she admitted. "How are you?"

"Hungry," he smiled, nodding at the bacon sandwich. "This is my third."

Morwenna paid attention, stationing herself at Rego's side, just in case.

Tamsyn yawned and pulled the teapot towards her. It was tepid but still half-full so she poured herself a mug and dumped in two spoonfuls of sugar. That was energy, right?

Rego passed a piece of bacon to Morwenna, then ate his

sandwich in silence, lost in his own thoughts as Tamsyn stole quick glances at him.

Suddenly, a phone in the house rang and Tamsyn jumped, her nerves jangling until she heard an old answer machine kick in.

"Yep, phones and power restored. Jago let me use his mobile to get in touch with Penzance nick."

"That's good," she said wearily, in no mood to think about work.

She became aware that there was a lot of noise outside, people's voices rising up from the quay.

"What's going on?" she asked.

"They're recovering the body."

The memories flooded back and she closed her eyes, pressing her hands to her face.

"Oh."

"The weather's cleared so the lifeboat from St Mary's came out along with Sergeant Hutton and his team from the islands police."

"Oh," she said again, opening her eyes reluctantly, her brain dull. "Shouldn't we be there?"

Rego gave a half-smile and shook his head.

"Nope. Nothing for us to do – they've got divers. And anyway, we have to wait for high water to get to the guy on the yacht." He peered at her. "I thought you had saltwater in your veins and knew all about this sort of stuff."

She tried to smile, but it felt stiff and unnatural.

"Do you know who he is? The man on the yacht?"

Rego shook his head.

"We've seen him. He's out there waving his arms and asking for help."

"Don't you need to question him?"

Rego sucked his teeth and gave her an assessing look.

"The quay is a crime scene and..." he paused, searching for the right word. "We don't want to re-contaminate it."

"Oh, of course," she said in sudden understanding.

"I can't get involved. And neither can you."

Rego gave a half-answer.

"Otherwise, the coroner would ask me all sorts of questions about why I returned to the crime scene. Same goes for you."

In theory, the Crown Prosecution Service could be looking at him and Tamsyn for murder; and there was sure to be another referral to the Independent Office for Police Conduct, but Rego didn't tell her that. He hoped that the video from the helicopter would tip the balance in their favour.

Despite what he'd said to Tamsyn about not getting involved, he'd already got up to speed. Sergeant Hutton was talking to the Police Search Advisor, and officers were checking for CCTV around the quay.

One good piece of news, there were no journalists on the island because the weather had only just improved and Sergeant Hutton was stopping any boats coming to the quay, as well.

"Once the body has been recovered, Sergeant Hutton will do a fingerprint scan. We should get a positive ID – he hasn't been in the water that long."

Tamsyn's pale face became ashen.

"Oh my God," she whispered, understanding dawning. "I'd forgotten. I mean, not forgotten but ... I killed him, didn't I?" She blinked at Rego, her mind slow to re-boot. "I was only thinking about you ... about not dying. I didn't think ... I thought... am I in trouble? I mean ... I killed him! I killed Besnik Domi!"

The panic started to rise inside her, but Rego reached across the table and laid his hand over hers.

"No, Tamsyn, you're not in any trouble."

"But ... but I killed a man!"

"I'm not sorry that the bastard is dead," Rego said, his voice low and tight. "Although I'd like to have seen him stand trial, but having him wiped off the face of the planet works for me, too. The only thing I'm sorry about is that you were the one who had to do it. But thank God you did, because you saved our lives. I have absolutely no doubt about that."

Tamsyn blinked, staring down at his hand over hers, and Rego pulled away, looking uncomfortable.

He cleared his throat.

"Look, there *will* be questions, and they might say it was a death in custody. There could be an inquiry..."

He looked down. He really hadn't wanted to bring this up so soon after yet another traumatic incident, but he wouldn't lie to her either.

"You're fine, Tamsyn. I promise. Apart from anything else, I'm fairly sure that the helicopter would have videoed the whole thing."

"Oh, yes! I remember the downdraft – they used it to blow us back toward the quay. God, my brain! But ... why was there a helicopter?"

"They gave me a lift over," said Rego simply.

"You came for me?" she asked, surprised, grateful, awed.

Rego paused, weighing his words carefully, keeping his tone neutral.

"I couldn't get in touch with you and there'd been a report of a yacht near St Mary's which they suspected had turned off its transponder: it fit with how Domi got away last time, so..."

"Yeah, that makes sense," she said, and Rego could see her putting the pieces together. "But why just you? Why not armed response, if you really thought it was Domi?"

Rego's expression hardened.

"There was supposed to be a sighting of him in Liverpool, but I didn't believe it."

"Why not?"

"Let's just say ... because it was gut instinct, a guess, because I had no firm intel. Besides, the weather was pretty bad and it was just luck that I could cadge a lift from Culdrose. And when they saw a yacht travelling up Tresco Channel, they were concerned, but it was too dangerous to land, so they used the downdraft to help us." He gave a wry smile. "I think that's what they were doing."

"Why were you dressed as Father Christmas?"

"I was undercover," Rego smiled.

Morwenna moved closer to Rego, staring up at him with adoring eyes, and he gave her the last bite of his sandwich.

"Thank you," Tamsyn said quietly. "I thought he was going to kill me this time. But I killed him instead – I can't get my head around that. It's so crazy..."

"I promise you'll be okay. There is no court on Earth that would charge you. He was armed, you weren't. It was self-defence, pure and simple."

He measured his next words carefully.

"Did Domi say anything to you while you were ... anything at all?"

"Yes," she said slowly, massaging her temples. "He wanted to know where *you* were."

Rego was surprised. "Me?"

"Yes, he said something like, 'where's that black man?'" and her cheeks flushed as she spoke. "And then, 'he's the one who put my brother in prison'. And he said something in Albanian after that."

Rego felt a cold finger of dread pressed against his heart, and he leaned forward.

"He definitely mentioned his brother?"

"Yes, is it important?"

Yes, Rego thought. *It's very fucking important.* To Tamsyn he simply replied, "It might be." Then he had another thought. "How did he know where *you* were?"

Tamsyn sat up straight.

"That's right! I'd forgotten. He said, 'I knew where you'd run to'. Do you think he's had people following me?"

"It's possible, although I don't see how he could have followed the trawler you were on. The guy on the yacht probably knows something."

Then Rego had an unpleasant thought: had Domi been able to track Tamsyn's phone ... or maybe he'd been in touch with someone else who had access. But the people who'd been doing that were the NCA: could they have a leak? Could Tamsyn's grandparents have mentioned it and word got around? Who else knew where she'd be? Rego had even told Tom Stevens where Tamsyn was going, and Tom had dropped her off at Newlyn harbour. But who had Tom told, if anyone?

A memory ticked over in his brain. He remembered that Mimi had a Polish boyfriend. What was his name? Luka. Yes, that was it: Luka. Could he be a member of the Hellbanianz, too?

Rego hated the uncertainty, hated that he suspected his own team. But no one had suspected Chloe Rogers either.

"I just need to make a quick call," he said.

He picked up Jago's phone and started to leave the room, then he stopped suddenly.

"You did well out there, Tamsyn. I saw you try to talk to him, and I saw you fight him. You did everything right; remember that." He smiled. "And you saved my life. I won't forget it."

Tamsyn watched him go, confused and a little hurt by his sudden departure.

Morwenna watched him leave too, disappointed that no more bacon had come her way.

Tamsyn wished she could call Joe, but her phone was deader than a dodo after being dunked in the sea. She could use the cottage's landline but she had no idea of Joe's number: who memorised mobile numbers these days? She didn't even have her laptop with her, and she knew neither Jago nor Edern owned one.

With Morwenna at her heels, she plodded upstairs to shower and dress, her movements sluggish. She was tired, so tired, and felt decades older.

I should feel grateful to be alive.

But all she felt was guilt.

When she was finally ready to face the day, there was nobody downstairs, and the cottage was empty. Morwenna looked up at her inquiringly.

"I don't feel like going out there, scruffalicious," she said, picking up the small dog and nuzzling her fur.

Her hands trembled as she held little Mo, her brain reeling from the buffeting it had taken. All her police training, all the ways she'd been taught to talk her way out of difficult situations, all the conflict resolution role plays, even the blue-light training where she thought she'd be chasing the criminal, it had all been for nothing, because the criminal had come looking for her.

"I'm okay," she said to Morwenna. "I'm okay. I'm alive, I'm alive."

She stared at the old-fashioned rotary telephone in the living room for several seconds before lifting the handset, hearing an unfamiliar dialling tone. She used the dial to call Control, identifying herself as PC Poldhu 1560, and asked to be put through to Joe Quinn at Scotland Yard, hoping, praying that he was on duty and could take her call.

She had to wait several minutes before he came on the line.

"Tamsyn! Thank fuck! Where have you been? What's happened?"

And she couldn't answer, she couldn't say a single word. She cried, letting out all the fear and stress and heartbreak that she'd been holding inside.

The quay was full of people. Just about everybody on the island was there, along with the police and lifeboat from St Mary's.

Rego stood at the back with Sergeant Hutton as two divers worked with assistance from the lifeboat crew to recover Besnik Domi's body.

Rego was glad that Tamsyn wasn't there to see it. The body had been bashed about during the storm and wasn't in the best of conditions. The corpse was loaded into a black body bag, then one of the officers scanned the fingerprints and gave a quick nod in their direction.

Rego watched as Domi's body was zipped up, and placed into the lifeboat.

One of the divers sank back into the water to try and find Domi's gun, but brought up Rego's canister of incapacitant spray instead.

He wondered what other items littered the seabed.

Both divers returned to the water, continuing to search for the gun.

"The body will be taken back to the mainland," said Hutton, momentarily distracting Rego. "Do you want to get a lift, as well, sir?"

Rego wasn't charmed by the thought of a boat ride the day after a severe storm, let alone with Domi's corpse, but the man was dead and gone at last. And Rego had a flight to catch. He hoped to make it and he thought he would because he was feeling pretty damn lucky right now.

"Yes, that would be good, thank you. I'd like to have a word with the man on the yacht first."

Hutton looked like he wanted to say something but then his mouth snapped shut.

"Yes, sir."

It was another hour before the lifeboat could get over to the yacht without getting stuck on the same sandbar that had grounded the larger craft.

The man was helped into the lifeboat, given a blanket, and taken to the quay to be checked over by one of the lifeboat crew who was a paramedic.

Rego prowled towards him and the man couldn't meet his gaze.

"Do you know me?" he asked.

The man stared at him dumbly.

"Do you speak English?"

Rego thought there was a spark of understanding in his eyes, but the man remained silent. So, he turned to Sergeant Hutton.

"It doesn't matter. He'll be found guilty of murder, attempted murder and a few other things. He'll never see the light of day again."

It seemed that the man did understand English because his eyes widened.

"I kill no one! I sail boat. Is all!"

Rego shared a look with Sergeant Hutton.

"Has he been formally arrested and read his rights?"

Hutton shook his head.

"I'll do that now, sir."

"And I want to know how he knew to come to Bryher."

Rego received a lot of answers in the next few minutes, but the man on the yacht would only tell them that Domi had ordered him to this island. Aderito de Jeles was a Portuguese national living in Madeira who'd been on their watchlist earlier in the year but they hadn't had sufficient evidence to link him to Domi at that time; in fact, they'd ruled him out.

The man seemed more upset that his yacht was in a sorry state rather than the fact that his boss was dead. Rego wondered if he might even be a little relieved.

Magio de Machico had been a handsome craft, but now it was storm-battered, holed below the waterline and still grounded on a sandbar.

But de Jele's information had brought him no closer to finding out how Domi had known to come to Bryher, and he had to concede that Domi may have taken the secret to his grave.

He hated loose ends, but it wasn't uncommon with a case of this complexity. At least Tom Stevens had been able to assure him that Mimi's boyfriend might have a Polish name, but he'd been born in Redruth and gone to school with her.

Rego was okay with ruling him out. For now. Discreet checks could be made at a later date.

And apart from anything else, it would have been a

severe blow to Devon & Cornwall Police if Mimi had been involved. No one from the brass would want to admit that a second employee had been working for the Hellbanianz.

There would still be significant fallout from the Chloe Rogers business: they'd have to assess every case that she'd worked on or been involved with. The repercussions would roll on over months, maybe even years.

A lot of good people could lose their jobs, and Rego included himself in that. He hadn't yet had a conversation with ACC Gray, although he knew it would have to be done. But whatever happened, he'd bet that Gray would survive. The man was as slippery as an eel in an oil slick.

His borrowed phone rang with an unknown number. Rego answered it cautiously.

"Hello?"

"It's Vik. Bloody hell! It's good to hear your voice. How are you, mate?"

Rego blew out a long breath, truly happy to hear his friend's voice.

"I'm alive."

"Vertical and sucking in air. Not a bad way to start the day," Vikram agreed sagely. "Listen, your DS Tom Stevens gave me this number. You said he was a solid bloke, so when I hadn't heard from you, I called him."

"Yeah, my phone is somewhere in 30 feet of seawater right now."

Vikram was silent for several seconds. Then Rego cleared his throat and filled him in on everything that happened, ending with Tamsyn diving into the water to save him, and how she nearly hadn't made it.

"Blimey, Rob. That was a close one."

"Too close," Rego admitted. "Don't tell Cassie."

"I wouldn't dare!" Vikram hesitated. "Rob, what made you go off the reservation like that?"

Rego's hackles rose.

"What are you talking about? It was ... an operational decision."

Vikram sucked his teeth.

"That's not what your ACC Gray is saying."

"What the hell are you talking about?"

"Look, this is unofficial at the moment, but I heard a whisper that he's saying you've been on an unsanctioned, one-man crusade, and he's 'worried' about you."

Rego was so angry, he didn't know which accusation to address first.

"That prize prick is setting me up!" Rego growled. "Jesus! It was so obvious to me that the alleged sighting of Domi in Liverpool was a deliberate attempt to wrong-foot us. There's no way that timing could be coincidental. Gray knows he was wrong telling me to stand down after PC Flowers was murdered, then not backing me up when I said Domi was after Tamsyn."

"Ah," said Vikram. "He's covering his arse."

"That's all he ever does," said Rego bitterly. "I'm going to make an official complaint! The man is incompetent and dangerous. I'm not letting it go this time."

Vikram's voice was calm.

"Remember our old sarge, Alan Fishwick?"

"Fishy Fishwick? Yeah, of course I remember him. What about him?"

"Well, he always said that if you're considering doing something out of your comfort zone, sit on it for 24 hours. The circumstances might look very different after a good night's sleep, and your course of action could be different when you've had time to reflect."

"Gray's throwing me under the bus!" Rego objected, his temper rising again.

God, wasn't the job hard enough without the top brass refusing to back you?

"He's questioning my professionalism, Vik!"

"I know, mate, and I'm on your side, so don't bite my head off. But the bugger has been clever and always said what he's said and done what he's done behind closed doors. You've got to remember that Gray hasn't gone that one stage further and actively sought to get you investigated or disciplined."

"Is that supposed to make me feel better?" Rego snapped.

"It's supposed to make you think," Vikram shot back. "Look at it this way: Gray's flown through the ranks without having much operational experience. You come along with a bucket load of commendations and your dashing good looks," Vikram laughed, "and you made him look like a sack of shit after that business last summer. So, him raising his voice, throwing his toys out of the pram making unfounded accusations and veiled threats is his way of trying to make himself look very important. It's all about chest-thumping and hoping the right people hear him."

Rego sat down on one of the benches lining the small quay.

"I could go over Gray's head, go straight to the Chief Constable," he said.

"Are you sure of where his allegiances lie?" asked Vikram.

Rego sighed.

"Not really. The man's a politician."

"That's what I thought."

"Anway," Rego said tiredly, "the Chief is skiing in France; Chamonix, apparently."

"Best place for him."

Rego wasn't sure if Vikram was joking.

"So, that's it? You're saying I've just got to sit on my hands and do nothing?"

"All I'm saying is to write your report very carefully. Gray is being a dick, but you've broken a lot of rules doing what you did. Gray knows he's on a slippery wicket, so keep your powder dry and keep this in your back pocket. You could make life very uncomfortable for Gray down the line."

"I hate all this politics crap," Rego groaned. "What's wrong with just doing the job?"

"Nothing, if you're a bloomin' boy scout," Vikram laughed cynically. "Come on, Rob, you know how the game is played."

"And if I'm played out in Devon & Cornwall Police?"

"Nah, I don't think so. But you could always go back to Manchester," he paused. "Although a little bird tells me that the NCA have been pretty impressed, and not just because you're a pretty face."

"You keep saying that, and I'll start to think it's not just your wife who fancies me."

Vikram laughed.

"In your dreams; definitely not in mine. But just think about it, Rob. There's more to life than being a copper. You could join my lot..."

"Thanks, Vik. I mean that. But I don't think I'm cut out for that spook squad stuff."

"I thought you'd say that, but don't rule it out. In the meantime, try not to do anything else stupid or life-threatening."

"I've got to tell Cassie that I didn't make my flight last night; does that count as life-threatening?"

"Abso-flippin-lutely," said Vikram. "But you're on your own with that one, mate!"

Rego glanced at his watch.

"Yeah, and on that note, I've got to go. The lifeboat crew are taking me back to St Mary's and I'm catching a flight to the mainland. Then I'll be driving like a bat out of hell to get a flight from Heathrow to Bermuda. I should make it there by Christmas morning. Just."

"Sounds expensive!"

"Don't ask, mate," Rego sighed. "Don't ask."

"Merry Christmas," Vikram laughed.

Rego headed back to the quay where the lifeboat crew were ready to go.

Tamsyn was waiting for him, her eyes red and puffy, but she seemed more alert.

"Are you going now?"

"Yep, got a flight to Bermuda this evening. I should make it." He looked at her closely. "Are you going to be alright?"

She shrugged.

"Yeah, I guess. We're staying here for Christmas. I'm not sure about New Year yet. I don't feel much like celebrating."

"You should," said Rego seriously. "If Rosie's death teaches us anything, it's that life is short and we have to make the most of every day. I didn't really know her, but she didn't seem like the kind of person who'd want you to stay home and feel sorry for yourself."

Tamsyn gave him a sad smile.

"She was great, she really was."

Sergeant Hutton walked over, his gaze flicking between them.

"Sorry to interrupt, sir, but the lifeboat is ready to head to the Main Island."

"Thanks, Nigel. I'll be there in a moment."

The man nodded and turned away.

"Well," Rego paused. "I know I've already said it but thank you for saving my life."

His words awkward, full of too many emotions.

"You're a very special person, Tamsyn, and a damn good copper."

She surprised Rego by giving him a big hug.

"You saved my life last Easter. I guess I owed you one."

She looked like she was struggling to keep her emotions in check, but trying to keep the moment light.

"Maybe we shouldn't make a habit of needing to be saved," he smiled, and she gave a threadbare laugh.

"Give my love to Maisie and Max," she said. And as an afterthought, "and Cassie and your mum."

"Will do. I've already said goodbye to your family, but thank them again for me." He looked down at his borrowed clothes. "And for this snazzy outfit."

She smiled and pushed her hands deeper into her coat pockets.

"It's really beautiful here," he said, his gaze drifting over the foreshore.

"Bryher is where God comes on holiday," Tamsyn laughed self-consciously. "That's what Edern says."

Rego smiled.

"I might have to bring the family over when the weather's better: maybe next summer. Well," he paused. "I'd better get going."

"Safe journey. See you next year."

"You, too."

And she watched him climb into the lifeboat, looking unhappy and seasick already.

Her grandfather came to stand next to her.

"This is no place for a city man, 'specially not one who gets seasick just looking at a boat." He paused, watching the lifeboat head down the Tresco Channel. "But he's a proper good 'un."

CHAPTER 28

It rained on New Year's Eve.

Tamsyn and her family had caught a lift from an islander going to the mainland, but none of them felt like celebrating. Jess had begged her to go out to party with their friends, promising it would be fun, but Tamsyn wasn't in the mood, and Jess couldn't persuade her.

She thought of her colleagues who were on shift, glad for them that the bad weather would make their job a little easier. People tended not to go so crazy if it was rainy or freezing cold.

She spent New Year's Day cooking up a storm in the kitchen with her grandmother, then taking Morwenna for a yomp across the hills, avoiding the popular beaches where families went to walk off their lunches. Still, everyone she met wished her a Happy New Year. She hoped it would be.

But first, she had a funeral to go to. And she was dreading it.

The day of Rosie's funeral was Tamsyn's first time back at the station since ... since everything. She wasn't sure how she'd be treated because surely everyone knew that Rosie was dead because of her.

But the atmosphere was muted, quiet, sad. All of C-team, Rosie's team, were attending the funeral, and another team were covering their shift. In fact, everyone who was off duty would be attending, along with half of Camborne and colleagues from across the two counties. Rosie had been well liked by everyone who'd met her.

Tamsyn greeted her colleagues, none of whom had much to say, then she slipped quietly from the room to go and change into her new Number Ones. She'd had to get a new best tunic from stores since her old uniform was still in an evidence locker in London for the Old Bailey case. Not that there was any case to answer now that Domi was dead, and not that she'd have been getting it back anyway. Her uniform had been contaminated with blood and whatever forensic tests had been done to it. It would be burned.

The Old Bailey seemed so long ago now. But the memories of the bomb and Domi and everything since, well, she didn't feel anxious today, just sad. Very, very sad.

She travelled to the crematorium in a convoy of patrol cars, sitting with Ky and Mitch, and an unusually subdued Jamie. She didn't ask him about Chloe; she knew the whole team had already been grilled by the Counter Corruption Unit. Jamie's interview had been the longest.

The four of them were helping form the guard of honour along with the rest of C-team. The coffin-bearers were five officers closest to Rosie and her father.

They drove up the A30 in silence, only the sound of the tyres on the tarmac providing a backdrop to their grief.

Treswithian Downs was Camborne's crematorium. The name meant 'farmhouse in the trees', and it lived up to its picturesque name.

The single-storey building was made of glass and wood, settling softly into the wide valley with green lawns fringed by trees. It was quiet and open and felt like a place where you could breathe; somewhere to say your final farewells to someone you loved.

Joe was there waiting for them, looking handsome in his uniform, his medals on display. Calvin was standing next to him, his face drawn, his eyes distant.

Tamsyn walked into Joe's arms and wasn't ashamed of the tears that welled in her eyes. He hugged her tightly and touched his hand to her cheek, careful not to knock her bowler helmet.

"Love you, Tam," he said.

She blinked up at him but couldn't say the words back. Not here.

Then she turned to Calvin, hugging him just as tightly as Joe had hugged her.

"I'm so sorry, Cal," she whispered. "You guys were really good together. I thought ... I thought..."

"Yeah," he said, his voice rough with emotion. "She was something special."

Jason walked over, quietly shaking hands and patting Calvin on the back awkwardly. Then they stood looking at each other with so much to say but no words to say them with.

Jess joined them, pretty in pink, her expression subdued. She smiled at Tamsyn, hugging her quickly, then she walked to Jason's side, taking his hand. He leaned down to kiss the top of her head.

Tamsyn was taken aback. When had this happened? Why hadn't Jess told her? But she knew why: because she'd been so caught up with her own drama that she'd let Jess drift away from her. And Tamsyn promised herself that she'd make it up to her oldest friend, because good friends were precious and you had to cherish them.

She saw the Traffic Officer Charlie Matthews standing at a distance talking to some of the older officers. He glanced towards Tamsyn and gave her a sombre nod.

Tamsyn was still thinking about going to speak to him when she noticed the Chief Constable's car coming down the long driveway, and she glanced up at Joe.

"The Chief," she said softly.

Chief Constable Evans was flanked by ACC Gray, the new woman ACC, and a number of senior officers Tamsyn didn't know. She hoped that she wouldn't have to speak to him, or to any of them.

She was relieved when Inspector Rego and the CID team turned up.

Mimi and Jen hugged her, and Rego introduced his DS to Joe and Calvin, shaking their hands and thanking them for coming.

His expression hardened when he saw ACC Gray, and they all watched as the senior officer turned his back on Rego to talk to the Crime Commissioner, another political appointment.

"Pal of yours?" asked Joe.

"Definitely not," said Rego grimly, but offered nothing more.

DCS Richards came over to talk to them, shaking hands with everyone, thanking Cal and Joe for coming down from London. All the things ACC Gray should have done if the man wasn't such an obnoxious prick.

Inspector Walters walked towards them, nodding at the others, her expression severe. Then she turned to Rego.

"Could I have a word, please, Rob?"

He wanted to say it wasn't the time, but felt too weary to have another argument with her.

They stepped away from the others, out of earshot, and Rego thought there was something furtive about Walters' behaviour.

"I know this isn't the best timing, Rob," she said, clearly choosing her words carefully. "I had coffee with ACC Gray a few weeks ago..."

Rego nodded, unwilling to admit that he already knew.

Walters looked deeply uncomfortable as she continued.

"He asked me to keep an eye on ... CID ... as he put it 'something that might not fit in with the way we like to run things down here'."

"I see. And was his concern with CID? Or with me?"

She didn't reply directly, but gave him a pointed look.

"Just watch your back, Rob," and she walked away, as if being seen talking to him would be a demerit.

Rego wasn't sure what to make of the conversation. It was common knowledge at the nick that Walters was hungry for promotion and looking for a ladder to climb to the next rank up. Did her advice mean that she'd decided not to hang her hat with Gray?

Rego wanted to think that he had an ally rather than an enemy, but decided not to trust her just yet. He'd sit on the information until he was sure about her motives.

He watched her as she chatted to some other senior officers, then he turned his attention back to the crematorium.

A cold wind blew across the valley, and clouds scudded in the sky. Rego shivered. He hated funerals; he'd been to too many.

"Time to form up," Jen Bolitho said quietly as she pointed out the hearse arriving.

All in uniform, they lined up in two cordons, solemn, silent, and several of Rosie's team were already shedding tears. The guard of honour would be the last to enter, following the coffin inside.

The hearse arrived at the entrance accompanied by two police motorcycle outriders, and another police car which had brought Rosie's family: her mother, father, little sister and an aunt. Her father couldn't stop crying and the little girl looked bewildered and lost as the bearer party marched forward.

Rosie's coffin was a simple wicker basket covered with flowers, jasmine and roses fragrant in the cool air.

There was a wreath with her collar number 1691: she'd taken a lot of ribbing about having '69' in the middle. She'd grinned and said, "if the helmet fits".

Tamsyn had laughed but now she had trouble swallowing back her tears.

Joe's elbow nudged hers, the smallest touch to say that he was there and that he cared.

Three more floral tributes were brought by the family: black and white roses in the shape of the flag of St Piran, Cornwall's patron saint carried by Rosie's aunt; a spray of delicate pink roses, carried by her mother; and finally, a design of yellow roses that spelled 'sister'. Little Karenza almost disappeared behind the large and beautiful blooms.

The bearers lifted the coffin carefully, the father's shoulders shaking with grief. You're not supposed to bury your child.

Charlie Matthews saluted as the coffin passed by. Tamsyn wondered if he'd known Rosie. Had he taken her for a ton-up blue-lights ride along the A30? Had he passed on his decades of wisdom to a young and nervous officer? Or was it simply respect for a fallen colleague, a deep-held belief that they all belonged to the same police family?

And as Tamsyn watched Rosie's friends following the coffin inside, she knew it was wrong, wrong, wrong. A funeral filled with young people. It wasn't right. It wasn't right. She'd never been to a funeral where the average age was under thirty.

Rosie's non-police friends had all been asked to wear colourful clothes. They looked like bright jewels amongst all the dark police uniforms.

Tamsyn bowed her head as the coffin passed by and said a prayer for her friend, a woman who had quite literally laid down her life for her.

She stood at the back of the large, airy room with Joe and her colleagues, a final cordon for Rosie's farewell.

She realised that there was a man taking notes at the back, probably a reporter for the local paper. Tamsyn didn't mind: Rosie had been brave and she deserved that the world knew it, too.

All the seats were taken, but she was okay with standing. From here, she could see the constabulary flag draped over the dais, the coffin on top.

The celebrant stepped up to the podium, and began to speak.

"We welcome you today to our chapel to pay our respects and celebrate the life of Jasmine Isobel Flowers, known to many of her friends and colleagues as 'Rosie'.

"She leaves behind her mother, Karen; her father, Ian; her aunt, Jennifer; and her sister, Karenza." She smiled kindly at the family. "I know this must be one of the most difficult of days for you."

Sergeant Terwillis read the eulogy, and Rosie's friend from school recounted through her tears an anecdote where

Rosie had ended up getting both of them detention. Several people laughed, but it was fleeting.

"Jasmine had recently met someone special in her life," said the celebrant, "and her parents have asked him to read Robert Frost's poem, 'Nothing Gold Can Stay'.

Calvin walked to the front of the room and Tamsyn turned her surprised gaze to Joe.

He shrugged and whispered, "He didn't want to mention it until he had to do it."

Calvin was a big man, and in that quiet space, he seemed to fill the room with his voice.

> *"Nature's first green is gold,*
> *Her hardest hue to hold.*
> *Her early leaf's a flower;*
> *But only so an hour.*
> *Then leaf subsides to leaf.*
> *So Eden sank to grief,*
> *So dawn goes down to day.*
> *Nothing gold can stay."*

His voice hadn't trembled and he hadn't hesitated, but as he left the podium, his face crumpled and he strode outside without stopping.

Joe squeezed Tamsyn's hand, then hastily followed Calvin.

The celebrant took over smoothly.

"Jasmine, your life we honour, your departure we accept, your memory we cherish. And although there is grief in our hearts today as we say goodbye, there is gratitude for your life, for your love, for your sense of duty, and for your service as a police officer. We are truly grateful for the privilege of having shared our days with you. You will be in the hearts and minds of all those whom you have touched in your too brief journey. And so, with love, we shall leave you in the final peace, the final farewell as we now commit your body to be cremated."

The coffin disappeared behind the heavy velvet curtains, the material swishing softly.

Rosie's father was inconsolable, and her little sister was being comforted by her mother and aunt.

Tamsyn wished it was over. It was too much, too many emotions, and her throat ached from trying not to cry.

The celebrant spoke one final time.

"For those who wish to make a donation, the family have chosen the charity South West Police Compassionate Fund in honour of Jasmine's memory. And as we leave, we will hear our final piece of music, a tribute chosen by Karenza, because it was one of her sister's favourite songs. I hope you will all find it as special as Jasmine found it to be, in your own journeys through life."

And when the music *Walking on Sunshine* started to play, Tamsyn wasn't the only one who gave up the unequal fight and was openly crying while the congregation began to file out of the chapel, the cheerful music leading them into the sunshine that streamed from between heavy, grey clouds.

"Thank you for coming," said Rosie's mother. "I hope you'll come to the wake."

The woman must have said it fifty times already, and it was clear that she didn't know who Tamsyn was.

Tamsyn tried to smile and mumbled something noncommittal. She wondered whether she'd be so welcome if Rosie's mother knew that her daughter had died because of Tamsyn.

But the well of Tamsyn's emotions had run dry, and she

felt exhausted. It was a relief to be outside and have a few moments of nothingness before she had to be PC Poldhu again.

When she saw the reporter taking discreet photographs, she made up her mind to talk to him.

He looked wary when he saw her walking towards him.

"Which newspaper are you from?" she asked, her tone borderline rude.

"Hi," he said, holding out his hand. "Jules Carter from *The West Briton*. I'm sorry for your loss."

"Thank you."

"Was she a friend?"

"Yes, she was," said Tamsyn. "A good friend and a good officer. She's a hero – make sure you print that. Make sure you write the truth. For her family."

He looked like he was about to ask her another question, but she turned on her heel, striding away from him, having said what she needed to say.

She saw Inspector Rego standing off to one side, sucking on a cigarette like his life depended on it.

After a brief hesitation, she headed towards him.

"I thought you'd given up," she said.

He nodded.

"I have," and he took a final drag, dropping the cigarette on the ground and grinding it out with his heel.

Then he bent down to pick up the stub and looked around for a bin.

"So, how are you doing?" he asked, when he'd disposed of the butt.

She shrugged.

"I don't know. It doesn't seem real."

"It might not help immediately, but this will give her family some ... I don't know if 'closure' is the word, but they'll be able to remember how many people came, how many people cared about their daughter. That's more than some people get."

"It's not enough though, is it?" said Tamsyn, not really expecting an answer.

"No, a thirty-minute service can't sum up a life. All we can do is remember her and live the best life we can ... because she can't."

They were both silent for several seconds, watching Rosie's friends and colleagues milling around in the car park.

"Rosie did my Secret Santa," Tamsyn said, her smile wobbling at the corners. "She'd put her name on it. You're not supposed to, but she wanted me to know it was from her."

"What was it?"

"A t-shirt that said *Hot Fuzz*," and she gave a small laugh. "What did you get?"

Rego was not going to tell her that someone had given him a set of fluffy, pink handcuffs, and that he had no idea who they were from.

"A tea towel with a picture of Land's End," he said, even as he wondered where that answer had sprung from.

"Useful," Tamsyn smiled.

"Always."

Tamsyn glanced across to where Joe was waiting for her, then turned back to Rego.

"How's Maisie?" she asked. "After that man tried to kidnap her? Did being in Bermuda help?"

Rego smiled.

"Honestly, we thought she'd need therapy, but she's good. What with her yelling at him and doing everything she was taught at school, and then seeing her gran fight him off with her handbag, that's what she focuses on. I think she's blanked out the fact that Mum got hurt." He frowned, but the emotion skated away quickly. "If anything, she's more confident than before." He smiled to himself. "But she wasn't above a bit of emotional blackmail. She said we needed a guard dog."

"Really? So ... you're getting a retired police dog?"

Rego grinned and shook his head.

"Not exactly, as of next week, we're getting a Labrador puppy."

He pulled out his phone and showed Tamsyn a picture of an adorable bundle of black fur, all chubby paws and huge ears.

"He's so cute! What are you going to call him?"

"Oh, I've got no say in it," Rego admitted. "The kids have already decided that he's going to be called Bill."

Tamsyn was amused, which wasn't an emotion she'd expected to feel today.

"Really?"

"Yep."

"Your dog is called Bill?"

"Yep."

"So, when he's an old fella, he'll be Old Bill?"

"Yep."

And they shared a smile.

EPILOGUE

Tamsyn didn't know what she'd expected from Besnik Domi's autopsy. Did she think she'd be able to see the evil stamped on his heart as Dr Blake removed it from his chest cavity? But it was just an empty carcass, and Domi was gone. At last.

The paper mask over her mouth and nose did little to shield her from the faint, sweet smell of putrefaction; nor did it conceal the satisfaction in her steady gaze.

Rego had been to many, many autopsies, and his prevailing thought was of Domi's older brother – the man who lived, breathed and plotted in prison. His reach was long and tenacious.

Rego knew he was right to be worried.

When the *post mortem* was finished and the cause of death given as drowning, Tamsyn wanted nothing more than to get away from the cloying, clinging smell of death. She drove back from Truro with all the windows open, parked the patrol car at Penzance police station and walked home, letting the clear, salty air cleanse her.

Morwenna greeted her at the door, intrigued by this new scent and not sure what to make of it.

"Come on, scruffalicious," Tamsyn said to the little dog, "we're going out."

Mo wagged her tail enthusiastically.

As the weak afternoon sun sank behind the cliffs of Land's End, the streets emptied, until only a few headlights followed their slow walk west along the promenade.

At Newlyn Harbour, the nightwatchman, Jonas Jedna, nodded but didn't speak as she headed down the pontoon to her grandfather's punt.

The *Daniel Day* had been in the family for 43 years, named for Tamsyn's father the day of his birth. The small craft was tired and careworn, but was all that remained of a man who'd drowned when Tamsyn was just a child.

The punt bobbed on the inky black water as she lifted Morwenna aboard, the little dog settling comfortably on a coil of rope while Tamsyn took in the lines and headed from the harbour.

She didn't go far, just past the Low Lee Buoy, stopping no more than a mile-and-a-half out and dropping the anchor close to where her grandfather kept his lobster pots in the summer months.

Where her father had been murdered.

The sea was still tonight, one of those rare millpond evenings, as if knowing that solemn silence showed respect for the dead.

Tamsyn stared out toward the lighthouse of Tater Du, the sweep of its light reassuring despite the lethal reef and hidden rocks that its presence warned of, lying just out of sight.

"He's gone," she said quietly. "Besnik Domi, the Albanian who got Uncle George involved in drugs in the first place. And he's gone the same way as Uncle George ... I hope they're rotting in hell."

Morwenna put a paw on Tamsyn's leg, asking to be picked up, and Tamsyn let the small dog nestle against her.

"It's over," she said. "You can rest easy now, Dad."

Then she weighed anchor and turned the *Daniel Day* for home.

THE END

WHAT TO READ NEXT...

Newquay: UK's surf mecca, and the Boardmasters competition where the reigning kings and queens are crowned.

Five days of surfing, partying and hanging ten with the top surfers in the world - until one of them is murdered.

With millions of pounds in sponsorship money, tourist visits and small businesses at stake, and the reputation of the Devon & Cornwall Police in tatters, Police Constable Tamsyn Poldhu goes undercover to discover the truth.

Out on 1st October 2025

www.berrickford.com

THE CORNISH CRIME THRILLER SERIES
SAMPLE CHAPTERS

There are four books in this police procedural crime fiction series so far, with more planned. Each standalone story features Police Constable Tamsyn Poldhu and Detective Inspector Robert Rego, along with a cast of recurring characters, all set in the beautiful seaside county of Cornwall.

Read the blurbs and sample chapters from each book.

Book #1, DEAD WATER

Book #2, DEAD MAN'S DIVE

Book #3, DEAD RECKONING

Book #4, DEAD SHORE

www.berrickford.com

ACKNOWLEDGMENTS

To Sue Nash, a great boss who died too soon.

To DS Dave Rennison: West Midlands Police (rtd) for the cockpit drill and driving system.

To DS Dave Stamp (rtd) for fact-checking and support.

To PC Nikki Buckland for explaining the professional help that Tamsyn would receive after her traumas.

To PC Teresa Boulden (rtd) for info on the new LEDs database and proofing help.

To Emily Humphreys for background info and hot chocolates.

To Rob 'Cookie' Cook for advising on Ozzie's punt, *Daniel Day,* the lights and buoys as you leave Newlyn Harbour, and all things fishing.

To Andrea Rego for wonderful touches of local dialect, and of course, for loaning her and Ozzie's names.

To Anne King, Lesley Exton, Peggy Moerman, Sarah Measham, Lesley Bown, and Kamla Milson for comments and proofreading.

To Stone's Reef for introducing me to smoked haddock rarebit.

To Sisu for the world's best chocolate brownies™.

To Tim, Karen and Buster, who stopped me in the street to tell me that Tim was nearly in tears when he thought Morwenna had drowned in *Dead Water*.

To Sharkfin Media for the website and all things techy.

And last but never least, to Coby Llewelyn: reader, editor, friend – as always.

FORENSIC FILE

In each edition of my monthly newsletter, I'll cover a topic of interest from the forensic files.

Topics covered so far:

Fingerprints
More correctly called 'finger ridges', these are formed on a foetus by six months, due to the movement of amniotic fluid, and even the fingerprints of twins aren't identical.

Digi dogs
Search dogs have been trained to locate drugs or explosives, but they can also be trained specifically to sniff out technology such as laptops, mobile phones, USB sticks and even SIM cards. First trialled in the UK by Devon & Cornwall Police, with assistance from the FBI.

Drones
At the beginning of 2023, more than 400 drones were

used in police forces across the UK. Drones are being trialled in remote rural areas: 'Drone as First Responder'.

Police Divers

How do divers work in murky or pitch-black underwater conditions? What precautions do divers have to make when working with Explosive Ordnance?

Learn more on my website and sign up for the monthly newsletter www.berrickford.com

Printed in Dunstable, United Kingdom